# Doc for the Mob

### by Arnold Klein

Copyright © 2012, All Rights Reserved

In accordance with the U.S. copyright Act of 1976, the scanning, uploading, and electronic sharing of any part of this book without the permission of the author is unlawful piracy and theft of the author's intellectual property.

# Acknowledgments

I profoundly want to thank the following for their dedication, help, and understanding: James Elens, my co-editor; Myra Murray, my friend and confidant; Jerry Murray; Tony Albarello, my old time friend and consultant; David Gartner, my official photographer.

*For my wife, Selma, who has borne the weight of my frustrations when writing this book over the three plus year period. Thank you for your patience, understanding, and love.*

# I

    I sit on Death Row in Sing Sing prison. My execution is scheduled for one minute past midnight and the clock on the wall outside of my cell reads 10:30 P.M. Death Row's walls are dimly lit and austere, casting about shadows of doom. A prison guard sits at a desk at the end of the hall. He is obligated to walk by my cell every half hour. The green door leading to the death chamber is only fifty feet away. The lights start to flicker as they make sure that there is the correct amount of current required for the execution.
    My pant leg is slit, my head and ankle shaved. My shoes have been replaced by paper slippers. I have had my last meal and have made my peace with God. I can't help but sit here and think of all the ways my life could have gone differently.

    My mother and father immigrated from the ghetto of Venice to New York's lower East Side shortly after marrying. They were seeking a better life economically and also to escape the restrictions of Ghetto life, and they were taken in by a distant relative who made room for them. I was born a year and a half later. My father, in order to make a living, sold the chocolates my mother handmade in their small shared kitchen, off of a pushcart surrounded by other vendors who sold all sorts of clothing, linens, fruits and vegetables, and even meats and fish. There was always a tremendous bustle of activity by the vendors vocally advertising their wares and the customers haggling over price. This was not only a method of doing business, but also a social happening. Friends met friends, and new friendships were made while price negotiations were carried out. The aromas of the flowers, fruits and vegetables, dairy products, meats and fish permeated the area, leaving a distinct pleasant potpourri scent. After four years of selling off of a pushcart, my folks saved enough money to buy a grocery store, known in Italian as *il negozio di alimentary*. We lived in three rooms in back of the store.

    The lower East Side consisted primarily of three ethnic groups: Chinese, Italian, and Jewish. They did not ordinarily intermingle. The Chinese occupied the area of Mott Street, the Italians in and around Mulberry Street, and the Jews resided and had their businesses on the neighboring Rivington, Allen, and Delancy Streets. Our store bordered on the Jewish and Italian areas. Because my folks grew up in Venice and spoke fluent Italian they were accepted as kinsmen. My folks also spoke fairly fluent Yiddish because their parents and grandparents left a ghetto in Russia to escape the Tsar's tyranny, and were also accepted as kinsmen by the Jewish community. So in addition to Italian, I also learned Yiddish. Incidentally, the store carried both Jewish and Italian products. Before long our Jewish customers were purchasing Italian staples and vice versa. The Italians really enjoyed the pastrami sandwiches and the Jewish customers loved the homemade pizza.

    My papa in his youth was a very strong, good looking fellow who worked for his uncle, Eli the butcher. Papa started out as an apprentice and after a time was promoted to meat cutter. As was the custom in orthodox Jewish homes, even in Italy, he was introduced to my mother by a *shatchun*, or marriage broker, whose job it was to arrange for prospective brides and grooms to meet each other. The broker extolled the virtues of each prior to their meeting and received a fee from the father of the bride if the marriage came to pass. According to tradition a marriage contract was quickly drawn up, listing all the monies and gifts that would be presented to the bride and groom once the marriage was held. After a suitable waiting period, my mother and father were married.

Although my parents were brought up in an orthodox Jewish community in Italy they could not continue this practice when they came to America, because of their economic situation. I was however circumcised and given a Hebrew name according to the Jewish tradition. My mama and papa did observe the Sabbath. They took time off from their work at the store on Fridays just before sundown to go back to the rear apartment and light the Sabbath candles, make a prayer and a wish. As I was growing up I also participated in this Jewish ritual. I was even Bar Mitzvah'd. When I was twelve and a half, my Papa said, "You need to prepare for your Bar Mitzvah, so I made arrangements for you to study with Rabbi Bernstein."

Papa and I went over to meet the rabbi the following Sunday to finalize the arrangements. Rabbi Bernstein was retired and lived with his wife Rivka around the corner from our store. He was a short, stout man with a white beard. His wife was also short, but thin. She had a gold tooth. The plan was that I would come for lessons twice a week on Tuesdays and Thursdays at three-thirty for forty-five minute lessons. I was to bring along seventy-five cents which the rabbi would charge for the Bar Mitzvah preparatory lessons. Included in the charge was the study book. The rabbi promised that I would be well prepared for my Bar Mitzvah by the time I was thirteen.

The Bar Mitzvah was held in the local synagogue, and it went very well. My parents kept a picture on their dresser of me wearing my *tallus*, or prayer shawl, and *yarmulke*, or skull cap, holding the Torah.

My parents worked very hard, and they did their best to raise me in a manner that would prevent what happened to me as an adult. It might have steered me to a different path than the one I chose. Looking back on it, I realize that I began on that path at a very young age.

It all started when I met Joe Mancuso. I bumped into him the first day upon entering middle school. He had previously attended the local Catholic elementary school. Joe was not a particularly good student or adaptable to the strict regime of parochial school. Upon graduation it was decided that he enroll in a public junior high school. I entered the same school and shared several classes with him. We struck up a strong friendship. After classes we played in the school yard, shooting baskets and competing with the other students in pick-up basketball, touch football, and baseball.

Time passed quickly and we both began high school as freshmen. Throughout high school Joe had constant problems passing his classes, mainly English, Math, and Social Studies. I, on the other hand, received A's or A-'s in all of my subjects. I spent endless hours helping Joe scrape through to get passing grades. On weekends we would meet and join with others to play stick ball, skate hockey, punch ball, or go to the matinee movies where, for fifteen cents, we saw two feature films, a cartoon, an adventure serial, and a news documentary. We became best friends.

In the summer time after school was out, on very hot days, the fire department opened the valves on the fire hydrants and the neighborhood kids would splash each other trying to cool off. But Joe and I had our own way of cooling off.

Joe and I couldn't wait to go to the neighborhood used tire store and purchase two used inner tubes. We had them inflated and went to a pier on the East River and tied them to the beams holding up the pier. We returned mostly every day and when the cops weren't looking, bundled our clothes and our shoes into the space between the beam and the pier. Stripping to our underwear, we jumped into the river and untied our inner tubes. What a great time we had floating in the river and diving off of the floating tubes and scrambling back onto them. Late in the afternoon we paddled back to our hiding place, secured our inner tubes, and retrieved our shoes and clothes. We then returned to our respective homes. Despite being sunburned and tired, we were so happy.

# II

    I had never been to Joe's house. We always met at mine. It was towards the end of our junior year that Joe asked me if I would like to come to Sunday dinner at his house. I immediately accepted. Dinner was always served at two in the afternoon, he said. Eating dinner at this hour was a bit strange to me since we never ate before eight in the evening, just after our store closed.

    Sunday dinner with an Italian family, especially one of Sicilian descent, is an event, an extravaganza. Joe's mother, Josephine, aided by his two sisters and two aunts who lived in the same building, did all of the preparation. The vegetables, meats, and fish were purchased the day before or that Sunday morning to ensure freshness. They set the tables using the special holiday dishes and silverware and did the cooking. Joe's sisters, in addition to helping in the kitchen, swept and vacuumed the entire apartment, made sure there was soap and fresh towels as well as new rolls of toilet paper in the bathroom.

    Bearing a homemade cake my mother made as a gift for Joe's family, I entered his building and walked to the third floor, where the Mancusos lived. I recall to this very day the wonderful aroma of the food cooking even as far as the first landing. I knocked on the door and Joe greeted me. He introduced me first to his father Carlo, then to his mother Josephine, his sisters, and his two aunts. His mother gave me a big hug and a kiss, thanked me for the cake and further thanked me for being Joe's friend and helping him through school. Joe evidently had told his family of my efforts in getting him through three years of high school.

An Italian Sunday dinner is centered on the family. There are aunts, uncles, nephews, nieces and cousins, be they first, second, or even third. Dinner without having at least fourteen relatives present is not considered a dinner, but just a snack. Around one-thirty members of the family began to arrive, bringing bottles of wine, flowers and all kinds of desserts. They greeted each other with hugs and kisses. It is a Sicilian custom for even the men to kiss each other on each cheek, a sign of love and respect. The relatives traveled from Staten Island, New Jersey, Long Island, and Brooklyn to eat and join in the festivities.

It was now close to two, and everyone was in the living room. The men were chatting, the women gossiping, and all were waiting for Vito Amatto, the "Padrone," or head of the family. It would be disrespectful to start the meal without his presence. The Amatto family arrived a little past two, and after a few minutes spent in greetings, we entered the dining room. Joe's Uncle Vito sat at the head of the table, Joe's father sat at the other end. Padrone Vito designated who he wished to seat in the chairs on his immediate right and left. The others were obliged to work out their own seating arrangement.

The meal started with glasses filled with wine. Toasts to health and prosperity were first offered to Uncle Vito, then to Joe's father, Carlo, and finally to all. On the table were mounds of Italian bread cut into slices sitting alongside bowls of garlic flavored extra virgin olive oil. Dipping the bread into this mixture was a delightful experience. Bottles of wine, Pellegrino sparkling water from Italy, green olives, black olives, and roasted peppers also graced the table. The antipasto was then served, and everyone took good sized portions of the variety of Italian-style hors d'oeuvres.

The next course was the *Primo Piatto*, the pasta dish. This was the test of the preparer's culinary skill. That day it was *filetto de pomadore* sauce, served over linguini. Preparations for the sauce started early in the morning. It was cooked slowly and consisted of olive oil, crushed tomatoes, garlic, and basil. A few minutes before serving the linguini was placed in boiling water, cooked just the right amount of time, then mixed with the sauce. The end result was pasta al dente, which means not too firm or soft, but just chewable for the teeth. Blocks of *parmigiano reggiano* cheese were passed around and grated onto the pasta dish. The proof of success was tested if second and third portions were asked for. Joe's mom beamed with pride as she heard the accolades about the pasta.

The time arrived for the *piatto secondo*, or second course. Tonight it was *Osso Buco*, a veal knuckle, slowly braised until tender and served with a highly flavored sauce. Next came *Pesci al Cartoccio*, fish baked in a parchment envelope with onions, parsley, and herbs, followed by *Busecca alla Milanese*, tripe flavored with herbs and vegetables. Bowels of salad were shared and they completed the *Piatto Secondo*. I really think that Joe's mother prepared the fish dishes because she knew I was Jewish and didn't know if I would eat the meat dishes.

For dessert there were dishes of *cannoli*, ricotta filled pastry shells, *zambawne*, egg based cream with sugar and Marsala wine, and my mother's cake, all placed on platters. While the desserts were passed around the espresso coffee was brewing and then served in espresso cups. Joe's mother and all who helped her were congratulated for their efforts in making the entire meal a great success.

No one left the table until Uncle Vito rose and went into the living room. All of the male adults followed, but Joe and I were not invited. The French doors were closed, and I later learned that this was when *familia* business was conducted. Cigars, Italian twist, and short brown cigarettes were lit and smoked. While the meeting was going on the rest of us pitched in, cleaning the table, washing and drying the dishes and silverware, vacuuming the carpet and sweeping the floor.

The meeting lasted about twenty minutes. The doors were opened and the men filed out. Vito's nephew, Paulie, told

Joe and me his uncle wanted us to come in and meet with him. We entered and closed the French doors behind us. We were then invited to sit down.

Mr. Amatto then told me that he was aware of the friendship that existed between Joe and myself and hoped it would continue. He also acknowledged the help I had given Joe scholastically and thanked me on behalf of the family. He asked about my family and was pleased to hear me respond in Italian. Although I was born here, my parents often spoke in Italian, especially when they discussed something that they did not want me to understand. I picked up the language anyway. Mr. Amatto inquired about our store, its location, the hours of operation, and our living quarters. He then asked what my plans were after graduating from high school. I told him I wanted to go to college and then on to medical school, that it was my dream to become a doctor. He then smiled and wished me luck, adding that I could call him Uncle Vito if I wished. I thanked him for the honor and then we were asked to leave and to tell Paul to send the men back in five minutes.

It was getting late and I had some studying to do, so I shook hands with the rest of the family I had met that afternoon, thanked Joe's mother and father over and over, and left for home.

# III

When I arrived at our store, my folks asked me questions about the Mancuso family and the dinner we had shared. Since it was late, I suggested that I give them a full report after closing, once we had retired to our living quarters. I helped my father put up the shutters on the front windows and doors, placed the perishables on ice or in the refrigerators, emptied the garbage, made sure all the doors were locked, swept the floor, and cleaned the slicing machine.

My mother, while making dinner for my father and her, made a cup of tea for me. I was so full from the food at Joe's house that I sipped the tea slowly rather than drinking it all at once. While they ate I related the wonderful time I had meeting all of the relatives that attended and partaking of real Sicilian food. While describing each dish, I noticed my mother nodding her head in approval.

Joe later told me that his entire family was very happy to meet me. He went on to tell me that Uncle Vito told his mother to invite me back in two weeks. This was a welcome surprise and I was overjoyed. Could this be what I had always dreamed about; an extended family?

Monday brought about the same old routine. Joe and I went to school, attended classes, and ate lunch in the cafeteria. We usually brought lunches prepared by our mothers. Joe normally had a different kind of hero every day and I had a variety of other sandwiches. Through the week we split them all between us. I especially liked his eggplant parmesan hero while Joe's choice was my corned beef on rye. He always was on the lookout for my half sour pickle and it was a contest as to who would get it first. Cans of soda and pieces of fruit completed our lunches.

After lunch, it was back to class. School ended at three in the afternoon, and I would meet Joe in the school yard. After some months, final exams were coming up the following week, curtailing our playing ball. The need to study was our main concern. We walked to my store and to the apartment in the rear, where I spent several hours tutoring Joe daily. I then hit the books myself. This schedule went on until Thursday of that week. Joe left my place around five-thirty that evening to go home, leaving two of his books behind. He needed them for class the next day, so I ran out to catch up with him.

When I spotted him on the next block I saw that he had a problem. I recognized two Irish kids from the Hell's Kitchen section were shaking him down for money. Those two kids had come to our neighborhood before and had reputations for threatening young kids unless they were paid off. Joe, who was around five-feet-seven and weighed a hundred and sixty pounds, was strong for his size. He had guts and was standing up to the Micks who were pushing him around and calling him a little Dago. I was six-foot-one, weighed a hundred and ninety-five pounds, and had experience handling myself. When Joe spotted me, he became more aggressive. Fists were being thrown by the time I joined the melee. The bullies tried to fight back, but they were outmatched, and after being considerably smacked around, they took off. Joe and I hugged each other to celebrate our victory. I then noticed that he had a bloody nose and the beginnings of a black left eye. He looked me over and spotted my swollen jaw and bruised knuckles, but we were happy. I picked up his books where I had dropped them, gave them to him, and we each went to our homes.

When questioned at school the next day, Joe claimed that he had walked into a door and my excuse was that I had a bad tooth that caused the swelling. The bruising of my knuckles was not noticed. Our scenarios were not really believed, just tolerated, and it was left at that. The code of the street on the lower East Side was never to squeal, even on an adversary.

# IV

I was working in the store the night after the incident when the public pay phone rang. This was very common. Most of our neighbors could not afford a private phone. The public pay phone was an important major means of communication. It was common practice that when a call came in, the message was taken and then delivered. If someone was available, the caller was told to hang on while a runner informed the person called that there was a call waiting. I participated as the runner as often as possible because it was customary to receive a tip, usually a nickel. This particular call was from my friend Joe telling me that Uncle Vito wanted to see me this coming Sunday in addition to the following Sunday as originally set up. I told Joe to hang on while I asked my folks if it would be all right. Sunday afternoon was their free time after the morning business rush to rest, read, write to their relatives in Italy, and to catch a movie. When asked, mama nodded yes. Joe was glad to hear this and said he would pass it on to Uncle Vito.

Sunday afternoon arrived and I once again climbed the steps to the Mancuso home. I was once more was taken in by the great smells coming from their apartment. Upon arrival, I saw that the family greetings were again acknowledged with hugs and kisses. This time there were about twenty family members gathered, some coming from as far as Connecticut and Pennsylvania. Uncle Vito took his usual place at the table, and to our surprise designated that Joe sit on his immediate right and me on his left. What an honor! I was so impressed, and so were some of the others at the table, except his nephew Paulie. He didn't look too happy.

The dinner from start to finish was fantastic. After the coffee and dessert were served Uncle Vito rose from the table and the ritual of the men entering the living room via the French doors was repeated. Again, Joe and I were not invited and we helped in cleaning up. Paulie, after all the men left, signaled us go into the room and join the Capo.

Uncle Vito greeted us warmly and invited us to sit down facing him. He then asked us to tell him, leaving nothing out, about the recent encounter with the Hell's Kitchen guys and our refusal to rat them out. When we finished, Uncle Vito rose from his chair and shook our hands. He told us something that I have never forgotten.

"You did the right thing and proved that you are honorable by abiding by the code."

He then dismissed us. In parting, Uncle Vito said he was looking forward to seeing me the following Sunday for dinner. He told Joe to send Paulie back to see him. I chatted with the family for a while, waited for Uncle Vito and his family to leave, and left along with the remainder of the family.

# V

The following Monday and Tuesday ran by quickly. It was late Wednesday afternoon around five. I was actually behind the counter. My mother and father were in the cellar taking inventory when two of Uncle Vito's other nephews, Tony and Sal, entered the store. I recognized them immediately as being part of the Brooklyn contingent of the Amatto family. They greeted me with, "*Comme sta?*" Italian for "How are you." They bought some candy and asked to see my father. They had a message from Uncle Vito for him. I had no idea what this was all about and called my father to come up. In a few minutes he appeared, and after having introduced Tony and Sal to him, they said that Uncle Vito asked them to come by with a business proposal. Tony then suggested a cup of coffee in the little coffee shop at the end of the block. My father said ok, took off his apron and they left the store. I didn't have the faintest idea as to what was going on and curiosity got the better of me. I waited a few minutes, left the store, made sure that they were way ahead of me but still in sight, and saw them enter the coffee shop. I sort of sauntered by the entrance and grabbed a glimpse of the three of them sitting at a table at the rear of the store. I didn't want to take the chance of being spotted, so I crossed over to the opposite side of the street and made my way back to the store, crossing over at the opposite corner. I was still in a quandary as to the message being delivered, but I felt sure that Uncle Vito would do us no harm.

Business at the store was not doing well. Times were really tough. Pushcarts and other street vendors were starting to sell similar merchandise at prices much lower than ours.

Their overhead was a mere pittance compared to ours. My folks were real concerned and so was I. I was counting on getting at least a partial scholarship for college, but the competition was keen. Additional tuition monies, cost of books, decent clothes and all the other expenses that are a part of college attendance had to be available. From what I could see, these funds were just not there.

My father returned in about an hour, alone. He would not answer my mother's questions nor mine regarding the meeting, stating that there would be enough time after dinner. It seemed like an eternity instead of two hours before the store was closed.

# VI

During dinner Papa said little. I was on pins and needles waiting to know what happened during the meet with Tony and Sal. Mama was also anxious. She fidgeted with her knife and fork all the way through the meal. Finally, Papa finished his two cups of coffee and had a second piece of Mama's cheesecake. He then pushed his chair back a bit and began to tell us what happened from the time he left the store with Sal and Tony and entered the corner coffee shop.

"The owner greeted us and ushered us to a secluded table in the back corner. I think he was expecting us. We all ordered double espressos and, although the store didn't have a liquor license, half cups of anisette were served alongside the coffee. Sal started off by telling me how much Uncle Vito thinks of you, Marco my son."

Papa gave me one of his big smiles and continued.

"Sal then went on to go over the details of the bully incident and finished by telling me that Uncle Vito considers you a stand-up guy. He feels great appreciation toward you since you helped Joe through junior high and high school. You know Marco, this is a great honor coming from a man like Vito Amatto. It also means you are honorable and can be trusted."

My papa was so proud that he got out of his chair, came over to me, and kissed me. Once he was back in his chair he continued by telling us that Tony now took over the conversation. He and Sal seemed to know all about our business and the financially difficult situation we were dealing with. Papa went on saying, "I was a little embarrassed when the facts came to light, played with my coffee cup, sipped the anisette and even bent the small espresso spoon I held. I wanted to compose myself. Tony smiled at me and said, 'I know where you are coming from. I was there once.' Afterwards he gave me a message that Uncle Vito told him to deliver. The message said, 'I want to help you and your family. My organization has a proposition for you. We would rent your apartment from nine to five daily. The organization would have the right to have two or three private phone lines installed. A messenger would be permitted to enter and exit the front and rear premises whenever necessary during rental hours. No one other than the immediate family would be permitted to enter the rental area during these hours. All expenses were the responsibility of Uncle Vito's organization and the contract could be cancelled by either party with a thirty day notice.' Sal then commented, 'Uncle Vito told us to offer you one hundred bucks a week as rent. In cash.'"

Papa continued, "I could not believe my ears. Did Tony say a hundred dollars a week? For a moment, I couldn't even speak. This money would make the difference between staying in business and having to shut our doors. When I got over the shock I knew I had to take the bull by the horns and ask them point blank, 'Is this a book-making operation?' Tony smiled again and answered, "In England it is called Turf Accountancy.' 'But bookmaking is illegal', I countered. Tony reassured me that there would be no problem, explaining that in this police precinct the cops were on the pad and all were well paid for their no-see, no-hear understanding. If anything happens Uncle Vito and his organization would take full responsibility, cover all expenses, and see that our family is protected. You know that he is a man of honor and his word is his bond. I acknowledged this immediately and then told them that I would have to talk it over with you and your mother. We then set up another meet, next week, same time, same place. I asked them to convey my thanks and appreciation to Mr. Amatto for his offer. We then went our separate ways."

When my father finished telling what had happened he sat back in his chair, fiddled with his pocket watch, and tugged on his moustache. I still see his lips quivering a bit. He had an eager expression on his face as if he was expecting a response. I said nothing. Mama also said nothing at first. Then I saw the expression on her face. It was getting grim and turning white. Her eyes showed fear. I was sure Mama was finally going to give her opinion. She looked directly at my father and in a very loud voice cried out, "Ivan, this is not for us! It is illegal! We will be arrested and wind up in jail! Lawyers will eat up all of our money! Everything we worked for all these years will be lost. These people are Mafia. They will own us!"

As Mama spoke, the intensity of her voice increased. It was near the screaming level. "Remember we are from Venice," she said. "They are from Sicily. *Sicilianos*! Remember my cousin Santo? He had a problem with them and had to leave Italy. It took five years until the matter was straightened out and he had permission to return."

Mama's voice was getting louder as she continued.

"Ivan, my *marito*, my darling, you don't know what you are getting us into. We don't want this. I want you to tell them NO, NO, NO! We can start over again even if it means selling off of the pushcart again. My mother was now close to raving and started to repeat what she said over and over. I tried to calm her down.

"Please Mama, stop now. It's no good for your heart and high blood pressure."

But she continued on repeating the same warnings. I heard her screaming at the top of her lungs. At the same time, I could see my father's face slowly turn red, his whole body tense up and his eyes ablaze with anger. And then it happened. My Papa lifted his arm high, made it into a fist and slammed it with full force down on the dining room table. The coffee cups jumped and so did I. I saw my mother trembling.

Papa, with a strong determined autocratic voice, said, "*Basta! Genug!* Enough! *Sono il capo de questa famiglia et sono fare los decisiones.*"

If you don't understand Italian, I will say it in English so that there is no misunderstanding: "I am the head of this family and I make the decisions. There will be no more talk about this. This conversation is over."

Papa got up from his chair, went to the bedroom and closed the door. After a few minutes, I saw that Mama was calming down. I will always remember her saying, "Papa is right. He is the head of the family. He makes the decisions. *Vass vert zine, vert zine.* What will be will be."

Mama rose from her chair, cleared off the table, then washed and dried the dishes. She said *buona notte*, gave me a big hug and a kiss, and joined papa in the bedroom.

# VII

When I awoke the next morning I was so happy to hear that things were back to normal with Mama and Papa. I heard them talking cheerfully while they were restocking inventory, accepting deliveries, slicing the cold cuts, and making salads. Listening to them chat and laugh made me feel that all was forgiven for the fracas last night. I felt a sense of relief seeing my parents back together in harmony.

I looked at my watch and had to hurry or I would be late for school. My brown paper bag lunch was waiting at its usual spot. I grabbed it, kissed my mother first, and then my father, and ran off to school. I met Joe as usual between classes and again during the lunch period. We, once more split our lunch, with Joe lunging and grabbing the half sour pickle. Joe asked me if I was coming to dinner this Sunday. I told him, "Not this week. I am going to mind the store Sunday afternoon so that my folks could have some free time for themselves. I want you to know I really love coming to your house. The food is unbelievable and your relatives are great. I really enjoy being with them, especially Uncle Vito."

Joe told me he would personally tell this to him, and said that I had a standing invitation for dinner at his house. We met after school, shot some baskets, and headed for my house to tutor Joe and study myself. I reminded him that we had the Regents tests coming up in a few weeks and that if we didn't pass those tests we couldn't graduate the following year. Joe then confessed he got the word that Uncle Vito was looking forward to attending not only his but also my graduation, so I kept on nagging him to study and review the Regents' subjects and he actually made the effort.

Sunday evening when my parents came back, both Mama and Papa told me how much they appreciated me minding the store. Mama told me they had a wonderful time.

"Papa took me to China Town to the House of Hunan. I always love the food there. After a wonderful lunch we took the subway uptown to 42nd street. Then we walked on 5th Avenue and looked in the fine shop windows until we came to Radio City Music Hall and we went in. We saw the stage show, the Rockettes dance, and then the movie, *A Day At The Races* with the Marx Brothers. Papa and I could not stop laughing. I want to thank you again, my son, for giving up your dinner at the Mancuso's. I know how much it means to you."

"Mama," I said, "nothing is more important to me than you and Papa, and I decided that you and Papa need your time off, and I will cover the store every other week." I heard Mama say no, but I insisted and she finally agreed. I heard her tell this to Papa and he said, "I knew that we raised our son the right way."

Monday and Tuesday ran by. Wednesday was the day Papa was supposed to meet with Sal and Tony to give his answer. I counted the hours and then the minutes. Would Papa say yes or no to the offer? I remember the meeting was at five-thirty at the corner coffee shop. I saw Papa leave the store at about five-fifteen. I had a feeling that Tony and Sal would already be there.

At about six o'clock I saw Papa coming down the street, back to the store. I called to Mama to come to the front of the store. There were no customers. We heard Papa come in and announce without being asked, "We have a deal, and we shook hands on it."

I learned that on the street with certain parties there is nothing in writing. The handshake is more binding that a written piece of paper. When Mama heard the news I could see that she was not very happy, but she said, "*Vas vert zine, vert zin.* What will be will be." I then saw her go behind the counter and start slicing cheese.

# VIII

Saturday came around quickly and Papa asked me, "When do you think we will hear from them? We made the contract last Wednesday."

I told him, "Don't worry. They will be in touch when they are ready."

Papa replied, "I guess you are right .This is all new to me." Papa then added, "Marco, would you mind the store for a while? There won't be many customers. It's slow this time of the day, especially on Saturdays. Mama is taking a nap and I need to do paper work. Call me if you need me."

Although I wanted to study I said, "Of course." I will never forget it. It was around three in the afternoon when we had visitors. To my great surprise it was Paulie followed by two of his boys. I remember him asking, "Where is your father?"

"In the back," I answered.

"Well get him out here. I want to talk to him."

I hollered, "Papa, please come up front. There are some people here we spoke about this morning."

I saw Papa coming out with a surprised look on his face. I guess he was expecting Sal and Tony. Paulie then introduced himself. Pointing to the two men who came with him, he said, "Meet Carmine and Louie." Papa told me later that he could never forget their names. Carmine had a scar running down the side of his face and Louie's face was pockmarked. Paulie then told Papa, "These are our associates and will be working here. We want to see the layout of the apartment."

Papa said OK, and added that my mother was asleep in the bedroom. Paulie answered curtly, "If her bedroom door is open, close it. We won't make any noise. We need to see where our stuff will go."

I looked into Papa's eyes. They seemed to say, "What did I get myself into?" Papa then led the men into the rear apartment.

About fifteen minutes later they came back and Paulie left without even saying goodbye. Just before he did he said to Papa, "Do the right thing and everybody will make money."

Carmine added, "We now know where to put everything and it will work out OK."

Louie chimed in, "We will be here to take care of everything and we will be in business by Thursday." He also said that he and Carmine would pay for all the food and drinks they bought from us and that we should keep a weekly tab which would be paid along with the rent. They then shook hands with Papa and me and left.

# IX

On the following Monday Joe and I split our lunches once more. He seemed to know about the visit to the store but said that he was surprised to hear that Paulie brought Carmine and Louie with him.

I replied, "You are my best friend and I really consider you a brother, so I'll clue you in on what happened. Paulie came in with an attitude. Wouldn't say hello. He then sort of commanded me to call my papa and was really not nice to him. Paulie told Papa that Carmine and Louie would be in charge of the operation there. I saw him leave, not even saying goodbye. After Paulie left, Carmine said to Papa, "Don't worry. Everything will work out fine."

I remember asking Joe, "Was Paulie trying to act like a hood? What's his problem?"

Joe then answered, "I also consider you like a brother and I will to tell you the low down on Paulie. Paulie does have a problem. He tried to copy Uncle Vito's ways, but couldn't, so he figured that, by instilling fear into others, he would get the same results. He really feels that if acting like this he could move up in the organization instead of just being a gopher for Uncle Vito. Besides that, he is jealous and afraid of anyone who he thinks is getting close to Uncle Vito. Marco, stay away from Paulie. Have nothing to do with him. If he is in your company, just say hello and walk away. The closer you get to Uncle Vito the more insecure Paulie gets."

I answered, "Thanks for the info. It proves that you are not only my friend but also my brother. We have to find another place to study because the contract calls from nine to five. Any ideas?"

Joe thought for a moment and came back with, "I got it. My father has an empty garage we can use. It's lighted and heated. We can move a table and chairs in."

I said, "We have some tables and chairs in our basement that we can use. I am sure my father's friend, Moshe, who has a truck, will move the stuff we need. I think we are all set, so let's get started after school today."

I saw that Joe was waiting at the entrance of the garage when Moshe and I pulled up and we unloaded two tables and two chairs. I also brought along two lamps and luckily found outlets near where we placed the tables. It was perfect.

Joe said, "I think it would be a good idea not to come to dinner this Sunday. Tell me that you need to work at the store and actually do this in case it is checked. I will pass it along and we won't be caught in a lie. This will give Paulie time to cool off."

"That's a great idea. Let's do it. Now let's get down to work and start studying. We have only two weeks until the Regents and have a lot of ground to cover."

It was Monday and I was back in school. Joe and I met as usual and I couldn't wait to ask him what happened the previous day. Joe replied, "The dinner was great as usual, and the after dinner meeting was held. Paulie again manned the door and seemed happy that you weren't there. I told Uncle Vito before we sat down to dinner that you couldn't come. He said nothing, but nodded his head. When asked, I told all the others you had to work in the store. Most of the eighteen that attended said they were sorry but understood. Many of them added, 'He's doing the right thing.' I glanced at Uncle Vito and saw a small smile on his face. I knew everything was ok."

After school on Monday, Joe and I didn't shoot baskets. We went to the garage and went over and over the material we thought would be on the test. My tutoring must have worked because Joe said, "I think I have it down."

I told him, "By helping you I also reviewed the

material."

At seven in the evening I said to Joe, "I think we had enough for today. I also want to help my father close up. We will keep going tomorrow."

Joe said, "Ok. You go on ahead and I'll lock up."

"Thanks," I replied. "See you tomorrow."

When I arrived at the store Papa was already cleaning up. I pitched in and helped. When we were through I asked Papa, "Anything new?"

He then said, "Carmine and Louie showed up around nine in the morning and waited for the telephone installers who were scheduled between nine and noon. Rather than hang around they decided to go to the corner coffee shop. They told me to call them on the phone when the installers came. 'Here is the number: CI7-2240,' they said. At eleven-fifteen the installers came. I called the number. Both Carmine and Louie came back and showed the installers where to put the phones and then they left. Louie then told me that some furniture was going to be delivered tomorrow morning and that they will be back to show where they want it put. Carmine and Louie both shook hands with me and said Ciao and left."

On Tuesday when I got home Papa said, "Two desks and two chairs came today and were placed where Carmine and Louie wanted them." On Wednesday, according to Papa, a new thick oak door with a deadbolt lock and peephole replaced the existing door. New wrought-iron bars were also put on the rear windows. Papa continued, "Louie gave me a key to the deadbolt lock and told me it was a Medeco key which can't be duplicated, so I have to be careful and be sure I don't lose it. Also, he said their bosses gave them a deadline to start up on Thursday, which they did."

I remember when I got home from school on Thursday around three-thirty Mama told me, "Our renters came at nine and went directly toward the rear. Louie came out about eleven-thirty and ordered a chopped liver on rye, a corned beef on a roll, and two cans of Dr. Brown's Cel-ray tonic. "Don't forget to keep a tab," Louie reminded me, and went back to work.

"It seemed like yesterday when a rough looking guy came in around four-thirty, knocked on the rear door, entered, and then left about five minutes later. A few minutes after that, Louie and Carmine came out, said '*Buona notte*' and left."

# X

Regents testing week came and went. The final exams were scheduled the next week. I told Papa that Joe and I were sweating bullets waiting to see if we passed or not. We received word that the Regents pass/fail results would be listed on the board outside of the main office on Thursday, the following day. We couldn't wait to get to school and find out where we stood. With great anxiety we approached the bulletin board. Crossing our fingers, we looked for our names on the alphabetical list.

Since my name started with 'F' and was before Joe's last name, I had first crack at the board. When I saw I had passed all of the tests I heaved a sigh of relief. Joe was next and I watched him biting his lip and actually shaking as he looked for his results. I heard his scream with joy and delight as he read that he had also passed the Regents test requirements. He started to do a little dance, then grabbed me by the shoulders and actually kissed me on both cheeks. He was elated and vigorously shook my hand and loudly thanked me over and over. I thought he would start to cry in happiness. He was so loud that the principal sent one of his assistants to tell us to leave the hall.

Once we were off of school property I reminded Joe, "We just passed only the first hurtle. Next week are finals, the second hurtle, and probably the most difficult one."

Since we had no school for the rest of the day I remarked to Joe, "We deserve a reward, so let's take the rest of the day off and go rafting. Tomorrow we'll start studying all over again."

Joe said, "Without a doubt," and off we went.

Our inner tubes were still in their original hiding places and, to our surprise, were still inflated. I remarked to Joe that it was like old times, paddling on our makeshift rafts, jumping into the East River and then returning the inner tubes to our secret hiding place to head home.

I told Joe, "We need to make a study schedule and stick to it. And since we have no school tomorrow let's start tomorrow morning at ten and work until noon, take a break until one and study until at least seven. Remember, we both have the English final Monday morning, Spanish final Monday afternoon, American history final Tuesday morning, Civics final Tuesday afternoon, Social studies final Wednesday afternoon, and the last final, Math, on Thursday afternoon." I remember telling Joe, "Let's just review everything but Math and once we get them down tight we can spend the rest of our time pounding on the Math."

We started reviewing English and Spanish first, all day Friday. On Saturday, we went over American history and Civics, memorizing historical dates and organization of the United States federal and local governments. We tried to guess questions that would be asked on the exams and spent time answering them. On Sunday, we reviewed Social Studies and had to miss the usual gala Sunday dinner. Once we finished the Social Studies review, around six in the evening, we decided to stop and get a good night's sleep so that we would be wide awake for the tests on Monday. I told Joe that the best way to take a test is to read all of the questions first and answer the ones you're sure are correct and then go back and go over the ones you're not sure of. Using this method it was believed that the subconscious mind will work on the unanswered questions while the positive answers are written down.

After the test on Wednesday I felt that I had done well on all of the exams so far. Joe told me that he felt he would get at least passing grades, but was worried that Math would be his undoing.

I said to Joe, "Let's get back to the garage and burn the

midnight oil if necessary."

We did just that. We went over and over formulas, equations, examples, and test questions listed at the end of each chapter in the book until we were exhausted. At around eleven I remember saying to Joe, "We have had enough. Let's stop now, have a big breakfast tomorrow morning, and a light lunch to be ready for the exam in the afternoon. In fact, let's meet for lunch as usual. You don't need to grab for the pickle. I will bring an extra one along."

When we met for lunch, and were eating the sandwiches, I could not help but notice Joe's palms. In small print Joe had printed many of the equations that might be needed to answer exam questions. I didn't know whether to laugh or get angry at what Joe was trying to do and said, "Joe, what the hell are you trying to pull off. You know this stuff and don't need crib sheets. It will be your ass if you get caught."

Joe replied, "I'm pretty sure I know the work, but I need the crib sheet as a back-up in case I get panicky and blow it."

At five minutes to one we entered the class room, and at one o'clock the tests were handed out. I looked the complete test over, answered the questions I knew were right, and went back and worked on the unanswered ones. I was finished in about forty minutes, handed in the completed test papers, and left the class room. I waited outside the door for Joe.

An hour after the tests were passed out our Math teacher announced, "Time is up. Hand in your papers."

Some of the other kids pleaded, "Could we have just ten minutes more?"

But the teacher said, "No, hand in your papers." Once all the papers were handed in the remaining students were dismissed.

When Joe came out, he was a little shaky and looked white.

"How you think you did," I asked.

"I'll answer you as soon as I wash my hands," he replied. "Wait for me outside the school."

He met me about ten minutes later with the cleanest hands I ever saw.

"Well, how did you do?" I asked again.

Joe then answered, "I can't swear to it but I think I just scraped through. My palm crib sheets sure came in handy. Let's get out of here and get something to eat. There is a good cheap Chinese restaurant right around the corner. Besides, I'm getting tired of the pickles."

"OK, with me," I replied.

I suggested to Joe that we split my portion of *egg foo yong* and his chicken *chow mein*. "Great idea," he replied. Over the meal we tried to remember the questions that were on the math exam, but we were so drained that we decided that we just couldn't do it. As we ate our pineapple and fortune cookies Joe leaned over and said, "The hell with the test remarks. We'll worry about them later. Let's finish here and go to the movies."

"Right on," I answered and, after leaving a small tip, we went to the movies.

I remember it like it was yesterday. We saw John Wayne in *Stagecoach* and Sidney Toler in a Charlie Chan mystery. We even had some money left over to buy some popcorn and a couple of Cokes. I reminded Joe that although tomorrow was the last day of school, if we did not attend school for at least the first three periods our report cards would be held up several weeks before being mailed. But students attending would receive their report cards the following week. Joe looked a little bugged and said, "I was going to ask you to play hooky tomorrow, but thinking of having to wait a couple of weeks for the report card would probably give me a heart attack, so I guess we better show up!"

"Amen," I answered. "By the way Joe, I planned on coming to your house for dinner on Sunday, but on second thought I think I will have to pass. I haven't spent much time with my folks these past couple of weeks and I need to do that. Besides, they need some time off again."

Joe said, "I got ya. I'll give your regards to all and a special explanation to Uncle Vito. See you tomorrow, Marco.

Oh, and forget the pickle. It has been giving me *agita*."

The next day, the official last day of school before summer vacation, was to us a joke. We piled into our home room, the teacher took attendance, and we were left to twiddle our thumbs or read or scribble, but not talk, for the balance of the period. We were then told to report to the auditorium where attendance was again taken, followed by a series of boring documentary films. After what seemed an eternity, the bell rang ending the second period. An announcement was then made that those who wished to remain in the auditorium for the third period could stay in their seats. The rest were told to go to the gym. Joe said, "Let's hit the gym. I don't think the gym teacher will take attendance and we could split early."

I quickly replied, "That's ok with me. Let's move!" And off to the gym we went.

Joe was right. No attendance was taken. We were lucky that we wore sneakers and were able to join in on a basketball game. Before we knew it the bell ending the third period rang, but the teams were so engrossed in the game that we didn't hear it. Before we knew it the locker room equipment manager chased us off the court and told us to leave the building.

"I guess we better head for home and get to know our folks again," Joe said.

I replied, "You're right. I have a lot of work to do at the store to help Mama and Papa prepare for Saturday's usual business rush. Let's stay in touch with each other by calling on the store payphone."

"Aren't you going to shower?" Joe wanted to know.

"I'll ask Carmine or Louie if it's ok. If not I'll use the washbasin in the cellar."

"Talk to you later, buddy," Joe said as he left.

"Give my best to all," I answered.

"Will do," Joe shouted back.

When I arrived at the store Mama and Papa were so happy to see me. They asked when I was going to get my report card, and I told them that it would be coming through the mail in a couple of days. I reassured them that I did ok. Just then Carmine came out, greeted me warmly, and ordered a piece of cheesecake and two cups of coffee. He seemed to know that Joe and I took finals and he hoped that we did ok. I said that I thought we both passed. I then took a chance by asking him if it would be all right if I took a shower although it was during the rental hours. He thought a moment and said ok, but not to make a habit of asking.

    I hit that nice hot shower and must have been under it for fifteen to twenty minutes. It felt great. The next thing I heard was a knocking on the bathroom door and Louie shouting, "Time's up! Get out! One, two, three, quick!"

    I did just that. I dried off, got dressed, and combed my hair in a flash. I didn't take the time to say goodbye. Just waived on my way out the door. Boy, it was so good to feel clean again.

    I put on my apron and went right back to helping Mama and Papa get ready for our Jewish Friday night *erev shabbos* customers. Out of respect for these religious people, we had to have everything ready before sundown. We then prepared for those that wanted food for their Saturday and Sunday breakfast and brunch, especially the appetizer delicacies. Getting ready for our Italian customers who came in early Sunday morning to buy for the traditional Sunday dinner was next on the list. In between we prepared cakes and food for neighborhood wedding parties, Bar Mitzvahs, confirmations, and other religious and organizational affairs. All this preparation required a lot of work and time since the great portion was made from scratch. We were able to do all of this work in less time than usual because Papa, using the rental money, bought some very good used additional kitchen equipment and had it installed in the cellar. He also bought a large Frigidaire refrigerator, and put it also in the cellar. No more having to buy ice and no more spoiled food.

    "I can now buy supplies in larger quantities at cheaper prices and can even compete with the push cart," Papa proudly announced.

    Papa was beaming when he said, "My decision to do

the rental wasn't such a bad idea after all. You see, it's starting to pay off."

I looked to Mama for her expression. She reluctantly gave a little smile.

As usual, we worked until past mid-night on Friday, got up at six on Saturday morning, ate breakfast, and opened the store promptly at seven. Business was brisk until around two in the afternoon and then dropped off until about 4:00 in the afternoon. It started up again a little after four and we were busy until we closed at eight. No cooking dinner for Mama. We were so exhausted that we just washed up and went to bed.

On Saturday, after breakfast, we ate for lunch and dinner what we had on sale. The same routine took place Sunday morning, with the slow period starting around two in the afternoon, and continuing until closing. I told Papa and Mama that one minute after five that evening they were on vacation. At first they said, "No!" But I insisted and finally they agreed. I also told them that I was going to open up at seven o'clock on Monday morning and take care of the early customers and that I would not take no for an answer. At that moment Carmine and Louie left, and Papa and Mama went into the back rooms. I could hear the sound of the shower and wondered if Papa and Mama were taking a shower together. The very thought of it made me turn red. No way. About forty minutes later Papa and Mama came out all dressed up. I told Mama how beautiful she looked, and to Papa how handsome he looked. Papa said, "Grazie, Marco." Mama then came over to me, gave me a big hug, saying, "Thank you my darling son." I saw them leave the store holding hands like two teenagers in love. It made me feel so good.

At eight o'clock that night I closed the store, saw that everything was ok, went to my room, and fell fast asleep with my clothes on. I was that exhausted. The alarm clock blasted off at five-thirty the next morning. I needed an extra half hour for myself and got out of bed at six. At seven o'clock I opened the store, ready for the morning business. Mama and Papa were still sleeping when I woke them up around eight. They rushed to get out of the apartment by the time Louie and Carmine arrived at nine. I then asked Mama how they spent their evening. She answered, "Let's wait until the rush is over and we have time to talk."

It wasn't until two in the afternoon that things quieted down. Mama, Papa, and I had cups of coffee, leaned against the counter, and Mama began to relate last night's happenings.

"We took the bus to 57$^{th}$ Street and walked over to the Russian Tea Room and had a wonderful Russian style dinner," she said. "It reminded us of the food my mama and grandmother made. Papa then added that the borscht also reminded him of his own mama's and grandma's cooking. Papa also ordered Russian tea and that we even had a glass of wine. The meal was so good."

"What did you do next?" I asked.

"Believe it or not, Papa discovered a movie theater that showed foreign films and they were featuring a film from Italy. We really enjoyed seeing it. It reminded us of our childhood in Italy. After the movie was over we walked over to Lindy's Restaurant on Broadway and we had coffee and shared a piece of their famous cheese cake."

Papa chimed in, saying, "Your mama's cheese cake is better"

"Would you believe it? When we left the restaurant and Papa hailed a cab, and we taxied home. This was really a night to remember."

It was about three when Mama and Papa finished telling me of their night out. I was hoping that Ozzie, our postman, who usually came by around three-thirty, would deliver the envelope from the school containing the report card. He came by around three-twenty but sadly there was no mail from the school. What a let-down. I had to sweat it out for at least another day. Just about then the public phone rang. I ran to answer it. Maybe it was an opportunity to get a tip for telling someone in the neighborhood there was a phone call for them, but it was Joe on the line.

After saying hello he continued, "Guess we got shut out

on the report cards today. I think until school starts we should devote our time from now on to a three letter word, FUN with a capital F, capital U, and capital N, and that includes girls with a capital G."

I interrupted him right there. "I agree all the way, and I know how to spell."

Joe continued, "For a starter, how about going to Coney Island tomorrow morning. I hear there are a lot of good lookers in sexy bathing suits just lying on the beach, waiting to meet two handsome guys like us. Besides, my cousin Sonny has a pizza joint right on the boardwalk. We can change there and hit him up for pizza and sodas. Let's meet at the subway tomorrow at ten, and don't forget to bring a couple of towels."

# XI

It was a beautiful day at the beach. The sun was shining, the ocean was warm and flat, and Joe was right. The opportunity to view and meet girls was great. We walked by, looking them over, and before long two beauties gave us the eye. We joined them on their blanket and had a great time. After a while we invited them to grab a bite with us and walked over to Joe's cousin's pizza place. I introduced Bev and Lynn to Sonny and he treated all of us to a large pizza and drinks. If the food wasn't on the arm we would have been in trouble, because we didn't have enough money to pay any tab. The girls seemed to be very impressed by our behavior, and after eating we went back to the beach and spent the rest of the day with them.

It was now late in the afternoon and it was now time to leave. We said bye-bye to Bev and Lynn, promising to see them again soon. On the subway ride home I leaned over to Joe and whispered, "I am going to tell you something, but you have to promise not to laugh or to repeat this to anyone."

Joe said, "I promise, I won't tell a soul. I'm all ears."
"Well, when Bev and I went into the water, and after we splashed around for a bit, I decided to float on my back. Bev sawthis and said, 'I always wanted to learn how to float. Will you show me?' I said, 'Sure, but you'll have to trust me and relax. I am going to stretch out my arm in front of me and I want you to lie down with your shoulders resting on my arm. I'll support the rest of you with my other arm. Don't be afraid. I won't let you sink. Just relax.' She said, 'Ok. I trust you.' She did just what I said, and before long she was floating, my one arm under her shoulders, the other under her ass. I could not help looking at her big *bazooms* and those great legs. In a

flash, I had a boner the size of an oak tree and just as hard. After a couple of minutes Bev said, 'I've had enough. Let's go back to the beach.' I thought quickly, still having this blown up wiener, and said 'You go on ahead. I want to swim for a while.' I helped Bev get to her feet and she headed for the shore. I actually swam to the jetty and back, concentrating on my strokes and finally the boner went away. It was so big at first that I would be arrested for indecent exposure. That's why I couldn't come out of the water with Bev."

Joe then exclaimed "That's some story. The best part of it is your bragging about the size of your boner. I know better. I've seen you in the locker room. Besides, you being Jewish, the rabbi chopped a chunk off."

With that Joe started to laugh so loud that I had to give him a little kick to shut him up.

He then said, "Do you know why I was laughing so hard? I have a better story to tell you. Lynn was lying on her back on the blanket. I looked at the guy and girl on the blanket next to us. He had his head on the girl's belly with his legs stretched out. It looked so good, so I asked Lynn if we could do the same and she said, 'Sure.'

"So there I am, head on her soft belly, legs out and able to turn my head to either side. The view was great from any angle. When I turned to the right my eyes took in the top of her bathing suit showing part of those two nice knockers. Turning my head to my left my eyes took in two long curved legs and the mound where the legs joined the bod. Talk about a boner! I had one also. Betcha it was bigger than yours and twice as hard. You were at least in the water and yours couldn't be seen. I think everyone that passed by slowed down, stared, and grinned. After a few minutes I got up quickly and with my back to Lynn told her I was going over to my cousins' to get a drink of water. I asked her, still with my back to her, if she wanted me to bring one back to her. She said, 'No thanks.' It took a few minutes to walk to the stand and get the boner to lay down. When I got back Lynn was sitting up chatting with Bev. I don't know if Lynn spotted the boner, but they both started to giggle when they saw me.

I then asked, "Do you think they spotted our boners?"

Joe replied, "I'm not positive, but if I had to bet, eight to five, yes. Were you embarrassed?"

"No way."

Joe snickered as he continued, "If they can't recognize a boner, it's time that they did. They're over sixteen and should be able to recognize one by now."

"Right you are, Joe. And hurray for the boner parade!"

As we exited the subway Joe said, "Today is just a sample of what we can do to have fun the rest of the summer. We have been girl-starved too long and we need to make up for it, so I vote girls, girls, girls! The more the merrier!"

"But where do we go and find those dolls?" I asked.

"At dances. They're holding them all over the place."

"But we don't know how to dance. Besides, I have two left feet when it comes to dancing."

"Don't give it a thought, my friend. My cousin Celeste works as a teacher for Arthur Murray. I already made the deal and we are all set. She'll give us lessons and we can pay her when we can afford it. With her teaching we'll be dancing like Fred Astaire in no time."

"When could we start and how do we dress?" I anxiously asked.

Joe replied, "I'll get all the details later on in the week. By the way, she is a knockout and likes to flirt a little. But she's spoken for, so don't even think of making any moves, no matter how she comes on. She does this just for kicks."

"Don't worry. I'm not looking for any trouble. Just want to learn how to dance." By this time it was getting a little late, so I said, "See ya. Talk to you later."

Then we went home. That night, after going to bed, I couldn't sleep, imagining how it would feel learning to dance with a knockout sexy professional dance teacher, and the boner reappeared. I had a big problem getting it to settle down. Finally I was able to fall asleep. I awoke in the morning too early to phone Joe, so I helped Papa and Mama prepare to open the store. At nine I phoned Joe and asked him when we could have the first lesson. Our future big plans depended on how fast we could learn.

"Hold on, my friend. Celeste is a very busy dance instructor, one of Arthur Murray's best. She don't have a lot of free time, but when she heard it was for us she was impressed and gave us time next Monday from four to six to see what she can do for us. She said we should wear comfortable clothes, and leather shoes.

Joe told me he knew where the studio was and that we could take the subway there. I told Joe to thank her for me and he said, "My friend, you will have the chance to thank her yourself when you meet her."

After speaking to Joe I thought I would go to the library and take out a book on ballroom dancing.

Wednesday came and went and still no report cards. I tried calling the school Thursday morning and didn't get any information. Joe and I called each other several times, each of us promising to let the other know if the envelope arrived. I hung around the store, just moping and looking out the window at the heavy rain coming down. Papa saw me doing this.

"Seeing as you have nothing to do and are bored, I want you to start painting the ceiling and walls of the cellar. Since we store food and cook there, it has to look like a kitchen. The paint, ladder, brushes, and everything else you need is in the basement storeroom. This job will take your mind off of whatever is worrying you."

I could never say no to Papa, so I went down to the cellar and went to work. The postman came, but no luck again. It was Thursday morning when Joe phoned me asking, "What should we do today?"

"I don't know. Want to go back to the beach?"

Then Joe said, "Not really. It looks like it's going to be a cloudy day. I've got it! Let's take the ferry to Staten Island! It's only a nickel and maybe we can meet some girls on it. Besides, I heard it's a swell ride. We can take some food with us and see the Statue of Liberty close up."

"Sounds like a winner to me. Let's meet at the subway at ten-thirty!"

"You got it! I'll bring the food."

It was a few minutes after ten-thirty when Joe showed up, dressed to the nines. He was wearing a cap, blue shirt, white pants, and white tennis shoes. Although it was a cloudy day he was also sporting sunglasses.

"What are you doing, looking like a guy from Park Avenue?" I asked.

"I'm sure to impress and draw dolls looking like this. It pays to advertise, and this is what I'm doing."

"OK," I replied. "Give it a try, Mr. Movie Star. But don't forget me."

"No problem."

The ferry docked and we boarded. There were cars and trucks loaded on and then the passengers. Joe kept an eagle-eye out for girls traveling by themselves. He was like a wolf hunting prey. Once the ferry left the pier Joe started out on the top deck with me in tow and went searching from rear to front and from side to side on that deck.

"Nothing doing here," he said. "Let's go down to the lower deck and cover that."

Again, no luck. We took a shot at the canteen, ate lunch, and struck out once more. A couple of older ladies, about forty-five, gave us the eye.

The ferry was now preparing to dock in Staten Island, and Joe whispered to me, "Let's save the nickel fare. We'll hide in the toilet until the ferry starts back."

"Are you nuts?" I exclaimed.

"We can do this," Joe replied. "We can go into the stall, lift up the toilet seat and straddle the bowl until the ferry is moving. It's a no-brainer and we can save a dime."

"Now I know you're off the wall. It's crazy, but it might be fun. Let's go for it."

The ferry docked. The cars and trucks drove off and passengers started to leave. As soon as we saw this Joe and I walked slowly, looking as if we were getting off. Coming up to a men's toilet we saw no one around and ducked into it. So far, so good. We chose the two stalls farthest from the entrance and hopped into them. We raised the toilet seats and lifted ourselves up and held onto the walls of the stall for balance. It felt like we were there for hours. My arms were getting cramped but the challenge was there. Could we pull this off? Finally I heard the sound of vehicles coming on board and foot steps and the voices of passengers. "We did it," Joe whispered.

"It was a blast," I agreed. "Let's get the hell out of here. This place stinks!"

I hopped off the toilet, put the seat down, and exited the stall. I heard Joe yell, "Son of a bitch!" He slipped coming off the toilet bowl and one foot landed in the bowl itself. And as he slipped, he grabbed the chain to the overhead water tank and the bowl filled up as if to flush. There was my *paisan*, Joe, one foot in the water, up and over his white shoe, soaking his sock, and up to mid-calf of his right pant leg. What a sight. I was howling with laughter. Joe was pissed and was using every curse word he knew. After a minute or so, I said, "We better go now before anyone comes in to take a leak. I'll grab some paper towels and you can try to dry up on deck. It's safer there."

"Ok," Joe said, "but I'm still pissed!" I took a bunch of paper towels and followed Joe out and up the steps to a higher deck. I had to bite my lip from getting hysterical again because I heard the squishing of his soaked shoe and sock with every step he took. When we reached the deck, we found an empty bench and I had an idea.

"Listen to this, Joe; I saw this in a movie. You start drying up after I walk out of sight. This move should attract, according to that movie, two inquisitive girls. If they're dogs give them a ball four. If they're dolls, concoct some hero story. Once I see you talking I'll come over and we act surprised to see each other. Then you introduce me to them and we go from there. It worked in the movie and both guys scored big time."

"Ok, I'll give it a go."

"See you later, sure foot."

"Well, uh, ball four to you, Twinkle Toes."

And off I went.

Well, I'll be damned if in about five minutes two good looking dolls didn't walk by and start talking to Joe. The taller one had blazing red hair down to her shoulders and wore a white skirt with a navy jacket. The other one was a blue-eyed blond wearing a tight white sweater that left little to the imagination and a black skirt that accented her great gams. I don't know what he said, but they seemed to want to stay. I waited a minute and casually walked toward them. When I was ten feet away I acted surprised.

"Is that you, Joe?!"

Joe replied, "It's been a long time. Meet two friends of mine."

I sped up just a little and Joe said, "Marco meet Jessica, Jessica meet Marco, Marco meet Louise, and Louise, say hello to Marco." During the introductions, I couldn't keep my eyes off of Louise's sweater. Greetings were exchanged and conversation returned to Joe's heroic act.

"Did you know your friend here is a real hero?" Louise asked.

"No," I said. "What happened?"

"Don't you see his wet shoes and pant leg"

"Sure I do. But what makes him a hero?"

"Well," chimed in Jessica, "it seems some girl was running to catch the ferry as it was pulling out, she jumped, missed, and fell into the water. Joe here saw her splashing, leaned over sidewise and pulled her out, getting his shoe, sock and pant leg wet. The girl he rescued just said thanks and ran off to another part of the ferry. Joe was so brave. Besides that he was so modest. He didn't even report it."

"That's my old friend, Joe," I said."Are you both from Manhattan?"

Jessica replied, "Yes we are. We both live on West End Avenue and 80$^{th}$ Street in the same building."

"And what do you do," I continued.

"We are both seniors at McKinley High School. What

about you guys?"

"Well, we just graduated from the High School of Music and Art and we are going to take a year off traveling around Europe."

"That's so terrific," the girls kept repeating.

The ferry was about to dock when Joe asked for their phone numbers, and they jumped at the opportunity to give them.

"Hope to see you soon," Jessica said, looking directly at Joe.

Louise said, "Want to see you again, Marco. Please call. We're going to have some parties this summer and want you to come."

"Look forward to it," I said.

Then Joe responded as he gave Jessica a hug and a kiss on the cheek. I had nothing to lose, so I bent forward to give Louise a kiss on her cheek, but she turned her head and gave me a wet one on the mouth. We said goodbye as the ferry docked, and hurried to the subway so that the girls couldn't follow us. While waiting for the train to come, we slapped each other on the shoulders.

"Success!" said Joe. "Success! Your idea was brilliant, Marco."

"And so was your toilet scheme! Fantastic. What a great day!"

The train came and took us to our station. I remembered it was now close to four and we wanted to rush home in time to catch the postman. I whistled all the way home. When I came in, Papa asked, "Did you have a good time?"

"Yes Papa. It was a very good time. We went on the ferry and saw the Statue of Liberty." I left it at that. Just then the postman, Ozzie, came by and said, "Marco, I have that letter from the school for you."

I rushed over to get it and he put the envelope behind his back. "Say pretty please, Mr. Postman," he said.

I made a lunge for it, but Ozzie jumped back, laughing. Then Papa got into the act, and said, "Ok, Ozzie. You had your fun for the day. Give him the envelope and my mail to me. I'll treat you to a cup of coffee and a piece cake."

"Ok, Ivan. I just wanted to kid around with Marco. I know he can take it. Where's the coffee?"

Ozzie gave me the envelope and I looked at it. Just then the public phone rang. When I picked it up I recognized Joe's voice.

"Did you get it?"

"I got it right here in my hand," I replied.

"Well, how did you do?"

"Haven't opened it yet. I'm just staring at the envelope. You open yours yet?"

"No, not yet. I'm sort of nervous."

"So am I. How about coming over here and we'll open them together?"

"Seems like a plan. See you in fifteen."

Sure enough, Joe was at the store in ten. He must have run all the way. He came in with a little smile on his face. I took a shot and asked him, "Did you peek inside the envelope?

"No, I didn't. I steamed it open and resealed it. How about you, Marco?"

"Well, I was taking the corned beef out of the steamer and the steam opened the flap of the envelope; so I took a peek and resealed it. I got an idea. Let's switch envelopes even though we both know how we did. We can make believe it's the first time. It will be, because I will know your marks and you'll know mine."

"Good thinking."

So Joe and I traded envelopes and opened them. In a happy tone I told Joe that I was proud that he had passed all his subjects, even scraping through math with a sixty-seven. Then Joe exclaimed with excitement, "*Marron*, Marco! You got over ninety in every subject! How the hell did you ever do it?!"

"I don't know. Studying and taking tests come easy to me. Let's tell my mama and papa and then go to your house and tell your family."

"I can't believe we're seniors and will graduate next

year. If it wasn't for you, Marco, I never would have made it this far. No one in my family went this far in school and once I graduate from high school, it will be a first for all the relatives."

Just then Louie and Carmine came out. "What's the big to-do here?"

Papa said, "The boys passed their test and will be high school seniors in the fall."

"That's *molto bene*," Carmine said.

Louie said, "I only got past the sixth grade and had to quit and go to work to help support my family. I always wanted to go back to school, but it was too late. Thanks to your Uncle Vito, Louie and I got good jobs and were making a living. You two have a real chance of making something out of yourselves by staying in school and graduating."

Louie took two tens out of his pocket and gave one to each of us. Carmine then came over and did the same. "This is a little present from us," said Carmine. "We are very proud of you and we'll take you out to celebrate soon."

Joe and I tried to give the money back, after thanking them over and over, when Papa stepped in.

"It is not respectful to refuse a gift when it is given for something well done and it comes from the heart. You must accept this gift and thank them both, showing appreciation. So do it now with gratitude."

Joe and I did just that. We then shook hands with Carmine and Louie and they left. Papa then turned to us and repeated, "This present represents appreciation on the part of their family for your and Joe's accomplishment. Refusing could mean a lack of respect."

After Carmine and Louie left we deep six'd the *gelt* in our pockets. I then told papa, "Joe and I are going for a walk."

We left the store and headed to the corner coffee shop. We ordered and sat down.

"What do we do with this money?" Joe asked.

I replied, "Have a good time! I got some way out ideas so let's leave it till tomorrow. It's Friday and it's getting late. I have to help my folks prepare for the weekend."

"Ok, let's talk and decide tomorrow. Just make sure girls are included in our plans."

"I am jake with that. I'll call you tomorrow around ten and we can go from there."

"Sounds like a winner to me. By the way, you are expected to eat with us on Sunday. See that you can work it out. Let me know tomorrow for sure if you are coming."

"I'll be there," I said. "Speak to you tomorrow."

"No problem."

Friday night was more hectic than usual and we didn't get finished preparing, waiting on customers and taking orders until about ten. We were so tired that we didn't even want our regular Shabbos dinner. We each grabbed a little something from the display case and that was enough to keep us going. We closed the store, turned out the lights, crawled into our beds and went right to sleep.

It was Saturday morning around five when I felt Papa shaking me and saying, "Marco, get up. It's time. We need to be open by seven o'clock sharp."

"Ok Ok, Papa. I'm getting up now. I'll take a shower and take some breakfast. Don't worry. We'll be ready by seven."

Starting around seven-fifteen, the usual mad rush came in. Customers ordered mostly bagels, cream cheese, lox, and coffee. The Italians came in after them and wanted all sorts of our Italian delicacies, like pizza, cheese, sausage, and other delights. Around noon, customers flocked in to get homemade chopped liver, chopped herring, pastrami, corned beef, and frankfurters. Business was steady until around two in the afternoon. when it usually quieted down. It began to pick up again around four. We stayed busy until closing time at eight. Mama had prepared dinner earlier. She heated it up and we ate around eight-thirty. After cleaning up and getting ready for Sunday, I told Papa I was going to get some air and possibly some gelato at Tony's ice cream parlor a couple of blocks away. I remember it was a beautiful night. The moon and stars were out and there was a slight breeze.

Tony's ice cream parlor had the best ices and gelato on the East Side. Everything they had was made by hand. Outside of his shop were a few tables and chairs where people watchers sat, talked, and ate their favorites. It was also a hangout for neighborhood kids, especially the girls who knew it was safe to flirt with the local guys. I was leaning against a lamp post in front of the store when two girls walked passed me, laughing and smiling. I recognized them from school. The tall one said, "Hi Marco. Nice night, isn't it?"

"It sure is," I replied. "Can I buy you ladies some refreshments?"

"Yes, thanks," they replied.

We went into Tony's and the girls ordered cups of lemon ices, and I had one too. I had the two tens on me, and I think I impressed the girls when I flashed the ten dollar bill to pay for the ices. We found the table outside and sat down. I felt foolish when I told the girls that although I saw them around school I didn't know their names.

"I'm Matti," the one that had the slight lisp answered. "And this is Angie."

Matti was not a beauty, being around five-foot-five with dark eyes and sexy lips. She was a little chunky, but not fat, and could be described as pleasingly plump.

Angie on the other hand was slim, and about five-foot-seven with black curly hair and large sexy eyes. She looked a lot like Sophia Loren, and had her body to match. We all chatted about school and the weather for a few minutes, but when Angie and I made eye contact the energy flowed between us. Matti must have guessed this and said, "I have to get up early and go to work tomorrow. Hey Marco, would you walk Angie home?"

"Sure will," I replied.

Angie said nothing, but I noticed she lowered her eyes and had a smile on her face. Matti then said, "Ciao," and split.

Angie and I talked and asked each other about our future plans. She was very impressed when I told her I wanted to be a doctor and I in turn was impressed when she told me she wanted to be a teacher. Time ran by quickly and before we knew it Tony was preparing to close the store.

"I guess we better leave," I said.

And she said, "I guess so."

Off we went. I held her arm as we crossed the street, even though there were no cars in sight. She lived on Allen Street, three blocks from Tony's, in a four-story tenement. I walked her up to the front door hoping she would invite me into the vestibule, but she didn't. She held out her hand, found mine, shook it, and said she had a great time and hoped to see me again. We looked into each other's eyes and the energy flowed again. Before we knew it we were kissing and our bodies sort of melded together. Abruptly, she stopped, pulled away, said good night, and ran into the building.

As I walked back home smiling, I said to myself, "Marco you dog. You are a real lady killer. I am going to see her again."

I arrived at the store, went to my room, washed up, got into my pajamas, and climbed into bed. This was a great day.

That night I dreamt of Angie and her kisses that nearly knocked me off my feet.

I got up early before Papa had to shake me awake. I showered, dressed, and had coffee and a bagel with Mama and Papa. We opened the store as usual at seven and went to work. Around two in the afternoon business became quiet, and since Mama and Papa knew I was going to Joe's for dinner, they told me to take another shower and get dressed in my new black pants. I asked Carmine if it was ok to come in and use the shower, since it was a special occasion, and he said "Ok, but don't take too long."

"Be sure to wear the white shirt that I washed and ironed for you," Mama said. "It is in your dresser drawer next to the black socks I want you to put on. Remember also to wear your good shoes."

I remember those black leather shoes with rubber heals, which were to be worn on *Shabbos* and other special occasions. "Ok Mama. Will do."

It took me fifteen minutes to shower and another fifteen to locate my socks, pants, and shirt. I had a problem getting the shoes on and had to squeeze them on using a table spoon for a shoe horn. My feet hurt a little bit at first, but I got used to them. Mama *qvelled* as she told me how great and handsome I looked. Papa had a broad smile as he wished me a good time.

On my way over to Joe's house, I stopped at Freddy Moskowitz' flower pushcart where Freddy greeted me with a big hello. He was a tall, heavy guy with a white goatee who loved his flowers and the people who bought them.

"Who do you want the flowers for?"

I told him it was for the Mancuso family, and that I was having dinner there in about an hour.

"Take the two dozen long stem red roses. They are beautiful and will last."

"How much for the two dozen, Freddy?" I asked.

"Well, since it's getting late and I'll be closing soon, and they're for the Mancuso's, I'll take a dollar."

"That's great! Will you pick them out for me?"

"Sure will, and I'll tell you what else," he said. "I'll give you another dozen for twenty-five cents. So you'll get three dozen of the finest for a dollar and a quarter."

"It's a deal Freddy. Thanks so much."

"You got the money on you, Marco?"

"I have it right here."

Then Freddy wrapped the roses in special paper, and even threw in some baby breath which made the bouquet even more beautiful.

"Thanks a lot Freddy," I said, and paid him. "I appreciate it."

"Any time, Marco. You're a good kid."

With the flowers nestled in my arm I went into Joe's building, climbed the stairs, and again smelled the sensational aroma of the food. In my heart I felt that this dinner would even surpass the previous ones.

As I knocked on the door to Joe's apartment, I could hear the bustle of activity, talking and laughing from every part of the apartment. Joe's mother opened the door and yelled out "Marco is here!" Josephine gave me a hug and a big kiss, nearly squashing the flowers. When she saw the roses, I remember to this day her yelling out, "Look everybody what Marco brought to the family. These roses are so beautiful, and smell so good. Did you just pick them, Marco?"

Grinning, I said, "Of course."

Josephine then called her eldest daughter Karen. "Put these beautiful flowers in the big vase on the mantle piece and place it on the dining room table. This way everybody can see what Marco brought."

"Ok Mama," Karen said.

The news of Joe and I passing the test and becoming seniors was now the main point of everyone's conversation. Joe and I received kisses and hugs from the women and hugs, handshakes, and even kisses on the cheek from the men, many of whom slipped Joe and me envelopes. Most of the men while doing this said, "You make the family proud, and keep up the good work." Even Paulie came over and reluctantly said, "Congratulations," and then quickly walked away. Just about then, Uncle Vito and his wife and daughters arrived. Everyone rushed to him, hoping to be first to hug and kiss him and shake his hand. I was always impressed by the way Uncle Vito looked. I am sure his clothes were custom made as they fit his five-foot-ten, 165-pound frame just right. Joe confided in me that his large cuff links were the real McCoy as well as the knockout star sapphire pinky ring.

Uncle Vito's eyes were steel blue. His hair was graying at the temples and styled up to the minute. He carried himself as a *padron* should, standing erect and tall, sure of himself, giving off the air of command and respect. His wife, Ida, was still an attractive woman, standing around five-foot-three and very quiet. I noticed that when she was asked questions, I seemed to think that she glanced at her husband to get his silent ok before she answered. I think that they had their own secret silent way of communicating. Because she was the wife of a *padron*, she was entitled to the respect befitting her station. As we prepared to sit down for dinner Uncle Vito designated that Joe sit on his right and me on his left.

The dinner was stupendous. I was always amazed at the variety of dishes that used the same basic ingredients. The table became laden with plates piled high with antipasto, which I remember included *bruchetta, caponata,* large black and green olives, marinated mushrooms, peppers, hard pepperoni, sliced tomatoes, and basil sitting in bowls of olive oil, plus an assortment of cheeses. I also remember the plates of warm crusty Italian bread used for dipping. Bottles of Pellegrino water and carafes of Sicilian wine were ever present and kept on getting refilled. Toasts were made by everyone, most of them directed at Joe and I. At the appropriate time, the table was cleared and steaming platters of pasta came out. For this occasion, *linguini d'aglio* mixed with cauliflower cooked al dente was served. I still remember the aroma and taste of the blending of the olive oil, loads of garlic, cauliflower and linguini. Crisp white wine replaced the red, and toasts and bravos were offered to Joe's mother and her helpers.

When the family was sated with the pasta - at least two hefty bowls for each - the third course was served. Platters of what looked like small sautéed garlic chicken came out with the salad. As I ate it, I turned to Joe's older cousin Al, who came in from Philadelphia, and asked him, "What kind of chicken is this?"

Al broke out into a big grin and let everyone in on what I had said. "Marco wants to know what kind of chicken this is." All started to laugh, including Joe. Even Uncle Vito had a small smile. After letting the family have a little laugh, Joe's mother broke in with "*Basta*! Enough! You had your fun. He didn't know!" Turning to me, she said, "It's not chicken. It's *coniglio*, rabbit. I don't know if Jews can eat it."

I replied, "I don't know either."

In any event, I ate it. I really enjoyed it with the salad.

Next came the *fruita fresco*, cannoli, and espresso for dessert. Before we drank the espresso and *sambucca* another round of toasts was made directed at Joe and I. It made us feel like heroes rather than two teenagers who finished three years of high school. It felt real good.

After dinner everyone waited as usual for Uncle Vito to get up from the table and go through the French doors into the living room. The men followed and the doors were closed. In about fifteen minutes the doors opened and the men exited. Paulie then motioned to Joe and I to go into the living room, which we did. Once in, Paulie closed the doors and remained on the outside.

Uncle Vito invited us to sit down facing him. He then personally congratulated Joe and me for our accomplishments in passing and becoming seniors. He then asked what hours we had to be in school in the fall and spring terms. He seemed pleased when we told him that since we have a very light schedule our hours are expected to be from eight o'clock in the morning until one-forty-five in the afternoon.

Uncle Vito said to me, "I have not met your parents yet and I am going to have a dinner party this coming Wednesday night at the Grotto Restaurant on Mulberry Street. I want you and your parents to be my guests. It's at eight-thirty and this will leave enough time for them to close the store and get to the restaurant. Tell them that I look forward to breaking bread with them. Joe and his mother and father will also be there. Now you can go back inside and talk to the family. On your way out tell Paulie to come in. I'll see you inside shortly."

We then thanked Uncle Vito and left. We also told Paulie to go in. We then made small talk with the family until Uncle Vito and Paulie entered the dining room. After a few minutes of chatting, Uncle Vito gathered his wife and daughters and left.

Once they were gone I grabbed Joe and said, "Are we still on for Arthur Murray's with Celeste tomorrow?"

"We sure are," said Joe. "I spoke to her last night. She has us scheduled from four to six, and told me not to be late.

Meet me at the subway at a quarter after three. This will leave us plenty of time."

"Ok. Will do. I am really looking forward to meeting Celeste."

After talking to Joe I said my goodbyes, thanked Joe's mother and father, and left feeling great. When I got home, I opened the envelopes that were stuffed into my pockets. I couldn't believe my eyes as I counted the cash. There was thirty-five dollars in the kick. What a family! I am so happy that they accepted me, except for Paulie and probably his little brother, Pete. I felt their resentment and it grew and became more evident not only to me but also to Joe every time I was near them. I listened to Joe and kept away from them as much as I could, but I could not ignore them all together. So what I had to do I did, and had just said, "Hello, *comme sta*, good to see you." Then I had walked over and started a conversation with other members of the family. I think Paulie got real uptight as soon as Uncle Vito invited Joe and me to meet with him, leaving Paulie sort of guarding the door.

# XII

I took my shower early that morning and put my clothes, shoes, and socks that I had previously put in the basement. Around two-thirty I took off my apron, ran downstairs, washed up in the sink, and changed into my dark navy pants, black socks, white shirt, and Sunday shoes. I carefully combed my hair and put some hair tonic through it. I also lightly splashed myself with a little of my papa's after shave lotion. Arthur Murray, here I come!

I met Joe at the subway station. He greeted me with a big "Hi!" and then declared, "You smell like a French *putana.*"

I knew he was just kidding, so I left it at that. We took the subway to Times Square, and from there walked to the Arthur Murray studio on 47th Street off Broadway. By the time we entered the building it was about ten to four. We went into the elevator and told the operator "Arthur Murray Studio." Since no one else was riding, he closed the door and took us up to the fourth floor.

"Have fun," he said as we got off.

There was a receptionist sitting at a large desk in the middle of the reception room. We approached her and gave her our names, and told her we had a four o'clock appointment with Miss Celeste. She buzzed someone and told us that Celeste would be out shortly. A few minutes later a door opened and she walked in. She was gorgeous. I couldn't take my eyes off her. About five-foot-five with short brown curly hair, olive creamy complexion, and beautiful large brown eyes. She wore a white jacket over a black blouse that matched her white skirt. She reminded me of a song, "Did You Ever See a

Dream Walking?" She went over to Joe, gave him a kiss and hug, and said she was so glad to see him and that she hoped his family was ok.

She then came over to me, extended her hand to shake mine, and said, "Hello, I'm Celeste and I'm happy to meet you. Let's dance, fellows. That's what you're here for."

She led us into a room with a polished wood floor. There was a table at one end of the room holding a phonograph and a pile of records. When she took off her jacket I saw a body that made Ann Sheridan look like a boy. "Let's get going. Joe. I'm going to start you off with a Lindy Hop. And you, Marco, will learn the Foxtrot. And once you get these down you will switch. I teach this way because some students can pick up certain dances better than others."

Celeste went over to the table and took two white pieces of what looked like cardboard and brought them over to us. She then told us that the Arthur Murray method of teaching beginners is to have the basic steps printed on the cardboard, so that the students can learn and practice these steps as fast or as slow as they can. She then placed the boards in front of Joe and me and told us to take a minute or two to look the steps over. Then she said, "I'll start with you. Joe. Marco, just watch."

She had Joe place his feet on the footprints on the board, showing him the basic steps. She made him do it over and over until she said, "Ok, I think you got it."

She then came over to me and went through the same routine. It was more difficult for me to pick up the basic steps, but Celeste was patient. After a while she said, "You got it down pat."

To my surprise, she said, "I'm going to leave now. I have a short lesson to give. I want you to keep practicing the basic steps over and over until I get back. We will then try it with music."

As soon as she left, Joe and I started practicing. We kept on doing it over and over until I said, "Let's take a break. It's starting to feel like work."

"Ok, Marco. Only ten minutes."

There was no place to sit, so we sat on the floor. At the end of ten we went back to the cardboards, and Celeste came in shortly afterwards.

"Let me see how you guys are doing," she said, and she watched us go through our paces. "Not bad for the first time," she said. "I think you'll do ok. Now, let's put on some music and see what you can do. You go first Joe."

Celeste went over to the phonograph, turned it on, selected a certain record and put it on the turn table. She then carefully placed the player arm on the record. I recognized the song she selected. It was "In the Mood" by Glen Miller. She then said to Joe, "OK, Hepcat, let's see what you can do!"

I could not believe my eyes. Joe was able to not only do the basic steps in time with the music but was able to improvise a couple of breaks, also in time with the tempo. He was a natural. I enjoyed watching him twirling Celeste around, and further enjoyed watching Celeste move, especially when the twirls revealed her legs and the white garters attached to her stockings. It was a sight to remember.

When the record was finished Joe said to Celeste, "I'm just getting started. Let's do it again."

And so they did, with Joe again doing the basic steps and throwing in some improvisation. What great legs Celeste had. When the record finished playing, Celeste said, "Now it's your turn, Marco. I'll put on something slow and sexy." The song she picked was "Stardust." When the music started she said to me, "Come over here and take me in your arms. Put your right hand on my back about two inches above my brassiere strap. That's good. Now take your left hand in mine and keep your arm about forty-five degrees below your shoulder and your hand about ninety degrees up from the elbow joining my hand. Dance is a body contact experience, and in order to dance correctly the bodies of both dancers need to meld into one, especially from the waist down. So, let's try it."

I did what she told me. It was a bit awkward and she corrected my position. "Now, let's dance," she said. "Start off on your left foot and do the basic."

When she said 'meld' she meant it. From the waist up we were just touching, but from the waist down her body was pressed into mine. I could feel her every motion as we sort of glided across the floor. The body contact was so close that I could hardly keep my mind on the dance steps. I felt beads of sweat coming out on my forehead, and it wasn't from the room temperature. Celeste could feel what was happening, and she whispered, "Keep your mind on the dance and the music, not on me."

It must have worked, because I started to concentrate on the steps and the music rather than on the mental pictures I had. When the song was over she said, "Marco, you did ok. Let's try a faster tempo song. It was "Dancing in the Dark." Celeste motioned to me and I joined her on the dance floor. I glanced over to Joe and he was enjoying the whole scene. Again, Celeste made me meld with her, and I concentrated on what we were doing. I was enjoying the contact and the music. It was really fun. When the song ended, Celeste said, "Time's up. You both did good. Tell you what. Take the boards with the basic steps home with you and practice. See you next week. Same time. Was good seeing you, Joe. Regards to the family. Marco, it was nice meeting you. It was fun." Then she left.

My feet were killing me, because they had grown since Papa bought me those Sunday shoes over six months ago. I took them off and sat on the floor massaging my toes. Joe had to rub it in, and started to imitate the way I danced with Celeste. He put his arms around an imaginary partner, grabbed an imaginary hand, pushed his pelvis as far forward as he could and glided across the floor. He then started to sing a few bars of songs he knew that would get my goat. He paraphrasing some of the lyrics, starting with "Peg of my Hard," continuing with "You are always in my Hard," and ended with a couple of lines of "Hardaches." I knew he was joking around but I threw my shoes at him anyway. Laughing, I shouted at him, "You grass-hopping *dago*. What do you know about contact dancing. I melded with Celeste and it was super, not only learning to dance but also getting a dry hump."

Joe then laughed along with me as I put my shoes on. Just then the receptionist came in and announced that the room was booked and that we needed to leave.

On the way out I asked Joe, "Should we leave Celeste any money?"

He replied, "We'll give her something on account next week."

On the subway going home, I asked Joe how I needed to be dressed Wednesday night for Uncle Vito's dinner. He told me he had only been there twice before and that all the older men came in suits and the younger ones came in sport coats with long sleeve shirts and ties. The ladies wore elegant dresses, sporting nice jewelry and mink stoles.

"Gee, I don't know if my mother has this type of clothing," I said. "I think my father has a suit that'll fit him. I know he has the shirt and tie. But I'll be dressed the right way. I got a few ideas."

"Be on time," said Joe. "But in case you get there early, wait for us outside the restaurant. We'll be there at eight-twenty. *Capich?*"

"Talk to you later, Twinkle.Toes."

"Talk to you later, Gliding Marco. Don't forget to practice."

"Will do. Ciao

# XIII

It was about two o'clock on Tuesday afternoon when I was able to get away from the store. It was only a few blocks to Izzy Cohen's store on Delancy Street. The sign outside read: *For sale or rent. Slightly Used Clothing for Gentlemen.* I went in and Izzy greeted me warmly. He had been our customer for years.

Izzy was a religious Jew, originally from Poland. He was *Shomer Shabbos*, meaning he was observant, and he closed the store before sundown on Friday and remained closed until sundown Saturday night. He wore his yarmulke all the time and attended orthodox services Friday night and Saturday during the day. He also closed the store for high holidays and even for the minor holidays. Izzy was a slight man, partially bald. He always wore a vest with an assortment of pins sticking out all over, a piece of tailor's chalk in the pocket, and around his neck was the tape measure for altering garments. He had a long table to lay out the clothes, shears to cut if needed, a couple of sewing machines, and steam irons to finish the work.

"How are you Marco?" he asked

"I'm ok. And you, Izz?"

"I'm fine. Still eking out a living. By the way Marco, I'm hearing some good things about you. You know that around here good news and bad news travels fast. So I hear you are going to be a senior in High School? That's some doing. Your mother and father must be real proud of you. You are giving them a *mitzvah,* some big pleasure. *Mazel Tov!* So Marco, how can I help you?"

"We are invited to dinner tomorrow night at the Grotto,

and I was told to wear a sport coat. I have a pair of gray pants. I also need a tie."

"Come with me and we'll see what we can do for you." We went over to a rack of sport coats and Izzy said, "Try this on for size." I tried it on. "Just as I thought," said Izzy. "The 40 long is too tight. Try on the 42." Once I did, Izzy said, "42 long is the right size. Now, let's pick out the color you like. Look at this navy blue double breasted beauty with the brass buttons. It's all worsted wool, and it's in your size."

I tried it on and Izzy said, "Look in the mirror. It looks like it was custom made for you. I just need to lengthen the sleeves about an inch and a half."

"But I need it for tomorrow night."

"Don't worry," said Izzy. "I'll have it ready by four tomorrow. You'll look snazzy in it. Ok, let's pick out a tie to go with the coat and pants."

We went over to a huge tie rack and I had trouble making a selection. So I said to Izzy, "You know more about this than me, so you pick one out for me."

Izzy looked through the rack and said, "This one is good," and handed me a blue knitted tie. "This one will blend with the jacket, pants, and shirt. This is the latest style and you'll look like a million. Trust me."

"Thanks so much, Izzy. How much will it be?"

"Well, to buy the sport coat it will be seven fifty. To rent it for the night will be a dollar-fifty. The tie to buy is seventy-five cents. To rent, twenty-five cents. I won't charge you for the alteration."

"I think I'll rent the sport coat and tie."

"Ok, Marco, I'll start working on it right away. You'll look like a movie star in this outfit. Let me measure you for the sleeves." He took out his tailor chalk. "Come tomorrow and you'll be all set. You can pay me tomorrow when you pick up the jacket and tie. Give your parents my regards."

I said, "Will do. Thanks." Then I left the store.

As I walked back to the store, I started thinking about seeing Angie again. So at about eight-thirty that night I walked over to Tony's, hoping to see her, but she didn't show up. I did see one or two of her friends and I asked them to pass a message to Angie that said, if it would be ok, I'd like to meet her here at Tony's on Thursday night around nine. The girls giggled when I asked them to deliver the message, but they said they would do it. I then gave them two nickels for the phone and the payphone number at the store.

Wednesday night came around quickly and around three-thirty I headed for Izzy's. I walked in and Izzy greeted me with, "It's all ready Marco. Let's try it on."

He brought out the jacket and I put it on.

"It fits like a glove," Izzy said.

He then brought out the knitted tie and laid it on one of the jacket lapels.

"Look how it blends in. A perfect match. Ok, Marco, you're all set. Let me put the jacket and tie on a hanger."

"Here is your money, Izzy. I'll have it all back by four tomorrow. Thanks a lot."

I said goodbye and went back to our store. It was four when I said to Mama, "Once Carmine and Louie leave at five I'll go back, take a shower, and get ready. I think then it would be good for you to go and get ready and when you are finished. Papa can go and shower, shave, and get dressed. I will have enough time to finish dressing once you are both done."

And so it was. It was close to eight when Papa stuck his head through the door and said, "Let's close up now. We don't want to be late."

"Ok, Papa."

I closed up quickly, went back to our place, washed up thoroughly, put some of Papa's aftershave lotion on, combed my hair, put on my pants, and white shirt that Mama had washed, ironed, and starched earlier. I had a little trouble tying the knot in the knitted tie, but finally got it right, and then put on the jacket. I looked in the mirror and admitted to myself that I looked pretty damned good.

I had not seen Mama and Papa dressed like this since they had their Sunday off several weeks ago. Mama looked beautiful in her black dress, wearing a pearl necklace and pearl earrings. Mama told me some time ago that these pieces of jewelry were handed down in her family for at least four generations, and were brought to Italy by her grandma. Papa looked like a Don. In his blue serge suit, blue shirt, and blue and red striped tie. I thought he put a little too much moustache wax on, however, since the points of his moustache resembled two spears ready for the attack. Both of them looked like royalty.

It was about ten after eight when we left the store and walked to the restaurant. We stayed outside waiting for Joe and his folks and Uncle Vito and his wife Ida to arrive. While waiting, we could not but help notice the limousines pulling up and the elegantly dressed women and smartly dressed men getting out to enter the restaurant. I recognized some of the men from their pictures in the paper. Shortly thereafter, Joe and his parents arrived in one of Joe's father's limos, I guess, because Joe's father was driving. He then gave the keys to the valet to park. Joe then introduced his parents to mine, and Mama and Joe's mother greeted each other in Italian and kissed. Joe's father shook hands with my father and they also conversed in Italian, most of which I didn't understand. It must have been good, because the four of them were smiling and laughing during the conversation.

It was a few minutes later when a big, black caddy limo pulled up and Uncle Vito and his wife got out. To my dismay, Paulie was the driver. Uncle Vito's wife looked like she was wearing an entire jewelry store. Uncle Vito looked chic in his shiny black suit. I guessed it was all silk. He also wore a white shirt with a black and white striped tie. I could see his large gold cufflinks and huge diamond pinky ring. He looked the part of a Capo. He greeted Joe's parents and then turned to mine.

"I am Vito Amatto, and this is my wife, Ida," he said. "We are so glad to meet you. You have a wonderful boy here. We are very fond of him. Let's go inside."

It is hard to describe the beauty of that restaurant. It had red velvet brocade walls with oil paintings hanging on them. There were lots of mirrors, chandeliers, and sconces. The tables were covered with crisp, white linen tablecloths and napkins. The silverware appeared to be the real thing. The chairs were high-backed and comfortable, covered in solid black velvet. It was quite a scene. All of the waiters seemed to be Italian and wore red mess jackets with black bowties. The maitre'd, Salvatore, wore a white dinner jacket, a red bowtie, and greeted Uncle Vito warmly. The head waiter, Mario, bowed and asked Uncle Vito and party to please follow him to the private dining room that was reserved for them. We in turn followed Uncle Vito and his wife. On the way several of the men at the nearby tables got up and came to Uncle Vito to say hello and shake his hand. A few even kissed him on both cheeks. Even some women came up with their men to say hello and pay their respects. There must have been a total of about a dozen of these people paying homage to Uncle Vito. Joe told me later that only those who reached a certain level paid their respects to men like Uncle Vito in a public place in this manner.

    As we entered the private dining room, it was like entering the dining salon of a palace. The walls were covered with the same brocaded velvet as the main dining area. The carpeting was thick. The chairs were also high-backed with a wooden scroll design and the seat cushions were soft, but not mushy. I could see the shinning mahogany table legs as we sat down, because the red table cloth only covered the top and part of the side of the table. Above the table was a beautiful antique chandelier that exhibited a soft glow throughout the entire room. Oil paintings mounted on the walls along with lighted sconces added to the beauty. Once in, Uncle Vito signaled where to sit. I remember the seating arrangement clearly. Uncle Vito sat at one end of the table, his wife Ida at the other end. Joe's mother and father were invited to sit at his left and my parents to sit on his right. Joe was asked to sit between his father and Uncle Vito, and I was motioned to sit between my father and Uncle Vito. I looked around the room and saw that Paulie was not there. I wondered where he might be, but let it pass.

Once we were seated, Mario, the head waiter, came over and introduced the staff that would be serving us for the evening.

"This is Alberto di Roma, Eduardo di Assisi, Nicky di Palermo and Frankie di Bari."

Uncle Vito then announced, "I selected several dishes for each course that I think you might enjoy. If you don't care for any of them, feel free to order off the regular menu."

Mario, with a great smile, approached the table and proudly announced that the owner Frederico di Grassi and master chef Benito Ramondi wanted to come to the dining room to pay their respect and personally offer the specialties of the house. Di Grassi was a short stout balding man. Chef Ramondi was a tall, dark, slim man dressed in a crisp white chef's outfit. I noticed that he didn't have a chef's hat on. Both of them greeted Uncle Vito with great respect and then greeted us all. In fact Mr. Di' Grassi kissed the hands of both Mrs. Amatto and my mother. Mama's face turned a little red after he did this. Uncle Vito thanked them both for coming and suggested that the chef go back to the kitchen and Mr. Di Grassi go back to his normal greeting of customers. Mario then took over. In English with an Italian accent he said, "Tonight I have for you, and recommend for the primero platto, the Sicilian Companata consisting of eggplant, celery, tomatoes, onions, and capers in olive oil. I also have Italian wedding soup. We have special for you the pasta dish imported from Italy, *Fusilli al dente* with *Cavolfiore*, served with a caper in aglio sauce. For those ordering the fish, as a side dish I will serve risotto al nero. For the main courses, I recommend *Tunno ala Palermitano* served with pan seared sardines. I'd enjoy making for you, if you wish, *Figato ala Venezina*. Our Osso Buco, slowly brazed with a flavored sauce, is a big favorite, as well as *Polla ala cacciatore*. We also feature *Anatra a la griglia* and *Bistecca a la fiorentina*. Might I also suggest Porcella cooked in the chef's special myrtle sauce? A wonderful fish dish is the sautéed sea bass baked in a parchment envelope with onions capers and herbs. For the salad can I suggest a special one consisting of radicchio, fungi, cipolle and arugula with green and black olives? The salad dressing is a mixture of twenty-five-year-old balsamic vinegar and extra, extra virgin olive oil. For the vegetables might I suggest asparagi, fegiolini, and cavolini de bruxelles?"

Uncle Vito ordered *Osso Buco*. His wife selected the Porcella. Joe's mother asked for the Anatra, and his father's choice was Bistecca. Joe and I also ordered that dish. Papa said, "I'll have the Tunno." And Mama's selection was the Sea Bass. All agreed on Sicilian campanata and, as this was served, platters of bruchetta were also placed on the table. Glasses were filled with sparkling Pellegrino water as well as the wines that Mario suggested that would complement the different entrees ordered. With the antipasto, since Mario anticipated that this would be selected, he already had the appropriate Sicilian wine opened in order to let it breathe, and it was poured as antipasto came out. Joe and I were passed up on the wine since we were not yet of age, but we did enjoy the Pellegrino water. To me it tasted a little like seltzer, but not as good. Once the wine was poured, Uncle Vito rose to make a toast, saying he was proud of Joe and me, and that he was happy to meet my family, especially since they were of Italian heritage. It was his hope that the family relationship would continue to grow. Next to make a toast was Joe's father, Carlo. He hoped that the families would continue to meet and enjoy each other's company as well. We all joined in with acknowledgment of the toast by saying "Salute, Salute," and then we sipped our drinks. Once we sat down again we started to partake of our food. Joe and I really attacked the antipasto and the bruchetta. The rest ate heartily.

The glasses were continually refilled and I noticed that Mama and Papa started to relax, especially since Uncle Vito began speaking to Papa in Italian. After the appetizer course dishes were picked up, napkins were replaced and even the wine glasses changed. Mario's timing was perfect. He allocated fifteen minutes before the *piatto primero* was served, which allowed a rest between courses and time for everyone to continue their conversation. I vividly recall Uncle Vito asking Papa questions in Italian and Papa replying also in Italian. Joe's father would also join in both as a questioner and a listener. Mama, Joe's mother and Uncle Vito's wife also had conversations in Italian, and seemed to get along well.

When Joe and I asked what was going on in the conversation, Uncle Vito said smilingly, "If you devoted more of your time to learning Italian instead of dancing, you could understand what we say." Upon Uncle Vito saying this first in Italian, and then in English, all started to laugh. Joe was a little embarrassed by this and so was I.

We got over this quickly as the door from the kitchen opened and Mario pushed out the cart carrying a silver tray and cover containing the pasta dish. The aroma from the pasta was like Italian nectar and made everyone look forward to partaking of hefty portions of this dish. Sprigs of fresh parsley and twigs of thyme adorned the dish. Mario brought the tray to Uncle Vito and served him first. Second was Joe's father, then Joe and me. The women were served last. This was in keeping with an old Sicilian custom. While the pasta was being served new bottles of Sicilian white wine were also placed on the table. This was to complement this special dish. As the pasta was placed on our plates, the waiter assigned to each station immediately asked permission to grate special imported parmesan cheese onto each individual dish, and then suggested the guest wait a few minutes so that the cheese could blend with the rest of the dish.

And so it did, magnificently. The al dente character of the fusilli and the softer texture of the cavolfiore made a great combination which was then enhanced by the small roasted garlic slivers. Once all the guests received their portion of the pasta and actually tasted it, it seemed that all in mass stood up and saluted Mario by saying "Milli Gratzi. Perfecto!" Second and third portions of pasta were consumed by all along with several glasses of wine by each of the guests, except Joe and me. When each guest had their fill of the pasta and wine, the dishes were removed along with the wine glasses and remaining bottles of wine. Again new napkins, wine glasses, and silverware were replaced. During the periods between courses Uncle Vito seemed to get into deeper conversations with my father. Joe's father said but little, although he did ask a question or two of my father. The conversations were in Italian and I couldn't understand much of what they were saying.

It was about this time that I leaned over to Joe and said, "I got to take a leak. Where is the toilet?"

"I'll show you. Just follow me."

And out of the private dining room we went. As we passed through the doors we saw Paulie, big as life, sort of keeping an eye on the door and carefully watching who came in and out. I felt sure that he was chosen to be not only Uncle Vito's chauffer but also his bodyguard. It was becoming more evident that Paulie had it in for me, big time. As we passed him in the hall, Joe and I said, "Hi, How you doing?"

Paulie's reply to Joe was, "OK."

But to me he sort of muttered something under his breath. I couldn't hear what he said, but Joe did. Joe then whispered to me saying, "Keep walking. Don't look back."

"What did Paulie say?"

"You don't want to know. Just stay away from Paulie. As far as possible."

I tried to press Joe to tell me, but he just kept repeating, "You don't want to know. Just forget about it and don't push it. This is not the time. Just wait it out."

"I did nothing to him. What's his beef?"

Joe came back and said, "He's jealous of you, and he thinks you are a threat to his position with Uncle Vito."

"That's ridiculous."

"It is, but not to Paulie. He considers you a real threat. Don't cause any waves and everything will be ok. Ok, Marco?"

"Ok, Joe."

We went into the men's room, took our leak, tipped the attendant a dime each, and went back to the dining room. Lucky for us, Paulie was nowhere to be seen. The festive air in the room was growing. The ladies were chatting and looked like they were having a good time. Uncle Vito, Joe's father and my father were deep in conversation, again in Italian. Again, I could not understand a word of it. After a reasonable time elapsed, and all were finished eating their main course, the tables were cleared. It was at this time that Uncle Vito got up and again welcomed me, my papa and mama. He hoped we were enjoying the food and more important the company. He again stated that it was proper for the families of the two boys like Joe and Marco to continue to bind together and stay fast friends. Uncle Vito then turned to Joe and me and said, "I'm very proud of both of you. You have proven yourselves to be honorable for watching out for each other's safety and well-being. Watching each other's backs keeps both of you safer than going it alone. For doing this, and doing this successfully, I have a little gift for each of you."

Uncle Vito then reached into his jacket pocket and brought out two small cases, and gave one to each of us.

He said, "You can open them now," and we couldn't wait to do so.

I couldn't believe my eyes. The box contained a beautiful gold wrist watch. Joe opened his package and said, "I can't believe this. This is fantastic."

We both turned to Uncle Vito and thanked him from the bottom of our hearts.

Papa and Joe's father came over and, with great expression of pride, helped put the watches on our wrists. Once this was done Joe and I had the same idea. We got up from our chairs and walked around the table, showing off the watches and enjoying the oohs and ah's from the family. We saved Uncle Vito for last. Joe leaned over and shook his hand and kissed him on both cheeks. I followed and did the same.

We then took turns in expressing our thanks and appreciation not only for the gift, but also for the support he gave us. Mario then announced, "Dessert and espresso will now be served." Bottles of anisette and sambuca were then placed upon the table, and hearty portions of the liquors were doled out. Then espresso cups were filled and refilled.

While we were enjoying the amazing desserts the entrance doors opened and the musicians from the main dining room came in and serenaded us with a medley of Italian songs. After they finished I saw Uncle Vito signaling the band leader over and thanking him while handing him a bunch of bills.

Uncle Vito then gave a signal to Mario to come over, and he whispered something in his ear. Mario nodded and quickly left the room.

A few moments later Paulie came in. I didn't want to make eye contact with Paulie, so I turned to papa and made some small talk with him. He kept looking at my watch, admiring it.

Joe told me later that he was able to overhear a portion of the conversation between Paulie and Uncle Vito. He saw Uncle Vito take a roll of bills out of his pocket and give it to Paulie, telling him to pay the bill and to take very good care of Mario, the waiters, the chef, the maitre' d, and the parking valets. He also instructed him to have the car in front when he and his wife came out.

The dinner came to a close when Uncle Vito stood up and thanked all for coming. Papa came over to him and said in English, "Don Vito, my wife and I want to thank you for this wonderful evening and the past favors you have bestowed upon us. I know my son Marco holds you in high esteem and values your friendship."

Uncle Vito replied, "It has been our pleasure, and we will be in touch."

All then said good night to each other and started to exit the restaurant. On the way out, the waiters, chef, head waiter and maitre'd made it their business to come over to Uncle Vito and thank him over and over for his generosity. When we reached the side walk, Paulie was already there at the wheel of Uncle Vito's limo. Joe's father's limo was right behind. As they entered their cars they waived and we waived back.

They drove off and we started to walk home. Once we arrived mama took off her shoes while papa loosened his belt.

Both were raving about the wonderful evening and the friendliness and warmth shown by all. I waited for the opportunity to ask papa the gist of the conversation in Italian with Uncle Vito and Joe's father. He told me, saying, "It's a small world. Part of the Amatto family lives in Venice. They are in the olive oil business and have been doing business with Mama's family who for many years has been in the import-export business. He further told me that the families even know each other socially."

The next day when things slowed down, I hurried back to Izzy's store and returned the jacket and tie and paid him. He asked, "How did things go last night?"

"Just perfect. Look at the watch Mr. Amatto gave me."

"Boy! That's some watch! Be careful who you show it to. On the other hand, you don't have to worry too much. If it is known that it comes from Vito Amatto no one will bother you. Wear it in good health. Give my best to your parents."

"Will do. So long, Izzy."

I left his store, returned to mine, and went to work.

# XIV

It was Thursday afternoon around four o'clock when the phone rang. It was Angie.

"Hi, Marco," she said. "I got your message, so I called. How are you?"

"I'm ok," I answered. "How would you like to meet me at Tony's tonight?"

"Funny you asked, Marco. I planned on being there around eight-thirty."

"That's great! See you there"

About seven-thirty I started to clean up. Papa said, "We close at eight. What's the hurry?"

"Well," I replied, "I thought I would go over to Tony's and meet some of my friends."

"Anyone in particular?"

"Well there is one girl."

"Marco, get cleaned up and get over there," he said. "I'll do the cleanup and close the store. Remember I was young once."

I hurried to the apartment, took a shower, even shaved, and put on fresh clothes. I put on a dab of Papa's aftershave lotion and combed my hair after applying a good amount of Brilliantine hair tonic. On my way out, Mama saw me and came over.

"Marco, you look so handsome," she said. "*Mein kind.* Have a wonderful time."

Papa looked up from his sweeping and said, "Have a wonderful time"

I hurried over to Tony's and waited for Angie to come.

It was nice outside so I got a little table on the outside under the awning. I kept looking at my watch with one eye and for Angie with the other. Around eight-thirty she showed up. She looked real pretty in her white skirt, black blouse, and saddle shoes.

"Hi Marco," she said as she sat down. "I've missed you."

"I've missed you too, Angie. How about some gelato or an ice cream soda?"

"I think I would like a chocolate ice cream soda. Bring some extra napkins. I don't want to get a stain on my skirt."

"Will do," I said, and hopped into the store and ordered an ice cream soda for Angie and a double lemon ice for me. I also remembered to bring the napkins. Once I delivered the goodies I sat down, and we started to talk. It was small talk at first, about school, and then the conversation went into more personal things. She told me about her mother and father, her brother and the rest of her family, where they lived and what they did. I, in turn, told her about my family, and how hard we all worked at the store. Of course I never said anything about our business with Carmine and Louie.

Time ran by quickly and before we knew it, Tony was turning off the lights and it was time to go. We got up and, arm in arm, walked to her home. When we got to the door of the tenement we went into the vestibule.

"I had a great time," I said.

"So did I," she answered. "I'd like to see you again."

"If you are free on Saturday, I'd like to take you to the Paramount theatre. They have Tommy Dorsey playing there and the singer is Frank Sinatra. There is also a movie with Ginger Rogers and Fred Astaire."

"I'd love to go there with you."

"Well, it's all set," I said. "I'll come to pick you up around one-thirty. We might have to wait an hour or so on line before getting in."

"It would be better for me to meet you by the subway at one."

"OK," I said. "Well, I guess I better be going."

Angie then moved closer to me and said, "Aren't you going to kiss me good night?"

I answered by putting my arms around her and pressing my body against hers. She did the same to me. She then pressed her lips against mine and I felt her tongue exploring every part of the inside of my mouth. She then pressed against the boner that I had. After a few moments of this she broke it off by saying, "It's late. I have to go. I'll see you Saturday." Then she ran up the steps. It took a couple of minutes for the boner to come down and I went home with a smile on my face.

Friday went by quickly. We were so busy that I didn't have time to think of my date with Angie. Of course, I told Papa of my Saturday plans, and he nodded ok. I added that I would run the store on Sunday so that he and Mama could take some time off. I even phoned Joe and told him I would not be going to dinner at his house on Sunday, but I didn't tell him why. I showered and shaved after work on Friday, and left my Saturday clothing in the basement storeroom.

I got up the usual time on Saturday morning, helped Papa open the store and worked with him until twelve. I then took off my apron and hopped down to the basement, washed up, combed my hair and got dressed. I looked in the mirror to see if everything was in place, and sure enough it was. I said to the image in the mirror, "You are a good looking dog, you!" I took some money from what I call my vault. It was actually a space behind a loose brick in the basement wall. As I left the store, Mama said, "Marco, have a good time." Papa gave me a smile and, when Mama wasn't looking, a big wink.

Thank goodness it was a beautiful day. I hurried over to the subway station. A few minutes later Angie arrived and gave me a kiss on the cheek. I had the change for the fare and we rode up to Times Square and walked the rest of the way to the Paramount. When we got close, we saw that there was a line around the corner waiting to get in. We hurried and got to the end of the line, and before we knew it, the line gathered behind us. During the two and a half hours we waited in line, we talked about school, our friends, and hopes and aspirations for the future. I again told Angie I wanted to be a doctor, and she again told me she hoped to become a nurse. She asked me about Mama and Papa, their background and about the deli. She seemed surprised when I told her I was Jewish.

"How can that be? I thought you were Italian."

I then explained to her that, in many cases, religion and nationality are not the same. She said, "I don't care if you are Jewish or not. I like you anyway." It was about this time the theatre let out and the line started moving, slowly at first and then faster. When we got up to the window the ticket lady said, "All we got left is the balcony."

I said, "We'll take two seats."

We entered the beautiful theatre and at the candy counter I bought some candy bars and popcorn. We climbed up the ramp and then the steps to the balcony. We saw seats two rows from the balcony top. "I hope we can get a good view from here," Angie said. "I want to see and hear Frank Sinatra."

We scurried up to get those seats before they were captured. As we got settled in, the lights dimmed and the stage lights came on. The next thing I saw was the stage rising up from the orchestra pit with the band on it. Halfway up, Tommy Dorsey's band, with him leading, started playing his theme song, "Sentimental Over You." The band reached stage level and continued playing the songs that Tommy Dorsey recorded. Angie and I could not stop stomping our feet to the music. After playing just music for fifteen minutes, Frank Sinatra was introduced and he went up to the mic. We were fascinated, and the audience loved him. When he finished he received a standing ovation. The audience wouldn't let him off and continued their applause and screaming.

"More! More! More!"

Sinatra glanced over at Dorsey who gave him a nod, and Sinatra came to the mic and thanked the audience. He said, "Although it's not on the program, we'll do an encore of one more song."

When he finished, the audience went wild. The applause was thundering. It took about five minutes to quiet down and then the band started to play again. While we were standing and applauding Angie turned full face to me and gave me a kiss that knocked my socks off. She said this was the best she had ever seen and that she loved me for taking her to see Sinatra.

After another fifteen minutes, Tommy Dorsey thanked the audience and the stage slowly lowered. Once it lowered completely the lights went down and the feature film came on. It was a musical starring Fred Astaire and Ginger Rogers. I was anxious to see Fred Astaire's dance routines. Maybe I could learn something. In the meantime Angie sort of cuddled up. She put her head on my shoulder and kissed me on my neck and even rubbed my thigh. I in turn put my arm around her and slowly inched forward toward her tit. There was no resistance, so I reached in and copped a great feel. I was on fire and so was Angie. I reached down, grabbed her hand, and directed it toward my crotch. Before I knew it, she was there. We continued kissing and hugging and touching, when all of a sudden she said: "Marco, what time is it?"

I told her it was a quarter after five.

She seemed to get panicky and said we have to leave. "I must be home by six. Don't ask questions, Marco. Let's just go."

Reluctantly I said ok, and we made our way down the balcony steps, to the main floor, and out onto the street.

I had to keep my coat in front of me, over my crotch, to hide the gigantic boner. I was hoping it would go away by the time we reached the street. It wasn't until the subway ride home that I dared take the coat away. Angie kept looking and teasing, saying such things as, "Why don't you put your coat on. Are you hiding something under the coat?" She whispered in my ear, "Aren't you worried that the buttons on your fly will come shooting off and hurt someone?"

By the time we reached our station the boner had cooled down. I went to walk Angie home and she said, "No, not this time. I'll explain some other time. I got to run. I had a wonderful time Marco, so please call me." She then gave me a fast peck on my cheek and took off.

I couldn't quite figure out the scenario but overall I had a great time. I got back to the deli and saw that there were many customers waiting. So I quickly put on an apron and went behind the counter to wait on the people.

Time passed quickly and before I knew it Papa closed the doors at eight o'clock. I know, because I looked at my new watch. As usual we went to the apartment and ate the dinner that Mama had previously prepared.

"Well, how was your date?" Papa asked with a smiling face.

"Where did you go, what did you do?" Mama asked

"Well, we went to the Paramount Theatre, saw Tommy Dorsey and heard Frank Sinatra. He was terrific and got a standing ovation. He even did an encore. The movie was also wonderful. Fred Astaire and Ginger Rogers. Boy, how they can dance!"

Papa then asked, "Is the girl very pretty?"
"She sure is."
"Did you do a little cuddling?"
"Leave the boy alone," Mama interrupted.
"Remember when we used to do that?" said Papa.
"That's enough, Ivan. You are embarrassing Marco."
"That's ok, Mama," I said.
Papa then asked, "Are you going to see her again?"
"I think so."

Mama then said, "Time to go to bed. We have a busy morning tomorrow. And thank you, Marco. Papa and I look forward to visiting friends in Brooklyn. Their cousins came in from Venice for a visit."

"Did you know them?" I asked.
"No, but I knew their family."
"Are they Jewish?"
"Yes," said Mama, "and I'm very anxious to hear about how the Jews of Venice are doing. I keep hearing rumors that

not too good changes are happening over there."

I went over to Mama, gave her a hug and a kiss, then went over to Papa and gave him a hug and a kiss and said goodnight. I got to the bathroom first, washed up, brushed my teeth, and went to my room. I put on my PJs and climbed into bed PDQ. I kept dreaming of Angie in bed with me and we were having a hot and sexy time in my dream. I could actually hear her moaning with pleasure when all of a sudden I exploded, wetting the sheets, PJs, and even the blanket. I never expected this to happen so quickly. I jumped out of bed and quietly went to the bathroom. I washed myself, the PJs and tried to wash the sheet and blanket so that no evidence would be left. It was uncomfortable trying to sleep on wet sheets and blankets, but I finally fell asleep.

I got up earlier than usual, and again tried to dry the now damp sheet and blanket. Since it looked like it was going to be a sunny day, I opened the window and I hoped it would help the drying.

It was Sunday morning and we were busy. Once the rush was over, Mama and Papa washed up, changed their clothes and said goodbye. They were on their way to Brooklyn. They left me a phone number in case of a problem. Evidently, their friends could afford their own phone. The rush was over around two o'clock. I made a sandwich, took a coke, and sat on one of our small customer tables. I was nearly finished eating when the phone rang. It was Joe.

"Hello," he said. "How you doing?"

"Ok."

"Busy?"

"Not right now," I said. "I have a little time to talk. If a customer comes in I'll call you back."

"Good. Where have you been, Marco?"

"I've been around."

"Sorry you can't make it today."

"So am I," I said, "but my folks need some time off."

"I called you yesterday. Your father told me you went

out, but didn't say where."

"Well, to tell you the truth, I took Angie to the Paramount to hear Sinatra."

"You took Angie Barrone?" said Joe.

"Yeah. Why?"

"Are you crazy? She is damaged merchandise. She got knocked up two years ago when she was fifteen. Her brother Bobo - he's the bouncer at the 42nd Street dance hall - he found a Jew doctor in Brownsville who took care of her. Bobo is about six-three and weighs over two hundred and fifty pounds. He found out who the guy was, waited for him, and beat the shit out of him. The guy was in the hospital for close to a month. When he got out, Bobo caught up with him and beat the shit out of him again. This time, when the guy got out, he left for parts unknown. Bobo will do the same to anyone he thinks is messing with his sister. His game is to marry Angie off as fast as possible. All Angie has to do is to mention to Bobo that you put a hand on her, and even Uncle Vito can't help in a case like that. Forget about her. Stay away from her. Give her an excuse that you need to work in the store more hours. You better hope that she meets someone else. Bobo already scared the last two guys away."

"But she's hot to trot," I said. "And I'd like to saddle her."

Joe came back, "Forget about it. Capiche?"

"For you, I'll give up probably the best hump I'll ever have."

# XV

With all the activity, before I knew it Monday afternoon came around, along with another dance session with Celeste.

I met Joe at the subway and we went to the dance studio. The receptionist recognized us and greeted us with a big smile. "Celeste will be with you in a moment," she said.

A few minutes later Celeste came out. "Hi guys," she said, and this time she kissed both Joe and me on the cheeks. She looked dynamite in here white sweater and black pants. The table and phonograph were in the same position as before.

"Well, let's see what you can do," she continued. "You first, Joe." She put on "Let's Dance" by Bennie Goodman. I was amazed by Joe's ability to do the Lindy. He had breaks that, by the look on her face, even surprised Celeste.

When the record was over, she gave Joe a big squeeze and said, "You are really good, the best I have ever seen for the time you have been taking lessons. You can hold your own with students that have been taking lessons for two or three years." She turned to me. "It is your turn, Marco." She put a new record on the phonograph. I remember the song. It was "Because of You," a nice slow fox trot.

Celeste melted into my arms as we started to dance. She told me that I held her in the correct position, and we glided across the floor. Keeping the tempo, I tried some fancy steps and Celeste followed in great style.

Before I knew it, the record was ending and I finished the dance by doing a bit sexy dip.

"Great job," said Celeste. "I loved the dip. I think you both are good enough to learn another dance. Joe, you are a good candidate to learn the Peabody. Marco, you will make a wonderful Rumba dancer. That's the new craze from South America. I am going to give you both the step charts. Take them home and practice. When you come next week, we will put them to music."

With that, Celeste left the studio and came back a few minutes later with the step outlines. "Let's see what we can do with these. You first, Marco." Celeste then faced me, saying, "Watch my feet just to get the beat." After watching her for about five minutes, she said, "Your turn, Marco. Let's see what you can do.

I put my feet into the step outlines while Celeste tapped out the beat. It didn't take very long before Celeste said, "You got it, you got it. You're next, Joe." The same procedure was followed, except the tempo was much faster and the steps were different. Joe caught on quicker than me and Celeste was thrilled. "Ok, guys, time is up." She spoke over her shoulder as she left the room. "Go home and study with your feet. See you next week."

"That was great," I said to Joe.

"Sure was, buddy. Since we did so good, why don't we try going to some dances in the neighborhood? Some of the churches and community centers hold weekly dances. It's a good way to meet some good looking dolls. Usually these dancers have good legs."

"We'll give it a try," I said.

"Let's look in the local papers and see what we can find. Flyers are also a good way to find out where the action is."

"Joe, you do some searching," I said. "As will I. Let's touch base Friday right after the papers come out and we'll compare notes."

"Sounds good," said Joe.

When we reached our station, we said 'so long' and went our separate ways.

I got back to the store and went back to work.

Tuesday, Wednesday, Thursday and Friday was the same old routine. I got a couple of calls from Angie during this time and had to tell her that I was so very busy at the store that I didn't have any free time. I told her I would call her when I could. I hated to do this because I really missed Angie, but the thought of her brother Bobo made me think twice.

Once the newspaper late additions were delivered, I grabbed them and pulled out the weekend entertainment sections that also had local and community activities. Scanning through the *Herald Tribune*, the *Daily News*, and the *Mirror*, I found exactly what we were looking for. There was a teenage dance that evening at the YMCA on 14th Street from eight to ten. Tomorrow, Saturday, there was one for fourteen to eighteen-year olds, close by at St Mary's Church on West Broadway. Sunday afternoon was a real winner. A live band dance was being held at NYU Downtown campus from two to five. The public was invited and the event featured the NYU dance band.

I called Joe with the news and he answered by telling me he had read the same papers as me. "We did our homework real good," he said. "Your choices were the same as mine."

"So let's do it," I said. "The YMCA dance is free. The Saint Mary's dance is fifty cents. The NYU dance is a dollar, but it's got a big band sound with live college orchestra."

Joe asked, "Can you get away from the store tonight by seven-thirty? I know it's your busy night."

"I'll ask and call you back," I said.

I asked Papa if I could get off work at six-thirty so I could have time to wash up, change and meet Joe.

Papa said, "You are a teenager, going to be a high school senior, and deserve to have a good time at this stage of your life. Besides, you earned it. I've been thinking that you're spending too much time working here. With the rental money coming in steady, I am going to look around for some part time weekend help. I spoke to Sol who lives around the corner. He's retired now but he was a counterman at the Stage Delicatessen for years and knows the business and seems interested. I want you to enjoy your weekends. It will also give Mama time to rest." He smiled. "And also give her time to gossip with the Yentas in the neighborhood. She might even learn how to play Mah Jong. Go and have a good time. Don't worry about anything. Tell me what plans you have for the weekend."

"Well," I said, "we were thinking about going to the dance tomorrow night at St. Mary's on West Broadway. It starts at eight o'clock and Sunday there's a live band playing at the gym NYU downtown, just a short bus ride away. It starts at two and ends at five."

"I'm sure you'll have a wonderful time," said Papa. "I hope your feet won't hurt from all that dancing. I think that if this dancing thing continues, I'll have to buy you new shoes." We both laughed. I hugged Papa and thanked him again. He then jokingly said, "Go now and get ready, before I change my mind."

I called Joe and told him, "It's a go for tonight and it's a plan for Saturday and Sunday. What do we wear tonight?"

"A shirt and pants should fit the bill."

"No tie?" I asked.

"Are you kidding? Just the shirt and clean pair of pants. Wear your Sunday shoes."

"Ok, I'll see you at the Broadway bus stop at seven-thirty."

"I'll be there."

We met as planned. Me with my gray pants and white shirt. Joe was wearing his white pants and black shirt. He looked like George Raft. We got to the YMCA and they checked our GO High School card and took our money. We followed the sound of the music to what looked like a large dining room. The tables were folded up and resting against the walls. There were chairs lined up in front of the tables. The phonograph rested on the table at the front of the room in back of the microphone and there were speakers on the right and left side. There was also a pile of records on the table. An older guy was in charge of spinning the records. I also saw a table off to one side holding two large bowls of what looked like punch.

Next to them were some cookies on paper plates. I remember Joe and I walking around casing the place for dance partners. He pulled me aside and said, "Don't even ask a beauty to dance. Ask a plain looking Jane, and the plainer she looks the better."

"Why?"

"It's simple," said Joe. "The doll will be asked a lot, the plain Jane not very often. Once they see you and I dance, all the dolls will be itching to dance with us."

"Sounds like a plan, so let's try."

Joe zeroed in on a girl fitting the description. He went over and said, "Hi, I'm Joe. Would you like to dance?"

"I'm Nancy," said the girl. "And sure, I'd like to dance."

The next record, fortunately for Joe, was "One O'clock Jump," a Lindy Hop number, and better still, Nancy was a good dancer. Joe and Nancy made such a good showing that all the other couples stopped their dance to form a large circle around them and egged them on. When the record was over, Joe escorted Nancy over to the punch table and they shared some punch and ate some cookies. Joe was watching me out of the corner of his eye as I approached a tall, skinny, not so good looking girl and asked her to dance. She readily agreed, told me her name was Bernice but everyone called her Bunny. To my surprise, Bunny was also a very good dancer who easily followed my steps including the brakes. We danced to the song "Moon Glow."

When the song finished, I walked Bunny back to her seat, thanked her and went to look for Joe. We hooked up and he said, "We did good. From here on the dolls who can dance will be looking for us." And so it was.

We just had to look at the doll and all of a sudden they were available to dance. We hit the doll jackpot that evening. Many of them asked if we would be out dancing Saturday or Sunday. When we told them yes, a lot of them said they would try to also be there. They just loved dancing with us.

Before we knew it, the evening was over. Joe and I

decided not to ask any doll for her phone number or try to take her home. I said, "Let's just play the field this weekend and see how we make out."

"That's a Si, Si," said Joe. "See, I didn't forget my Spanish."

We laughed, caught the bus, got off at our stop, said 'Ciao' to each other and went on our way home.

Before I fell asleep that night, I reviewed the time at the dance and fell asleep with a big grin on my face. I hadn't sleep very long when I felt Papa shaking me. "Marco," he said. "Time to get up. It's five-thirty. We need to get the store ready by seven." I reluctantly got up and got prepared to help Papa open and operate the store, even though I was still half asleep for the first two hours. Two cups of strong coffee helped to bolster me up.

I worked with Papa and Mama all day Saturday until around six, when Papa said, "Don't you have a dance tonight at St. Mary's? What time does it start?"

"Eight o'clock, Papa."

"So what are you doing here behind the counter in your apron?" he asked. "Go take your shower, shave and get ready for the dance. I got reports that you did good. Try to stay away from the *shicksers*. They are always trouble."

"I will, Papa," I said with tongue in cheek as I started to get ready.

I changed into my only pair of pants and had the white shirt I wore the previous night as my Saturday night shirt, and of course wore my Sunday shoes which were still a little tight, but I was getting used to them. I met Joe on the corner of Delancy Street at about a quarter to eight, and we walked over to St. Mary's. As we came up to the church, we heard music coming from the recreation center next to the church itself and saw a lot of kids standing in line waiting to get in. The line moved slowly but steadily, and after waiting for fifteen minutes, we paid our entrance fee of fifty cents and went in.

The room was pretty big and was probably used for

church meetings. It was the same setup as last night, table in front with a phonograph and speakers and a pile of records. Chairs were lined up against the walls. There were fans on poles in the corners. The table next to the phonograph held cokes and cookies that were being sold. It was ten cents for a bottle of coke and the cookies were two for five cents.

As Joe and I looked over the crowd, he said to me, "Let's use the same plan as we did last night and pick out wallflowers to dance with. They are either good dancers or put out, maybe both."

We then hunted our pray like two blood hounds. When we found what we thought was a good choice, we waited until a new record was put on and then made the move. Lucky for me, it was a slow fox trot, and I walked over to the mark and said, "Could I have this dance?"

She looked unsure at first, then said, "Ok. My name's Janet."

It must have really been my lucky night, because Janet was a pretty good follower. I tried some breaks but it was tough for her to follow.

When the song ended I walked her back to her chair. "Thanks," I said. "See you later."

The next song was a lindy-hop and there was Joe doing his thing with a real doll and she was keeping up with him, breaks and all. Many of the other dancers noticed them, especially the dolls, and Joe was loving it.

I was good at the fox trot and two steps, but just fair on the lindy, but I used our wallflower system and got through it pretty good. On the next slow dance, my partner was real good and I got noticed. From then on Joe and I were kings of the dance. The dolls even came over to us and asked if they could dance with us. The evening came to a close faster than we thought and we left with pockets full of dolls' phone numbers.

When we went to the toilet, we decided not to tell anyone where we were going to be on Sunday, since this was a college dance with a live band. We didn't want to be hampered by kids from the YMCA and St. Mary's.

On the way home, I asked Joe, "How do you think we should dress for tomorrow night?"

Joe answered, "Since it's a college, I think we should wear jackets. We can always take them off."

"You really think so?" I asked.

"Yep!"

"Ok," I said. "I guess I'll have to see Izzy tomorrow morning. I think it would have been cheaper to buy the jacket."

"Talk to you tomorrow," said Joe. "Ciao."

"Ciao"

When I awoke the next morning, I glanced at my watch. It read eight-forty-five. I looked at it again, it still read eight-forty-five. Why hadn't Papa woken me up to help open the store and wait on the early morning customers? I jumped into my clothes, brushed my teeth, and hurried into the store. To my surprise, there was Papa, Mama, and Sol behind the counter taking care of the customers. I grabbed Papa on the side and said, "What's going , Papa?"

"Mama and I decided to let you be a teenager on weekends from now through your senior year," said Papa. "We felt the store was taking up too much of your time. Sol is now retired and was looking for some part time work, because he loves the business. He is experienced in making the corned beef, pastrami, tongue, potato salad, and coleslaw. I told him just enough about using the toilet after I cleared everything with Carmine and Louie. I told Sol they were working for the government. He really doesn't know too much about the Italian side of our business. This I can teach him real fast. See, so we are all set. He will work from Friday afternoon until we close on Sunday night."

"But Papa," I said.

Papa interrupted me. "I made the decision and this is the way it is. I want you to have a senior year that you'll always remember."

"Thanks so much, Papa," I said. "I really appreciate what you're doing for me. I know that when I get to college,

I'll be concentrating on my studying and won't have much time for socializing."

I hugged and kissed both Mama and Papa, then said, "Now that I have some extra time, I'll go by Izzy's store, rent a jacket for tonight. I think I still have a clean white shirt."

"Don't worry," Mama said. "You'll have one ready for you."

I hopped over to Izzy's, and he greeted me with a big hello. He had a few customers and asked me to wait a few minutes and said, "Look around, maybe you'll find something you like. I just got some shirts in that are beauties in you size. I got some ties also that are practically brand new."

I looked around and before I knew it, Izzy was by my side saying, "What can I do for you, Marco? And by the way how are your folks?"

"They are fine," I replied. "I need a sport coat, maybe a tie for tonight."

"Big doings?" Izzy asked.

"I'm going to a college dance."

"You are getting up in this world," said Izzy. "First a high school senior and now a college dance. If I remember right, I still have the navy blazer with your alteration. Let's see."

Sure enough when I put it on, it fit as well as before.

"How about a shirt to go with it, and a tie?" Izzy suggested.

"No, I think I'll just take the jacket," I said.

"Ok, you know Marco, you already paid me a dollar-fifty for renting the first time and you'll owe another dollar-fifty now. Why not buy the jacket? I'll give you a special price because you are going to be a college boy next year. When wearing this jacket, people will come over to you and ask, 'Where did you get this beautiful jacket?' You can tell them that you got it at Izzy's. Tell them to mention your name and they'll get a special price."

"Ok, how much for the jacket?" I asked.

"Give me five dollars and it's yours."

"I'll take it."

Good thing I had the fiver on me. I gave it to him, folded the jacket over my arm and said, "Thanks, goodbye."

When I came into the store, Mama said, "Your change of clothes is waiting for you in the basement, including the shirt and one of Papa's ties."

I zipped into the basement, washed up and got ready. I ran to the phone to call Joe. When he heard it was me, he yelled, "Where the hell were you? I was waiting to hear from you!"

"Joe, it's only twelve o'clock," I said. "We have plenty of time."

"Ok, I'll meet you at the subway at about quarter after one."

"Alright, but I think we need to plan strategy. I think most of the girls are going to be older than us and probably college students. They may not like to hook up with guys younger than them. So here is what we do. We ask the dolls where they live. If they say they live in Manhattan, then we tell them we live in Brooklyn and go to Brooklyn College. If they say they live in Brooklyn, we say we live in Manhattan and go to City College. This way we are covered age-wise."

"Good idea," said Joe. "It will work. See you later."

"Ok."

We met on time and on the way up we rehashed our plan, and decided it would work.

The dance was being held in the basketball court of the college. When we got there the seats were being filled up and the band was warming up. When we looked around it was like seeing a gallery of dolls, most of them in sweaters, skirts, bobby socks, and saddle shoes. What a sight to see, and I was energized. The band started to play and it was an up number.

Joe sized up a good looker and made his way with her to the dance floor. They were good and notice was taken. The next number was a two-step, and I picked out a sweetie and we did just fine. And so it went.

During an intermission, the band leader came up to Joe and me and said, "I'd like to talk to you guys once this gig is over. So, will you hang around?"

Joe shrugged and nodded ok, and I said, "Sure."

He went back to the band stand and the band started to play again. Our strategy worked great. For some we lived in Manhattan, and for others we lived in Brooklyn. Pretty soon we had choice of the girls for dance partners and Joe and I were having a great time.

Before we knew it, the band was playing "The Party's Over," and this was the last number. Some of the dolls went around to find out if we would take them out after the dance.

Joe and I told the same story; that we were very sorry but we had to meet with the band leader on some special business. We then asked them for their phone numbers saying we'd be in touch. We hugged them, gave them a little kiss, and headed to meet the band leader.

He greeted us with a big smile and said, "It's too hectic here. There is a coffee shop down the street on the right called Charlie's. I'll see you there in about ten minutes."

I looked at Joe and he looked at me. Since it was not out of our way going home we said, "Sure."

We found the store, grabbed the table, and ordered coffee and donuts. A few minutes later, the band leader came in and sat down. He introduced himself as Gary, telling us further that he was a music major and would continue to lead the band for at least another year.

"How come you wanted to see us?" I asked. "If you were looking for musicians, you got the wrong guys."

"No, it's nothing like that," he said with a wave of his hand. "We are going to have a big dance contest in three weeks, the week after the semester starts. I saw the way you two made it on the dance floor and I think you have a shot of getting into the finals. First prize gets a six months pass free to Saturday matinee to Roseland ballroom, second prize is one hundred dollars, and third prize is fifty. You know that

Roseland is the top in the city for live music, great bands, and sensational dancers. You two have a shot at winning one of the prizes, so get some partners and start rehearsing."

"What do you think Joe?" I asked my friend.

"Sure, we can do it," said Joe. "And we will."

"Gary," I said, "you can count on us to deliver."

"Here is my phone number," said Joe, writing it on the napkin. "Call me and give me all the details."

"Will do, Joe," said Gary.

"It's all set then," said Joe. "Call me tomorrow night around seven-thirty."

"No problem."

With that, Gary got up, left some money for his coffee, and took off. I said to Joe, "How can you ok a deal like that? We don't have partners and we've got no time to find them."

"Don't worry, I got it all figured out," said Joe. "When we see Celeste tomorrow she will hook us up with partners that will be the cat's meow. We are going to win that contest, no doubt about it."

"Let's pay for the coffee and get out of here. I got to get home."

"So do I," Joe said.

"See you tomorrow, same time same place."

"You got it."

It was nearly six before I got back to the store. Mama, Papa, and Sol were behind the counter taking care of a lot of customers. I watched the way Sol worked.

He was a big guy, about six feet tall, over two hundred pounds, with a ruddy complexion. His hair color was hard to tell because he always wore a straw hat.

He was a real pro and knew how to handle customers as well as how to fill their orders. I guess the many years at the Stage Deli gave him the experience. He actually rearranged the items in the display counters and made them look more appetizing. Papa and Mama were pleased with what he was doing and how well he fit in, and the customers loved him.

Believe it or not, I was a little jealous of him being there instead of me. I got rid of that thought quickly when I came to my senses.

Although Joe warned me to stay away from Angie, I still sort of missed her. I wandered over to Tony's hoping that she would be there. I looked around but she was not there. I didn't know whether to be disappointed or to heave a sigh of relief. I had my lemon ices, said hello to some guys, and took off for home.

When I came back, the store was about to close and Mama had prepared dinner. She even invited Sol to stay for it. He readily agreed.

Sol was an interesting man, having emigrated from Hungary when he was eighteen. He told us that he had actually met his wife Bessie on the ship bringing them to America. She was from Romania. Their common language was Yiddish, so they were able to converse. They got engaged on the ship and were married three days after getting through Ellis Island. The newlyweds moved in with Sol's uncle and aunt, and had to live in a large closet that was converted into a bedroom. There was only one toilet and this was on the floor they lived on, and was shared by four other families. Because hot water was at a premium, baths were allowed once a week. Most of the men tried to save up the fifty cents that allowed them to go to the Turkish baths. Here they could enjoy steam rooms, dry heat, showers, and if money was available, even a massage.

Sol's uncle had found him a job delivering meat from a wholesale kosher butcher to neighborhood kosher meat stores and delis. He was given a bicycle to carry the meat. He had to deliver quickly so that the meat would not spoil and he was often seen pedaling fast up and down the East Side. Sol further told us he hated this job but needed to put food on the table. Bessie, in the meantime, got a job in a garment factory sewing ladies' blouses. Sol said he and Bessie scrimped and saved , trying to get enough money to get a normal-sized room. But the money just wasn't there. Then he saw the ad in the Jewish daily newspaper *The Forwards*. It called for an experienced counterman at the Stage Delicatessen, one of the best known delis in New York. Interviews were to begin at eight o'clock the next morning. Sol said he was there at six, wanting to be first in line. Sol was in luck, as the interviewer was from the same town in Hungary and knew of Sol's family there. Sol's father and brother had a kosher meat market which also made pastrami, corned beef, and pickled tongue. Sol, having worked there, learned to prepare and carve these specialties and got the job. He worked at the Stage steady for thirty-eight years. When Bessie got sick, however, he had to quit and take care of her.

Bessie's condition got worse and worse. After a year in a half, Bessie passed on. Sol had no desire to go back to the Stage, so he just hung around the little apartment they had rented over thirty-five years before. He then told us that he was getting depressed and lonely and wanted to do something that would keep him busy. He also told me he felt it was a Godsend when Papa asked him if he would consider some part time work, so here he was at the dinner table.

It was a Jewish style feast. I don't know when Mama had the time to make the food, but I knew it was homemade because Mama would never buy prepared food. She had to make it herself.

First we had chopped liver, then chicken soup with matzo balls, followed by salad and then potted chicken and vegetables, and to my utter delight, potato latkes. Dessert was sponge cake and tea.

We all thanked Mama over and over again for the great meal. Sol was so overwhelmed that he actually had a tear in his eye when he said, "This was the best dinner I have had since before my Bessie got sick. She was a wonderful cook." He then added with a little smile, "But not as good as you." After dinner, we all helped clean up.

Sol then said goodnight and started to leave. Papa said, "Wait, I have to let you out and I also want to pay you for your time." They both then left the apartment. When Papa returned, he said, "Sol is a mensch. He told me outside ,'I feel like a young man again working here, and I will be glad to come in on a moment's notice any time you need me.'

"You are lucky, Marco," Papa continued with a chuckle. "Now you have somebody to cover for you, Mr. Fred Astaire Jr. O.K., time to go to bed. We have a store to open tomorrow".

I kissed Papa and Mama, said goodnight, and got ready for bed. Because I wasn't asked, I didn't volunteer any information about the dancers. I hit the sack and fell right to sleep. Next thing I knew, as usual, Papa had to wake me and we went through the same routine.

Since Papa and Mama knew I was going to meet Joe and go with him again to the dance studio, Papa said, "Since you have a watch, you should know it's time to quit now, Mr. Dancer, and get ready. So go." He smiled. "Marco, this is what America is all about. This could never happen in Italy and Mama and I are so proud of you. So go and enjoy. Now hurry. By the way, when we have time this week, we'll go to Thom McCan and get you a new pair of shoes."

I washed up, got dressed, said goodbye to Mama and Papa, and met Joe.

We took the subway and then walked over to the studio building. I don't know why but the elevator operator recognized us when we got on. "Arthur Murray Studios, right?" he said.

"Right," we replied.

He then added with a giggle, "After a few more lessons , you two will probably be waltzing in and out of here."

"Very funny," Joe replied.

When he let us off, we saw the receptionist at her desk. "Hello you two" she said. "Have a seat. Celeste is running a few minutes late."

I said to Joe, "How should we talk to Celeste about the contest? You and I didn't talk about it on the way up here. All we spoke about were the dolls we met."

"Let's tell her we were asked to enter a dance contest and if she could leave us enough time to talk about it after the lesson, even if the lesson has to be cut short."

"Sounds like the way to go," I said.

Celeste came in looking just terrific. "Hi guys," she said. "Did your feet do the homework? Let's get started. I look forward to seeing what you can do. You amaze me how quick you pick up the dance steps."

"Hold on a minute, Celeste," said Joe. "We have to talk to you, and need your help. It'll only take about fifteen minutes. So how about cutting the lesson time down by that much? It's important."

"Ok with me," said Celeste. She turned to me. "This time you first, Marco." She put a foxtrot on the phonograph. I took her in my arms and we danced. It felt like our bodies became one and we blended to the music. Our spins were smooth and our breaks clever. When the song was ending, I put her into the dip position and she ended by putting one leg in the air. It was terrific. Celeste turned to me and gave me a big hug, saying, "Marco, you did that dance great. Now let's move on to the Rumba. Let me show you how to hold your position for this dance. It is a little different than that in the foxtrot. Ok, once the record starts you use the basic steps from your side of the room and I will do the same from my side and we will meet in the middle. This is a little more of a professional way of approaching this dance. Remember to first get the feel of the tempo. Once you do that, you can improvise. I'll put the record on now. Once again, get the feel of the beat and get your body into it."

As soon as I heard the song "Besame Mucho" it went from my head to my feet and I started to react to the music. It seemed so natural to me that I could in tempo, glide over the dance floor and meet Celeste coming from the other way. We met and I took her in my arms in tempo, twirled her around twice, again in tempo, and we continued to dance. Celeste, once she knew that I had the steps down pat, did some exciting sexy breaks while I kept to the basic ones. She made me look good as her partner. We then got into the basic step routine when the song ended.

"Super job, especially for the first time," she said. "Joe,

let's see your style now. First the lindy. I'm going to change the tempo to see if you can get into the beat. Here comes "After you've gone.""

Once the music started, Joe began to snap his fingers in time to the music and after a moment or two his body began to move with the beat. Celeste was standing close by when Joe grabbed her and they started to jump and jive. They looked as if they were partners who had danced together for years. Joe was so loose and could improvise breaks, and Celeste kept up with him. They did a great job.

I was, as I'm sure they were, sorry to see the record end.

Celeste was a little winded and so was Joe, but he wouldn't admit it. Celeste, being the teacher, said, "Let's take five." She had some bottles of water under the table holding the phonograph and gave one to both Joe and me, keeping one for herself. "You need to drink this, else you could get dehydrated. Don't ask questions, just drink all the water."

After a three or four minute break, she said to Joe, "Peabody man, let's get cracking. This is really a good dance, and Italians love to dance it."

"Why didn't you give it to Marco instead of me?" said Joe. "He's Italian."

Celeste was so cute when she said, "Your family is the real goods, they come from Sicily. He's only from Venice."

We all laughed at this quip. She then said, "Times a wasting. Let's do it Joe, and do it smoothly, body erect and small steps. The tune she selected was "Avalon", and Joe tried to get into the beat and the step routine but was having a little trouble. Peabody was a pretty far cry from the lindy hop. Celeste shot over to him. "These are not the same steps as the Lindy," she said. "Think Peabody, and you'll get it." It must have worked because Joe grabbed Celeste and started to move her across the floor doing the Peabody. Joe did the basic steps for a while and then came up with some fancy breaks. Celeste followed suit. She was a terrific dancer and teacher.

I could have gone for her in the big way, but that wasn't

possible. She was at least five years older than me and had a boyfriend.

When the Peabody was over, Celeste came back to me and said, "We need more time doing the Foxtrot, then the two step, and finally the Rumba. I want to be sure you do the steps right"

And we did them all, over and over again. The same went for Joe. The Lindy and the Peabody were practiced and re-practiced with Celeste alternating the dances with Joe and me.

I was surprised when I glanced at my watch and saw the time. We had been dancing for over an hour. When the song finished, Celeste said, "Time for a pit stop, some water and a short break. So take fifteen and we'll do some more dancing."

I started to protest, but Celeste responded, "I know, I know, you want to have a confab with me. I left fifteen minutes of the session for it. See you in fifteen." She then left, I guess to go to the ladies room.

Joe and I took long drinks from the water fountain, went to the toilet, and then peaked into some of the other studios where dance classes were going on. Some of the dancers were amazing and some were just ok.

The next thing we saw was Celeste coming down the hall. When she saw us she said, "Let's go guys, time to dance." And we followed her like sheep back into the studio.

Again Celeste alternated dancing with Joe and me. I was amazed at her stamina. I was getting knocked out and she was fresh as the daisy.

When the music stopped around a quarter to six, Celeste said, "Ok guys, what's up?"

"Well," said Joe, "we had this offer..."

And I followed up by saying, "We went to a dance at NYU Downtown and did so good that the band leader asked us if we were interested in competing in a dance contest that is going to be held on the first Saturday night after the college resumed for the new semester."

"So?" asked Celeste.

"My buddy here," Marco continued, "said we'll do it. The band leader then followed up with 'go find yourself some dance partners, you only have about three weeks to get ready.'"

"What do you want from me?" asked Celeste. "I can't do it. I am a pro and I am damned sure they wouldn't allow me. Besides, I have other things to do on a Saturday night."

"No, no," Joe broke in. "We need you to help us find a couple of girls that would make us look good on the dance floor."

"I got ya," said Celeste. "Let me think for a minute or so."

She then started to walk around the studio and seemed to be mumbling to herself, then she turned to us and in a loud voice said, "Yes, I think I got you both covered."

Joe and I in unison said, "Great"

"Can you both stick around for another hour or so?" said Celeste. "I have an idea and since my six o'clock student had to cancel, I have the time. There are two girls coming at seven o'clock that I think would fit the bill. They have been dancing for years and are now training to be Arthur Murray dance instructors, and they are not yet professionals."

"Sounds good," I said.

Joe came in with, "What do they look like and what kind of bods do they have?"

"Are you kidding?" said Celeste. "Would I recommend two dogs to you? They are gorgeous and are dream-built. In the meantime, let's go down and get something to eat. If you want you can use our phone to call home and tell them you'll be late, if you have to."

Although we were past seventeen and in about three weeks would be seniors in high school, out of respect we each called home and told our folks we would be late. Celeste took us to a little sandwich shop off Broadway, where she had a salad and Joe and I went for the tuna fish and cokes. It was hard breaking old eating habits. About five to seven, I paid the check, Joe left the tip, and we went back to the studio.

We waited in the reception room while Celeste spoke to one of the other instructors in another studio. She came out a few minutes later with a smile on her face. "It's ok with Marsha, the girl's instructor. If they want to be your partners, you and they could have up to a half hour to try out and see how it works. It's up to the girls."

Just then the elevator doors opened and two dream boats walked out. Could these be the girls?

Before we could say anything, Marsha came out and said to the girls, "Good to see you girls. Come back to the studio with me, I have something to talk to you about. How about joining us Celeste?"

All of them walked back to the studio, leaving us like two bumps on a log, and closed the door. A few minutes later they all came out and Marsha said, "The girls agreed to audition you for a half hour. So you better hurry up and get started. This is Patty, and this is Margo. Say hello to Joe and Marco. You already met Celeste." She turned to Celeste. "They are yours, Celeste, for the next twenty-five minutes, then send them back here."

We went back to Celeste's studio where she questioned the girls, asking, "Who feels most comfortable doing the Lindy, and who really likes doing the Foxtrot and Two Step?"

The girls looked at each other and Patty said, "I like doing the Foxtrot over the Lindy."

"The Lindy is my very favorite dance," said Margo.

"Ok, we need to move fast, time is running by," said Celeste. "What we'll do is this, starting with Marco and Patty, a Foxtrot, halfway through I'll stop the music, put on a jump number and let Margo and Joe go at the Lindy." And this is what happened.

Both girls were good lookers and great dancers. After we all danced to two rounds of records, we each bonded into dance partners and we moved great.

Before we knew it, Celeste said, "Ok, time is up. You girls can go back to your studio, and you guys wait in the reception room."

Celeste left with the girls. We went to the reception room and waited.

"How do you think it worked out?" Joe asked.

"Mine worked out terrific," I said. "You bombed! I'm just joking. I think we did Ok."

Celeste came back. "You two scored big time," she said with a smile. "The girls said they were looking forward to being in the contest with you both and they recommended that we keep the same set up. Patty with you, Marco, and Margo with Joe as partners. I have the schedule of available time so work it out between you when you can get together. I got a special rental price for the studio of ten dollars an hour but you will have to spin the records and pay for them in case they get damaged. I'll try to come in if I'm not busy with other students. So, go to work and get your times picked out and I'll let the studio scheduler know. Sorry about the ten dollar charge but that was the best I could do."

I grabbed Celeste, gave her a big hug, and said, "We don't know what we would have done without you. Don't think we don't appreciate it. You are the best, Celeste. See, it rhymes!"

Joe then said, "Stop with the jokes. Let's figure out a schedule."

Patty joined in. "How about waiting for us," she said. "We have about a half hour left on our dance instruction time. When we are through, let's get a cup of coffee and see what we can work out."

"Good idea," I said. "We'll wait."

The half hour went by and the girls joined us. We found the Automat Cafeteria nearby and Joe and I sprang for the coffee.

"Run this by us again, this contest," said Margo.

I explained it to them again.

Patty then piped up, "From what you told us, am I right, the contest is broken down by category, lindy, foxtrot and two step, latin, waltzes, and polkas. Right?"

"When I spoke to the band leader this is what I was

told," I said.

"All Marco and I were interested in was the lindy, foxtrot and two step," said Joe.

"Ok, that's good," said Pattye. "I have an idea. You guys have four to six on Monday and we have seven to eight. Why don't we talk to Celeste and Marcia and see if we can meet with Celeste from six to seven and Marcia from seven to eight for just these three weeks. Let's see the schedule again."

We laid it out on the table.

"How about Thursday at seven?" said Pattye. "It's open."

Margo agreed by saying, "It sounds good. How about you, Marco?"

"I think it will be ok," I said. "But I have to check it out."

"How come?" Margo asked.

"My folks have a grocery deli and I usually help them at the store those hours," I said. "But I think it will be ok. I can let you both know tomorrow. Is there any way we can get in touch with you?"

"Sure," said Patty. "I am a receptionist in a dentist's office. You can call me there. I'll give you the phone number." And she did. "One other thing. Margo and I have steady boyfriends, so don't get any ideas about starting a personal relationship. We are doing this for the experience and also to win. It goes without saying that we will split the winnings fifty-fifty. By that I mean if one couple wins, they will split 50/50 with the other."

"Agreed," Joe said.

"Agreed," I said. "It's getting late, so let's get going."

"Look forward to dancing with you, Margo," said Joe.

"Same here, Joe," she answered

"Look forward to dancing with you, Pattye," I said.

"Me too, Marco," Pattye said with a smile.

"I'll phone you tomorrow about the 'ok,'" I said. "I feel real sure it's a go."

With that the girls left and after a couple of minutes, we

did also. On the way home, I said to Joe, "What kind of simps are we? We never found out anything about the girls; where they live, where they come from, what they do, and how old they are."

"We'll ask them the next time we meet," said Joe. "Lay off how old they are. Once we ask them, they'll ask us. In fact let's not ask any questions. This way they won't ask us."

When we reached our stop, I said to Joe, "Same routine as last week, checking the papers on Friday to see where we want to dance."

"Sounds good," said Joe. "I think you need to go to dinner at my house Sunday. I want to see Paulie sweat. Besides, Uncle Vito mentioned to my father that he hasn't seen much of Joe and Marco lately. That's his way of saying come Sunday."

"Tell your mother to set a place for me," I said.
"She'll be glad to see you and so will my father."
"Talk to you tomorrow."
"For sure, for sure."

When I got home the store was closed, but I had the key. I opened it and saw that the light in the apartment was still on. I went in and saw Mama and Papa sitting around the table sipping tea and eating what looked like corned beef sandwiches. Papa said hello and added, "Sol really makes good corned beef. You want some, Marco?"

Although I was sort of hungry, I said no. "I need to ask you something, Papa," I said. "Joe and I were asked by the band leader at the college to enter a dance contest in three weeks' time, and we need to practice. Our teacher, Joe's cousin Celeste, hooked us up with two very good dance partners. We just danced for a half hour with them and we think we could win."

"So get to the asking," said Papa.

"You said it was ok to take lessons on Monday from four to six. Can I switch it to six to eight? And also I'd like to have Thursday from seven to eight maybe till nine. We really have a shot at winning. The first prize is a hundred dollars, the second is fifty dollars, and a third is a six-month Saturday afternoon pass to Roseland Ballroom where the best dancers in New York come to dance. What do you say, Papa?"

"I thought you wanted to be a doctor?" said Papa. "Now a dancer?"

"Papa, this is for fun, and it's only for three weeks. Once school starts I won't have time for this it's only three weeks and I really want to do this."

Papa tugged on his mustache, turned to Mama, and asked, "What do you think Sarah?"

"Ivan, it's only three weeks," said Mama. "Let Marco have his fun. We can get Sol to come in. If Marco wins, he can pay us back out of his winnings." Mama said this with a twinkle in her eye. "Ok, it's all right, so go ahead. Since you are now in a contest tomorrow when it slows down we'll get you a new pair of shoes."

"Thanks so much, Papa and Mama, for being so understanding and helpful."

"You are a good boy and deserve it," said Papa.

"One more favor," I said. "Is it ok if I go over to Joe's house for dinner this Sunday? Uncle Vito said in a roundabout way that he wanted us to come."

Papa looked up and shrugged, saying, "Anything else I need to know about your social life?"

"No, Papa."

"Ok, go and send our regards to all and especially Mr. Amatto. Now let's go to bed, we have a store to run tomorrow."

On the way to the apartment, I heard Papa tell Mama, "I'll call Sol to fill in for Marco. He can use the money and I'm sure he'll jump at the chance to put in a few more hours. Especially if you'll invite him to Saturday dinner with us."

I couldn't wait to tell Joe that the Monday and Thursday times were ok with me and to confirm that these times were still on for the girls. Joe said he would check with Pattye and she would then contact Margo. He also said he needed a couple of hours to get in touch with them and call me back. "Don't worry" Joe said. "They'll do it."

"Where could these two gems find partners like us?" I said. "Rest easy, it's going to be in the bag."

Joe called me back one hour later and elatedly stated, "It's a go, Amigo! First session is this Thursday at seven through eight. Maybe a little later if the studio is available. Pattye is going to ask Marcia to give us a few pointers if she is available."

"Sounds good," I said. "Let's meet at the subway at six-thirty. We might be caught in rush hour, so let's leave a little earlier. I almost forgot, I'll be able to come to your house for dinner Sunday. So I guess our Sunday dance session is out. Let's see when the paper comes out on Friday what's happening and if we see there is a chance of catching one on Friday and maybe one or two Saturday."

"Right on," said Joe. "Talk to you."

"Gottcha."

Tuesday passed by as did the many Tuesdays before. On Wednesday, when things slowed down, Papa said, "Let's go to McCann's and get you the shoes you'll need for the contest. It'll be slow here for a couple of hours and Mama can handle things." So off to Thom McCann's shoe store on Allen Street we went.

As we approached the store, we looked in the window and saw loads of shoes for sale, and some on special sale. My eye caught a pair of black, shinny penny loafers that were reduced from $12.99 to $9.99.

"Let's try them on, Papa," I said. And he agreed.

We entered the store and were greeted by Mr. Waldman, the owner. "Good afternoon," he said. "How can I help you?"

"I'd like to see a pair of shoes you have in the window," I said.

"Point out which ones you like and I'll see if I have them in your size."

We walked outside and I pointed out the shoe.

"That's a very nice shoe," said Mr. Waldman. "It's soft leather, comfortable, and will give you lots of wear. Sit down take off your shoes and I'll measure you for the right size." When I did, he brought over a metal foot measurer that measured both the length and the width of the foot. After using it, he said, "Eleven C should do it. Now let me see if I have it."

He went to a different part of the store, looked at the rows of boxes in the cabinets, then turned and said, "You are lucky, this is the last Eleven C left in this style." He brought the box over and opened it and took out one shoe. "Feel this leather. It's just like butter, and it's a handsome shoe."

Mr. Waldman took out a shoe horn and eased my foot into the shoe. "Stand up, walk around," he said. "How does it feel?"

"It feels ok," I said.

"Now try on the other and walk up and down the store to get used to them. They must fit right. Not too short, not too long, not too narrow or too wide."

I walked up and down a few times, flexed my toes and bent my feet from side to side. The shoes felt very good. Papa sat quietly, and when I came back to where we had been sitting, he said, "Well, how are they?"

"They are good Papa. I'll take them."

"You'll take them?" Mr. Waldman asked.

"Yep!"

"You got a great shoe there," said Mr. Waldman. "Especially since they were reduced from $12.99 to $9.99. Do you want to wear them or should I box them for you?"

"Box them and I'll wear my old shoes home," I said.

"Will do."

As we approached the counter, Mr. Waldman asked, "Do you need any socks or polish to go with the shoes? Our polishes are made special for your kind of leather. Using it will keep the leather soft and shiny. It's only twenty-five cents."

"Ok, I'll take a polish," I said.

Mr. Waldman wrote up a bill, and I paid him. Papa wanted to pay this, but I told him I still had gift money left and wanted to use my own money for this. Papa and I thanked Mr. Waldman and hurried back to our store.

On Thursday late afternoon, Sol came in to work at four, and I actually worked alongside him until Carmine and Louie left at five. Once they were gone, I made a beeline for the shower and took a nice long hot one. Once finished I shaved and got dressed. I decided to wear my old shoes to and from the studio and wear the new ones only while I was rehearsing there.

When I stuck my face out of the door leading from the apartment into the store, Sol motioned to me and then said, "I made a nice tongue sandwich for you on a roll and put some potato salad and coleslaw as a side, on the plate. You'll enjoy this and it'll give you extra strength to do your thing. Take a Dr. Brown with it to drink and don't gobble it down. You have plenty of time. Your Papa told me all about the contest and rehearsing, so you have to eat to stay strong."

I was hungry and although I tried to eat slowly, I ended up eating everything fast and quickly attacked the Dr. Brown. It was so good. I thanked Sol again and thanked Mama and Papa and hurried over to the subway. And sure enough there was Joe pacing up and back.

He greeted me with, "I thought you would be late, but my watch shows you are two minutes early. You seem to get in under the gun all the time."

"Let's go," I said. "I'm looking forward to a fun evening."

When we arrived, the elevator operator recognized us with a slight smile on his face and said, "I know it's Arthur Murray, 10th floor. Are you taking the ballet classes?"

Joe looked him right in the eye and said, "Ride this thing to the 10th floor without any stupid remarks. It ain't funny. Just do your job and stop with the comedy. Do we understand each other, friend?"

I never realized that Joe could come on this way. His whole manner and expression had changed while talking to the elevator operator. He looked and sounded like a hood. The elevator operator turned a little white. "I was just kidding around," he said. "I meant no harm. I'm sorry if you took it the wrong way."

Joe replied, "Apology accepted. But from now on, the only conversation I want to hear from you is 'What floor please.'"

We were let off on the tenth floor and the girls were waiting. We all said hi and went into the studio that the girls usually used. To our surprise, Marcia was there setting up the records.

"Good to see you, Marcia," said Joe. "Are you going to stay?"

"Just enough time to see you get started and how good you are doing," said Marcia. "I want one of you to win this contest. It will be good for business here. Marco, you and Pattye go first. If I don't see what I like, I'll stop the music and give you some pointers."

Before we knew it the song was playing. I think it was "Dream." I took Pattye in my arms, holding her as I was taught, and started to lead her around the dance floor. As we made a spin and then a full turn, the music stopped and Marcia came over and said, "That's no way to make a spin, and certainly not the way to turn your partner around. Keeping good posture is very important. It'll give you poise and elegance. When you make a turn, both of your heads need to be square on your neck and shoulders to give the impression of oneness. Your turns, your spins must be sharp but executed smoothly. I heard you have a nickname, "Gliding Marco," so let's see how close you're to living up to it."

Marcia put the music back on and Patty and I started to dance, trying to follow her instructions. She had to stop us three or four times before she said, "I think you got the idea. You already know the steps. I want to see sharpness in doing them and proper posture. Let's try it once more and see if you really got it." Which we did.

"That's better," said Marcia after the song was over.

"Keep practicing. Remember, knowing and doing the steps doesn't make you a good or great dancer. It is the dance presentation by the performers that wins the gold.

"Ok Joe and Margo," she said, turning to the other pair. "The same goes for you two. The lindy takes up more room than a couple doing the foxtrot and the tempo is faster than the two-step. When you get on to the dance floor, you have to mentally pick out your dance space. Bunking into another set of dancers will eliminate you both pronto, so you have to work out a system of keeping out of the way of other dancers and other dancers out and away from you. Once you pick out your space, stick to it. After the first dance or two, other contestants will realize it's your territory and will keep to their own. If, however, you stray out or some other couple comes in, a simple trick is to do what I call a "short arm," and I'm not being cute if you know what I mean, fellows." She grinned at us.

"Instead of using the hands in the breaks," she continued, "move your hands up onto her wrist, lower arm, elbow or even upper arm. By doing this, your partner will be closer to you and further away from the couple who came into your territory. Try never to breach someone else's space. This is a no-no, especially in a contest. Now, the Lindy is a lot less formal than the Foxtrot, but similar rules apply, such as sharpness of execution, positioning of head and elegance of performance."

She looked over at Joe. "Joe, your partner is not just a bag of something you throw over your shoulder, slide between your legs, or gyrate across your back. The dance is not a phys-ed or gym experience, but needs to be a well thought-out production with rehearsed and practiced routines. Now get out there and do it."

Marsha then put on a jump tune "After You've Gone" and Margo and Joe started to do their thing. They evidently didn't hear the music stop about halfway through the song, but I did.

"Joe," Marsha said, "you're not Tarzan, Margo's not

Jane. Lead her with grace. You look like you're pushing her and then pulling her in. Margo, you have to anticipate Joe's moves and the breaks he wants to do. Practice will bring that out. On the breaks, I want to see gymnastics, but with grace, style, and poise. Now let's do it over."

After Joe and Margo practiced this over and over, Marsha said, "I think you got the idea, now work on it. I know you are scheduled for two hours on Monday and one on Thursday for the next three weeks. It would be to your advantage if you speak to Jason, our scheduler, to see if there would be some more studio time open so that you could practice more. All of you did pretty good for the first time but you need a lot more work if you want to be able to win a contest. See ya." She left the room.

Joe said to the girls, "How about grabbing a cup of coffee at the Automat again and we can make plans? But before we do, I'll stop off to see Jason and see what studio time he has open. Maybe we can get our routines polished."

"Ok," the girls responded in unison. "But make it quick. We have to get home and don't want to stay out late tonight."

"Ok, ok," Joe said. "You both go with Marco and I'll see you there."

I met the girls at the Automat and bought four coffees, found a table, and waited for Joe who arrived a few minutes later.

"I got the open time schedule and it don't look too bad," Joe said. He then laid the schedule on the table where we could all look at it.

Patty said, "Monday six to eight still looks ok. Now let's look at Thursday. Margo and I have seven to eight. See here, Thursday at six and nine are open. Should we take either six to eight or seven to nine on Thursdays?"

We all seemed to agree that six to eight on both Mondays and Thursdays would be the way to go.

"Maybe if we spent more time rehearsing," I said, "we will have a better chance of winning."

"Maybe we would," Patty answered. "But we other

things to do, so let's leave the time slots as we agreed upon and just to set the record clear, you two are just our dance partners, nothing more. This is more or less a business arrangement and not a social one. Once the contest is over, it's over. If one pair of us is lucky enough to win, we split it four ways, as we agreed. After that we say goodbye, so long, and ta ta."

Margo then added, "We really don't know you both and we don't want to get involved. If for some reason you guys don't believe us, we call it quits now."

I looked at Joe and saw a surprised look on his face and he quickly replied, "If you both want it that way, it is jake with us. Am I right, Marco?

"That a 'Yes,'" I said.

We finished our coffees and split.

On the way home, Joe said, "Those two are weird but are good dancers so let's do what they say, although I would like to have taken a shot at Margo."

"I could have sworn that Patty had a thing for me," I said. "So let's let the cards fly and see where they land. Maybe we can get lucky, after all. Don't forget, you are Twinkle Toes, Joe, and I am Gliding Marco."

We got off at our stop, said 'so long,' and started to walk home. Turning back, I yelled to Joe, "Tell your Mom I'll come to dinner on Sunday. In the meantime, let's see what dances we can dig up for Friday night and Saturday."

"Ok, let's check the papers out and be in touch."

"You got it!" I said.

I reached home, went through the store to the apartment and saw the lights out except the one in the kitchen. Mama and Papa's door was closed. I guessed they had gone to bed early. I was sort of tired myself, so I quietly got ready for bed, hopped into it, and feel asleep right away.

Having had a good night sleep, Papa didn't have to wake me in the morning. I was up at five-thirty, took a shower, dressed, had some breakfast, and was ready to open the store at seven. Business was the usual mad rush, then slowed down, then became madness once more. Sol came in at four wearing his straw hat and smiling.

"Hello, everybody, I'm here," he said.

Papa looked up and said, "Sol, we know it, so now let the customers know it."

Papa said this not sarcastically, but in a joking manner.

"Ok Ivan, it's around the counter I go," said Sol. "Bring on my friends, the customers."

Just then the newspapers came. I grabbed them, took out the entertainment sections, and looked them over. Didn't see too much going on for us dance-wise. Before I could phone Joe, he called me.

"Well, what do you think?" he asked.

"Don't see too much tomorrow afternoon," I answered.

"You're right, think we should pass."

"Good idea," I agreed.

"We still have rehearsals with Patty and Margo to look forward to," said Joe. "I gotta say, I'm going to enjoy dancing with those dolls again."

"Me too," I said. "So let's be ready for rehearsal with the girls and make the most of it."

It got to be late Monday afternoon, and I was really excited for rehearsal with the girls. I couldn't wait until Carmine and Louie left so that I could get ready and fortunately for me they left right on the dot of five. I hurried in and stepped on the gas. I had to meet Joe at five-thirty. I don't know how I did it, but I did it.

Joe was already waiting outside the entrance to the subway and greeted me. "We are cutting the time for getting there short," he said. "If we miss a train, we'll be late."

"You're right," I said. "I'll have to make it my business to meet you by five-fifteen."

We scooted down the steps to the subway, paid the fare just in time to catch our train, and we got to the studio by six.

Patty and Margo were already there and ready to start rehearsing, and we felt good when we saw both Marsha and

Celeste coming over to us.

"Look," Marsha said, "Celeste and I talked it over and believe it or not, getting you to win is now a challenge for us."

I couldn't help but feel a little insulted when I heard that, and Joe looked like he felt the same way.

"We still don't know why we got so excited about this," Marsha continued, "but we are going to give it our all to see that you win. So I'll tell you what we decided. We arranged for two studios instead of one. Joe and Margo will go with me and practice the Lindy and Peabody while you, Marco and Patty, will go with Celeste and work with her on the Foxtrot and Two Step. We don't have much time to get ready, so let's get going."

With that, we went into the different studios. For two hours, without even a ten minute break, Celeste kept us practicing and correcting things she said would make the difference between winning and losing.

Patty was a great partner and was able to rapidly pick up Celeste's pointers, sometimes even faster than me. We were very comfortable and loose with each other and got to the point where we could even anticipate each other's moves.

Time ran by fast. Celeste stopped the music and said, "Time's up. You did fine. I think you really have a chance. Remember the things you learned tonight. We will go over everything again on Thursday."

Patty, Celeste, and I walked out of our studio and saw Marsha, Margo and Joe waiting for us.

"How did it go ?" Joe asked Celeste.

"They did good," Celeste answered. "They might have a chance after all."

I, now acting a little annoyed, answered, "What do you mean 'might have a chance.' Patty and I are going to win . No doubt about it."

Celeste said, "I'm glad you both feel that way. That's the extra punch I was looking for. When you get on the dance floor, put that punch into your performance."

Marsha then remarked to Joe and Margo, "You both did

good but I want you to also mentally have the zip that will separate your dance routines from the other dancers. Now get out of here. Celeste and I have other things to do."

We didn't even ask the girls to go for coffee. Instead we said 'so long' and took the subway to our station and parted ways.

When I came in to the store I saw a light coming from our apartment. It was the dining room light. I guessed that Mama and Papa were sitting up waiting for me. There was tea and cheesecake waiting for me also.

"Sit down and eat," Mama said while Papa looked on. "You must be tired and hungry." . "Thanks, Mama," I said, and I took a hefty piece of cheesecake and a big cup of tea.

"Well, how did the dance practice go?" Papa asked.

"It went real good for me and my partner Patty," I said.

"How did Joe make out with his partner?" Papa continued.

"He did real good also," I answered. "I think we have a good chance of winning."

"I hope you do. Mama and I spent a lot of money paying Sol so you could have the time to dance. When is the contest? Tell me again, I forgot."

"It's this Saturday night at the college and we hear there will be a lot of good dancers trying to win, but we will beat them all."

"I hope so," said Papa. "Should Mama and I come to see you perform?"

"I don't think so," I said. "The place will be filled with kids and college students and you might not like the way they act."

"What do you mean 'the way they act?'" asked Papa.

"Well sometimes they get loud and even boo the ones they don't like. They might even go further than that and stamp their feet to throw the dancers off the beat and tempo. They can be real cruel."

"How did you find this out? "

"The band leader told up this the other night," I said.

"Joe called him for information about how the contest was to be run and after doing that the guy clued him in on possible down sides."

Papa was serious when he said, "No matter what happens, don't lose your temper. Always be the gentleman. Tell me, how does the contest work?"

"The leader told Joe he would explain everything to all of us the afternoon of the dance contest at a meeting. I know you want to come but after speaking it over with Joe, we think it best that our parents not come. It might make us nervous. Besides we have to be there at six o'clock for the meeting."

"All right, all right, so we won't come," said Papa.

# XVI

Thursday afternoon came around real quick. Tonight was going to be the dress rehearsal without the dress up part. Joe and I met as usual and we managed to get to the studio fifteen minutes early. The elevator operator was still polite since Joe spoke to him.

"Hello there," greeted the receptionist. "The girls are not here yet but Celeste and Marsha are. Should I let them know you're here or do you want me to wait until your partners come?"

"We'll wait," I said.

Just then the elevator doors opened and Patty and Margo walked in with Patty saying, "Hi guys, you're here early. Guess you both are getting anxious about Saturday. Don't worry, you two, we got you covered."

As if on cue, Celeste and Marsha came on the scene with Marsha saying, "Good to see that you are all here. Let's get started. Patty and Marco, this time you come with me. Celeste will check out Joe and Margo. So let's go dancing." Then she stopped turned to us and said, "I have a better idea." She pointed to Patty and me. You two are going to spend an hour with me and then you'll switch and work with Celeste. Joe and Marsha will then come to my studio and I can check them out for the other hour. These are your finals, so give it your all."

When the two hour session was up, we met in the reception area to say goodbye to Celeste and Marsha and we thanked them over and over for what they did for us.

As we rang for the elevator, we got a hug and a kiss

from both of them and Celeste added, "You all did great. We really think you could win this thing. Keep your wits about you and remember what we taught you. Come and see us Monday and let us know how you did."

I saw Marsha then turn to the girls and she said, pointing to Joe and me, "keep these two focused and I think you will make it. I'll see you both next week, regular time."

Celeste then chimed in, "Treat these guys with respect for what they did. They came from nowhere to somewhere. Now get out of here, we have students waiting."

When we got to the lobby, I remember asking the girls, "How about coffee?"

Patty answered quickly. "Not tonight. We both have things to do. We'll see you Saturday. Since the band leader called the meeting for six o'clock, lets meet at five-thirty."

"That's a go," Joe said with me shaking my head in approval.

Turning to the girls, I said, "We'll look for you. See ya."

"Ciao," said Joe.

"So long," said Marsha.

Well, Gumba," Joe said as we got out of the subway. "Be careful what you do between now and Saturday. Don't take any foolish chances".

"You too. Don't make any dumb moves, Joe. Remember the ferry thing.

"Are you going to come to my house for dinner Sunday?" Joe asked.

"I don't know yet," I said. "I'll have to let you know."

"Anyway, let's check with each other between now and the time we meet on Saturday. Remember, we have to meet the girls at five-thirty so we meet here at five. Ok?"

"That's jake with me," I said. "Give me a call tomorrow. I think I have to work in the store all day so I'll be easy to reach."

"Will do," said Joe. "Say hello to your folks."

"Same here."

And we both went our separate ways.

When I got to the store, Papa and Sol were still preparing for Friday. I walked in, said hello, and asked Papa, "Where's Mama?"

"She's in the back resting. It's been a busy day."

Sol then asked, "How did the dress rehearsal go?"

I wondered how he knew about dress rehearsals but then it came to me. There were a lot of show people coming into the Stage to eat. He must have heard them talking.

"Everything went good," I said. "Our teachers think we have a chance of winning but I'm not counting on it."

Papa broke in, "If you go as a loser you'll be one. Go like you're going to win and you will.

Sol added, "Your father is right, go positive and you'll do positive."

Papa then came back to me with, "Now grab the broom, Mr. Contest Winner, and dance around the store and sweep the floor while you're at it."

We all started to laugh when I got the broom, and I pretended it was a dance partner and danced around the store and swept as I did the steps. I actually hummed a tune to myself as I did this.

When I finished my sweep dance, Papa and Sol were finishing up their prep work.

"Ok, let's call it enough," said Papa. "We have a busy day tomorrow and if we all work together we won't be tired by the time it is Shabbos." Turning to Sol, Papa then added, "Want to stay for Shabbos dinner tomorrow night? Mama always makes enough for an army."

Sol, with a big smile, said, "That would be terrific but I have to leave early."

"How come?" I asked.

Papa came back with, "Hey Marco, it's none of your business."

I felt a little embarrassed and went back to the apartment and told Mama that Sol was coming for dinner. I then went back to the door to the store and opened it just a little so I could hear them talking.

I heard Sol tell Papa that he was invited by Mrs. Eidem, one of our good customers, to come over to her place for coffee and cake. I also found out that Mrs. Eidem came into the store a few times when Sol was alone behind the counter and they got sort of friendly. I waited on her several times and remembered she was a very nice lady, good looking too. We all knew from the neighborhood that she had been a widow for about six years.

The next thing I heard was Mama telling me to call Papa in for dinner. Instead of calling him, just to be cute, I went up to them saying, "Mama wants you to come in now." As I started to go back to the apartment, I began singing sort of loud, the song "Isn't it romantic." When I got to the door, I turned around and took a little bow. The next thing that happened was Papa throwing a bagel at me, hitting me in the chest. His throwing arm was not the greatest. It didn't bother me at all.

I then heard Papa say to Sol, "I guess he heard us talking. The boy really doesn't mean anything by this. He is still young, I hope you don't mind his *narishkeit*." That means 'foolishness.'

"It's ok," said Sol. "I don't take it personal."

Sol then left after saying goodnight. Papa locked up and came in and we sat down for dinner.

I was going to go for a walk after we ate but it started to rain and besides that I was tired from the two hectic dance sessions, so I went to bed and fell fast asleep.

Papa let me sleep until eight o'clock the next day but I was behind the counter ready go by eight-thirty.

The day went by quickly and before I knew it, it was time to close the store. Once Carmine and Louie took off, Mama went back inside and began to prepare the Shabbos meal.

When it was around sunset, Mama came and told Sol and Papa to come in while she lit the candles and they all said their prayers. After they returned from doing this, I went back with Mama and lit another set of candles and said my Shabbos prayers.

The Shabbos meal was as good as ever and just before Mama was going to bring out the dessert and coffee, Sol got up and said he had to leave. Mama asked, "So early?"

But before she could continue any further, Papa said, "Sol has something to do later on, so let's not hold him back."

Mama then replied, "If you have to, you have to. I'll see you tomorrow morning."

"Thanks so much, Sarah, for having me for Shabbos," said Sol. "It means so much to me. It's just like being with *Mishbocher*. I'll see you in the morning." With that Sol left after saying goodnight.

After letting Sol out the door, Papa returned and said to me, "It's a nice night. Maybe we should take a walk." He turned to Mama and said, "Sarah, do you want to come with us?"

"No Ivan," said Mama. "I have to wash my hair and then write a letter to some of my family in Italy and see how they are doing. I hear things are not going good over there."

"All right, if that's the way you want it," Papa answered. "We'll be back soon."

"Good. Have a nice walk."

"Come Marco, let's go," Papa said, heading for the door. "A nice stroll will be good for both of us and we will be able to sleep good tonight."

Once outside, Papa remarked to me, "What a beautiful night, so clear. Look up, Marco, you can see the stars. I dreamed of this when we lived in Italy. We are free here to look up at the stars if we want to. In Venice, we had to be confined to the ghetto, even though Jews have lived in Italy for hundreds of years. Now let's talk about tomorrow. I think you should shower early tomorrow morning and put the clothes you are going to wear during the contest in the cellar."

"Good thinking, Papa," I replied. "I can work the busy morning up to about one."

Papa interrupted me saying, "Tomorrow, no work for you. Take your shower and get dressed in your work clothes. You then are going to take yourself with your dancing clothes and shoes over to Sol's place and stay there until it's time to go. He was the one who came up with this idea and it makes sense. He has a nice couch and a radio and you can take a nap or listen to the radio. Mama will fix you a nice lunch and something to drink. You come over to the store before you go to meet Joe so we can wish you good luck."

"Are you sure it's ok with Sol?" I asked.

"It's ok, it's ok. He already told Henry the super that you are coming over. Sol said you were his nephew. That should satisfy the Yentas, especially the neighbor on the floor, Mrs. Waxer. Sol has an extra key and he'll give it to you tomorrow morning, so you are all set. Don't forget to thank Sol for doing this for you. He must like you a lot."

"He must like *us* a lot," I said.

Papa then said, "Enough walking and talking for tonight. Let's turn around and go back, close the store, and make ready for bed."

When we got back, rather than wait until the next morning, I brought the clothes I was going to wear down to the basement. Next step was going to be getting a good night's sleep, which I did. I didn't need much coaxing to sleep a little later than the usual five-thirty, so I repeated the same wake up at eight and deliciously remained in bed until eight-thirty. This, I remember, was so good. I then hopped out, grabbed a fast but thorough shower, shaved, put my work clothes on, and hurried into the store just as Carmine and Louie were coming in.

They both said hello to me and Louie said, "Tonight is your big night and we want to wish you good luck. We heard you and Joe are good dancers and your girl partners are knockouts."

"Hope you guys win," Carmine added.

"Thanks," I replied. "We'll do our best."

Carmine answered, "You do that and Louie and I will add a little extra to your prize. You know why?" He laughed as though he was telling a big joke.

So I said, "Why?"

Louie answered, "Because I got two left feet and Carmine is as clumsy as an ox."

I remember they both broke out in peals of laughter and I didn't know why, but I went along and faked my laugh with them.

Abruptly Carmine then said, "Time to go to work. Can't keep our customers waiting." And they went into the apartment.

I said good morning to Mama, Papa, and Sol. I took some breakfast and was getting ready to put on my apron when Papa said, "No work today. Get your stuff and go over to Sol's and spend the day there. Mama already has your lunch ready, and something extra if you get hungry later on. Here is the key that Sol gave to me to give to you. Don't forget to thank him for doing this."

"Thank you so much, Sol," I said. "I promise I won't mess up the apartment."

"Don't worry about it," said Sol. "It's my pleasure. It's been many years since anyone stayed at the apartment. I left a clean sheet and pillowcase on the bed. The apartment is small but we found it comfortable. Too bad the toilet is on the floor, but that's the way it is."

"Again, I can't thank you enough, Sol."

"It's ok, it's ok," Sol came back.

Before I knew it, I was on my way to Sol's with my lunch and clothes. His apartment was small but kept real neat. I settled myself in on the living room couch and fell asleep. Waking up about three hours later, I ate the lunch Mama gave me, turned on the radio, and listened to a Dodgers-Giants game. I didn't want it to be known, but I was secretly a Brooklyn Dodgers fan.

Around four I washed up in the kitchen, changed my clothes, slicked my hair, took the remains of my lunch, and went back to the store for Mama and Papa's inspection, especially Mama's. Fortunately, the store was not busy when I got there and Mama and Papa came from behind the counter to look me over.

"You look great," Papa said. "The jacket and pants are a good match and that white shirt looks even like a tuxedo shirt."

Mama said, "Turn around," and she looked me over also. "You look beautiful. That red tie goes so good with the jacket. So go now." And with that Mama gave me a hug and a kiss. Papa came over and gave me a bear hug and a kiss and said, "Good luck, I know you'll do fine."

Sol said, "Good bye," as I gave him his key back, and he then added, "Boychick, mark my words, you'll be a winner."

I exited the store and hurried to the subway station. Joe was already there and when I saw how he was dressed, I stopped and actually stared. I couldn't believe my eyes. There was my friend Joe, stacked out in a zoot suit with a reap pleat, fifteen-inch cuffs and about twenty-two-inch knees. His jacket was nearly down to his knees and I saw the chain from his belt to his pant pocket. He had a wide brim fedora on his head. He was dressed to the nine yards. This was the latest style and it was the symbol of the swing era.

"Holy shit," I said. "Where did you get those duds? You look like you came out of a Howard Clothes window. You can win on just having the balls to wear that outfit."

"Let's go," Joe said, and we went down the steps to get the train.

Joe got some side glances from other people waiting for the train, including some pretty-looking babes. Even while walking from the station to the college, Joe was a head-turner, and it wasn't from amazement, but from jealousy.

We got to the door marked "Contestants," gave our names at the desk, and were directed to the auditorium where we met Patty and Margo. They loved Joe's outfit, but said mine looked perfect for the type of dance Patty and I were going to do.

As the auditorium filled up, I was struck with the sight

of many other guys coming in with the same zoot suit style as Joe had on. He was not so dumb after all. The auditorium filled out fast and it was just a few minutes after six when the band leader, Gary, came on the stage with a few more people who sat down in back of him.

I remember Gary saying, "Hello, you contestants. Are you ready to dance and win?"

The contestants yelled, "Yeah!"

Gary continued, "First I want to introduce our sponsor and judges and their assistants. I ask you to save your applause until I introduce them all and then give them a big round. I want to hear some whistling, some hooting, hollering and feet stamping as well as the clapping of hands. First, our sponsor is Mr. Wally Kemp, manager of the Roseland Ballroom, the finest dance ballroom in the country. Roseland has been kind enough to donate the prizes. Now we meet and greet our judges. Miss Marlene Hammond of Dale Dance Studios, Mr. Steve Andrews, assistant choreographer of the Radio City Rockettes, and Mr. Jamie Larson, associate director of the Harvest Moon Ball Competition, and last but not least, their assistants who'll have the mean job of picking out the ones the judges designate to leave the dance floor.

"Don't try to dance away from them if they are heading your way. They'll find you. Here is how it's going to work. The lindy hoppers will report to the men's locker room. The Latin dancers will go to the ladies locker room and the fox trotters will stay here. There will be plenty of time for each category to get to the dance floor. We limited each category to thirty couples. There will be plenty of room on the dance floor. Each category will dance to three songs and the judges will disqualify fifteen couples at the end of the first set. They will then cut the number of contestants down to five at the end of the second set and pick winners one, two and three from the remaining five at the end of the third set. To make it more exciting for everyone, the lindy hoppers will start off, followed by the Latin dancers, and last will be the fox trotters. On the second set, the fox trotters will be the first, the lindy hoppers second, and the Latin dancers third. On the third set, the Latin's first, the fox trotters second, and the lindy third. Now let's hear it for our sponsors, judges, and assistants!"

After the accolades were heard, Gary said, "Ok, let's go to our assigned places. In the meantime, the band will play a number or two until you all are ready. Good luck and go dancing." And so it was.

Joe and Margo and Patty and I were able to survive the first round and then the second. And the more we danced, it seemed, the better we got.

I had the willies during the third number of the second set, especially when I saw an assistant heading our way. But lucky for us he passed and tagged the couple behind us.

We made the final round. It was unbelievable. One more round to go. We were next after the Latin's finished and then the winners were going to be picked. We were confident since we had made it this far. We could go to the top, and we did. Nothing could stop us. Our intricate steps were perfect, our breaks exciting, and Patty's dips were sexy deep. She sure had great legs. The third song was being played and there were three pairs left. When the song ended we were told to stay on the dance floor. Two of the assistants came out. One tapped the couple next to Patty and asked them to take three steps to their left. The other assistant walked toward us but then turned to the couple next to me and directed them to take three steps to the right.

Gary got on the mike and announced the winners of the fox trot contest. The couple on our left won third prize. We held our breath as Gary announced the winners of the second prize. It was the couple on our right. We won first prize! I couldn't believe it. I really couldn't believe it. This was official. Patty and I were announced as the winners of the fox trot first prize.

At our meeting all winners were told to report to the teachers' lounge. As we made our way there, we came past an empty classroom, the door was slightly open and Patty said, "Let's go inside. I have a surprise for you." Once we got past the door, she closed it and grabbed me by the neck, pulled me close to her, and before I knew it her tongue was exploring every part of my mouth. Her body felt like I was welded to mine. I exploded and returned her kiss with lust. My hand started to explore her body when she abruptly stopped and backed away saying, "This is a mistake. I have a boyfriend, but I couldn't help myself. I had to do this. I do like you Marco, but can't do anything about it for now. Let's calm down for a minute and go to the teachers' lounge."

"Ok," I said. Once we exited the door, I said to her, "Let's sneak back to the entrance to the dance floor and see how Joe and Margo are doing."

"Ok," Patty responded while straightening her clothes. We then walked back and were able to see Joe and Margo doing their thing. They were terrific. This was their third number and Joe was going crazy. He put Margo through flips over his back and even pulling her under his legs, and she did some of these breaks to him. The audience was standing and applauding. When their dance was over, the assistants came onto the dance floor and pulled the same routine as they did with us. One couple on the right and one on the left with Joe and Margo in the middle. The first prize winners came as no surprise when announced. It was official. Joe and Margo!

Patty and I were so happy that we hugged each other and when I went to kiss her, she backed off.

"No Marco," she said. "Let's just stay friends for now."

"But I love you, Patty."

"No you don't," she said. "You're just hot for me. Let's let it go for now. Here come Joe and Margo."

Joe and Margo actually came dancing down the corridor as we ran up to meet them. Joe stopped every few steps and hugged Margo and twirled her around and even kissed her.

"Hey Champs" I said

Margo responded, "Hey Champs yourself."

We went to the teachers' lounge where all the winners were assembled and we all congratulated each other. We were then told to go back to the dance floor and to go up on the stage. Which we did.

Mr. Kemp was introduced and he presented the winners, starting with the third place and ending with the first place with their prizes. As first place winners, the four of us each received a three-month pass to Roseland Ballroom, good on Saturday matinees, and a trophy. I thought to myself *I'm in luck, at least I can see her on a Saturday. Maybe we can even dance together.*

After we left the stage, Joe came up and said, "This night has been sensational. We need to celebrate. I got it. The Hotel Piccadilly has a roof garden café and the Three Son's are playing there. We can get in."

Margo interrupted, "Not tonight partner. We told you from the beginning, we have boyfriends and they are waiting for us."

Joe then shrugged his shoulders and said to me: "If you say so."

Patty then said, "After we tell Marcia and Celeste on Monday night what happened we could have a cup of coffee with you guys and say goodbye."

When the girls left, Joe turned to me and shrugged his shoulders and said, "Hey Marco, sometimes that's the way it goes. By the way, wipe the lipstick off your mouth."

I came back with, "It must have happened during one of the breaks."

"Yeah, and my name is Abraham Lincoln."


Needless to say, Papa and Mama were thrilled and so was Joe's family. I know because I was there for Sunday dinner where we were congratulated by all, including a "That's nice" by Uncle Vito. Even Paulie reluctantly nodded in agreement.

On Monday we met the girls at seven o'clock at the studio. Celeste and Marcia came out to greet us.

"Well," Marcia asked, "How did you do?"

Joe, being cute, said, "We did terrible. We both won

only first prize."

"You all should be proud of yourselves and we are proud of you," said Marcia. "We would like to use you in our ads telling that in only three weeks Arthur Murray studios taught you to be first prize winners of a New York Dance contest." We all agreed and Marcia continued, "You are going to hear from our advertising agency in a little bit." Turning to the girls, she then said, "Let's go girls, you are back to your normal time frame. Your fun three weeks with these guys is over."

Both girls turned to Joe and me. Patty said, "We are sorry. We'll take a rain check on the coffee. We will have it maybe before or after the Roseland dance session."

Joe then said, "That's OK with us. We'll see you."

We then hugged Celeste and Marcia and rang the elevator as the girls went with Marcia.

As we sat on the subway going home, Joe saw my dejected face and tried to cheer me up. "Marco, my man," he said. "Girls at this stage of our lives are like trolley cars; you miss one, there is always another one behind it. These are our fun years, so let's sop them up. Quantity, not quality is the theme going here. Remember Angie and how you pined for her. She's just a memory now, right?"

"I guess so," I answered, and Joe was right.

School started the next week and the weeks passed quickly. Joe and I continued to go to dances, especially the ones on Saturday at the Roseland. We met lots of dolls, terrific dancers who taught us new steps and breaks. While dancing, we bumped into Patty and Marcia once in a while. They were always with the same two guys. I guess these guys were their boyfriends.

# XVII

I remember it was about the middle of the first semester when I received a message from my grade advisor Mr. Kramer to meet with him in his office.

When I came in, he invited me to sit down and began by asking me if I still intended to go on to college after graduation. I assured him that I was really looking forward to it.

"What colleges are you looking to attend?" he asked.

I replied, "NYU Uptown, Columbia, Princeton, Dartmouth, and University of Pennsylvania."

"That's an impressive list," Mr. Kramer replied. "Are you considering City College and NYU downtown?"

"Not really. I think going to any of my first choices would help get me accepted to medical school."

"I see," Mr. Kramer answered while he stretched his hands over his head and leaned back in his chair. "So you want to be a doctor?"

"Yes, it's been my dream. I want to help people."

"That's very admirable. So let's see how I can help you get started on your way. Have you contacted any of the colleges on your list?"

"Not yet," I answered.

"Well, don't waste any time, and write for applications right away, including City College and NYU downtown. They could be backups for you. You have a very good grade average and you need to ask Miss Weiner in the office for transcripts of those grades. Talk to as many teachers as possible and see if they would write letters of recommendation for you. Once you get them, see if Miss Hanson could make copies of them for you to send along with your applications. I see here that you don't have too much in the way of after school activites. I think it is important for you to participate in as many as you can, so that they could be listed on your application. Let me caution you not to just join and not show up. Many times the admission office at the colleges contact the school to see if the applicant is a no-show."

"I never joined any school clubs or teams," I said. "Do you have any suggestions, Mr. Kramer?"

"Well, there are always openings on the debate teams and theatre. I see you took three years of Spanish, so look into participating in the Spanish club. There is always a very good Math club here. Talk to Mr. Hay about getting in. You can also get a list of our after school clubs at the office. Just ask one of the secretaries for it." Mr. Kramer then added, "I see you have a very easy schedule for your entire senior year, so if I were you I would spend a lot of time getting accepted into as many clubs as you can.

"By the way," Mr. Kramer continued, "A lot of the colleges and universities you picked have high tuition costs. You might check them out and see if you can afford to go there. Also figure in the cost of books and living expenses if these schools are out of town. You have a lot of work to do, so I suggest you get to it right away."

"Thanks a lot Mr. Kramer. I'm glad you took the time to get me started."

"That's Ok, Marco. Now go. I have other students to see."

On my way out, I got a list of after school clubs and made it my business to run them down during the next couple of days. I guess I got lucky, because there were openings on the Yearbook committee, publicity for the Senior Prom Committee, Pan American club, Math club and even a spot in Mr. Kramer's office. And they all fit in great with my schedule. I said to myself, "I'm set."

Over the next few months, I was busy sending for and

sending back college applications. Many of them required fees for up to fifteen dollars. The transcripts cost one dollar each and Papa came up with the money. He was so proud to have a son who was applying to college. The "after school clubs" and activities were fun and productive, especially the one working in Mr. Kramer's office since I was allowed to use a typewriter to fill out my college applications. During that time, Joe and I saw each other every day at school for lunch. We even had time to spend together on Tuesday, Thursday, and Friday right after school. Monday and Wednesday I had to attend after school committee meetings. I was lucky to have my last period as a free period.

Friday nights we spent at local dances and most every Saturday afternoon we were at Roseland, where we had the chance to meet and dance with semi and sometimes real pros. Every other Sunday, it was dinner at Joe's.

Days ran by and before I knew it, it was Christmas and Chanuka. Papa, true to his word, would not let me work in the store unless he caught me doing nothing. Then it was back to sweeping and cleaning.

On New Year's Eve, Joe and I went to 42$^{nd}$ Street and Broadway and joined the thousands there waiting to see the ball come down. I remember all of us counting: ten, nine, eight, seven, six, five, four, three, two, one, and then screaming "Happy New Year!" and shaking hands with everyone around us. Joe and I actually hugged each other. 1940 was here and we were starting the last half of our senior year. It was hard to believe we would be graduating in six months.

During the next three months, life was good. I was accepted to Columbia, Dartmouth, NYU both Uptown and Downtown, the University of Pennsylvania, and City College. It was hard to decide which college to choose.

Joe was very happy for me and didn't want to influence me, but sort of mentioned that he hoped I would go to a New York college. I was caught in a quandary, but this was solved when at the next dinner I attended at Joe's house. After Uncle Vito finished the business with his associates, Paulie signaled

Joe and me to join him. Once we were seated, Uncle Vito leaned back in the chair and said, "Joe told me you got in to several colleges. That's very good. Mind telling me which ones?"

I quickly told him.

"What do you think you are going to do?"

"I don't know," I said. "I would like to go to University of Pennsylvania or Dartmouth, but I don't think Papa can afford to send me there."

"How about NYU or Columbia? Both have very good medical schools also. You can do what you want, but I'd like to make you a deal. Since you are like a part of the family now, and would be the first to go to college and then on to medical school, your tuition and books could be paid by a scholarship loan from a union, probably the Cement Masons Union. I think NYU Downtown would be better for you because it's closer to the neighborhood. You can pay what you owe back when you become a doctor."

I couldn't believe my ears. Did I hear right? My tuition and books might be paid for from a scholarship loan fund, and NYU was a good school and had a top notch medical college.

"Think about it Marco," said Uncle Vito. "Talk it over with your folks, and get back to me. When do you have to let the school know?"

"I have ten days to give them an answer."

"Well, let me know in a week."

"I'll do that."

"Tell Joe, and we'll start making arrangements if you decide to take up my offer." He added, "Ok you two, on your way out, tell Paulie to come in."

After saying goodbye, I started to leave when Joe said, "Wait up, I'll go down with you."

Once we reached the street, Joe turned to me and said," That Uncle Vito, he must love you. What an offer. What are you going to do?"

"I don't know yet."

"Are you crazy? You can't turn that down. It's an offer

of a lifetime."

"I've got to talk to my parents. It's too big a decision to make by myself. I've got to go, Joe. I'll call you later."

"Ok, I'll be waiting."

I rushed home and hung around until the store closed, swept up, and joined Mama and Papa in the apartment after Sol was paid and had left.

While Mama and Papa ate, I filled them in with what had happened and told them about Uncle Vito's offer. Mama's jaw dropped when she heard the details. Papa just leaned back in his chair and twirled his mustache.

It seemed to me he was deep in thought, and then he started to speak. "Let's look at this from every angle," he said. "Our experience with Carmine and Louie through Vito Amatto has been good. He has kept his word with us 100%. If it wasn't for him, we would have had to close our doors."

Mama then asked me, "Why would Mr. Amatto do this? What are you to him that he should spend this kind of money on a practical stranger? My mother taught me that if it sounds too good to be true, it usually is, and she also taught me that if you take you've got to give back."

Papa said, "Joe and Marco are like brothers and Marco is considered as one of the family. The proof is the way they treat him. Besides, they want one of their own to go to college and then on to be a doctor. No one in their family has ever done this before. I think you should take up Mr. Amatto's offer, but I'm not telling you to do it. This is your choice and only you must make it."

"But Papa," I said, "If I decide I want to go to the University of Pennsylvania, those colleges are out of town and the living expenses are higher there than here. Their tuition and books cost more."

Papa continued, "Marco, if you really want to go to the out of town schools, I think I have the answer. You know Sal Rizzo, he owns the Negozio di Generi Alimentari. He came to see me and invited me for coffee. He told me his lease in his store was coming up soon for renewal, and instead of renewing, he'd like to be partners with Mama and me. He probably heard about Louie and Carmine and said it would make no difference to him, but he would want a piece of the rent that was being paid by them. If I make the deal with Sal, he would own half the business, but I could get enough money from selling half to him to send you to the out of-town colleges and maybe medical school."

It was then that I made up my mind. I didn't want Papa and Mama to sell one half of their business, especially to a guy like Sal, who had a not so good reputation in the area. I told Mama and Papa that no way did I want them to sell a half of what they worked for all these years.

"I'll tell you what, Papa, let me think about his until tomorrow," I said. "I don't want to rush into things."

"All right, all right, that's enough thinking for tonight," Mama said. "You'll wear your brains out. Let's go to sleep, and Marco's right, we'll talk tomorrow."

Papa started to interrupt when Mama said, "Ivan, that's enough. Leave the boy alone, and let's go to bed." And we did.

I couldn't sleep that night. I tossed and turned all night thinking about whether I should take up Uncle Vito's offer or pass it up. Should I go to Columbia, which is in town, or to the University of Pennsylvania, which is out of town? If I go out of town, how can I afford the tuition, books, and living expenses? One thing I knew is that I didn't want Mama and Papa to take in a partner. NYU is the best choice, just a subway ride from home. It had a good pre-med course and its own medical school. Besides, how can I pass up Uncle Vito's loan offer? He said I could pay it back once I became a doctor. No doubt about it. NYU was the right choice. I heaved a sigh of relief, turned over, and fell back to sleep.

Next thing I knew, Papa was shaking me, saying, "Marco, it's past seven o'clock, you'll be late for school."

"Ok, Papa, thanks for waking me."

I jumped out of bed, got dressed, ate breakfast, and

raced off to school, nearly forgetting my lunch.

When I met Joe before our first class, he couldn't wait. Didn't even say hello but asked instead, "Well, what are you going to do?"

"What do you mean, 'going to do'?"

"I'm asking you, what are you going to do about college? What do you think I'm asking about? Not if you're going to shack up with Pattye. Well, let me have it."

"I haven't made up my mind 100%. I'm going to think about it today."

Just then the bell rang and we were off to the first period class. All through the morning classes, Joe kept bugging me. It was during lunch when I had had enough and I told Joe to lay off by saying, "You're not helping me. I know where you're coming from and that means a lot to me, but I got to do this on my own. You are like my brother, so I know you'll understand. Don't be pissed, just understand."

"Ok, Ok, brother, but I hope you make the right decision, and we both know it's NYU."

"You always have to have the last word."

"That's right," Joe answered.

That son of a bitch, he got the last word in, as usual.

I got home a little after five from school, having had to attend a Pan American Club meeting. I didn't want to hang around the store because Papa would always find something for me to do, so I went over to the library and started to read the papers. I picked up the *New York Times*. This was the first time I read the *Times*. Usually I glanced over the *Daily News* and the *Daily Mirror* since we sold them at the store. I knew there was war in Europe. Germany had taken over Austria, then Czechoslovakia, and then Poland. I felt bad for all those people. It was scary but I wasn't afraid. America was safe and could beat any country in the world. I was just about finished reading the papers when the librarian came over and softly announced, "We will close in 10 min."

I returned the papers to the rack and left for home. I got

there just in time to miss having to do any prep work or cleanup. Papa and Sol had already done it.

Sol said goodnight and left, and as he had done for so many years, Papa locked the front door and turned off the lights, leaving just the night security lights on.

We sat down to eat and halfway through the meal Papa asked, "Where did you go earlier when you left the store?"

I told him and Mama that I went to the library to bring myself up to date with what's going on in the world.

Papa grabbed my hand, looked me straight in the eye, and said, "That's good. You should know what's happening. It doesn't look good for the Jews over there, and I'm worried about some of our relatives and friends in Italy."

"But Papa, Italy is not in any war," I said.

Papa came back with, "Not right now, but Italy is in with Germany and will go to war with anyone Germany tells them to. Let's hope it's later than sooner." Papa then turned to face me and continued, "We can't solve the world situation, so let's see what we can do to solve the college situation. How about it Marco? What did you decide?"

"Well Papa, I thought about it and thought about it, and I think the best thing for me to do is to take up Vito Amatto's offer and go to NYU. It's a great college with a famous medical school and I don't want you and Mama to have to take in a partner, and also I don't want to give up my family and friends for at least four years if I go out of town to college. Believe me, Papa, and you too, Mama, this is the best way to go and I want to hear what you think."

Papa leaned back in his chair, stretched his arms high, and then twirled on his mustache. He usually did this while coming up with what to say. Mama made herself busy by cleaning off the table and putting the dishes in the sink. This was her way of considering things.

"Please sit down, Mama," I said. "This is very important for us to discuss now." And Mama sat down. "Papa, please let us talk about it."

"Ok," Papa said, and turning to Mama he said, "Sarah,

you go first."

Mama replied, "I really don't know what to say, but I know how I feel. I'd love to have you stay here for at least college, but I don't know what to think about Mr. Amatto's offer. It just doesn't sound kosher to me, but I might be wrong. Marco, my son, you know Mr. Amatto best of all. If you think it's the right thing to do, then do it. If you want to go out of town to college, don't worry about the money, we'll manage it." Mama turned to Papa saying, "Ivan, what do you think?"

Papa rubbed his hands over his face and once again tweaked on his mustache, looking like he was still in deep thought. He then lifted up his chin and faced me and said, "You know, Mr. Amatto has kept his word with us all the time and Carmine and Louie have been gentleman. From what you tell me, Joe's family treats you like one of their own. What have you got to lose? If it doesn't work out for some reason, Mama and I will pay the money back. Just think an opportunity like this doesn't come very often. I think you should take it and thank your lucky stars that you got somebody who is willing to do this. Vito Amatto is a big name in this neighborhood and has a good reputation. He's called an honorable man and that's good enough for me."

I said to Papa, "You're right, he's known as an honorable man and is well respected all over the neighborhood." I then turned to Mama and said, "Everything is going to be great. I'll go to college not too far away. I will study and get good grades so I could get into medical school."

"So it's settled then," Papa said. "How do you go from here with Mr. Amatto?"

"I think I'll call Joe right away or maybe I'll wait until I see him in school tomorrow."

"It's close to ten, so maybe waiting till tomorrow morning is the right thing to do," said Mama

"I think you're right, Mama," I said.

"So let's go to bed," said Papa. "We have to open the store regular time tomorrow morning."

I went to my room and left Mama and Papa talking

quietly between themselves. Waking up in time was easy because I was so excited I couldn't sleep. I met Joe just as we were entering our home room.

"I gotta talk to you on our way to first period," I said.
"What's up?" Joe asked.
"I'll tell you later."

Just then the home room teacher declared, "Take your seats and quiet down." After the teacher took attendance and made some announcements, the bell rang and the class emptied out and headed to the first period classes.

"What's the problem?" Joe asked.
"I got some bad news."
"What's going on? Is it really bad?"
"Sure is."
"What is it?"

With a real anxious look on my face, I said, "Well, you're gonna be stuck with me and me with you for another four years, cause I'm gonna take up Uncle Vito's offer and go to NYU."

Joe gave out a yelp and did one of his fancy dance steps. "You son of a bitch. You scared the hell out of me. This is the best news I've heard since we won the contest." He held out his hand, saying, "Put it there partner." And I did, and we hugged each other.

Just then the hall monitor came over and told us to stop carrying on and get to class. The rest of the day was a breeze. At lunch, I asked Joe how I could get my decision over to Uncle Vito. Joe said he would contact him and give him the message. I wanted to hang out with Joe after school but I had to go to the Math Club meeting.

When I got to the store, Papa told me that Joe called and left word for me to call him. And I did.

"I got in touch with Uncle Vito," said Papa. "He told me to tell you to come to dinner on Sunday. He also said to tell you he was pleased to get your message."

Friday night seemed to roll around fast. Joe and I hit some new dance territory; a dance in the Bronx. The Bronx

141

girls are different from the ones in Manhattan. I couldn't figure it out, but we had a good time and increased our inventory of babes. Saturday afternoon was our usual stint at Roseland, where we always had a great time watching and dancing with the best of New York. After a while Joe and I got to be known and we were asked to dance by some real good looking, sexy dancers. It was so much fun.

    I saw Pattye there almost every Saturday and tried to ask her to dance or even talk, but she always gave me the cold shoulder. The more she did this, the more anxious I was to talk and dance with her. The memory of our kiss and her body grinding into mine still remained with me. Seeing her caused my heart to speed up, my longing for her to increase, and a little sweat to break out on my forehead.

    Joe, on the other hand, was as cool as a cucumber when he saw Margo. He didn't even make an attempt to approach her. He played it smart and casually said, "Hey Margo" while he was dancing close by.

    Margo always answered him, "Hi Joe," and Joe danced away. To me Margo seemed jealous seeing Joe dance with other girls. And that was that.

    Saturday night, Joe and I decided to go to Madison Square Garden and see the Harlem Globe Trotters. It was great.

    Sunday morning at five, the same routine, clothes in cellar, work behind the counter until two. Then I washed up, changed into my Sunday clothes, and started off for Joe's house. I was looking forward to my meet with Uncle Vito. I was going to buy some roses for Joe's mother, but Mama gave me a big bag of apple strudel that she had baked the night before, and she knew how to make a terrific strudel. When I got to Joe's, I was warmly greeted as usual and by this time knew every member there. It was wonderful having an extended family. Uncle Vito and family arrived and we sat down to eat. Joe was told to sit on Uncle Vito's left and I was told to sit on his right.

    The entire meal was as stupendous as usual and everyone loved Mama's strudel when it was served along with the desert.

When he was ready, Uncle Vito got up and went into the living room followed by his male family associates. It was getting to be a practice that when this happened and Joe and I were not asked to go in along with the others, we would help clean up.

When the French doors finally opened and the men started to come out, Paulie went over to Joe and said something to him that I couldn't hear. Joe put his broom away and motioned to me to go with him into the living room where Uncle Vito remained. Once we were in, Paulie closed the doors and remained outside.

"Have a seat," Uncle Vito said to us. "Having fun this last half of your senior year?"

We both replied that we were.

He said, "Good, but the real fun starts when you get out of school this summer." Turning to me, Uncle Vito said, "Did Joe tell you he doesn't want to go to college?"

"He didn't," I said.

"I tried to talk him into trying it out for only six months, but he said he had enough of school and he wants to go to work. If that's what he wants to do, I'm sure he'll find something that he'll like. So, Joe told me that you decided to take up my offer and go to NYU."

"I thought it over, spoke to my parents about it and decided it was the right thing to do," I said.

"I'm sure it will be. Now let me tell you how it will work. In a few days you will get a letter from a union in New York telling you that you are a candidate for a scholarship loan. The letter also tells you to come before the loan committee for an interview. Be sure to bring along your high school transcript. If all goes as expected, you'll hear from them in a couple of days that you got the scholarship. Once you get the OK, you will have a second meeting and arrangements for the money will be made. Just a word of caution, there are several others competing for this, so do your best to make a good impression. I'm sure you'll have no problem. Now go and tell

Paulie I want to see him."

Joe and I stood up and started to leave, then Uncle Vito beckoned me over to him and said, "Put your right hand out palm-out." He then put his left hand over mine saying, "Now, put your left hand on top of mine." Once this was done he put his other hand over mine and said, "Press your hands against mine as I press mine against yours." While doing this he continued, "This is our sign of friendship. Honor it well."

I was stunned and for a moment couldn't say anything, but then regained my senses and said to Uncle Vito, "I thank you for this sign of friendship. I will respect it forever. I also want to say thank you for the trust you have in me. I will never let you down."

"Well put," Uncle Vito answered. "Don't forget to send Paulie in, and don't forget to give my regards to your mother and father."

Joe and I left the room, gave the message to Paulie, then chit-chatted with some of the family. We waited for Uncle Vito and his family to leave and then I left. When I got home, I helped around a little at the store and before I knew it Papa and Sol were closing up.

After Sol left, Papa, Mama, and I sat down at the dining room table as we usually did and Mama served dinner. I couldn't eat a thing because I had stuffed myself at Joe's house. While sipping his coffee, Papa asked, "Well, aren't you going to tell us what happened today?"

I replied, trying to be cute, "I thought you would never ask." And then I related all the details of the meet with Uncle Vito.

When I finished and before Papa could say anything, Mama said, "Why all this rigamarole, this beating around the bush. Either you get the scholarship or you don't get it. I don't understand."

Papa came up with, "You don't have to understand. This is the way they do things. Take it or leave it. Let's just wait and see what happens."

"All right, all right, we'll wait and see what happens."

Papa turned to me saying, "You go to sleep now. Mama and I have some paperwork to do. Say goodnight to your Mama and go to bed." And I did.

I waited anxiously for the letter from the union to come. It reminded me of the time I was waiting for the final test mark report. It was on Thursday that I got the letter from the Cement Masons Union inviting me to meet with their executive committee the following Wednesday at four o'clock and I was to bring my high school transcript with me. There was also a note for me to call if I could not make it.

Four o'clock was perfect for me. I raced back from school, changed into clothes that I had left in the basement the night before, and took the subway to the union office. I remember it well. Their office was on the fifth floor. I'll never forget the first floor was a funeral parlor show room full of coffins. What a shocker this was. It got off at the fifth floor. It was about a quarter to four. There was no one there. I sat down and waited in the little reception room. It seemed like hours just sitting there staring at the four walls and checking my watch. Around four, the door opened. A guy came out and pointed a finger at me and asked, "You Marco?"

I stood up and said, "Yes."

"I am Tony. OK, follow me."

And I followed him. We went into a large room that had nothing but a big round wooden table and six chairs. The walls were bare. There were tan window shades hanging half way down the windows. The windows needed a washing. I was introduced to the two men, Ray and Al, who were sitting at the table.

"Sit down, sit down," Ray said to me. "Do you want a cuppa coffee, a coke?"

"No thanks" I answered.

"Ok, let's get to it," Ray started out. "You come well recommended, else you wouldn't be here. Vito Amatto is well respected and his recommendation means a lot. Now, whattya going to take up in college?"

"Pre-med."

"So you want to be a doctor?" Ray asked.

"I've dreamed of being one since I was a little boy."

"That means after you finish four years of college you'll have to go for another four years to medical school," Al remarked.

"That's right," I said. "But I'll try to go to college in the summertime and I think I can finish in three years."

"I didn't know that," Ray said. "That's good if you can do it. Did you bring your school records?"

"Sure did," and I handed them over to him.

Tony and Al rose and looked over Ray's shoulder at the transcript and the other information I brought along. As they peered over these records, I heard them commenting, "This looks good. These grades are first class, and what's more he's an all around guy."

When they finished, Ray asked, "Can we keep these?"

I said, "Sure."

"Good. Go out into the reception room and wait there till we call you. It won't be very long."

With that I went back out the door and sat down and twidled my thumbs, flexed my toes, stretched my arms, twisted my body, and flexed my elbows and wrists in an effort to keep busy. None of this worked, and after a while I stopped and just stared into space. It seemed like hours, but it was actually like fifteen minutes when the door opened and Tony motioned to me to follow him back into the other room.

I was again asked to sit down, and Tony pulled up his chair and sat down next to Ray and Al. Ray then put his hands behind his neck and Tony and Al followed doing the same.

I was wondering what was coming next. After their exercise bit was over, Al took out a cigar from his inside coat pocket, bit off the end, and lit it using a lighter that was on the table. "Want a cigar?" he asked me.

"No, thanks," I replied, "I don't smoke."

"That's good," Ray replied. He took a Phillip Morris from a pack that was also on the table. "I heard smoking was no good for you."

I was going to say "so why do you do it?" but I decided to keep my mouth shut. Ray took a big drag and blew the smoke out slowly. When he finished, he took the cigarette out of his mouth and laid it in an ashtray next to the pack. He then looked at me and said, "We have talked it over, and the scholarship loan is yours. Congratulations." He then reached over to shake hands with me. As he finished Tony and Al did the same. I thanked each one of them as they shook my hand. Ray continued, "You got the points needed for the loan scholarship for mainly two reasons. Reason number one is Vito Amatto. He let us know that you are a friend. And second, you have the marks and extra things to go with it. You'll get a letter in a day or two telling you that you were awarded the four-year loan scholarship which will cover tuition and books. In order to keep getting the loan funds, you need to maintain a minimum of a 3.5 average." All this information he read from a card.

Looking at me, Al asked, "Understood and agreed?"

I answered, "Yes."

Ray continued, "You send us the bills from the college along with the bills for the books and they will be paid directly to the college in your name. Does that sound ok to you, Marco?"

"It sure does," I said. "And I won't let you or Mr. Amatto down. I also want you to know that I will repay the loan as soon as possible."

Al came back with, "I'm sure you will. Remember, do the right thing."

And with that, Ray got up from the table, reached across it, and shook my hand again. "Good meeting you. Say hello to Victor Amatto for us."

I thanked all three again and left. Once I got out onto the street, I heaved a sigh of relief and started for the subway, when I saw a Chock Full of Nuts shop. I went in and had a cup of coffee and a nut and cream cheese sandwich.

This gave me the time to recover from had just happened. When I finished the sandwich and coffee, I hopped the subway and went home. When I got there I said hello to Mama, Papa, and Sol and went into our apartment. I didn't know what it was, but I had a strange feeling. I went to my room, took my shoes off, and laid down on the bed. I was tired but couldn't sleep. I just laid in my bed thinking that I would be graduating from high school in a few months and then I would be going to college, and my money problems would be over. I smiled to myself, turned on my side, and went to sleep.

# XVIII

Time just flew by. Joe's eighteenth birthday came in early April and mine was soon after. There were no really special birthday celebrations, just the regular feast at Joe's house ending with a birthday cake. For my birthday, after the store closed, Mama, Papa, Sol, and I went to the Chinese restaurant and had a special "off the menu" dinner in my honor. This was topped off by a beautiful birthday cake and lycee nuts.

School was a breeze, but I was still busy with after school activities. One of the tough ones was helping to get the yearbook ready for the printer. Photos of the faculty, graduates, description of their accomplishments, class officers, and other designations usual to high school yearbooks had to be taken and/or determined. I was on the coordinating committee and it took up a lot of time, more than I ever thought. Because of this, I didn't see Joe that often, but I had an idea and I conned him into joining with me to work on the yearbook. I convinced him this was the best way to meet all of the girls that would be graduating with us, by helping the photographer take their pictures and also interviewing the grads for their piece in the yearbook. Joe hopped at the chance and did a great job, never guessing that he was conned into doing this. We devoted a lot of time to getting these projects completed and before we knew it, our yearbook committee finally got all of the work done.

It came as a complete surprise couple of weeks after our birthdays when Carmine and Louie approached me, and Louie said, "Carmine and I want to take you out for your birthdays, so keep this Tuesday night open. I already cleared this with

Joe. We'll pick you up around seven o'clock and then get Joe. We have something nice in store for you."

"Gee, that's awful good of you guys," I said.

"Forget about it."

This was the Sicilian way of saying, "You are welcome."

The weekend and Monday came and went. On Tuesday, as Carmine and Louie were leaving, Carmine said, "Be outside at five to seven. We don't want to double park."

"I'll be there," I said, and I was. On the dot of seven, their car drove up and I got in the back seat.

"You look good," Louie said.

"So do you," I said, since both were wearing nice suits but no ties.

"You can take the tie off, where we are going it's not that formal," said Louie

Carmine said, "True, true." And he smiled as I took off my tie.

We pulled up to a waiting Joe and proceeded uptown to 52nd street off of 7th Ave to Tony's Restaurant. We lucked out, as there was a parking spot right down from the restaurant.

We went in and were warmly greeted by the owner, Tony. Once we were seated, we ordered dinner and Carmine ordered a bottle of wine. The waiter brought four wine glasses but Louie told him to take two away. He did the right thing because the drinking age in New York was twenty-one and the chance of getting caught serving minors could cause a problem with Tony's liquor license.

Dinner was very good and it was interesting listening to both Carmine and Louie talk about their childhood, their parents and grandparents, and their reasons for leaving Italy and coming to the United States and growing up on the lower East side. Before we knew it, espresso and desert was served. Tony presented us with his special home-baked cake with two candles inscribed with "Happy Birthday Joe and Marco."

"Now at the count of three, blow out all the candles and

make a wish," Carmine said to Joe and me. After he counted one, two, and three, Joe and I blew out the candles. Tony then cut the cake and served us. It was delicious. After we had our fill, Louie signaled Tony for the check, which was paid from a big roll of bills.

"Let's go guys," said Louie, "and we'll see if we can make at least one of your wishes come true."

We got into the car and Louie drove uptown to a street in the 70's and parked in front of a brownstone house.

"Let's go," Louie said, waving to us as he rang the doorbell.

Joe looked at me and I looked at him as to say, "What the hell is going on here?"

Joe, Carmine, and I got out of the car and went up the steps just as the door opened and a 50-ish black lady dressed in a maid's uniform greeted Carmine and Louie as Mr. C. and Mr. L.

"So nice to see you again," she said. "Come on in. You and your guests are expected."

We all entered the foyer and then up the steps to a sitting room where the maid, Clarisse, invited us to sit down. As she left she said, "You will be joined shortly."

Quite frankly I didn't know what in the hell to expect. Joe, on the other hand, had that shit-eating grin on his face that told me he was wise, but I didn't want him to think I was a shmuck so I smiled too.

Carmine and Louie were having a good time watching us and giving hand signals to each other that I couldn't figure out. This went on for a few minutes before the door opened and two beautiful girls entered. They went over to both Louie and Carmine, hugged and kissed them, and told them that they were missed. The taller one said, "When are you going to introduce us to these handsome men?"

Carmine said, pointing to me, "This is Marco and the guy over there is Joe."

"So nice to meet you Marco," said the tall girl, and turning to Joe, she said, "It's a real pleasure. I'm Brigette and this is my friend Tammy. Tammy is from South Carolina and has a real Southern accent." Tammy then came over to me and Joe, leaned over, and gave us big hugs. When she bent over towards me, I could see the outline of her tits and I began to sweat.

 Brigette was a tall slim dark haired girl that was really stacked, and was not afraid to show it. Tammy, a willowy blonde with a great bod, followed Brigette by coming over to me and saying, "Hi Marco," and then she kissed me on my neck with her tongue running up and down it. I nearly came.

 In the meantime, Brigette went over to Joe, sat on his lap, and started to run her fingers through his hair. Seeing this, both Louie and Carmine stood up and Louie looked at Joe and me and said, "We got some things to do, so we are going to leave you boys here."

 With that, Carmine added, "You are going to be in good hands."

 Louie then came back with, "You're going to be in good legs." At this they both laughed.

 "Don't worry," said Brigette. "By the time you come back, these boys will be men."

 "See you in an hour?" Carmine asked.

 Tammy coyly replied, "Make it in an hour and a half. We want to have some fun too."

 "Ok ladies, and hour and a half it is."

 As Carmine and Louie left, Louie turned with a big smile and said, "Have fun boys. Make sure you put in our regards."

 Once the door closed, the four of us were alone. Tammy, who had been sitting on Joe's lap all this time, changed her position and was now astride him and started to gyrate her body against his. I could hear Joe's breaths getting faster and faster but this was drowned out by my own breathes as Brigette continued running her tongue along my neck. It was just a moment later that Bregette stopped and leaned over to where Tammy was working Joe over said in a stage voice, "Tammy, I do believe we have two cherries here."

And Tammy replied in a deep Southern-accented voice, "I do believe you are right. These Yankee boys are cherry. It's been a long time since we have broken in cherries. And besides, I hear this is their birthday present. So let's make it a real happy birthday party."

With that Tammy hopped off Joe, took him by the hand, and said, "Come with me honey, and I'll show you how a cherry gets to be a tree." And they went up the stairs.

Once they were gone, Brigette said to me, "I'm really going to enjoy making a man out of you. Don't be shy or afraid. We can do anything that you every thought about doing in bed with a girl. I'm here to please you in any way and every way you want. Are you ready to have the time of your life?"

All I could do is nod.

"Ok, let's go." And we went out the door at the rear of the sitting room and entered a big bedroom. There were soft pink lights and the room had thick tan carpet which felt soft on my feet, which made it feel so sexy.

"Sit on the lounge chair or sit on the edge of the bed," Brigette said.

The bed was big, but I picked the lounge chair. I didn't remember too much about the rest of the room since my mind was too occupied with looking at her and then looking away because I was a bit embarrassed. Brigette tried to tantalize me with her movements as she slowly took off her dress leaving her in her black bra, black underwear, black garter belt, and black silk net stockings. Brigette then sort of glided over to me, leaned over, and whispered, "Reach in the back and unhook my bra and take it off."

I could hardly catch my breath. In fact I remember my hands were so shaky that I had a hard time doing this. I remember Brigette was very patient while I struggled. I finally unhooked the bra and took it off, and the next thing I saw was two beautiful knockers staring at me in the face. Briggette then took my hands and slowly guided them over them, and the same time guided my mouth over her nipples. I nearly exploded with desire. She sensed this and abruptly pulled away and said, "Why not go to the bathroom and wash up, especially down below. Just think of what's waiting for you while you are doing it. Take your jacket, shirt, and pants off and leave them on the chair."

I turned my back while doing what she asked of me. When I finished, she said "Now turn around and face me. I want to see how big the bulge is in your underwear." Once I did this, she said, "My, my, that's nice. Now go, wash up good. Take your time."

I hurried to the bathroom, took down my shorts and started to wash the area. As I soaked up my pecker, I couldn't help it, I came. I cleaned it as best as I could. What do I do now? How can I face or tell Briggette?

I put my shorts back on and sheepishly went back into the bedroom. Briggette was there waiting, lying face up on the bed, her top still bare, only difference being that her bottom underwear, garter belt and stockings were gone. She was completely naked and looked just beautiful. She looked better than the pictures I sneaked a look at in the Police Gazette.

"Come lie next to me," she said, and I climbed in bed with her. She smelled real good. "Did you do as I asked and wash up real, real good?"

"I did what you told me," I answered.

"Did you pop? Did you come in there?"

I couldn't face her and turned my face saying, "I couldn't help it. I'm sorry."

"Don't be sorry," she answered. "I wanted you to do just that. You are eighteen, strong and full of juice. You'll be ready to go again full strength but lasting longer in about fifteen minutes. Take off those boxers and we can start playing with each other. Don't be shy, just let your hands glide over my bod while I do the same to you."

It was an experience I will never forget. I will never forget the pleasure. Briggette saw that I was hesitant in moving to the love mound between her legs. She took my hand and made me run it up inside and outside of the area. She then took my middle finger and placed it on a particular spot and said,

"Rub this gently up and down, and around and around. This is the 'clit' and it gets big and hard when it's rubbed. This is what gets a woman really aroused. Once you get her this way, she'll do anything you want."

I did what she told me, and the part got hard. In fact I remember her giving out a groan.

"Now let's get to it, but first, I want you to always remember, never enter any woman until you put on a rubber." And with that she leaned over and took one out of her night table drawer sitting next to her bed and she actually showed me how to put it on. "This little thing will save you from being a papa, but most importantly from catching a disease. Now let me get you hard again."

And she did and then rolled me over on top of her and guided me into her. It was amazing. If there was a seventh heaven, I was in it. I did what came naturally and she countered everyone of my thrusts with unbelievable strength, and then it happened. I came and it was something else. What a feeling. It was fantastic. I couldn't believe how great it was.

After a moment or two, Briggette rolled me off her. I looked down at my pecker. It looked like a contented sleeping baby. Briggette leaned over and took the rubber off, tied it up and laid it on the night table.

"Stay right here honey, I'll be back in a mo," and she bare-assed went into the bathroom and came back with a moist towel and washed me all over down below. This wasn't a bad feeling either.

She then climbed back in bed with me, hugged me and held me close.

"I usually don't do the after care," she said. "But since it is the first time, and it is a birthday present, a little romance is my gift to you." She then ran her hand through my hair, massaged my face and neck and then my toes. I was so comfortable, I wanted to go to sleep with her lying next to me, but this was not to happen. A couple of minutes after she did the toes, she said, "Time to get up and get dressed. We don't want to keep Carmine and Louie waiting."

I got up and got dressed. Briggette did the same, and we went back to the sitting room. Joe and Tammy were sitting on the couch. Joe looked starry eyed. He was in a daze. Once Briggette and I sat down, Joe and I just looked at each other. We didn't know what to say. I guess Tammy sensed this and started a conversation about her looking to buy a little dog and then Joe asked what kind and this cut the tension down as we all talked about dogs.

We were in the middle of the dog discussion when Louie and Carmine came in, said hello, and looking at us Louie said, "Say bye bye to the ladies. We got to go."

Tammy came over to Joe and gave him a hug and shook hands with me. Briggette gave me a big hug and a kiss on the cheek and shook hands with Joe. Turning to both Carmine and Louie, Briggette remarked, "You brought us two boys and now we are returning two men to you. I know Tammy feels the same way I do. You can bring these guys back for a second lesson. It will be a freebie. That's our birthday present to them."

Louie then answered, "That's a first ladies, and it's ok with us. Am I right, Carmine?"

"You are right," Carmine replied.

We then went down the steps to the first floor where Clarisse was waiting, said goodnight to her, climbed into the car parked at the curb, and drove home. Joe was left off first and me second. As I got out of the car, Carmine rolled down the window and asked, "Did you have a happy birthday tonight?"

I said, "You bet."

"How about the food?"

"It was great."

"And how about the *special* desert?" Carmine asked.

"Sensational," I said. "Would like to come back and get another piece."

Carmine laughed. "Night, Marco"

"See you Carmine, bye Louie," I said, and went into the store, back to the apartment. I washed up and went to bed. I think I was smiling in my sleep all night, going over the escapades with Briggette. It was a hell of experience, better than being Barmitzvah'd.

# XIX

The next couple of weeks passed; same old, same old. But I'll never forget the beginning of the third week. It was on Tuesday when I got home from school. Carmine came up to me and said quietly, "Uncle Vito wants to see you, so be outside on Thursday at seven o'clock and I'll pick you up. It won't be longer than about an hour. If anyone asks just tell them you are meeting Uncle Vito about the loan scholarship."

On Thursday at seven, Carmine was waiting in his car at the curb. I got in and we drove uptown. The neighborhood seemed to be the same as where Brigette and Tammy lived. Carmine pulled up in front of a brownstone and said, "This is where we get out."

As we went up the steps to the front door, I saw a bronze sign on the side of the house. It read *Sicilian-American Cultural Society*.

Carmine rang the buzzer and someone I couldn't see looked through the peephole at us and asked, "Carmine? Who you're with?"

"Marco, he's expected by Mr. D."

"Just a sec."

A moment or two later, the door opened, the chain lock removed, and we were let in.

"I'll wait down here," Carmine told me. "You go up the stairs, turn right, and knock on the first door on your left."

I did just that and after knocking on the door, I heard Uncle Vito say, "Come in, Marco."

I walked into a big office with walls lined with expensive-looking paintings, I guessed of Sicily, and thick carpeting on the floor. The lights were soft, making the whole place look like the office of the president of a big corporation. Uncle Vito sat behind what I later found out was a mahogany executive desk. He was sitting on a big leather swivel office chair. He looked very impressive.

I went over to Uncle Vito, leaned over the desk, and shook his hand.

"So nice that you could come," he said.

"My pleasure," I answered.

"I understand you are all set with your funding."

"Thanks to you, I am."

"You are a good boy and deserve it. I know you'll continue to do the right thing. I'll tell you why I asked you to come here. But first of all, what are your plans this summer?"

"Right now I don't have any," I said. "I guess I'll work back at the store and my folks could then take some vacation time."

"That's good, but let me run this by you. How would you like to partner up with Joe and both of you work for my organization this summer? It will pay good money and I'm sure you could use it when you start college. The reason I'm doing this is because Joe is a good guy, honest and loyal, and will do what he's told. He'll also follow through on any assignment he gets. You know, he's like a bulldog that never gives up. So why am I telling you this? You got the same traits like Joe, but you got one thing extra. You can think on your feet and make quick decisions if changes are needed. You two have been a great team and that's why I think it would be a good deal for everybody. I'm sure you won't mind going to a driving school with Joe and get your driver's license. Because when you do, we'll buy a car for you both to use while you are working for us. If you agree, you'll get $25 a week to start and then we'll see what happens.

"Come to dinner on Sunday. If this offer is ok with you, I'll speak to you and Joe after we eat. If you don't think my proposition is for you, tell me now and the matter is closed. The talk we just had never happened because you were never here. If for any reason you need to come up with an excuse to be here, just say that I called you to go over some details of the scholarship loan. Capishe?"

"Capisco," I said. "And I will be proud to work for you and happy to be working with Joe. And doubly happy to get my license and a car. This is another one of my lucky days. I don't know what to say except Milli Gratzi."

"I think you made the right decision," said Uncle Vito. "I'll see you on Sunday."

I was sure that this was the signal that our meeting was over. So I got up from the chair, shook Uncle Vito's hand, thanked him again, said good night and left the room. Carmine was waiting in the foyer. We left the building and Carmine drove me home. He didn't ask any questions.

Sunday came around real fast and again I enjoyed eating at Joe's house. As we finished dinner, I was surprised when one of Joe's teenaged cousins Alicia from Staten Islands asked Joe, "When is the graduation and when is the senior prom?"

Joe answered, "The prom is a week from this coming Wednesday and we graduate in two weeks."

She then turned to me and coyly asked, "And what lucky girl gets to go to the prom with you, Marco?"

"I'm not going to the prom," I answered.

"How come?"

"I don't know, just have no interest in going."

"I know why," she said with a smile. "Is it because you don't know how to dance?"

"That's right," I answered, putting a close to this repartee.

Joe then started in, turning to me, "You know, it's funny, we never talked about going to the prom. And I'm glad you made no plans to go. Neither did I. After Roseland, the prom is like going to an amateur hour thing."

Turning to Uncle Vito, I said, "We got only four tickets each to the graduation. Joe was going to use his for his mother, father and two sisters. My mother and father are the only ones going, so I have two extra tickets, and I'd like to offer them to you and your wife. Joe and I would really love for both of you to be there and see us graduate."

"That's very nice for you to ask us, and we will be proud to be there," said Uncle Vito. "And by the way, I'm throwing a little graduation party for you both next Sunday. So instead of coming here, you are all invited to my house. Make it around three. I would like your mother and father to come also. Carlo can pick you and your parents up. I'm sure he'll be using one of his limos. Am I right, Carlo?"

"You are right, Vito," said Carlo.

By this time desert and coffee were finished and Uncle Vito got up and as usual went into the living room followed by the men. Joe and I were not invited, and Paulie closed the doors and stood on the outside like he was on guard.

Again, Joe and I had to join in cleaning up. When we were about half way through, the living room doors opened, the men exited and Paulie motioned for us to join Uncle Vito. Once we were in, the doors were closed and we were asked to sit down facing him.

"Want to tell you again how proud we are of you both," said Uncle Vito. "Now to business. I know that you both are free once school is over. I have jobs for you two. You'll need a car to get around, so I'll send you both to driving school. Then you'll both take the test and get your licenses. Once you get them, we'll pick out a car for you to use. You'll each get $25 a week to start. Any questions? Good. Marco, thanks again for the invite. Give the tickets to Joe, he'll get them to me. Joe, ask Paulie to come in as you go out."

As we left, Joe motioned for Paulie to go meet with Uncle Vito.

We all waited for Uncle Vito and his family to leave, as was the custom. And after saying goodbye, I left and went home.

When I got home, Sol had left and the store was already

set up for the next day. Over a cup of coffee, I told Mama and Papa about Uncle Vito's job offer to Joe and me, our acceptance, and our getting the driver's license and a car.

"What are you going to do with the car?" Mama asked.

"I guess drive around."

"Drive around and do what exactly?"

"I don't know," I said. "I'm sure we'll find out later. By the way, I hope you don't mind, but since I have two extra tickets to the graduation, I asked Uncle Vito and his wife to come and see Joe and me graduate, and he said yes. He's also having a little party in our honor on the Sunday following the graduation at his house in Seagate. Uncle Vito wants you to come also. Joe's father Carlo will pick us up in his limo. Uncle Vito wants us there at three."

Papa replied, "I don't know if we can do that. We can't close the store, even if it's for an occasion like this."

"Sol can easily run things," I said, "and if you put up another sign asking the customers to cooperate because it is a graduation party for me, they will be patient and nice."

"Ok, I'll talk to Sol tomorrow and if he says he can do it, we'll go to the party." Papa paused and then continued, "Now tell me about the plans for the graduation."

"Well, I have to be at the school by six. It's two hours before the ceremony starts. All the graduates were told "Don't be late" and we need to report to the gym. Papa, you and Mama can get to the school about seven thirty or so. The actual graduation is at eight and it's being held in the auditorium."

"Ok, we'll close the store at seven," said Papa. "I'll put up the sign Wednesday night and I'm sure the customers won't mind since it's a very special occasion."

"Good idea," I said.

Time has a habit of running by quickly and it was hard to believe that gradation day was actually here. And then time slowed down and it felt like minutes turned to hours as I waited for five o'clock to come around. I had an hour to get ready so as soon as Carmine and Louie left, I shaved, showered, combed my hair and got dressed. Since we were going to graduate in caps in gowns, I didn't think I would need to put a tie on, but I put one on anyway. I didn't think I would need a jacket, but I put one on anyway. A little dab of Papa's after-shave lotion completed the dressing. By this time it was a quarter to six and I had to get going.

Mama, Papa, and Sol told me how nice I looked as I left for the school. Once I got there, I reported to the gym where we were issued our caps and gowns. But we were told not to put them on until announced.

Mr. Kelly, one of the gym teachers, called out our names in alphabetical order and told us to line up that way just before marching into the auditorium. We were also assigned seats so that one row followed the other in the same alphabetical order. Before we knew it, Mr. Kelly told us to put on our gowns and caps. Once this was done, we were told to line up in the order he had gone over before. We were also told that after the graduation we were to report back to the gym and turn in our caps and gowns. Failure to do this would result in a $10 fine.

"OK, ARE WE READY TO GRADUATE?" Mr. Kelly yelled.

And we responded with a wild "YES!"

"So let's do it. Try to keep in step with the music and the person in front of you."

We then marched to the doors of the auditorium which were then opened and we marched in time to the music the school orchestra was playing. We took our seats in the assigned rows and waited for the graduation to finally begin. And then it did.

The principle, Dr. Carroll, asked all to rise and join him in reciting the Pledge of Allegiance. Then Miss Nelson from the music department led the singing of the Star Spangled Banner.

I will always remember the actual graduation exercise. Diane Patashnik was called up. She was the class valedictorian. She was chosen because she had a straight "A" average and got a full scholarship to Hunter College. She delivered a great speech thanking the teachers for their dedication, and she then said, "Speaking for the entire graduating class, we will go on and achieve our goals and make all of you and especially the school proud of us." She then took a seat on the stage.

Dr. Carroll then introduced the guest speaker, Stanley Isaacs, the Borough President of Manhattan, who gave a real down to earth message about the opportunities available in public service. The speech was short and to the point. After receiving a big round of applause, he returned to his seat on the stage.

Dr. Carroll then started to call out the names of the graduates. He was assisted by Mr. Kramer, who handed out the certificates while Dr. Carroll shook hands with the graduates.

It didn't take very long before my row was called and a minute or two later I was up on the stage to receive my diploma. As Mr. Kramer handed it to me, Dr. Carroll announced, "Marco Falcone, in addition to graduating, I'm proud to tell you that you have been accepted into the National Honor Society."

While saying thank you, I looked at the audience and saw Mama and Papa smiling and applauding. I was so proud. I looked to their left and saw two empty seats. My knees nearly buckled. These seats were for Uncle Vito and his wife. What could have happened? I had a funny feeling in my stomach as I exited the stage and took my seat. I tried looking for Joe but couldn't catch his eye, and I couldn't talk to him because he was not close by.

The graduation finally ended and we marched back to the gym to turn in our caps and gowns. I couldn't wait to grab Joe.

"What happened?" I asked him. "Uncle Vito didn't show. Is he ok? How about his wife?"

Joe answered, "Nothing to worry about, just a little problem that needed to be straightened out. Let's not talk about it now. I got to go home with my family. What are you going to do?"

"I guess I'll go home also."

"Talk to you tomorrow."

"That's a go," I said.

I met Mama and Papa in the school entrance and they gave me hugs and kisses.

"How come the Amattos didn't show?" Papa asked.

"I really don't know," I said, "but Joe told me that there was a little problem that needed his attention."

"Where would you like to go to celebrate?" Papa then asked. "How about Chinese food or some other place you would like? After all, this is a very special night."

"To tell you the truth, I rather go home and have some of the brisket Sol made," I said.

"Anything you want."

When we got to the store I noticed a car parked in front and a truck in the back of it. As Papa took out his keys to open the store, Carmine and Louie came out of the car, both said hello to us all, and then Louie added, "Open the door Ivan. We have to talk to you. Nothing to be worried about."

I could not help seeing the scared look on Mama's face, but I said nothing.

Once inside, Carmine said, "Let's go back to the apartment. Maybe, Mrs. Sarah, you'll put up some tea." Mama just nodded her head.

Once we were seated and the tea came out, Carmine started to tell us: "Since LaGuardia became mayor, he's had a "madon" to change things in New York. So what did he do? First he closed down the burlesque theatres which threw people out of work. Then he started out trying to break businesses that have been here for years and years, including bookmaking. He appointed Dewey as district attorney and ordered him to close down bookmakers, numbers operators, and other forms of entertainment. Dewey had nothing else to do and beside that LaGuardia needed headlines to keep him in office. Dewey started to shut down some places that were ratted on by paid squealers looking to make deals with the D.A.'s office. Twenty-two of our sports rooms were shut down this week. So what Louie and I are going to do is move everything of ours out tonight so that the place will be clean."

Louie said, "If you get some visitors from the D.A. office and they ask about us, just say we were good customers, nothing else. If you have any more problems with them, call this number." He handed Papa a card. "Ask for Don Sanders. He's one of our attorneys and he'll tell you what to do. There is no charge ever for you. By the way, you'll continue to get the rental fee every week. Any questions? Good."

Carmine said, "Don't worry, this will blow over soon, so just go about your business as if nothing happened. Ok? Now why don't you all go out and get some coffee and come back in about an hour. We should be finished by then."

"Good," Papa said. And we left. We walked down to the coffee shop on the corner, sat down, and Papa ordered coffee for all of us. Mama was about to say something when Papa turned to her and whispered, "If it's about what happened, we don't discuss it here. Let's talk about the graduation."

I told him how I felt from the moment I arrived at the school until I got the diploma and Honor Society Certificate. I deliberately left out the feelings I had when I saw the two empty seats. Mama and Papa each kept telling me how proud they were of me and how they were so sure that I would be outstanding in college and medical school.

We finished one cup of coffee and ordered another, and the conversation about me went on. Before I knew it, the hour was up and it was time to go back to the store. When we got back, the truck was gone and Carmine and Louie were waiting for us.

Louie said, "We rushed but we were able to get things done in an hour. Let's go back to the apartment and you tell me and Carmine if everything looks ok."

When we walked through the door into the apartment Mama said, "I can't believe it. It looks just like it was before you rented."

"You are right, Sarah," said Papa. "They took all their stuff out including the telephone connections and brought back the same type of furniture we had."

Mama then commented, "Yeah, only the style and colors of the furniture you brought really doesn't match with our furniture."

Carmine laughed and turning to Louie said, "Louie, Mrs. Sarah thinks we are interior decorators." He added, "This was a special order. We did the best we could. I feel sure you could doll it up. Everything is going to be ok, and by the way, don't believe everything you read in the papers or hear over the radio. As I said before, it's a chance that you'll might get a visit from the D.A.'s office. Don't volunteer any information, and if you feel you are being pushed in any way, tell them you want an attorney and call the number on the card I gave you."

"Ok," Papa said. "I'm sure everything will turn out all right."

Louie and Carmine then left after telling us good night.

I looked around and thought to myself that it was nice having things they way they were before Carmine and Louie came on the scene.

I remember Papa locking the store and coming back to the apartment and joining Mama and me at the table.

Papa then turned to Mama and facing her said, "I see you are bursting to say something, so get it off your chest now."

Mama, looking at both of us, answered, "We got into this with our eyes open. We took their money which we knew wasn't kosher but we needed it. I always had the feeling that some day this rental thing would come back and bite us in the tuckus. Remember one thing, they will look to protect their own and we are not their own. So if push comes to shove, we'll be thrown to the wolves. This is what I'm worried about and this is all I have to say."

Papa then came back with, "I can understand how you feel and you might be right but what other choice did we have then and now? The best thing is to do what they tell us to do. I am sure they will protect us, especially because of their good feelings towards Marco." Papa turned to me and asked, "What do you have to say about this"?

I replied, "I trust Uncle Vito and know that he will do the right thing for us. So let's go on as before and if anything does happen, Vito Amatto will take care of it for us. Now, let's go to sleep. We have a store to open tomorrow."

Papa left saying, "Mama, he has been a high school graduate for four hours and right away he thinks he's a boss and can give orders. He's right about calling it a night, so let's get some sleep."

## XX

    I climbed into bed, but could not fall asleep right away. I went over the graduation and the events that followed. I hoped that my faith in Uncle Vito was right. I could not help thinking what could happen if I was wrong. Finally I fell asleep and slept late, since I remembered that Sol was coming in to help Papa and Mama. In the morning I showered, got dressed, took some breakfast, and went into the store.

    There were a lot of customers waiting when Papa, having a moment, said, "Grab the News and the Mirror."

    I did, and there it was in the headlines on the front page: "D.A.'s Office Raids Gambling Ring Locations. 22 Arrested In Sweep." The news story went on to describe the action. There were also some photos of the ones that were arrested, and I recognized most of them as members of Uncle Vito's family. It was about then when the phone rang. Sol grabbed it and called out to me, "Marco, you got a call."

    When I picked up the phone, I heard Joe's voice. "How're doing?"

    "Ok I guess."

    "I think we got to meet," said Joe.

    "Where and when?" I asked.

    "Twelve o'clock, where we kept our rafts."

    "That's an OK," I said.

    "See you."

    "See you."

    It was a few minutes to twelve when I saw Joe at the pier. He was throwing small rocks into the river. He still had a strong arm, better than mine.

"Hi ya," he said. "We need to talk. I guess you heard all about it."

"Yeah, and I read the papers also."

"These things happen every so often," he said. "It don't mean a thing. The guys that got pinched are already out on bail. They'll pay a fine and go back to doing what they do. It's just some politicians making noise to get re-elected, or they have a beef about not getting enough payola. By the way, Uncle Vito told me to tell you he couldn't go to the graduation because he was tied up straightening out the situation. He said he would also tell you this in person when he sees you. Capishe?"

"Capisco."

"Now down to business. We start our driving lessons on Monday at eleven o'clock at the EZ Learn Driving School. It's on 10th Ave and 12th Street. We can go by subway to 14th and walk over or take the bus. What do you think?"

"Let's go by subway," I said.

"Ok, I'll meet you at ten-fifteen. Any problem?"

"No, not really," I said. "I have to do a selling job with my folks about the driving school and the job."

Joe then replied with the strongest tone I ever heard from him, "Marco, you gave your word, so you have to do this. You got your scholarship and a good job. Don't be stupid. It will be a very big mistake to let this pass by."

"I guess you're right, I'm not a kid anymore, and it's about time I stood on my own two feet. Besides that, I am a man, I got laid, and what a good hump it was."

"Louie told me this was the first time he heard that hookers gave freebees," said Joe. We both laughed and hugged each other. "One more thing, if you would have backed out, you would have given the ammunition Paulie was looking for. He collared me the other day at our hangout, and said he was pretty sure that you and your folks were the ones who ratted the family out and caused the problem. I told him, 'You must be crazy, where's your proof?' and he said, 'The proof is that someone did it and they're Jews.' So I said, 'They're also

Italian.' And he said, 'That makes no difference, a Jew is a Jew no matter where he comes from.' I told him 'You're 100% wrong, Paulie. The Falcones are stand-up and honorable and I vouch for them. I think you better keep this to yourself because Uncle Vito might not like what you say about Marco and his folks. Uncle Vito's brothers and Marco's family have been doing business together in Italy for a lot of years and from what I was told the two families are very friendly. Closer to home you know that Mr. Lucky and Mr. Meyer are very, very close. So for your sake, clam up unless you got the goods on the Falcones. I don't want to hear any more bullshit about them. Remember Jimmy the Geek? He spread some rumors about one of the family that wasn't true. That was about five years ago. Jimmy walked out of his house one morning and hasn't been heard of since. Be smart and shut up.'

Joe continued telling me, "Paulie then spit on the floor and started to walk away saying, 'Ok, ok, maybe you're right, but I still don't trust them.'"

"Thanks Joe," I said.

"Look Marco, what started with Paulie not liking you is turning to hate. He's making it personal, so be on your guard around him and be careful what you say. He will twist it around so that you look bad and he looks good. He's a snake. Got it?"

"Got it."

"I guess you figured it out that there's no party at Uncle Vito's on Sunday, and there is no big dinner at my house. Just my mother and father, my two sisters, and me."

"I kind of guessed that."

"What about Roseland on Saturday?" Joe asked. "Think we should give it a go?"

"Sounds good," I said. "Meet you regular time."

"Yep, talk to you tomorrow. One more thing, until this blows over, be careful what you say over the phone."

"No problem." I said

"Ciao"

"Ciao"

I didn't want to go back to the store because Papa would put me to work, so I went over to the library and looked through the papers I didn't read in the morning. The New York Times had just a little article on the fourth page about the arrests. The Herald Tribune and the Village Voice had stories on page two. I was glad Uncle Vito's name was not mentioned anywhere.

Once I read through all the papers, I still didn't want to go home, and since it was a nice day, I got on the bus and took a ride uptown and got off near Central Park and went to the zoo. I always wanted to go there, but never got around to it. It was really fun going through the different animal houses and seeing the animals. Before I knew it, it was time to leave. I made a promise to myself to come back and spend a lot more time there.

On the bus ride back, I kept thinking about how the animals must feel about being captured and caged up. Little did I know I would find out myself.

I got home ok, saw there were a lot of customers, so on went the apron and behind the counter I went. I worked until closing, then helped clean up while Papa and Sol prepared for tomorrow. Once this was done, Sol left saying he had something to do. Mama, Papa, and I went back to the apartment and sat down to eat, but for some reason we were not very hungry. So we noched on some leftovers from the store. As we finished our coffee, Mama asked me, "What are your plans for the weekend?"

"Well," I said, "I made plans to meet Joe and go to Roseland. We don't have many free weeks left. On Sunday I think you both should take the day off and have some fun. Sol and I can handle things. Also because of what happened, the party at Uncle Vito's is off. Joe and his family are going to eat by themselves. You haven't had any time off for yourselves for a long time, so go out and enjoy. You deserve it.

"I think there is something else I have to tell you. In spite of what's happened, I'm going to take the job Uncle Vito offered. Joe and I start taking driving lessons this Monday. I don't know all the details about the lesson times and days. I'll find out on Monday."

Mama, I remember, screwed up her face and came back with, "Are you sure you want to do this? Are you misugar? Don't we have enough to worry about now? What'll you be doing after you get your license? I'm sure it won't be on the up and up. Papa and I are worried sick now about what could happen because of the Carmine and Louie thing. Now you are giving us more to worry about. I want you to tell whoever that you changed your mind. Do you hear?"

Papa then said, "Listen to your mother. She's right. We don't need more aggravation, worrying about you and what might happen."

Facing both of them, I remember saying, "I have to follow through. I told them I'd do it. I can't back out now. With these people a word is a contract and must be kept. If I change my mind, I'm sure I'll lose the scholarship and maybe more. Look, I'll be working with Joe and Uncle Vito wouldn't let him do anything that might get him or me in trouble. It'll be ok. I promise you that. Wait and see."

Mama looking me straight in the eye said, "I don't care what you say, I don't want you to take that job. Do you understand?"

I said, "Mama, I love you and Papa very much, and I tried to be a good son. You both have been the parents anyone would wish for, but please understand that I can't go back on my word. And I ask you to please, please go along with me on this. It will work out ok." Turning to Papa, I said, "Where're you taking Mama on Sunday?"

Papa looked back at me and said, "Maybe you should go into politics instead of medicine. You changed the subject pretty good."

"Thanks for the complement, Papa," I said. "I want you and Mama to know I'm doing the right thing. Now tell me what you think you'll do on Sunday?"

Papa replied, "Mama and I will make plans. I'm sure we'll have a good time. I'll let you know when we know."

"Ok, that's fine."

Papa, rising from his chair and opening his collar, said, "Let's get some sleep. Come Sarah." Then he turned to me and said, "Say good night to your mother."

And I did, not only to her but also to Papa.

The next morning, Papa woke me up and I got ready to work when the store opened. Around eleven-thirty I took off my apron, made myself a sandwich, grabbed a soda, and ate. I then got ready to meet Joe at twelve-thirty. We took the subway and walked over to Roseland as the doors were opening. The dance session was nice and we danced with a lot of girls, some of whom were great dancers. Didn't meet anyone that I wanted to see outside of Roseland. We left as the band played the last number and we took the subway to our stop. I remember telling Joe, "We'll talk tomorrow."

"That's a yes," he said. "But be careful what you say over the phone."

"Alright, alright, I understand," I said. "You told me this about ten times."

"I want to impress on you the rules of the game."

"Ok, I'll watch what I say, and you do the same."

Joe came back, "If we don't touch base for some reason, I'll meet you Monday at ten-fifteen as we planned. Bring your birth certificate."

"You got it."

"So long."

"See ya."

I went home and helped with the prep work and cleanup. Had a nice dinner Mama prepared, made some small talk, said goodnight, and went to bed. I got up early and went to work behind the counter. After the morning rush was over, I insisted that Mama and Papa get ready for the rest of their day off and they left about an hour later.

I didn't hear from them even after the store closed. Sol and I went back to the Greek restaurant where we had another fine dinner. I walked Sol home and went on to the store. When

I got there, some lights were on other than the night lights, telling me that either we were getting robbed, investigated, or Mama and Papa had come home.

I unlocked the door and cautiously looked in. Everything seemed ok. I shouted out, "Papa, are you home?"

I heard Papa's voice loudly coming back with, "Where do you think we are, Philadelphia?"

I locked the door and went into the apartment. Mama had made some coffee and I was just in time to get some.

"What did you do today?" I asked them.

"You're not the only one who goes to the zoo," said Papa. "We had a good time seeing all the animals, especially the monkeys."

"And then?"

"Once we left the zoo," said Papa, "we went to Tavern on the Green and had dinner and half a bottle of wine. It wasn't Italian, but it was good. I think it came from California. And then we went to the Metropolitan Opera House and we were lucky enough to buy two tickets for the opera Carmen. The seats were way up in the balcony, but we could hear and see real good. And then we came home."

Mama chimed in, "It was a wonderful day. And how was your day?"

"Worked and went out to the Greek restaurant with Sol," I replied. "I also made the bank deposit."

"That's good, that's good," said Papa. "What time is your driving lesson tomorrow? If I'm allowed to inquire."

"That's not fair, Papa, but it's at eleven o'clock. In any case, I'll keep in touch."

"Monday is Monday," Mama said, "And it's back to work, so lets go to bed."

Once in bed, I kept thinking how great it's going to be driving a car. Could hardly wait.

Once I fell asleep I kept dreaming of myself driving a race car at the Indy 500, taking the turns sometimes on two wheels, then bouncing not only the sides of the track but also other race cars and coming across the finish line first. I must have smiled in my sleep when I was awarded the trophy.

I guess this dream must have tired me out, because Papa had to wake me. "What time is it?" I asked.

"Twenty after nine," he said.

"I better get up and step on it." And I did, and I met Joe on time.

It didn't take us more than twenty minutes to get to the driving school. Our two instructors were waiting for us. And they wasted no time telling us that if we paid attention we would pass the test and get our licenses. We spent the next three weeks taking lessons. We also got instruction books because we had to take the written test in addition to the driving test. The written instruction was easy. Even Joe didn't have a problem learning it. We took and passed the written tests. The school even got us our learner's permits. The three weeks flew by and our instructors said we were ready to take the real driving test. I was sort of unsure because I had a problem parallel parking. Joe had no difficulty doing this. It came naturally, just like the Lindy did. We both thanked the instructors, who wished us luck and assured us that we would pass the tests. They even made appointments for us to take them.

I didn't hear from Joe until the next day when he phoned me saying, "Be outside at twelve o'clock tomorrow. Have your learner's permit with you. I made arrangements for us to practice in the car we'll take the test in."

"That's great. I'll be waiting."

On the day of the test, it was about twelve o'clock when a car pulled up. Joe was sitting in the passengers seat. I got in and Joe introduced me to the driver saying, "Say hello to Phil." I said hi, and he just turned and said hello.

Phil drove over to 24th Street and 10th Ave and parked the car. He turned over to Joe and said, "Ok, you first." Phil got out of the driver side and switched seats with Joe. Looking at Joe, Phil said, "I want you to get familiar with driving this car. Every car handles a little different."

Joe and I took turns driving up and down avenues and streets.

Since it was Saturday, there wasn't too much traffic, except for the taxi drivers who nearly scared the hell out of us. We parallel parked over and over until we felt comfortable doing this. It was around two when Phil said, "Time's up, we gotta go." He dropped me off at the store and he and Joe drove away.

The rest of the weekend was quiet with nothing much doing. Again, there was no mention of dinner at Joe's house. It was Monday around one-thirty in the afternoon. when Joe and Phil picked me up and we drove up to the place where the test was given. We took the driving test and we both passed. We were going to get our driver's license. In a few days I got mine in the mail, called Joe, and he told me he got his also.

He also told me to meet him on the corner of Allen and Eldridge Streets the next day at three-thirty. I told him I'll be there.

I met Joe and we both walked down Eldridge Street to a store front. Above the door was a sign reading "Eagle and Tarpon Social Club." I saw that the windows had pull-down shades that were three quarters down. I noticed that on the sidewalk outside the store three or four guys were just hanging out talking, laughing, and smoking. I recognized one of the guys from the dinners at Joe's house. As Joe and I went into the club, I turned to face him and said, "Hi." He just picked up his hand, recognizing my hello.

I think the club might have been a restaurant at one time. It was big, holding a pool table and three or four big card tables. Off to one side was a pretty large bar and in the back I could see the kitchen. There was a closed door on the other side of the kitchen. And Joe and I headed toward that door. As we walked through the club, some of the guys playing cards and even some at the bar said 'Comme Sta' to Joe, who answered 'Bene Grazie.' When we got to the door, Joe knocked and we heard, "Come on in." We walked in and I saw behind the desk a guy that I wouldn't want to meet in a dark alley if he had a beef with me. He was big, slightly balding, muscular and had piercing eyes that could scare the shit out of anyone. "Sit down," he said

Then I noticed a scar running down his whole right cheek. I remember how the conversation went as if it was yesterday.

"I hear you two got your driver's licenses and are ready to go to work," he said. "But first, I gotta talk to you." He pointed to me. "Whatcha name again?"

"Marco," I said.

"Ok, I'm Tony A., and you'll be a member of my crew to start." Looking at Joe, Tony continued, "You can go out while I give Marco the scoop or you can stay."

"I'll stay if it's ok with you."

"I already said it's ok," said Tony. "Listen with both ears and let my words sink in. It might make the difference between whether you live or get whacked. Capishe?"

"Si," I answered.

"Do you know what "Omerta" means?"

I shook my head no.

"Then you're not Siciliano."

"No, my folks are from Venice," I said.

"It figures. Omerta was brought over from Sicily. It means the code of silence and must be obeyed. I'm going to give you just a few of the rules.

- You never cooperate with the law.
- If you get busted, never answer any questions.
- If someone commits a crime and you get blamed for it, don't answer any questions or point any fingers.
- If you see a crime committed, keep walking, don't get involved.
- If someone wants to kill you and you find out about it, keep the law out of it.
- If you want justice, take care of it yourself. Never get mad, get even.

Tony continued by asking, "You got it down good? Make sure you understand every word I told you."

"I understand," I said.

"I just told you about Omerta. Now I tell you about our rules. Never ask anyone in our crew or anyone we do business with their last name or what they do. If you violate this you're liable to get a smack in the mouth or a kick in the balls. When you're doing our business don't come on like a wise guy. Act like a friend. You got to balance this by the situation. People gotta know you're not a pussy, that you got the strength and can stand up with the best of them. Most important, your word is your bond. Never forget that. Got it?"

"Got it."

"Now go see Sallie. He's waiting for you." Turning to Joe, Tony A asked, "You know him, don't you, Joe?"

"Yeah, I know him," Joe replied.

Tony nodded. "Sallie is your captain and he'll give you the low down."

Joe and I said good bye and started to leave when Tony A said, "Remember, do the right ting, and everybody makes money."

We left Tony A in the office and I followed Joe over to the bar where a guy was sitting drinking some espresso. Joe said, "Hi Sallie, long time no see."

Sallie replied, "Yeah, long time." He then got off the bar stool and walked over to one of the empty card tables. He sat down and told us to sit down. Sallie was about five-foot-six, nearly bald, and must have weighed around two hundred and fifty pounds. He was a real Rolly Pollie. "Ok, here's the deal," he said. "You pick up slips every day after two p.m. and deliver them to where we tell you. You know the heat is on and you two are new faces on the scene and that's good. Here's what I want you to do. When you come to a stop, one of you goes in, the other stays in the car. You can take turns driving. Work that out by yourself. If you think there's a tail on you, skip the spots and call into the number on your route sheet. You'll be told what to do. If you take a pinch, call the number on the card you'll get from Phil. You're not gonna have any trouble. This is just an 'in case.'"

Reaching into his pocket, Sallie pulled out some business cards and gave one to each of us. "Now I'm going to tell you how you two are gonna work. Every day at two o'clock you're gonna pick up the routes for that day and you go to the spots on the rout sheet, when you finish the last stop you'll drop all the slips off where it says on the route sheet. The route sheet will also tell you where you pick up the info for the next day. Capishe? If you think there is a tail on you, tear up the route sheet and the slips. First see if you can lose the tail. If you can't, the driver slows down and lets his partner out and drives off toward the Holland Tunnel or the Lincoln Tunnel. Cops are lazy and don't like to tail if they have to go through tunnels. Once you shake the tail, come back over one of the bridges and hook up with your partner across from the pick-up place. Meantime, the other guy once, he makes sure that the tail isn't on him also, goes to the phone and calls the number on the card I'm gonna give you. They'll tell you what to do. This is just a 'in case.' Also it ain't gonna happen, but I'm gonna tell you again, if you get pinched, tell the cops you want to use the phone. They gotta let you make one phone call. Call the lawyer, he'll take care of everything. Remember, keep your mouth shut. Don't fall for the cops' bullshit. They come in and tell you that your partner ratted you out in order for you to talk. This is one of their friggin moves and they're good at it. Don't get sucked in. Just remember the Omerta, and you'll be ok. See Phil and he'll take it from there. Stay in touch. Ciao."

    We walked out of the club and Phil was waiting for us. "Let's take a walk," he said after greeting us hello.

    We followed him up Eldridge and turned onto East Broadway. "See something familiar?" he said.

    We looked around and Joe spotted and yelled out to me, "Look over there, it looks like the car we took the test in."

    "You're right," I answered.

    We both turned and looked at Phil who had a big smile on his face and said, "This is your Fourth of July present from our crew to you guys." With that he took out two sets of keys and gave one set to each of us. Phil continued, "The registration is in the glove compartment along with the insurance card. The car is registered to the Monty Oil Corp. and you two are listed as company drivers so you are covered.

Since Thursday is the Fourth of July, we are giving you guys till Monday to get used to the car and to have a little fun too. Pick me up Monday at two o'clock in front of the barber shop on Delancy Street. I'll be waiting. I'll go around with you until I'm sure you know the ropes. So you got a nice few days off before you go to work." He then jokingly added, "Ok, Hot Shots, here's your car, so what are you waiting for. Get outta here. See you Monday. Try not to smash up the car over the weekend." Phil then left with a wave.

Since both Joe and I wanted to drive, we tossed a coin, and I won. The first half hour was mine and the second was Joe's turn. The hour ran by quickly and it was fun, but before we knew it we were in the middle of rush hour traffic and I was glad Joe was at the wheel. That we didn't get into an accident was a miracle. Between the taxi's, the big busses, and the nuts crossing the streets trying to beat the lights, it all scared the hell out of us. We must have been lucky and made it back to Joe's house where we parked in the garage that we used to study in. Joe locked the garage door and turned to me saying, "Well, that was fun, wasn't it?"

"Some fun," I said. "We nearly got killed or worse, damaged the car."

Since it was the Fourth of July, I remember asking Joe, "Want to see the fireworks tonight?"

"Yeah, let's meet around eight. We'll go over to the river and watch."

"Sounds good," I said.
"Ok, Ciao."
"Ciao."

We met, saw the fireworks, went over to Tony's for gelato, spoke to a few girls and Joe and I split and went home.

We had decided to go to Brighton Beach again and see if we could get a replay of the fun we had the last time we were there. But this time we drove. Joe called his cousin Sonny who owned a pizza joint and he arranged a parking spot for us. So we left Friday morning around ten-thirty and drove out, taking

with us some good sandwiches and drinks. When we got there, Sonny showed us where to park and we changed into our bathing suits in the car. We spent the afternoon soaking up the sun, looking to hook up with girls, and swimming. The ocean air must have made us very hungry and thirsty because the sandwiches and drinks went very fast.
Our search for girls wasn't too successful. We found out that the day after July Fourth was a family day and girls that normally made themselves available had to hang around with their entire family. We even walked from Brighton Beach to Coney Island's Luna Park on the girl prowl, but even over there it seemed it was also family day.

  It was getting sort of dark by now and we should have been heading home. Joe asked me if I wanted to drive but I said no. Joe then told me it would be a great idea for us to stay for the night because the chances of meeting girls would be much better the next day, since family day would be over and girls would come by themselves or with their friends.

  Then it came to me. Joe didn't want to drive because neither one of us had ever driven in traffic at night. So I agreed with him to stay and we could sleep in the car.

  We had a great day on Saturday. We met a lot of girls and when they found out we had a car, they became more friendly. In fact, Joe took one of them back to show her the car and came back with her about an hour later smiling from head to toe. Before I could ask, Joe whispered, "I'll tell you later."

  We had invites to a lot of parties and we had a lot of phone numbers, and most of these girls were dolls. Our social and sexual calendars looked good. Maybe we wouldn't go back to visit Brigette and Tami after all. Although, a freebee with a pro is something not to turn down. We left for home before it got dark and I spent Sunday trying to ease the discomfort I got from the sunburn over the weekend.

  On Monday, we picked up Phil and he directed me to drive to a drug store on Delancy Street. Once we parked, Phil said, "Both of you come with me. In the future, just one of you go in. I want to introduce you to the owner."

We did what Phil told us. We entered the store and met the owner. "This is Joe and this is Marco," said Phil. "They're with us and we'll be seeing you."

"I'm Ben," said the owner. "Good to see you. I have something to give you." He took out an envelope and gave it to me.

"Give me the envelope," said Phil, and he put it in his jacket pocket. Since there was no one else in the store, Phil continued to us, "If you are here and there are customers, Ben will slip you the envelope but buy something to keep everything looking kosher. Understand?"

Joe and I nodded yes and we followed Phil out the store after saying goodbye to Ben. Once we were in the car, Phil, while handing Joe the envelope, continued, "When you pick up the envelope, always wear a jacket and keep the envelope in the jacket. Also keep two or three paper bags in the car. The slips you'll be picking up will be in white envelopes with rubber bands around them. Once you pick them up, put them in the paper bags. It's easier to get rid of a paper bag than a bunch of loose envelopes. Got it?"

"Got it," we answered.

"Ok, let's get going," said Phil, and I started the car. "Look for a parking spot by a bank, a park, a school, an office building or a place where you won't stand out. Here's a post office. Pull up into their lot."

Once parked, Phil pulled out the envelope, handed it to me, and said, "Open it and tell me what you see. Joe, you lean over and see what Marco has."

I opened the envelope, took the sheet out, and leaned over to Joe so that he could see what I had. I then told Phil there are fourteen places listed on the sheet with initials next to each name and address.

"These are the places that you'll make the pick-ups today. The initials are the guys who will give you the slips. You'll go in, knock on the door, and when asked who's there you'll give the initials. The guy at the door will give you the envelopes and you split and move on to the next pick-up. You drop off the slips at the last stop." Phil paused. "What else is there?"

"On the bottom is another name and address also with initials," I said.

"This is where you will pick up the route sheet for the next day," said Phil. "This is very easy. I got some dummies in my crew and they learned this right away, so it should be a breeze for you two high school graduates. No mistakes are allowed. Making one could cause a big problem. Understand?"

"We understand," Joe answered.

Phil looked directly at me and said, "I didn't hear anything coming out of your mouth."

"I understand, I understand," I said.

"Let's get started," said Phil. "As I told you before, I'll go with you until I feel you know what the hell you both are doing."

We left the car and went into the barber shop, which was the first one on the list. Phil said hello to the barber who was giving some guy a haircut. The barber nodded hello back as we walked through a curtain at the back of the store to a door. Phil knocked on it and a voice answered, "Who's there?"

Phil said, "N.L."

The door opened a bit and a hand came out with some envelopes in it with rubber bands around them. Phil grabbed the envelopes and stuffed them in his jacket as the door closed. "Let's go," he said. "The party's over."

As we walked out, Phil nodded to the barber who was still cutting the same guy's hair. Back in the car, Phil put the slips into the paper bag and we drove off to the next stop. And this is what we did stop after stop after stop. When we reached the last stop, we took the paper bags holding the envelopes and dropped them off.

We then drove back to Allen Street and dropped Phil off. As he got out of the car, he said, "Pick me up tomorrow, across the street from the barber shop. Don't be late."

Joe and I drove the car back to the garage.

We met Phil the next day and we went through the same routine. Picked up the route sheet, made the run, and dropped off the paper bags. We also looked for and found the address for the next day's pick-up place at the bottom of the route slip. We continued to do this all week including Saturday and Sunday. When we finished on Sunday, before we dropped Phil off, he handed each of us an envelope, saying, "Here is your money for the week. You get paid every Sunday. You guys did OK, but I'll stay with you on the route for at least another week just to make sure the guys know you." Phil got out of the car. "See you tomorrow across the street from the route pick up stop." And he left.

Joe drove and dropped me off at the store. I invited him in to say hello to my folks and he said ok while parking the car. When he came in, my Mama came from behind the counter and gave Joe a big hello followed by a hug.

"My my," she said. "How you have grown since the last time I saw you. How are your parents? Be sure to send them our regards."

Papa, who had just finished waiting on a customer, also came from around the counter and shook hands with Joe. "It's been too long since we saw you last," he said. "Do you want to stay for dinner? We close in about an hour."

"Sorry, I'm expected home," said Joe. "But I'll be glad to come again."

"Make sure you give our regards to all your family," I said.

The next couple of weeks was a repeat of the first week with Phil. We picked up the route sheets, made the pickups, and did the drops. It seemed like we picked up at all different kinds of places. Barber shops, auto part stores, dry cleaners, shoe makers, candy stores, hardware, cigar stores, haberdashers, delis, gas stations, and newsstands were just a few of the types of pick-ups, drop-offs, and the next day's schedule. Phil told us that we do different types of locations because it made it safer for us to operate.

It was the end of the third week, and while Phil was paying us, he said, "You two are on your own from now on. I don't have to babysit you guys any more. If you have any trouble, you know what to do. And I don't want you to hang around the club. Your faces are fresh, and we don't want them to get mixed in with the rest of our crew. Sooner or later you'll be recognized as belonging. Capishe?"

Joe replied, "Capisco." And I nodded ok.

Phil left and then we drove off. As Joe was dropping me off, I remarked, "This is a great job, but we don't get a full day off."

"What it is, is what it is," said Joe. "Besides, the money is great."

"But we got no place or time to spend it."

Joe, with a smile, came back with, "Then we'll have to find some places to spread the cash around. For a start lets call some of the numbers we have and see if there are any parties going on."

"Good Idea." I said. "By the way, between you and me, do you see Uncle Vito at all?"

"With all the shit going on from the D.A.'s office, we don't see much of him, but we get messages. He's ok. So is his family. He even asked about you."

"Well, send him my best regards," I said.

"Ok. About the parties, I'll make some phone calls and see what we can latch on to."

"I forgot to ask you how you made out with the girl?"

"What girl?"

"The one you took back to the car," I said.

"Oh, Marci? Yeah she was something."

"What happened?"

"No sense going through the whole story," said Joe. "The bottom line is that she gave me a hand job."

"You're kidding?"

"No, for real. Afterword she told me she wanted to see me and we could really get to know each other."

"How about giving her a call and maybe we can set something up for the four of us," I suggested. "You, me, Marci, and her girlfriend Robin. She seemed to come on to me."

"Will do," said Joe. "Should be no problem. We have wheels and dough and good looks. What else could these ladies ask for? Leave it to me, I'll set it up. I'll try for Saturday or Sunday night."

Joe dropped me off and said he would pick me up by the subway station.

And he did.

This was the first day we did the route by ourselves. And everything went A-Ok. As did the following days and weeks. Joe and I were a good team together.

In the middle of the first week, I asked Joe, "How about the girls? Did you get a hold of Marci?"

"I was going to tell you," said Joe, "she was thrilled to hear from us, and also said Robin would like to see you again, but Marci is going away this weekend with her folks. Robin was not available either, so I made it for us for next Saturday night."

"Sounds good," I said. "So we are free so far for the weekend."

"So far," said Joe. "I got an idea. Why don't you call Brigette and see if she and Tammi want to go out with us either on Saturday or Sunday. We can take them for dinner and dancing and then go back to their place. This way we're sure to score."

"Good thinking," I said. "I'll make the call tonight. I got their number at home."

When I got home I said hello, went to the dresser in my room, and pulled out the number Brigette gave me that I had hidden in a sock. I didn't want to use the payphone in the store, so I told Papa I was going to take a walk. I went to the payphone on the corner, dialed the number, and as soon as the phone was answered, I said, "Hello Clarise, this is Marco. My friend Joe and I met you a few weeks ago when we came by with Carmine and Louie."

"Yes, I remember you and your friend," said Clarise. "How are you?"

"Good. Is Brigette busy? I'd like to talk to her."

"If it's for an appointment, I can handle this for you."

"No, it's nothing like that," I said.

"All right, let me see if she can talk to you now."

Clarise got back to me in about a minute telling me that if I could hold on, Brigette could get on the phone in about ten minutes. I was sort of ashamed to tell Clarise that I was calling from a payphone, so I told her I would call back in ten minutes. Clarise said, "I'll tell her but make it fifteen just to make sure."

"Ok, thanks Clarise," I said. "I'll call back in fifteen."

This was a long fifteen. I walked up and down the street, looking in store windows and glancing at my watch. Time seemed to crawl. At about five minutes before I was going to call, I went back to the payphone and, my frigging luck, someone was using it. I made a mad dash down the street to another payphone booth on the opposite corner and nearly got run over crossing against the light. I called the number again. Clarise answered, recognized my voice, and said, "Hold on, I'll get Brigette for you."

A few seconds later, I recognized Brigette's lilting voice. "Hello Marco," she said. "How's my cherry boy doing?"

"Doing great," I replied.

"You didn't have to call me personally for an appointment. Clarise handles this for me."

"I really didn't call for that kind of appointment," I said.

"What then, to take me to dinner?" she asked jokingly.

"How did you guess?" I said. "My friend Joe and I want to take you and Tammi out for dinner and dancing this Saturday or Sunday night."

"I don't believe what I'm hearing," she said. "You and Joe actually want to take two working girls out on a date?"

"You heard it right. What do you say?"

"I can't fucking believe this. It might be fun. Let me

ask Tammi. Give me your number and I'll call you back in a few."

I gave her the number and hung up. My three-minute phone call was about up. I didn't want to go out of the phone booth right away, and made believe I was still talking on the phone. I didn't want anyone to leave it until after I got my phone call. After five minutes of doing this, the phone booth got hot and I started to sweat. So I got out and hung around the booth. I was thinking of putting an "OUT OF ORDER" sign up, but I didn't have paper or crayons. I prayed nobody would come and use the booth while I waited.

Just then, the phone rang and I beat it into the booth and picked up on the third ring. It was Brigette. "Is that you, my Cherry boy?" she asked.

"It sure is."

"Well, I spoke to Tammi and dammed if she didn't say ok. So now you both have dates with two hookers."

"Joe and I don't look at you that way," I said.

"Ok, you have dates with two ladies of the evening."

"When can you make it?"

"We will make ourselves available this Saturday night," she said.

"Great, I'll give you a call tomorrow and tell you what time we'll pick you up. What's a good time to call?"

"Any time after six. Just tell Clarise and she'll pass the message through."

"Will do."

"Believe it or not," said Briggette, "Tammi and I are looking forward to Saturday night."

"So are Joe and me," I said.

"So long for now, Cherry boy."

I then called Joe. His mother answered saying he wasn't in, so I left word for him to call me. After saying goodbye to her, I went back to the store. Since I wasn't really tired, I picked up some of the newspapers left over from the morning and decided to catch up on what was going on in the world.

# XXI

    I thumbed through the papers and I remembered what Papa had told me. He was right. Since Germany had now conquered most of Europe, their Axis partner, Italy, declared war on England. Hearing rumors about the bad treatment the European Jews were getting by the Germans made me want to get more information. So I decided to go to the library the next day and see what I could find out. Once there, I was able to get backdated newspapers and also copies of reports from independent agencies. I could hardly believe what I read. European Jews were being blamed for all of the economic problems suffered by not only Germany but the rest of Europe, and a lot of Europeans believed it. Jews were dismissed from the universities and schools, their medical and dental licenses revoked, fired from government jobs, and even forced to wear a yellow star denoting that they were Jews. Positions in the arts were terminated and from all reports, the restrictions against Jews were getting tougher and tougher. The reports about Italian Jews were not as bad. However, Jewish officers in the military were forced to resign and Jewish acceptances to professional schools were drastically cut.

    This was all the information about the Italian Jews I could find. I made a promise to myself that I would come back every few weeks to try to find out what was happening. I felt sorry not only for the Italian Jews but for all the Jews in Europe who were suffering at the hands of the German Nazis and the Italian Fascista.

    I also read reports that a large number of Americans did not want our government to get involved in the affairs of

Europe. They felt it was none of our business. And they claimed that isolationism was the right path for America to follow. Others felt it was a big mistake to leave Britain to stand by herself facing the Axis hoard. America, however, did sell Britain food, ammunition, and fuel. This was for cash, and this was business.

It was getting close to time to go to work on the route, so I left the library, went home, had some lunch, changed clothes, and waited for Joe to come pick me up.

When I got in the car, Joe said, "My mother told me you called last night. I came in too late to call you. What's up?"

"We got dates Saturday night with Brigette and Tammi," I said.

"You're kidding?"

"No, it's all set. I got to call them and tell them what time we'll be picking them up."

While we were on the route, we talked back and forth as to where we should take them.

"I got it," Joe said with a big grin. "We'll take them to the Copa. Nat King Cole is the star there and he's great. The girls will love him. Where should we go after the Copa?"

"I think we should take them dancing," I said. "So let's go to the Café Rouge, at the Hotel Pennsylvania. Benny Goodman is playing there."

"How do you know they can dance?" asked Joe.

"I'll bet my bottom dollar."

"You got a bet."

We picked up the ladies, drove to the Copa, and the valet took our car. After mentioning our names to the valet, he escorted us through an alley to the back of the Copa and knocked on the door. When answered by the security, Joe whispered something to him, and we were immediately escorted by another person through the kitchen to a table right in front of the stage.

Joe said to me, "It's good to have the right connections."

The show was great. The dinner was very good. And the girls were well dressed and looked beautiful, really beautiful. No one, I thought, would ever guess what they did for a living. After the show, and in order to beat the crowd waiting for their cars, we were led back through the kitchen into the alley and there it was, our car waiting for us.

I saw Joe reach into his pocket, take out some bills, and give it to the guy standing there with the keys. We got in and I drove downtown to Hotel Pennsylvania. We gave the car to the doorman and went into the hotel to the entrance of Café Rouge. Someone must have known we were coming, and when Joe mentioned a name to the guy at the door, we were ushered in to a table right on the dance floor. Benny Goodman and his band were sensational, and the girls were good dancers.

During a moment when the girls went to the ladies room, I said to Joe, "I bet we'll be invited to come in when we take them home, for payback. What do you say we tell them since this is a first date and we don't expect to get laid? This should shake them up and might be fun seeing how they handle this. Push comes to shove, we'll go in and get laid. I'm sure there will be some extra thrills in store."

Joe looked at me as if I was crazy and said, "You must be kidding, we went for all this dough with two hookers and all we get for it is a thank you and maybe a kiss? I got a thing for Tammi and I want to sock it to her."

"I'll tell you what, let's see what happens when we tell them," I said. "We'll play it by ear. I'll bet this never happened to them before, so lets see how they handle it."

Joe responded, this time not smiling, "Handle it, not handle it, I still want to get into Tammi's pants. I got a boner the size of a baseball bat."

"I read you, it will work out. You'll get your action. Don't worry about it. I'm using psychology."

"Don't give me the psychology mumbo jumbo, tell it to my boner and see if it understands it."

I leaned over and sort of looked down at Joe's crotch, softly whispering, "Mr. Boner you won't be disappointed tonight."

Just then the girls came back to the table. We danced a few more dances and then Goodman played the last number. It was time to leave. We paid the check and gave a good size tip to the waiter and maitre d'. This way we would be recognized when we came back and also we were sure the guy who made the reservation for us would get a call that we did the right thing. Once outside, we gave the car ticket to one of the parkees and the car was delivered one, two, three.

I thought to myself, being part of the organization had some pretty good privileges.

While driving home, I glanced in the rear view mirror and saw that Tammi had put her head on Joe's shoulder, and I wondered to myself if this was the way hookers work. When we parked the car and went up to the door, Tami said, "Come on in, you two."

I replied, "We had a great time tonight and you don't have to do anything other than kiss us goodnight. It's that simple. You owe us nothing."

Brigette came back with, "We had a great time too. And I'm sure Tammi will agree with me. In our profession, business is business, but tonight, pleasure is pleasure. We wanna have some fun, because we have needs too. Besides, we like you two and we will always remember our two cherry boys. So come on in and this will not be business, but passion."

Brigette then opened the door and we went into the lounge, sat down, and spoke about the events of the evening. The girls were impressed that we were able to get the wonderful table locations and super service we had.

Tammi then said, "I guess you two have some 'very good people' in your corner."

Joe didn't answer her, and I took his lead and said nothing also.

To break the silence I asked, "I know it's not right to ask anything about how, why, and where you two ladies got into your business. It's none of our business, but I'm curious to know where you both learned to dance that good."

Tammi said, "Well, while growing up down South, I went to dancing school until I was fourteen years old, and even appeared in some high school musicals. I guess once you learn something, you can pick it up again real easy."

"My parents were in show business," said Brigette. "They were in vaudeville and traveled all over the country. And I was brought up traveling with them. I even was part of their act. I learned to dance from them and other members of the vaudeville circuit.

"How about you two guys?" asked Tammi. "What can you tell us that would not seem to be asking too much?"

Joe said, "I grew up on the Lower East Side, met Marco in school and we've been like brothers ever since. That's all I got to say."

"Joe told you the whole story," I said. "We are like brothers."

Again there was silence. Then Brigette said, "Believe it or not, I got the hots for you, Marco. It's been a long time since I had this kind of feeling, so let's do something about it."

She then grabbed my hand and in a way pulled me upstairs to her bedroom. As I left, I turned and saw Tammi actually pull Joe close to her, grab his chin, and start to passionately kiss him.

Once we got into Brigette's bedroom, we started to undress each other and at the same time kissed, hugged, and bit. What happened once we got into her bed to this day remains a blur. First I think it was lust, then passion, and then tenderness and caring. We each tried and successfully succeeded to please each other in every way possible, and I mean in every way possible, and we did this over and over until we were both spent but content. Brigette in fact crawled into my arms and we both fell asleep, her beautiful, sensual body encircling mine. This entire experience gave me a sense of bliss that I could not have even imagined.

It seemed it was just a few minutes afterward that I heard a light knocking at the bedroom door. It was Joe whispering, "Marco, we gotta leave, it's nearly four o'clock."

I groped for and turned on the light on the night table next to me and said to myself, "Holy shit, it's ten to four." I crawled out of bed, trying not to wake Brigette, who was sleeping like a baby, and grabbed my clothes and tip-toed bare-ass out the room. Once outside, I saw that Joe was fully dressed and I jumped into my clothes.

"Let's go," I said.

"Let's go now," said Joe.

"What's the hurry?" I asked, "I can hardly walk after all that action."

"We gotta get some shuteye so we can stay awake on the route."

"Ok, ok."

When we got to the bottom of the stairs, we were amazed to see Clarise standing there ready with two paper cups of coffee.

"Don't you ever sleep?" Joe asked in a nice way.

"Thanks for the coffee," I said, and handing one cup to Joe, I asked Clarise, "When do you sleep?

"When there is more than Brigette, Tami and me here, I can't sleep," said Clarise. "The only time I can is when the three of us are alone. Has nothing to do with you two personally. Just a habit, I guess."

Joe and I said goodnight to her and left. On the way driving home, Joe and I said very little to each other. I think we were both relishing over the events of the evening. And I'm sure that Joe would like to do other evenings like we had tonight with the girls.

As Joe dropped me off at the store, he said, "See you regular time, regular place."

"Ciao," I said.

After opening and closing the store doors, I quietly washed up and climbed into bed. At first I couldn't fall asleep. I was thinking about what happened and how great it was. The sex was fantastic and fulfilling. The way Brigette climbed into my arms, still moaning as we fell asleep, I had the feeling that she cared for, trusted, and respected me and that she felt safe.

And off to sleep I went. I woke up around eleven. Got ready, met Joe, and went on the route. Everything went well for the next few days. During stops, we had a chance to go into surface details about our dates. We both agreed that we wanted to see the girls again.

"This time Joe, you set it up," I said. "You have a home phone. I have to use a payphone."

"It will be my pleasure," Joe mimicked. "I almost forgot, we got dates Saturday night with Marci and Robin."

"Where do you want to go?"

"Don't think we should do a places replay of last Saturday night," said Joe. "Since the girls live in Brooklyn."

"What do you mean, the girls leave in Brooklyn?" I interrupted. "You must be kidding."

"Don't get your balls in an uproar. They live right over the bridge in Red Hook, near the Navy Yard. It ain't far and I know how to get there. And I know where we can take them that's not far from where they live."

"And where's that, my nightclub reporter friend?" I asked.

"Hotel St. George. They have a good band and the food is also good and won't cost a lot of dough. I found out about the place because one of my cousins got married there. The hotel also has a big indoor pool that hotel guests can use up to about nine at night."

"So what do you want to do?" I asked. "Take them swimming?"

"No, this is for future reference."

We picked the girls up, drove to the St. George, parked, and took the elevator to the top floor. When the doors opened, we found ourselves in a very nice night club-style restaurant. The dance floor was lively and a good dance band was playing. We were seated at the table on the second tier of the place overlooking the dance floor. I glanced around and saw the room was pretty full but not packed. We were handed our menus and then we ordered. When asked if we wanted drinks, we all ordered Cokes. While waiting for the food to be served, we made small talk. Marci asked if we were still in school and if not, then what did we do.

I beat Joe to the punch by answering, "Where're out of high school and we are working in the delivery business."

"What do you girls do?" Joe asked.

Robin answered, "Both Marci and me are starting our senior year at St. Mary's."

"Isn't that an all-girls Catholic School?" Joe asked.

"That's what it is," said Robin. "Marci and I had no choice. Our parents decided that's where we had to go."

Marci added, "At first we hated it, but now we sort of got used to it, and we have just one more year to go."

Joe asked, "What are you going to do once you graduate?"

"We both haven't made up our minds yet," Robin said.

"By the way Robin, what does your father do?" I asked.

"He's a conductor on the Long Island Rail Road."

"Really?" I said.

Joe turned to Marci and asked, "And what does your father do?"

"He's a cop," said Marci. "He works out of the four-two in Williamsburg."

Glancing at Joe, I said, "That's nice."

The food started to arrive and between courses we danced. Robin was a fair dancer. A little too stiff for me. Must have been the St. Mary's influence. I glanced over at Joe and Marci on the dance floor and if she would have been any closer to him she would have been behind him.

The band took a break and the girls headed for the ladies room, probably to plan strategy for the rest of the night's activity.

At the table, Joe and I did the same thing. I told Joe, "We got a problem here, these girls are just beginning their senior year and I'm betting they are not 18, so they are jailbait. To top it off, there is also a cop in the picture. So figure it out for yourself. It's not trouble, it's double trouble."

"Yeah," Joe replied, "but Marci is hot to trot and so am I, even if it's for another hand job or maybe something better."

"I'll tell you what," I said, "let's leave after dessert and we take Robin home first then you take off with Marci, and I'll take the subway home. It's just a few stops."

"Are you sure you don't mind?"

"I'm positive, it's ok with me," I said.

And we did just that.

I walked Robin up to her door and told her that I had a great time and would call her again. I leaned over to kiss her, and she grabbed me and kissed me passionately and said, "Next time let's you and I go out just the two of us. I really want to be alone with you. Really alone."

"I want to be alone with you too, and I'll arrange it really soon." I kissed her again, and left. Grabbed the subway and went home.

By the time I got home, Mama and Papa's bedroom door was closed. Since I couldn't talk to them, I went to my room and went to bed.

I got up early Sunday morning, grabbed something to eat, put on my apron, and went into the store expecting to go behind the counter and help out until I had to meet Joe and go on the route. When Papa saw me, he waved me off, saying that I didn't have to work and that he would explain why later.

The store was crowded, so I couldn't understand why Papa said I wasn't needed. I picked up the Sunday News and the Mirror, went back to my room, and read them. The news about the war in Europe was terrible. Both newspapers reported that cities in England, especially London and the major industrial communities, were being bombed night and day by German aircraft. The reporters called this period The Battle of Britain. The papers continued describing that as soon as the alarm was given, residents ran to the nearest subway stations or air raid shelters for safety, bringing pillows, blankets, food, and water with them preparing to spend hours and hours there until the all-clear sounded.

These German bombing attacks, although destroying the physical parts of the cities, only made the resolve of the British people stronger to take it, to keep Britain safe and to eventually destroy the Nazis. These sentiments were reported by many American correspondents stationed in Great Britain.

From what I read, it didn't look too good for the British, but I hoped they could hold their own.

I was about to read the funnies when I glanced at my watch. It was time to go meet Joe. I mouthed down some left overs, said goodbye, and met Joe just in time to do Sunday's route.

As usual, we stopped in a Chock Full of Nuts Shop and got our daily orange drink and date-nut-bread cream cheese sandwich. We also were able to take leaks there.

Once we got back in the car and I started driving, Joe turned to me and asked, "How did you make out with Robin last night?"

"Nothing really," I said. "Took her home, kissed her goodnight, and left. She said she would like to see just me and her go out the next time. She wants to be alone with me. I told her I'd call her. And that's what went on. And how about you, lover boy?"

"Well, how can I put it?" said Joe. "We drove over to the docks and parked behind one of the terminal buildings and started to play around with each other. I must have really turned her on because it was a minute or two later when she said, 'I want you and I want you to know it.' She started to crawl on top of me, but the steering wheel and floor gear shift got in the way, so we got in the back seat. She went back there first and I got a couple of rubbers from the glove compartment."

"A couple?" I said. "What are you, a superman?"

"By the time I got into the back," Joe continued, "Marci had nothing on from her waist down and she sure looked great. She also unbuttoned her blouse and unhooked her bra. She told me that she wanted me since the first time she met me at Brighton and that she had been hoping I would call and take her out. With that, she started working me over and I was loving it. After the hot foreplay, it was time for the main event. She wouldn't even give me time to take off my pants, so I did the next best thing, opened my pants and fly and took my stick out. Marci grabbed the rubber for me, tore off the wrapper, and put it on me while kissing me. When this was done she hopped on me and guided me in her. It was sensational. She rocked back and forth, moved sideways, turned around and I did her dog style. She must have come at least seven or eight times. I tried to hold back coming, but it was so good I could only hold out for a minute or two longer and then Ba Ba Ba Boom. I think I came from my toes up. After some more hugging and kissing, Marci got off my lap, sat on the back seat and stretched her legs over the back of the front seat. And once I took off the rubber I did the same.

"We were silent for a few minutes staring ahead, not looking at each other, when Marci turned to me and said, "If you haven't got the strength to go another round, take me home." This was a challenge I couldn't turn down. So we started in again with Marci helping me to get the old pecker ready for action. Good thing I had the second Trojan. Once we were both hot, we went at it again, this time a little slower and not as fast. This was also great, but to tell the truth not as exciting as the first round. After we rested and came back to reality, Marci asked me if I had any towels because she wanted to clean up a bit. I said no, but then remembered we had a stack of napkins from Chuck Full of Nuts, Nedicks, and the Automat. I got some out of the glove compartment and gave a bunch to her. And then she said, 'Don't look back till I tell you. I got some areas I need to clean up and it's none of your business.' And I said, 'You mean I can't sneak a peak?' and she said, 'You can't sneak a peak so don't even try. If I catch you, you'll feel three inches of hat pin being stuck in your ass.'

"In a few minutes Marci came up front and we drove off to her house. When we got to the door, she whispered, 'No heavy kissing now, sometimes my mother or grandma sneaks a look to see what's going on. Kiss on the cheek will work just fine.' She whispered, 'Suggest you get rid of the used napkins in the back seat and send your pants to the cleaners.' Then laughingly she said, 'I left a little of me on them. And most important of all, get a decent supply of you-know-what from the drug store for the next time we go out.' I kissed her on the cheek and did what she suggested and dumped the used napkins in the garbage can on the way home. And that's the story, the whole story."

# XXII

Sunday we went back on the route and continued working it Monday, Tuesday and Wednesday. Same old, same old. When I met Joe on Thursday he had a worried look on his face.

"What's up?" I asked. "You look like you just came from a funeral."

"I think we have a problem," said Joe.

"Watta ya mean?"

"I got a message from Sallie. He wants us to meet him tomorrow at eleven at the lawyer's office."

"What lawyer?" I asked.

"Tepperstein, on Madison Avenue. Sallie said don't drive, take the bus or subway."

"Any idea what the meet is for?"

"No, but I got a feeling it ain't good."

"Well, we can't worry about it now," I said. "Let's do the route and get it over with."

As Joe dropped me off after our work was done, he said, "I'll meet you tomorrow at ten by the subway. We gotta be sure we're there on time."

I met Joe as planned and we took the subway. We got to the lawyer's office building in plenty of time. In fact we had a half hour to spare, so we went in to a luncheonette and had some coffee. At ten to eleven we went into the building and rang for the elevator.

The elevator operator asked, "What floor?"

"Twenty," said Joe.

We got off on the twentieth and Joe said to me, "Look

for an exit sign."

"What for?" I asked.

"Tepperstein's office is on the eighteenth floor. So we have to walk down two floors. Sallie wants us to do this and we don't question what he wants us to do."

We found a stairway and walked down two floors. As we came out of the stairwell we saw on our right two big glass doors, and etched on the doors was "J. T. Tepperstein, Attorney at Law, Managing Partner." And under his name were about twenty other names listed as associates. Joe and I walked in and up to the reception desk where a young lady asked, "Can I help you?"

"We are here to see Mr. Tepperstein," Joe replied.

"Your names please."

We gave them and after looking in a book on her desk she said, "Yes, you are expected. Mr. Tepperstein's personal secretary has the first office on your left after I buzz you in."

With that, the receptionist pressed a button and a door to her rear right buzzed. We proceeded through the door into what seemed to be a human bee hive. People were scurrying in and out of offices all around us. I could hear typewriters clicking all over the place and phones ringing. We entered the office on our left as instructed and we were pleasantly greeted by Mrs. Loewen (her name was on the name plate on her desk).

"Mr. Mancuso and Mr. Falcone?" she asked.

We nodded yes and she said, "Mr. Tepperstein is expecting you, you may go right in." We entered the office door behind her desk. As we walked in, we saw, seated behind a big desk, a balding round-faced man in what I guessed was his early sixties. He had a trimmed white beard and wore a beautiful suit complementing his white shirt and red tie.

"Hello," he said. "I'm J.T. You boys have a seat."

As we took our seats, we turned to our right and saw Sallie with his back to us looking out the window. In contrast with J.T., Sallie wore a zip jacket and an open collar shirt with his stomach protruding over the belt holding up his baggy pants. He was chewing on an unlit cigar. As Sallie sat down, both Joe and I said hello and he just nodded back. J.T. made small talk with just Joe and me for a couple of minutes. He knew we had just graduated from high school and asked general questions, nothing specific. Sallie just sat there chewing on his cigar, looking around the room and out the window. Then Sallie got up, followed by J.T., who while walking opened the door next to his office and said, "This is our conference room and you are welcome to use it. It's quiet here and you won't be disturbed."

Sallie walked in and we followed. He took a chair at the head of the large table and motioned for us to take a seat on either side of him. Sallie took the cigar stub out of his mouth, laid it in the ashtray then looked at Joe first and then turned to me and said, "Tell me, did you two clowns have a good time a couple of Saturday nights ago? Tell me, how did you like Nat King Cole? Was the table good enough for you? You assholes! And by the way, did you two jerks enjoyed Benny Goodman's band at the Café Rouge? Did the waiters do the right thing by you?"

Joe looked at me with a strange look on his face. Sallie turned to him and said, "You look at me when I talk to you, Capishe?"

Joe nodded.

"Who gave you permission to call our contacts and get you in at the Copa and the Café Rouge? You got a lotta fuckin balls."

"But Sallie," Joe started to answer, "when I called for the knock-down to the places, the guy said 'Ok, it's done, don't worry about it.'"

"Whose name did you use?" Sallie asked.

Joe squirmed in his chair and Sallie asked in a louder voice while pointing his finger at Joe.

"Whose name did you fuckin use?"

"I used your name," said Joe.

"You used my name, you jerk-off. Did I give you permission, DID I GIVE YOU PERMISSION? Did you even ask me if you could get my ok?"

Joe sunk lower in his chair. I thought he would faint. Sallie continued with his tirade.

"You both deserve good slaps in the face, if not more," he said. "Then the crowning stunt. What you two, the Jews have a word for it, "Schmucks," pulled off and took out two of our hookers..." At that point, Sallie looked at me and continued. "Remind me which one of these broads you took out."

Sheepishly, I replied, "Brigette."

"And you, Fancy Dan," Sallie said the Joe. "Who was your friggin date?"

"Tammi," Joe answered.

Sallie then continued in a very quiet but convincing manner. "Well, you two are very stupid or got more guts than I thought you got," he said. "I gotta believe you're just stupid. You two morons took out our best earners on a Saturday night, the night that they earn the most. They usually do four or five tricks each on a Saturday night at two hundred dollars a pop. That comes to about a "G" note each that they gave up and we lost on our end. I don't know what you did to get them to go out with you, but that's their problem and we'll deal with them and teach them a lesson they won't ever forget." He paused. "Listen to me and listen to me good. We own these whores lock, stock and barrel, and I mean we own the two broads lock, stock, and barrel, which includes their tits, asses, and their cunts. You got it?"

Joe and I nodded yes.

"I ain't asking you, I'm telling you both stay away from those broads. Don't call them, If you want to get a hooker get two others, not them. If you see them on a street or in a restaurant and they approach you, tell them Ball Four. In other words, forget them. Capishe? Now, getting back to the 'G' you cost us. We could take it out of your pay, but we're not going to do that. We know that putting somebody against the wall denaro-wise and sometimes guys who are hard up for the green get bad ideas, like becoming a paid rat for the cops."

I interrupted Sallie by saying, "We would never..."

Sallie turned to me and said very slow, "Shut the fuck up. Just thank your lucky stars we're gonna give you a pass on this. Remember what I told you, stay far away from those two broads. You won't be told again. If we even smell that you have anything to do with them, it's all over for you two and we are holding you both responsible for what either one of you does.
Now get out of here."

We both got up and I tried to shake Sallie's hand but he waived me off. Joe came over and said something to him in Italian which I couldn't understand. From what I could see, Sallie didn't answer.

We started to walk toward Mr. Tepperstein's office when Sallie said, "Use the door in back of me and go out the building the same way you came in."

I wanted to run to get out of there but Joe came up behind me so that Sallie couldn't see and grabbed the back of my belt slowing me down.

Once we got through the door, I saw Sallie pick up his cigar butt, put it in his mouth, and head towards Tepperstein's office.

Joe and I left the attorney's building and headed for the subway. On the way there, I noticed that Joe was wobbly on his feet and he was turning green.

"Are you ok, Joe?"

He started to reply but all of a sudden ran toward a garbage barrel that was on the curb. He barely lifted off the cover in time and puked his guts out into the can. He was shaking while he did this. Once he finished and I could talk to him, I asked, "Are you ok?"

"Yeah, I'm ok," he said. "Don't know what came over me."

"Yeah, I guess our meeting with Sallie had nothing to do with your puking," I said. "It could have been worse. You couldn have shit in your pants."

"Very funny," Joe answered.

We reached the subway, got off at our station, and we

was rough. While driving the route, Joe and I had to keep our eyes and ears on the alert for anything that seemed not kosher. Was the car behind us tailing us? Were the joints we picked up at being watched by not only the cops but also guys from our own crew checking up on us? We were also told the feds were looking to hook the operation into income tax evasion stuff and had our bosses as targets. Every day, seven days a week, we had to be on our toes, and if caught, we had to keep our mouths shut no matter what.

It sounded easy at first, but when push come to shove, it was a mental ball-breaker. It was close to eight when I heard the rattling around in the kitchen. I got up, put my shoes on, and went in and asked Mama if I could help her. She put me to work setting the table. When I was just about finished, Papa came in and said to me, "Hello stranger, you look just like my son Marco before he graduated high school and before he became a big shot. Oh, it's you, Marco, so come over and give your Papa a hug and a kiss." Which I did.

We sat down to eat. The brisket that Sol made was terrific, and so was the kasha and escarole that was one of Mama's specialties. Over coffee and cake, we had a chance to chat. Papa asked me how the job was going, but was smart enough not to ask details.

Papa then shared with me that Carmine and Louie had stopped by the previous day to say hello, eat a sandwich, and give us the news that there would be no more rental money coming in, and this was the last week.

I said to Papa, "I can't match what you were getting from them, but I can give you $15 a week from my pay."

Papa smiled and said, "That's very nice of you my son, but we got lucky. Sometimes in life, you lose something and something else comes along to take its place, even better."

"What do you mean?"

"It's Sol. Believe it or not, he's bringing in a lot of business. It seems the single ladies, divorced ones and widows, found out he's not married and they are flocking into the store to buy stuff just to talk to him. They even openly ask him to come to eat whenever, and Sol is smart enough to tell them that he would as soon as he gets a day off. He's a charmer that Sol. I get a real kick of seeing these ladies come in all phaputzed like they were going to a party just to impress Sol. If he was a restaurant he would be booked up all the time."

Mama then came back with, "The best of all that there is no more bookie business in the back. I tell you the truth, every time some stranger came in and walked to the back, I got a pain in the heart. Not that Carmine and Louie were bad, but what they were doing was not legal. I'm glad we got our whole apartment back. So let's clean up here and get some rest."

We were all helping with the clean up when Papa looking at me said, "I forgot to tell you, Marco, you got a letter from the college today." Papa took an envelope from his back pocket and handed it to me.

It was from N.Y.U.'s admitting office. I tore the envelope open and read the letter that was in it. It told me to report to the college for orientation and selection of courses the following Wednesday at ten a.m. This worked out good because I still would have time to make the route.

On Wednesday I went to the college and was directed to the auditorium and sat through an hour of orientation bullshit. We were then directed to the gym where we lined up based on the first letter of our last name. Mine being "F" got me into the "A-G" line. When I got up to the desk, I was asked, "What is your major?"

"Pre-Med," I replied.

I was then told to get into one of the lines marked Pre-Med. I kept looking at my watch as the line slowly moved. I still had two hours to go before I needed to meet Joe. I had my fingers crossed that I could get to the desk, get my courses set, and meet Joe in time.

Finally it was my turn. I was asked to sit down and a nice looking gray-haired man sitting behind the desk extended his hand said, "Hello, I'm Dr. Quiring, and I will be your advisor during you time here. And what is your name?"

"Marco Falcone."

Dr. Quiring looked through a pile of folders on his desk and picked one out. "Here it is," he said, and opened it. Looking it over he said, "You have an impressive record and I think you can carry a full load starting with your first semester." And he started to fill in some sort of form, I guess listing subjects, date, day, and time.

Before he could complete it, I said, "Excuse me sir, I need to tell you I have to work in order to stay in school, and my job hours are from two p.m. to six p.m. and I need about a half hour travel time."

Dr. Quiring remarked, "I admire a student that has to work while going to school. Let's see what we can do to fit your classes with your work hours. You realize you'll have to attend classes at night." It took about ten minutes to fill out another form and handing it to me he said, "Well, I think I worked it out for you. It will be somewhat tough, but I'm sure you can do it."

I took the form and without glancing at it put it in my jacket pocket. "Thank you very much, Dr."

"Here at the university, I prefer to be called professor," he said.

"Thank you, Professor."

"I'm here to help you throughout your college career. If you need any advice or help, just call my office."

"Thanks again, Professor," I said as I shook his hand. Then I left the college.

# XXIII

The days flew by quickly, and before I knew it, it was time to start college. My first class was at eight o'clock on Monday, Wednesday, and Friday. And the last one was at twelve-forty, leaving me just enough time to grab a fast bite and meet Joe. Tuesday and Thursday my schedule was nine in the morning until noon. I had night classes five nights a week, Monday through Friday, from six-thirty until ten-thirty. It wasn't easy, but I was determined. I got very little sleep because I had to study once I got home, sometimes until three in the morning. Mama always had something for me to eat when I got home a little after eleven from my night classes.

Joe and I saw each other every day doing the route. It looked like everything was getting back to normal. There were no more raids on our places by the cops and the D.A.'s office. Maybe it was because of the war in Europe that the cops were instead looking for spies that were tipping the offshore German U-Boats about our ships bringing supplies to England.

I remember it was about two weeks before Labor Day when Joe told me that Uncle Vito was having a party at his house and we were invited, and so were my parents. I asked, "What about the route?"

"Don't worry, it's being taken care of," said Joe.

"I'm sure my folks can't make it," I said. "Labor Day is one of the busiest days of the year and as good as Sol is, it will be too much for him."

"Ok, I'll get word to Uncle Vito that you'll be there without them. I'm sure he'll understand, and you'll go with us. My father is taking one of his limos."

The two weeks ran by without a hitch, and on Monday as planned Joe's father picked me up in his limo. I was real happy to see his parents and sisters again. It had been a long time.

The ride out was nice through Brooklyn to Uncle Vito's house in Seagate. Once there, we had to pass through a guard house where Joe's father spoke to the guard and then the gate lifted. We drove a few blocks to the end of a road where there was a big house surrounded by a large fence and another gate. There were two or three guys guarding the gate and checking the cars looking to get inside. They must have recognized Joe's father because they waived to him and raised the gate and we entered the property.

I couldn't believe the size of that house. It was a mansion. The big lawn was cut, green and beautiful. There was also a big garden with all kinds of flowers and I never saw this before, there was also a green house. When we drove to the house, two young guys came out to welcome us. They helped us out and then took the car.

We walked into the house and were warmly greeted by Mrs. Amatto, who told us her husband was out on the beach in back of the house. She said to follow her to meet him and join the party. She led us through the large foyer toward the back and through the glass sunroom to the door leading to the beach. When we got on the beach, Joe looked at me and I looked at him. We couldn't believe our eyes. There was a large swimming pool, a tennis court, a bocce court, cabanas to change clothing, and shower and umbrella topped picnic tables and chairs that could hold maybe a hundred people were set out around the pool. There was also a large bar and a portable dance floor. Two bands took turns playing. One was playing Italian music and the other popular American tunes. At one side was the cooking area, and chefs dressed in the starched white clothes and hats were cooking Italian delicacies. There was even a whole pig being roasted on a spit. Joe and I made it our business to make it through the crowd of guests to greet uncle Vito, who seemed very happy to see us and actually said, "Glad you're here. Have fun. We'll talk later." And then he was off to meet other guests.

"How about taking a swim?" said Joe. "They have bathing suits and towels in the cabana."

"Let's hold off for a while," I replied. "I want to get the lay of the land."

Joe said, "How are you going to get the lay of the land by just sitting here on your ass under an umbrella?"

"Ok, but let's wait ten minutes and see who else comes to the party."

And we did just that.

Some of the guys from our crew saw us and came over to say hello. There were others from families that I had recognized from the newspaper. Others I had heard their names mentioned around. Some of the guests were even big shots from the other families who brought their wives and kids. It was a social affair although at times a small group would walk off and talk by themselves and had one or two guys seeing that the group was not disturbed.

Sitting at the table gave me a chance to look the whole place over. At the perimeter of the property, a wood fence ended and a chain-link fence took over. I guess it was about six feet high and it ran around the rest of the property including the beachfront. There were two gates leading to and from the ocean, and I saw a couple of guys walking around and letting people back to the ocean and back through these gates.

Off to one side was a gated large enclosed kennel that housed four big Doberman pinchers. I asked Joe about them, and he told me that they were guard dogs and were let out at dusk and put back in the kennel at sunrise.

"Well my friend," Joe said, "take your choice, ocean or pool?"

"Let's do the ocean. It's been a long time since I swallowed some sea water."

We changed into suits in one of the cabanas where there were plenty of different sizes and colors. Towels were also there and so was a shower with soap and shampoos. *What a set up,* I thought.

As we approached one of the gates leading to the ocean, one of Uncle Vito's men unlocked the door and Joe and I raced to the ocean.

"Last one is an old maid!" I yelled. I tried to beat Joe, but I lost.

We swam, floated, and belly-dived. We also took turns climbing each other's shoulders and then diving off. It was fun. After doing this for about half hour, we had had enough and headed back to the gate. We were let in and then showered and got back into our clothes. The party was going strong and everyone seemed to be having a great time eating, drinking, and dancing. Toast after toast was made to Uncle Vito, who accepted them with grace.

I looked around and asked Joe, "Not that I miss him, but where's Paulie? I don't see him anywhere."

Joe came back with, "He ain't here."

"How come?"

"You gonna love this. He and Phil are covering the route for us."

"You're kidding?" I said.

"Nope, Uncle Vito made the decision and that was that. Paulie didn't like you before, so just imagine how he feels about you now. I don't think he's too happy about me either, but I'm blood, and you are not."

Just then Uncle Vito came by and sat down at our table. "Having a good time?" he asked.

"The best!" Joe responded.

I added, "I want to thank you so much for inviting us. It's a real pleasure."

"The pleasure is mine," Uncle Vito said, and then he asked me, "How are you doing in school?"

"It's a lot harder than High School," I said, "and that's why I have to study longer hours, but I love it so far."

"You got a lot of people betting on you," said Uncle Vito. "I know you'll do the right thing, and do what you promised some very good people, and become a doctor. I'm sure you won't disappoint them, or me either."

I replied by saying, "I'm very thankful for what you're doing for me, and I won't let you down."

"That's good. Keep me informed as to how you're doing in school. Or if you have trouble with the work or anything."

"I'll do that, Uncle Vito," I said.

Turning to Joe, Uncle Vito said, "It's going to be nice having a doctor in the family."

"It sure would," Joe replied.

With that Uncle Vito got up and said, "I have to say hello and visit with some of my people and other friends. So I'll say goodbye to you both now. But you can stay until the party is over. I guess that will be when the food is gone." Uncle Vito smiled.

As he got up to leave, Joe and I got up, came over to his side of the table, and each of us gave him the customary hug and kiss on the cheek. Doing this was a sign of respect.

As Uncle Vito walked away to greet other guests, Joe's mother and father came over and sat with us. Joe's mother, in her typical role of an Italian Mama, said, "Boys, you must be hungry, so get yourself something to eat. There's plenty, so take big plates full."

We were in fact hungry, so we took Joe's mother's advice and piled our plates, not once but twice. But we left a little room for espresso, biscotti, and gelato.

By this time, some of the guests had started to leave and Joe's father signaled to us that we needed to also go. We made the rounds of saying goodbye, and as we walked back into the house through the foyer towards the front door, there were packages of food waiting for us to take home. I saw one package with my name on it, and one of the chefs told me there was no pork included in the package. I thanked him and took it, then got into Mr. Mancuso's limo with the rest of his family. During the ride home we each talked about the great time we had. As I left the limo, I turned and thanked the Mancusos for picking me up and taking me home.

Once inside, I gave Mama, Papa, and Sol a rundown of the afternoon and how nice it was, without going into great detail. I had studying to do and didn't want to take the time to describe the whole picture. I gave Mama the package, and she was very pleased. When she opened it, there were lots of special Italian pastries, homemade of course. Italian espresso coffee beans and lots of home grown fruits and a bottle of wine made by a member of our crew's grandma. Mama and Papa and even Sol were very happy with the gifts and Mama said she would call Mrs. Amatto the next day to thank her.

I had to buckle down that night and get my mind on studying, and it took hours. Once I felt ready for the two big exams I was going to take the next day, I also spent some time reviewing for the exam I had at the end of the week.

The next day, as Joe and I were doing the route, something came to mind and I asked him, "How come we went to Tepperstein's office instead of going to one of the Italian lawyers that represented our crew?"

"Well," he replied, "when it comes to little things like minor pinches, getting guys out on bail and things like that, we use the Italian guys. But if it comes to big stuff, we figure we want to use a Jew lawyer. They're smarter and have the right connections with the judges. The same goes for doctors and accountants. We use them for the big things."

"You must be kidding?"

"Nope, that's the way it is and it's always worked out good for the family."

"If that's the way it is, that's the way it is," I said.

The following weeks all was going well, when suddenly all hell broke loose. The D.A.'s office and vice cops were raiding a lot of our stops, not only bookmaking operations but also gambling joints and even some of our cat houses. Joe and I nearly took a pinch but were lucky enough to shake off the tail.

Then Joe got a message for us to stop making the route. The newspapers were full of stories about the police and the

D.A.'s office clamping down on organized crime in Manhattan. The following week Joe called me and told me we had to meet with Phil the next day at three o'clock inside the Greyhound bus station on 34th street. We were also told not to come together, and not to come by car. He further said that there was a bus scheduled to leave for Boston at three-fifteen, and we were to meet him by that bus, but not get on it.

I met Joe and Phil as planned. Phil checked around to see that we weren't followed and, finding everything ok, had us follow him into the waiting room. He found a couple of empty benches and motioned for us to sit down.

"There is a lot of heat on us now," said Phil. "So lay low and no more routes 'till we tell you. We think there is a rat involved. And I'm here to tell you to keep your eyes and ears open. We gotta find the scumbag quick. Any ideas, fellas?"

Joe looked at me and I looked back at him and we both looked at Phil and we both shrugged our shoulders.

Joe said, "I ain't got the slightest idea who could be doing this."

"Neither do I," I said. "We hadn't noticed anybody sniffing around or asking questions, but we will keep our guard up."

"You can bet on that," Joe said.

"Ok," said Phil. "And don't use the car until I tell you."

"Ok," said Joe, with me nodding in agreement.

Phil nodded. "Now leave separate and remember keep your eyes and ears open."

The next three weeks was like being on a vacation. With no route to deal with, I had plenty of time for school and studying. I even thought of asking a girl out on a date or going to some dance.

Joe and I were in touch every day but we didn't actually get together in person. We felt it was safer that way. The raids kept on and more and more places were shut down, our guys pinched. The rat was still out there. It was in the middle of the forth week since we were told to stop the route when I picked and that will piss the cops off more, so they'll try harder to get someone to squeal."

"Well, while we're here," I said, "let's find some girls and do some fancy footwork."

We lucked out. There were lots of girls there without partners and Joe and I had a good time dancing. Some of the girls were worth a recall and we took their numbers.

On the subway ride home, we compared notes and decided that the two girls we met that lived in the Bronx - although we didn't like to go to the Bronx - were good candidates for our lust. We also made up to meet that night and try the roller rink, although we hadn't been skating for years. It might be fun and maybe we could meet some girls with great bodies and good legs. We went and it was little difficult to get going with the skating. In fact I nearly fell, but two girls skated over and grabbed me. They were not bad looking, and Joe and I skated with them.

After the session was over, the girls said they were being picked up by car by one of their fathers since they live in Yonkers. We waited with them until their ride came and promised to see them again. On our way home we congratulated each other of getting a new list of possible conquests.

Before I went to bed that night, I asked Papa if he needed me to work the next morning, since it was always busy on Sundays. Papa smiled and replied, "No, college boy, we have Sol Baby, the Casanova, who can do the job of two like you. Besides, you need to study, right?"

"Yes Papa, I have two exams this week."

I grabbed something to eat and studied for three hours, then decided to take a walk to clear my head. On the way back, I picked up a copy of the *Sunday Daily News*. The front page was full of goings on about the war. The Battle of Britain was in full force, and hundreds of German aircraft dropped bombs nightly over many of the British cities, especially London. From what I read, it didn't look good for England. I continued reading and on page three, there was a news story that caught my eye.

I'll never forget the caption: "Roosevelt Signs Selective Service Act. The draft for the military is now "law." The article continued: "All men between the ages of 18 and 35 have to register. Failure to register could result in jail time. Once registration began, lotteries will be held and numbers drawn. Those holding the drawn number will be the first to be called. In addition to getting the draft law passed, Roosevelt declared "U.S. Neutral Status In The War", and ordered the navy to patrol American territorial waters to protect shipping."

How would this affect me if my number was drawn? Would I have to leave college to go into the Army? I tried to sleep but also tried to think of what would happen.

At the university there was a lot of discussion about the war. Many felt that it was none of our business, and that we didn't need to save Britain's ass. It was argued that Great Britain was the largest imperial nation in the world and by helping the Brits we are helping them maintain their dominance over their empire. Another group held rallies in support of Roosevelt's policies. By helping Britain, they claimed, the war is being kept over there. If Britain fell, we would be forced to defend ourselves on our own soil. On the streets, on the radio, and in the newspapers both sides voiced their strong opinions. "Don't get involved in European affairs," some said. The other side was determined to save Britain: "In order to avoid our physical participation. It's better to sell Britain supplies than to send troops." And so it went on.

Word was sent down that we would start the route on Wednesday. It worked out well for me because I had a couple of days open to study for exams that I had to take toward the end of the week. I actually felt a little guilty that I didn't do much, if at all, during the time of the route.

Joe and I started up on the route again and time ran by quickly. School was getting harder and harder and I had to spend more sleepless nights studying. I started to take No Dose pills a couple of times a week to keep me from falling asleep while studying, or even while in class. Many times I fell asleep on the route when Joe drove. He had to constantly wake me up to make the pick-ups. He told me over and over that he wouldn't let me drive because he was sure I would fall asleep at the wheel. I started to lose weight and bags were beginning to become noticeable under my eyes and I was a little shaky in my walk.

It was two days before Thanksgiving when I got a phone call just as I was leaving for school. It was Joe's mother. She told me that Joe was not feeling good and was up all night with diarrhea and vomiting. She added that he was going to see the doctor that day at three and wouldn't be able to meet me, but said I was to go to the same place and at the same time. I thanked Joe's mother and said I would call later to see how Joe was feeling.

Right after school, I grabbed a sandwich and hurried to our usual meeting place. Sure enough, the car was there and I saw Phil behind the wheel.

"Get in," he said, and we drove off.

During the time we were working the route, we didn't speak much, except for him to say when I got into the car, "You look like shit."

I remember it clear as day, I had just finished coming out of the spot next-to-last with a pretty full bag in my hand, when two big bruisers came up to me before I reached the car. One of them called out, "Marco Falcone?"

Taken by surprise, I nodded. One of them flashed a badge, and said, "You are under arrest." And the other one took the bag out of my hand. "Turn around and put your hands behind your back." And I did just that. I felt my hands being secured by what I was pretty sure were handcuffs.

Out of the corner of my eye, I saw Phil drive off. The two that pinched me walked me to a car, opened the back door and one of them helped me get in. I was both scared and embarrassed, and hoped that no one I knew recognized me. I was really worried that if the news got out that I was pinched I might get thrown out of college. I got really scared when we passed the police station and the car didn't stop.

"Where are you taking me?" I asked.

"Shut the fuck up," said the cop in the passenger seat.

We got onto 10$^{th}$ Avenue and headed south, and stopped at what looked like a row of garages and small warehouses. The car turned into the driveway of one of the garages and the guy sitting next to the driver got out. He unlocked the overhang door, raised it and we drove in. By this time I was panicking. *They're gonna kill me, they're gonna kill me*, I kept thinking.

The car came to a stop inside the garage and the guy that opened the overhead sliding door closed it, came to the rear car door, and told me to get out. I did, with his help. I was pushed toward the rear of the garage and told to sit at a table which was at the back. Once I did this, the two cops sat down. The guy on my left, facing me, spoke first. "My name is Pat," he said, "and this is my partner, Russ."

I didn't know what to answer.

Pat then continued, "We know all about you and we know all about the store your Mother and Father have and what's been going on there and they are gonna be in a lot of trouble. We even know about Carmine and Louie and the bookmaking they did out your back rooms."

Russ then came in by saying, "We know your folks and they are good people and we can give you a chance to save them from getting arrested and probably losing the store, and maybe even going to jail. No matter what happens, they'll need a lawyer and lawyers don't come cheap."

Pat then took over. "As far as you're concerned, you'll need a lawyer too, and if you are convicted, you can kiss college goodbye."

Russ then said, "We heard you're a good kid, and maybe we can figure a way for you and your family to get out of this problem. That's why we brought you here, instead of the station house where you will have your picture taken and be fingerprinted and a record made of your arrest. How does that sound?"

I thought quick to myself and asked, "What do I have to do for my Mama and Papa and me to walk away?"

"It's simple," Pat replied. "All you have to do is to meet one of our guys every couple of weeks and sort of acquaint him with what's going on and what will be going on with your crew, and any other information you think we can use. By the way, in addition to all of you getting a pass, you'll get paid cash for the info. The amount would be depending on how important the stuff is. We know you are a smart kid and can do this for us and for your family. And you are clever enough to pull this off without anybody ever finding out."

With that Pat turned to Russ and said, "It's hard to think things out with handcuffs on. Take them off the kid so he can see we want to be in his corner."

Russ took the handcuffs off.

Pat continued, "We know this is an important decision you need to make and we'll give you a couple of days to make up your mind, and we are sure you'll realize what we are offering you is a hell of a deal. To ensure that you'll do the right thing, if you don't take our offer, we'll get word out on the street that you agreed to become a C.I."

"What's a C.I.?" I asked.

"Confidential Informant."

"You mean a stool pigeon, a rat, a squealer?" I said. "The answer is no, no way, never, negative. You want me to rat out people. It'll never happen. I won't do it even if I have to go to prison."

"What about your folks?" said Pat. "They can end up in jail and that would be sad."

"We are stand-up people that would never get involved with this C.I. business even if we had to take a fall."

"Don't rush into things," said Russ. "Think it over and we'll be in touch with you in a couple of days."

"Don't waste your time," I said. "Not interested in doing anything for you or with you. I ain't no rat, and neither is my family. So do what you have to do."

Pat came back with, "Ok, if that's the way you want it,

that's the way it'll be. Let's go."

We walked to the car and Russ opened the back door and I got in, no handcuffs. Russ then opened the garage door and guided Pat in getting out, then got in once the door was clear of the garage. As we neared the police station, Pat slowed down and called out, "Last chance to cooperate before we take you in."

"Do what you have to do," I said. "I said it before and I'll say it again, I ain't a stoolie and I won't rat anyone out no matter what."

To my amazement, they drove past the station to a subway, slowed down and Pat told me to get out. Russ said, "You're free to go, because we said we'll give you a day or two to think our proposition over and talk it over with your folks. We'll be in touch."

And they drove off.

I was in shock, but I knew I had to report what happened to Sallie. The only place I could think of where he might be was the Eagle and Tarpon Club, and I hurried over there as fast as I could. When I got to the door of the club, I knocked and the door opened slightly with a pug-face guy asking me, "Who are you and what do you want?"

"I'm Marco Falcone and I need to see Sallie or Tony A. It's important."

"Wait here," said the man, and he closed the door in my face.

A few minutes later - it seemed like hours - the door opened and I was let in. I spotted Sallie sitting with Tony A and a couple of other guys. They were playing cards. They saw me and motioned for me to sit down at an empty table at the back of the room. I waited and waited and waited, and they were still playing cards. Finally they came over and Sallie said, "This better be important because we left a card game where we're both winning."

They sat down and I told them everything I could remember. And they listened good.

When I finished, Tony A said, "You did good. Don't

worry, these cops won't bother you anymore. Now beat it and get some sleep and if Joe is ok, you hook up with him. Otherwise Phil will be there to do the route with you."

"Ok, will do, so long," I said.

On my way home I kept thinking, *how come I got busted*? Was Joe really sick and I got set up? Funny that Phil had the motor running and was able to get away. I stopped in the middle of the street and shook my head from side to side. Passersby must have though there was something wrong with me because they sped up as they passed me by. There is no way Joe could jake me out. I trusted him with my life, and Phil is part of Uncle Vito's crew. If I could I would have kicked myself in the ass for even thinking this way, and I put it out of my mind, not being mentally assured that my being pinched was just an unlucky break.

I felt I needed to talk to Joe, so I found a phone booth and dialed his number. Once his mother answered, I asked her how Joe was doing.

"Just a minute," she said. "I'll let you talk to him."

Joe got on the phone and said hello.

"How you feeling?" I asked.

"I'm feeling a lot better," said Joe. "I had the shits so bad I must have lost fifteen pounds. What made it worse I was also puking every time I took something, even water. The medicine the doctor gave me did the job. I think I'll be able to go back on the route in a day or two. I wanna make sure I'm over the shits before I go back to work. What's doing with you, Marco?"

"I'll tell you when I see you."

"You want to come to my house for Thanksgiving dinner?"

"I'd like to but I haven't spent too much time with my family, so I'm going to eat turkey with them. I also need to catch up on my studying. I got finals coming up in the next couple of weeks. Give my best to your whole family, and I'm sure they'll understand why I turned down the invite."

"Ok, will do," said Joe. "So I'll see you on Saturday. If there's a problem, I'll let you know."

"Ok Joe, see you on Saturday. Same time, same place."

# XXIV

    Papa, as he did every Thanksgiving, closed the store at five in the afternoon. Then we all, including Sol, sat down to eat. From what Papa told me, Sol had so many invites from the single ladies that he told them that since Papa was his boss, he was expected to come and eat with us, especially since he was cooking the turkey. This little white lie saved Sol from making a choice and pissing off the other ladies that asked him to come. Papa didn't mind this at all, since it made the ladies more anxious to try to snare Sol, and thus more likely to come and buy more often.

    On Thanksgiving day, I slept a little later than usual and spent the rest of the day studying, up until the time we sat down for dinner. I had to take a little break after we ate, so I walked over to Tony's hoping to bump into some of the girls, but Tony's was closed so I went back home and back to the books. Then caught some sleep.

    Saturday, I left for work at the regular time and spotted our car where it was supposed to be. When I approached it, I saw Joe was sitting behind the wheel.

    "Hi, what's up?" I said as I got in.

    "All is Ok," said Joe. "Let's get going."

    Between the stops, I told him about the pinch, and he had no comment other than saying, "You're a lucky son of a bitch."

    The days and weeks rolled by, and I was really knocked out by the time Christmas time came. Between working, attending class and studying, I was more exhausted than ever. I started to look like a zombie. Once again, Joe noticed the way I looked and kept on telling me, "You better get a lot of sleep and regular eats over your break from school. You look like hell."

And I took his advice. I slept late and rested up when I wasn't working. Between Christmas and New Year's, Joe and I double-dated some girls we met previously, and I got laid with one of them a couple of times. I think her name was Lucy. For New Year's Eve, Lucy invited Joe and me to a party at her house and we had a great time. And I got laid again. Joe didn't, and he was really pissed off about that.

1941 arrived and things were changing. I kept on seeing more and more guys in uniform in the neighborhood. Draft boards were being formed and draftees started to be called based on the national lottery. The news about the war in Europe was getting from bad to worse. Especially what was happening to the Jews.

I started the Spring semester and was lucky enough to get my class schedule to fit in with my work one. But it was a tight call. The weeks ran by and once again, the pressure mounted, and I was exhausted. It was harder than ever keeping up with my grades and working the route seven days a week. Joe again would not let me drive. He was sure that I would fall asleep at the wheel and kill us both. I had a hard time keeping my eyes open in between stops sitting in the passenger's seat.

A couple of weeks later, Joe gave me some news that perked up my day; Paulie had one of the draft lottery numbers and he had to report for his physical in ten days.

*What a relief it would be to see him drafted into the Army*, I thought. *What a swell feeling*. As elated as I was with the prospect of Paulie serving, I took a 180 and went far down in the dumps when Joe called and told me that Paulie couldn't pass the physical. He had flat feet and they wouldn't take him and sent him home. I felt I got fucked by the fickle finger of fate.

It was around the middle of March that I got word that Tony A wanted to see me. I was at the Eagle and Tarpon club as directed. It was lucky for me that I didn't have classes that night. When I got there, Tony A motioned for me to sit down and a few seconds later, Sallie and Phil showed up and joined us.

Sallie opened the conversation by saying, "You don't look too good. Are you sick or something?"

"No, but I'm sort of beat," I said. "Doing the route and going to college ain't easy, but I can handle it."

"Ain't sure that you can handle it," said Phil. "I had to wake you up a couple of times while we were on the route and that ain't good."

I didn't say anything. I just sat there expecting the worst. Tony A then took over, saying, "We called you in for a reason. Since you proved yourself to be a stand-up guy, we are going to make your life easy."

I took a shot and asked, "What do you mean I proved myself? Did it have something to do with the pinch?"

Tony A looked at Sallie and said, "Tell him Sallie."

"The bust you took, we set up, because there are rats around," said Sallie. "We had to make sure. Those cops are on our payroll and were told to check you out."

Phil added, "You passed the test good, and you are a fuckin' man."

"The draft has taken a lot of our guys and we need to replace them," said Tony A. "Because you did the right thing, we're going to take you off the route and give you something to do that will give you a lot more time to study. We got a big investment in you becoming a doctor and we don't want to take a chance of you dying on us. So here's the plan. We're gonna give you a list of places and days that you go each week and pick up the *vig*. Most of these places are small businesses, so you can get there any time that they are open. If they have a lot of customers when you come in, don't hang around for more than a couple of minutes. Just make sure the guy that owes the money sees you. Just tell him I'll be back to pick up the order in fifteen minutes. When you go back, and you get an excuse and you don't get the vig, don't argue. Just say, 'We'll be seeing you,' and walk out. You are going to earn a piece of everything you pick up. Phil will clue you in and take you around and get you acquainted. Any questions?"

"Just one if you don't mind," I said. "Joe and I have always been together. What's going to be with him?"

"Don't worry about Joe, he'll be in good shape," said Tony A. "Stay in touch, we're counting on you. Oh, by the way, when we think you're ready, we'll get you a car. Just remember, do the right thing."

Phil then added, "I'll be calling you soon. In the meantime, stay on the route with Joe."

"Will do," I said, then I turned to Tony A and said, "Thanks." And I walked out.

When I left the club I could not help but think, *Son of a bitch, they set me up and I fell for it. I hate to think what would happen to me and my folks if I agreed to cooperate. I felt real sure I would have wound up like Augie.*

I met Joe the next day and told him what happened. He sort of hinted he knew something and told me we could have a cup of coffee after our last stop and he would fill me in. And we did just that.

I started conversation by asking, "Did you have anything to do with us breaking up?"

"I sort of did," said Joe. "Uncle Vito was at our house for Thanksgiving dinner and asked about you, and I told him that you were out on your feet and looked like shit. He then asked me if I knew how you were doing in college. I told him I didn't know, but didn't see how you could take the pace for much longer. Uncle Vito thanked me and the conversation was over.

"Uncle Vito was killing two birds with one stone. He got a message from one of our relatives in Umbria. I think it was a cousin. He has a son who's around fifteen and asked Uncle Vito to get his son out of Italy. He thinks Mussolini is

232

crazy and that the Italian Army is getting defeated everywhere. So they are down to drafting kids as young as sixteen. He doesn't want his only son to be cannon fodder. Well, Uncle Vito pulled some strings and the boy is being smuggled out of Italy and should be here in about a week. I was told he speaks a little English, enough to get along, and we're gonna try to break him in to take your place."

"Joe, I don't know whether to get real pissed at you or say thanks."

"You shmuck," said Joe. "You were killing yourself and since we are like brothers, I had to save your ass even from yourself. Now you gonna have time to study and also stay involved with your family. Don't worry Marco, we'll still see each other like before and have some fun again. You've been a real drag for months."

"Ok Joe," I said. "I think I'm supposed to stay on the route with you until I'm told not to."

"Yeah, let's leave it at that," said Joe. "Now scram, go home and hit the books."

"Need to do that. Got quizzes coming up in the next few days."

"What's quizzes?" Joe asked.

"Little tests," I replied. "See you tomorrow, Brother."

"See you tomorrow. Ciao."

"Ciao."

Joe and I did the route for the next three weeks and all was going ok. I didn't hear anything from Phil during that time until one day toward the end of the third week as I came up to the route car we used, when I saw Phil leaning against it with a young guy standing next to him. When he saw me, he pointed for me to get in the back seat and motioned to the other guy to get in next to Joe, who was behind the wheel.

Phil then sat down next to me. "Say hello to Vinnie," he said. "He got in from Italy last week."

"Hi Vinnie," I said to the new guy.

And he in fairly decent English responded, "Good to

meet you."

Phil then said, "Vinnie here is gonna learn the route from you and Joe, mostly from you because he can't get a driver's license for now, so he'll make the pickups. The sooner he learns the score, the sooner you can move on." Turning to Joe, Phil said, "Let's move. I stay with you three until I see that Vinnie can handle things. And then I'll show you the ropes."

I didn't ask Phil what the score was, thought it better to keep my mouth shut. About two weeks later after we made the last stop on Friday, Phil said to Vinnie, "You learn quick Vinnie, so starting tomorrow you and Joe go it yourselves. If you have a problem, give me a call." Turning to me, Phil said, "You, Marco, meet me at the club tomorrow two o'clock. Got it?"

"Got it," I said.

I was outside the club about ten to two. I knocked on the door and was surprised when the guy that opened the door recognized me and said, "Come on in Marco, you're expected."

I walked in, said hello to a couple of guys I knew and went over to the table in the back where Sallie, Tony A and Phil were sitting. I said hello to them and they nodded back hello. But I remember they didn't ask me to sit down. Phil then got up and motioned for me to follow him.

We wound up in a small office room in the back. We sat down and Phil began by saying, "Tony A gave you a rundown of what we want you to do. We got a good loan business going and you are going to be part of it." He then asked me, "Do you know anything about our type business?"

"I think so," I replied. "Years back when my father needed some money to get started, Hunchback Hymie lent him five hundred dollars. My father had to pay twenty-five dollars a week interest until he paid the five hundred back."

"So you do know something," said Phil. "We call the interest *vig*. That's short for *vigorish*. And your father paid five points a week. That's what we charge. The difference between us and Hunchback is that his top loan is five hundred dollars, our smallest loan is a one thousand dollars. We don't want to be bothered with the small potato loans, so we leave Hunchback alone. He don't bother us, and we don't bother him as long as five hundred is his limit. We gonna start you off with ten vig stops. Tony A told you how to work with the customers. Just do as he told you and you'll be ok. Every week you'll drop the last week's vig off to me at the club Monday at five o'clock. This gives our customers a week's time to get the vig together.

"And something else," Phil added. "We don't take partial payoff. If we lend a *g-note* we get a *g-note* back. Capishe?"

"Capisco."

Phil continued, "So here's how you earn. We are going to give you one piece of everything you collect. We're starting you off with only ten one-thousand-dollar customers, so your end will be fifty dollars a week. Ain't bad for a few hours' work right?"

"Right."

"Now if you get your own customers and use your own money to push out, you can keep two points. You use our money and you get the one point. Let me tell you that before you push out any money, even if it's yours, you need to get an ok from me or Sallie. I don't have to tell you what will happen if you do any secret service work and hold things back from us, especially money. Understood?"

"I would never do that, Phil," I said.

"One more thing, don't keep any records in writing. Doing this can get you and us in a lot of hot water. Any questions?"

"None I can think of," I said.

"You got time Monday at two o'clock?"

"I'm ok with that."

"Then meet me outside here on Monday and we'll get started."

# XXV

    The ten stops were not too far apart and could be done in a couple of hours. The customers were mostly small business shop keepers. On the way to the first stop, Phil turned to me and said, "I'm going to introduce you as John or Johnny. This is your name in the loan business, so don't forget it."
    I said to myself, *if that's the way he wants it, that's the way it'll be*. I spent the next two weeks riding with Phil and everything went real good. I had time to attend classes, study and get some rest, as well as the time to eat Mama's home cooking, get sleep, and even get to the gym. Joe and I also had the chance to get together on weekends and have some fun. We took Vinnie along and introduced him to some girls who immediately fell for him. We nicknamed him the Italian Stallion, and he played the part real good. Put us to shame on the scoring with the girls.
    I had a real problem concerning where I could keep the vig money. I had to find a place where no one, especially Mama and Papa, could find it. All of a sudden an idea came to me. There was a hole in the wall behind the Frigidaire in the cellar left by the electrician when he put in the wiring. I next turned my attention for a way to keep a record of my vig collections. This was easy. I just created a code made up of numbers and since I was taking Calculus, I put them in with my lecture notes and homework.
    At the end of the second week, as we pulled up in front of the club, Phil said, "I think you can go on your own starting Monday." He turned off the engine and gave me the keys. "The car is yours to use for the business, but it's ok sometimes to use

it socially, especially to get laid." He laughed. "That's a good one."

 I drove home and parked the car around the corner from the store. I didn't want Mama, Papa, or Sol to see me with the car. I wanted to tell them but first I had to figure out a way, without lying, to explain how I got a car. My change in working hours would be explained after.

 For the first time in what seemed like a year, I was able to sit down and eat dinner with Mama and Papa. The food was terrific and the conversation centered about how I was doing in college, the war, and the terrible rumors about the treatment of Jews in Europe including Italy. It kept bothering me about telling Mama and Papa about my new job and about the car. Well, I thought, the car was not a new one. It was s a 1935 Nash that had dents and could use a paint job, but it ran real good and I wanted to wait and see how things worked out in the new situation. I thought it best that I would go to the college library, study there, and come home at my regular times. Making these decisions actually took the pressure off me. For next month or so, everything went great.

 At dinner one night I sort of eased into telling Mama and Papa about the car, and said that Joe's father let me park it in his garage. I told them it was a hand-down gift for doing good and besides, the owner is going to buy a newer one, which was true. Telling them also about the vig business was a little more difficult. I wanted them to hear it from me, rather than from one of my customers or maybe Hunchback Hymie. I decided to wait until I thought the time was right, and said that I got a sort of promotion and I was now doing only the pickup of loan money payback. The new job gave me plenty of time to study and I expected to get straight A's from then on.

 Mama and Papa, after I told them this, said nothing, neither approving or disapproving. When we got up from the table, Papa said to me, "Let's go into the store. I want to check out some supplies and see if I need to order more."

 I said ok and followed him.

 Once inside he turned to me and said, "Marco, you

think you have a dumb greenhorn Papa?"

"No, Papa," I answered.

"Don't you think I know what you are now doing?" he asked. "It was bad enough you were working with bookmakers, but now you are even looking for more trouble, being a shylock's collector. Tell me what you do when your customers don't pay. Break their kneecaps or worse? I never thought my son would turn out to be a gangster."

"No, Papa, it's nothing like that," I said. "The clients are small business men just like yourself, and they couldn't get a loan from the bank. So we lend them the money on just their word that they'll pay back. I know Papa, the interest is high, but they have no place else to go. I haven't had any problem collecting, and if I do I try to work it out. If I can't, I'm out of it. I'm not a loan shark, just a collector for one. And Papa, I'm very upset you think I'm a gangster. I'm not and will never be one. I want you to know that I'm saving every penny so I can pay the scholarship loan back as soon as possible and put all this business behind me. I'll be a doctor, Papa, and I want so much for you and Mama to be proud of me." With that I went over to Papa and hugged him.

He hugged me back. "You are our life Marco," he said. "If we had to sell the store and pay back the loan, we would do it in a second."

"No Papa, I can handle this and I promise I'll let you know if I have a problem. I love you and Mama so much. I would never hurt you."

"I know and let's leave this just between us. Mama doesn't need to know. Now let's get back and have another cup of coffee."

And we did.

# XXVI

  Christmas break came and went. It seems that the time just flew by. Joe and I saw each other as often as possible. We went to dances, went bowling, ice skating, had dates with a lot of good looking girls. I had Christmas dinner at Joe's house. It was a big celebration with about eighteen of Joe's relatives attending, including Uncle Vito and his family. As usual I brought flowers, but this time I presented three dozen red roses. The meal was great and I actually was asked a lot of questions about college. Uncle Vito seemed pleased to see me.

  When it came to the seating arrangements, Joe and I were not invited to sit opposite each other next to where Uncle Vito was sitting. Instead Uncle Vito motioned for Vinnie to sit on his left and Paulie on his right, the seats we had previously sat in. He motioned for us to sit on either side of the table between two of his close relatives who were also members of our crew. I couldn't help but look at Paulie as he sat in the seat Uncle Vito chose for him. I caught him looking in my direction with a smirk on his face followed by a shit eating grin as if to say *you're not so high and mighty, you Jew bastard*. I looked away quickly so as not to show the anger I felt. I would talk it over with Joe at a later time.

  This time after coffee and desert, there wasn't the usual behind-closed-doors meeting. Presents were then taken from under the Christmas tree by Joe's mother with the help of Joe's sisters.

  It took about an hour of oohs and aahs and thank you's before Uncle Vito signaled to his family to get ready to leave. A few minutes later they did, after receiving the customary hugs and kisses accompanied with wishes for Merry Christmas and Happy New Year.

  School started up again the week after New Year's, and I think it was around the second week of the semester when I got a letter that Professor Quiring wanted to see me, giving me a day and time he wished me to come in. He must have checked my class schedule because the appointment was the hour break I had between classes.

  When I opened the letter and read its contents, I had a panic attack. He must have found out that I was a collector for a loan sharking operation. What else could it be? Was I going to be suspended or maybe even expelled from college? What was going to happen to my dream of becoming a doctor? What would Papa and Mama say? If this happened I could just see Mama shaking her finger at me while saying, "I told you no good was going to come out of this. I had this feeling from the beginning starting with bookmaking, then your so called 'route,' and now this. What are you going to do now since they chased you out of college? Graduate not a doctor but a real gangster? Or maybe it's better the Army will get you and send you off to war."

  It took a little bit of doing to get myself back to reality. Thinking of woulda, coulda, or shoulda couldn't help the situation. I made up my mind to just sweat it out and see what happens.

  The day and time of the meeting with the professor arrived and I was ushered into his office. I couldn't help it, but I was really nervous.

  "Sit down, Mr. Falcone," the Professor said.

  And as I sat down, my heart was in my mouth.

  The Professor continued, "I have a matter of vital interest to discuss with you."

  Now I was sure the axe was coming and I wasn't sure how I was going to handle it.

  "Are you alright, Mr. Falcone?" he asked me. "You look a little pale."

"I'm fine sir," I said. "Just a little indigestion."

"Well," the Professor went on, "since the start of the war, it was determined by the government that there will be a vast shortage of doctors. Hundreds and hundreds, possibly thousands of experienced doctors need to be available to treat our military and therefore these doctors have to be replaced in order to fill the void. This burden therefore lies on the medical schools to turn out more graduates, without cutting corners in their curriculum and quality of their education. Some of the undergraduate schools that have medical schools as part of their university were consulted and asked to submit a plan for the granting of a degree in medicine in a shorter time span than customary.

"With the cooperation of this college and our School of Medicine, the federal government has approved our plan to cut the time from eight years to five, two years college and three years medical school. This is a pilot program, limited to just a few universities. If this program works out, it will be offered to other universities. This is what brings us to you. We are offering this five-year program to just fifty second semester freshmen and I'd like to know if you have any interest in participating in it. It won't be easy In fact, it will be extremely difficult. We expect that between ten and fifteen percent will drop out, and go back to their normal four-year undergraduate courses."

I found myself very relieved that this conversation was not about my 'extracurricular' activities, and the difficulty of what he was proposing to me now started to sink in.

"If you accept this challenge," he continued, "you'll have to increase the number of courses you are now taking and need to take. You will be required to take a full course load over the summer. You can also forget about vacation breaks, including Christmas and Easter. Classes for this program will be held and attendance will be mandatory. You don't have to give me your answer now, but I expect to hear from you within a week. Yea or nay, either way. Any questions?"

"No sir," I replied.

"All right Mr. Falcone, when you decide, ask my secretary Mrs. Ault to set up an appointment. Good day."

I got to my feet and managed to say, "Good day to you, sir. Thank you for the opportunity." I think I staggered out of his office and nearly bumped into a classmate of mine, a real brain who was probably on his way into the professor's office for the same reason I was called in.

I couldn't believe my luck. What I thought would be a disaster, turned out to be a bonanza, albeit a challenging one. I gulped down a cup of coffee at the school cafeteria and just made it to my next class. While in class, I couldn't help but go over what had just happened, and I kept going over and over again. I tried taking some of the lecture notes, but I just couldn't concentrate. I was doing great in this class anyway, and would get the subject matter from the textbook.

After my last class, I hurried home, did my homework, and ran out to do some collections. Dinner was a little after eight; just Papa, Mama, and me. Sol had a dinner invite from one of his many lady friends. I told Papa and Mama of my meeting and they were thrilled, but Mama, just like all Mamas said, "Is this going to be too much for you? One of our customers, Mrs. Fano, told me she had a nephew who was so overworked in college that he got sick and had to drop out for a year."

"Don't worry, Mama," I said. "I can handle it."

After dinner I called Joe, telling him I wanted to make a meet with him the following night after he finished the route. "Just you and me, like old times," I told him. "I got something to tell you that's important."

I suggested that we meet at Katz's and get some real Jewish delicatessen, and it was agreed that we meet at seven.

The next night we met as planned ordered our pastrami on rye, half-sour pickles, and potato salad with a couple of Dr. Brown's Cel-Ray Soda. I remember Joe starting to wolf down the food and I jokingly asked, "The way you are gobbling down the sandwich, are you sure you're not Jewish?"

Between bites, Joe responded, "You never know. I heard a rumor that's been going on for a long time, that the lost tribe of Israel wound up in Sicily." We both laughed at the thought.

After we finished eating, I told Joe of my meeting with the Professor and of his offer. Joe was delighted and clapped me on the back. "This is great," he said. "Becoming a full-fledged doctor in five years. I can't believe it. You got to take this deal even if you have to break your balls doing it. Are you sure he said five years? Don't make sense and then it makes sense. The Army, Navy, and Air Force are going to need every doctor they can lay their hands on and the schools have to hurry up and graduate doctors."

"I know, I know," I said. "But I think it only fair that I run it by Uncle Vito and get his ok before I make the decision. I owe it to him. So, Joe, I'd like you to call him for me and set up an appointment. Don't tell him what it's about, and if he asks, just say that I need some advice from him. If you could ask for a night appointment so I don't have to miss classes, that would be great."

"Will do it," said Joe. "I still can't believe it, becoming a doctor in five years. Maybe I should have paid more attention to school and not screwed around. I think I would've made a great woman's doctor." And we both laughed.

"Now," Joe continued, "I got something to tell you that will knock your socks off. It has to do with Paulie."

"Since you are bringing him up, I was wondering why Uncle Vito sat Paulie and Vinnie next to him when those seats were ours since the first time he told us to sit there?"

"I got to let you in on a little secret, and what I tell you doesn't even get repeated."

"I'm all ears," I said. "Especially when it's about Paulie."

"Paulie's getting rejected on his military physical was a set up," said Joe. "He doesn't have flat feet. One of the examining doctors was on the take, and he was reached on Paulie's behalf. And this doctor came up with the flat feet diagnosis. So he was sent home. But this doctor was so greedy that the other legit examining doctors got pissed and put in a complaint. First thing that happened was that the doctor got transferred and is now under investigation. On top of that, all of the guys this doctor examined and rejected are going to be called back and re-examined. I heard that the military cops and F.B.I. are looking into this matter, and once they get involved, they are like blood hounds. Some of the rejected guys, rather than have a problem with the Feds or the M.P.'s, are enlisting in the Army, maybe the Navy, the Air Force, and even Marines. Others are going for the Merchant Marine. Your pal Paulie will probably sign up for the Merchant Marine. He got the idea if he does this, our connection with the Long Shoreman's Union will land him a cushiony job. I'm pretty sure that Uncle Vito knew this and invited Paulie and Vinnie to sit where they did. Uncle Vito is very smart in doing what he did. I think Vinnie might take over for Paulie if Paulie has to go in, and Uncle Vito wants Paulie to teach Vinnie the ropes. But Uncle Vito changed his mind. He decided to replace Paulie with "Donald Duck" Lugano, who just got out of the joint after eight years. He's an honorable stand-up guy. He wouldn't rat anybody out no matter what the D.A. offered, so he did the max. Besides, he can't get drafted. He's too old. Meantime, Vinnie stays with me."

    Joe, as promised, set up an appointment for me to meet with Uncle Vito at the Sicilian-American Cultural Club a couple of nights after I asked him to do this for me. It was at seven-thirty, and since my last class finished at five, I had time to go home, change clothes, grab something to eat, and head uptown to make the meet. I got to the club a little early, and was let in after giving my name and told to wait in a downstairs reception room until I was called. I waited about ten minutes until some guy came in and said, "Mr. Amatto will see you now."

    "Thanks," I said. I went up the stairs right up to his office door and knocked on it.

"Come in, come in, Marco." Uncle Vito got up to give me a hug and I kissed him on the cheek, always showing my respect. "So nice to see you, Marco. Tell me, how are your parents?"

"They are fine and they send their regards," I said.

"Send mine also," said Uncle Vito. "They are nice people." By this time he had taken his seat behind the big desk. He clasped his hands behind his neck and said, "How can I help you Marco? Joe said you needed my advice. If it's to help you pass a test or something like that, I would have to say no."

"It's nothing like that." And then I told him of the offer and that I wanted his advice as to accept it or not.

Without a moment's hesitation, Uncle Vito told me in no uncertain terms that I should take the offer and accept it right away. "This is a wonderful opportunity, so grab it."

"I might have a problem with collections," I said, "because I'm going to get a very heavy class schedule and may not be able to get to the customers as usual."

"Are you going to school Saturday or Sunday?" he asked.

"I don't know what my schedule will be."

"Well, let's wait and see what the schedule will be and we'll work out something. Most important is for you to get into that program, and we can go from there." Uncle Vito then got up from his chair, reached over the desk, and offered me his hand. I got up and we shook hands, which was a signal that the meeting was over.

I thanked Uncle Vito for his advice and started for the door. As I opened it, Uncle Vito said, "Marco," and I turned as he continued. "Again, send my regards to your parents. I hope to see them soon."

"I will give the message." I thanked him again and left.

The next day between classes, I stopped in at the Professor's office, saw Mrs. Ault, and asked for the earliest appointment. She looked at the calendar and glanced up at me, saying, "Are you free today at four?"

"My last class is over at four-fifteen," I said. "Would that be ok?"

"That's fine," she said. "I'll schedule you for four-twenty. Your name is…?"

"Marco Falcone."

"Ok, Mr. Falcone. See you then."

I got out of class at four-fifteen and hurried over to Quiring's office and got there a few minutes before four-twenty. As soon as I entered, Mrs. Ault said, "Hello, go right in. The Professor is expecting you."

I entered the office and greeted the Professor. "Hello sir," I said.

He motioned for me to be seated opposite him. "Well, Mr. Falcone, I assume you came to a decision. Are you here to share it with me?"

"Yes sir, I am."

"And it is?"

"I will be proud to accept your offer and participate in the program, and I want to thank you for this wonderful opportunity."

"I'm glad you took me up on this and I'm further certain that you'll do well," he said. "We'll get started with the rescheduling of your classes right away. The committee responsible for this will start over the weekend, and each participant will receive his new set up by the end of next week. There will be little if any room for schedule changes. Any questions?"

"None I can think of," I replied.

"Good. If you think of anything or have a problem, contact me. I think you made the right decision, Mr. Falcone. Good luck."

I knew this was my clue that the meeting was over. I left after saying goodbye and thanks.

The following days ran by, and I was kept busy with schoolwork and making the collections. At the beginning of the following week, I was notified to attend the rescheduling committee meeting that was held in one of the small lecture halls in the college. When I got there on the date and time assigned, I saw many of my classmates waiting also. Once we were all seated, the committee came in, sat down in front, and the chairman started with a recap of the program and how lucky we were to have been chosen. His talk was repetitive and started to get boring, until he said, "We have your rescheduled classes all set up for you and will divide you into groups alphabetically and go over them with you now." So we divided into five groups and received our new schedules once the committee men went over them with us.

When I got mine, I looked it over and over saying to myself, "This ain't going to be a piece of cake. They are really piling it on." But I made up my mind right then and there that I was going to make it.

I saw that my classes were eight-fifteen until late in the afternoon, with a couple of Tuesday and Thursday labs at night. One class was even scheduled on Saturday morning until noon. I figured out that I could still make the Saturday morning class and do the collections on Saturday afternoon or even Sunday when I had no classes. I caught up with Joe on Saturday night following the meeting with the committee, and he couldn't wait to see my new schedule.

After looking it over, he said, "This schedule is a bitch. How the hell do they expect anyone to get through this and stay sane?"

"That's not the whole story," I said. "Not only do we have to pass the courses, but we have to have a minimum of 3.75 average or out of the program you go."

"Holy shit!" Joe exclaimed. "How are you going to do it?"

"I don't know, but I'll do it no matter what."

"So," Joe said, "I guess we won't be seeing each other so often."

"We'll work it out. I'll have Saturday afternoons off and I'll have my collections done fast and I have all day Sunday, so we have plenty of time to get together."

"That's a plan. How about tomorrow at my house?"

"I'd love to, but need to pass. I gotta get things lined up for Monday and spend some time with my family. This new setup won't give me much time to see them. Hope you understand."

"I capisco," said Joe. "Give me a call Monday and let me know how you're doing."

"Ok, let's leave."

"Ok." Joe then dropped me off at the store and took off.

Keeping to the new schedule for the first two weeks was difficult, but it seemed all of my classmates in the new program and myself seemed up to the challenge. We were all fired up and took on our extra burden ambitiously. The professors were doing their part also. Since we were all ready into the third week of the semester, they organized seminars to give to those students in the program the first two weeks of instruction. By doing this, the students would be up to date in the subject matter. Days ran into weeks and weeks into months. The usual Easter school break came and went. The "Program Guys," as we were labeled, attended classes during this vacation period. I was really in a whirl of activity; early morning classes, a short break for lunch, then back to class after class after class, getting finished after five and sometimes six-thirty.

From college I tried to make at least two or three collection stops and once done, I went home, had dinner, and then hit the books. There was so much to learn, and so little time available to learn it. Sleep was the reward for completing the assigned study material and reviewing past lecture notes. I had science class followed by a lab class on Saturday morning, which ended at twelve noon. I hurried out of school and made rounds to make the other loan collections. I was usually finished by six. It seemed to be happening more and more often that one of my customers wanted to recommend one or two potential clients to me. Remembering Phil's instruction that anyone recommending a client is responsible to pay that client's loan in the event the new client couldn't pay, I explained this carefully. When the recommender heard they were responsible, they usually backed off. The ones that vouched got the loan for their friend or relative from us after I checked and got the ok from Phil.

I remember it was half way through the semester when the guy our group called The Brain cornered me after our physics class and said, "Marco, I had a brain storm. How about we ask some of the other guys that excel in a particular subject in our curriculum if we could meet once or twice a week and go over the material, clearing up any stuff that we don't understand or are unsure of. Since there is no competition among us, this will be a win-win situation. We could meet at my house if we can't find a more convenient place. We live in a brownstone right over the Brooklyn Bridge and there is a subway stop two blocks away."

"Sounds great to me," I said. "Count me in."

The Brain and I met the next day and we picked out potential candidates with backup choices in case any of our first picks weren't interested. During the next few days, we clued in our first picks and they all accepted. I think it was our "no competition" approach that swung the deal. We started the following week and it worked out great. Because the meeting proved so fruitful, we decided to meet at least twice a week, especially when there were quizzes and exams. This group kept together through college and even into medical school.

The end of the semester was coming up, and after naming ourselves "The Octets," our group felt real confident about doing well on the final exams, and we all passed with flying colors.

We had a week off before the summer session started. I got my collections over as early as possible and Joe and I met every chance we could and had dinner and hung around together as much as we could. It felt like old times. Joe told me everything was going great on his end. The route was a snap, and Vinnie was working out real good. Joe further told me his social life was even better. He was dating three or four different girls and was screwing two of them on a steady basis, and was sure he'd be fucking the other two shortly. I was jealous. It seemed I hadn't gotten laid for an eternity. I even thought of calling up and making an appointment with Brigette, but decided it might not sit right with Tony A.

# XXVII

School started up again, and we had to cover an entire semester in five weeks. The pressure was on, and because of "The Octet" meetings, we were all able to cope and do well on our finals. This time we had only five days off before the next semester started, and I decided to catch a movie matinee one day. When I came out of the Roxy Theater, I stopped in at the Automat to grab a bite.

The Automat, I remember, was always a lot of fun. Getting nickels from the cashier, dropping them into the slot next to the dish you wanted, and seeing the door open was a sight to see. I selected my customary "Chicken Pot Pie" dropped in my four nickels and put the dish on my tray. The place was jammed. I couldn't find a seat anywhere. All of a sudden a lady got up and I was just able to get her seat. As I sat down, I saw a nice looking lady sitting opposite me. She must have been around twenty-five, not beautiful but nice looking. Brownish hair, brown eyes.

"Would you mind holding my place here while I get silverware and a cup of coffee," I asked.

"No, I don't mind at all," she said with a smile.

I then noted her accent. It wasn't American. It sounded like English. I hurried back with the coffee and silverware and we started to chat. I remember sipping my coffee slowly because I wanted to get to know her better, and I noticed that she just lifted her coffee cup to her lips but didn't drink any. If she did, it was just a drop. I guess she also wanted to stay.

"Can I buy you a cup of coffee?" I asked.

"No thanks," she said. "But I will have a cup of tea."

"I'll be right back with two cups of tea." When I returned and placed the cup before her, I remarked, "From your choice of tea and your accent, I'll bet you are English."

"Good guess," she responded, flashing a smile that showed her beautiful set of teeth.

We both sipped our tea as if we were drinking in slow motion as we talked. It got to the point when I decided to take the bull by the horns and said, "It's a nice day, would you like to take a walk with me on Broadway?"

"I'd be delighted."

And so we walked up The Great White Way. She told me her name was Pamela, but her friends called her Pam, and her home was in Manchester.

"I'm Marco and I live here in New York," I told her.

"Tell me, Marco, what do you do?"

"I'm in a special accelerated college medical school program"

"So, you are going to be a doctor?" she asked.

"Hopefully."

"I'm sure you'll make it."

"And how about you, Pam?" I asked her.

"I'd rather not talk about it now. I'll tell you later."

Not wanting to take the chance of screwing things up between us, I said, "It's up to you, whenever you are ready to tell, I'll be ready to listen."

Before we knew it, we had walked to 59th Street, and I asked her if she would like to go with me to the Tavern on the Green in Central Park.

"Not today, Marco, maybe some other time," she said. "I better be going now." And she hailed a cab.

"Can I see you again?" I asked.

"I'd like that."

"How about tomorrow night for dinner?"

"Sounds wonderful," she replied.

"Can I pick you up?"

"No, I'll meet you."

"Since we didn't make the Tavern on the Green today,

how about tomorrow night at seven? I'll make the reservation in the name of Marco Falcone."

"So you are Italian?" she asked.

"I'll tell you all about it tomorrow night."

"That's cute," she said while entering the cab. Once seated and as the cab started to move, she waved and blew me a kiss. For the first time, I noticed she was wearing a wedding band.

*What the hell was this about?* I thought to myself. *Was she divorced, widowed or still married and is a cheater?* No matter what, I wanted to see her again. The only fly in the ointment was that if she was a cheater, the guy she was cheating had better not be connected.

I was at the Tavern on the Green at six-thirty, in case Pam showed up early. I wouldn't go to the bar because I wasn't twenty-one yet, and I didn't know what connection the families had here. I also couldn't take the chance of screwing up their liquor license if they got caught serving an underage guy. So I paced up and down in front of the restaurant. I think the doorman was getting a little suspicious, because he started giving me strange looks.

At about five to seven, a cab drove up and I saw Pam was in the back. I beat the doorman to the cab door and helped Pam out. I glanced at the meter and before she could open her purse, I paid the fare and included a nice tip. Pam looked very attractive. She had a sexy bod and great legs. Coupled with her other assets, she was a knockout. We had a great table right off the dance floor, enjoyed a fine dinner, and we danced a lot. She was a good dancer. Not great, but good. After the first few dances, she relaxed and melted her body into mine. It was a great feeling. I felt myself getting excited and realized she was getting excited too.

Over coffee and desert she said, "You asked me what I do. Although we just met, I know we have good energy between us, so I will trust you. If I'll tell you my story I want your word that you won't repeat anything I say to anyone. Do I have your word of honor?"

"You do," I replied.

"The reason I'm in the States is that I'm a ferry pilot," she said. "I fly war planes from here over to England for use by the RAF. When a plane is checked out and is ok to fly, I get all the flight instructions and go on my way. Once I deliver the plane to the designated English airport, I wait until a group of other ferry pilots is assembled and we are flown back to the States to pick up other planes."

"You mean you fly these planes all by yourself?"

"Not all the time," she said. "Sometimes, but not often, I have a co-pilot. I'm a good pilot. I've been flying for years. My father was a stunt flyer and gave me lessons since I was fourteen. I was licensed when I was sixteen and have been employed as a commercial pilot since I was eighteen. Once the war started, the Battle of Britain was forced upon us. Your president got the Lend Lease program into law. Since our country was dangerously short of aircraft, the Lend Lease program provided the planes. Pilots were now needed to fly them. British-licensed, mostly women pilots were recruited, including me, to sign up for the ferry program. The pay is fair, but the benefits are very good. We get to fly, eat decent meals including steaks and chops in the States, and have lodging in good hotels. Any more questions?"

"Let's dance some more," I said. "I'd like to feel your body against mine."

"Let's do it then," she said with a wry grin.

And we danced and danced until the band took a break. Once we were seated, I took a shot by saying, "Pam, it's question time."

"Marco, just two or three more, and question time is over."

"Is that a wedding ring you are wearing?" I asked.

"Yes, I'm married."

I was shocked that she said it so matter-of-factly. "So, how come I'm out with you and you are out with me?"

"You see, my husband is a tank commander and was

one of those that stayed behind to see that the maximum number of British troops could escape at Dunkirk. He and his group were captured by the German's and he is now in a P.O.W. camp in Germany. I know he's ok because the Red Cross inspected the camp and reported he's unharmed. The Germans treat officers a little better than privates and non-commissioned officers. I love him and can't wait to see him again. Next question."

"I don't know how to put this," I said, "but I'll say it anyway. So, why me, and what are we doing here?"

"Marco, my darling," she said. "I have needs. I have not been with anyone for a long time, and I am unfulfilled. I'm in love with my husband, but I want a lover basically for not good, but great sex. And I want someone who is not interested in romance, just great sex. I won't get involved with anyone at home because all of the young studs are away fighting the Nazis, and besides that, our country is small compared to yours and news travels fast. The gossip about me and another bloke would not be too good. Interested in becoming a hero's wife's lover?"

I was stunned but kept my head on my shoulders, and quickly yet confidently replied, "You got your wish. I'm just what you ordered. When do you want to get started?"

"How about tomorrow?" she said.

"How about when we leave the restaurant?"

"Tonight is no good," she said. "Tomorrow is better. Are you available tomorrow around lunch time?"

"Can make it any time you want," I said, trying to fully comprehend my good fortune.

"Let's meet tomorrow around twelve."

"I can pick you up," I said.

"No, it's better if I meet you."

"Ok, twelve it is. Say you meet me at the restaurant at the Hotel New Yorker."

"I know where it is," she said. "I'll meet you in the lobby at twelve."

"Let me at least drop you off tonight at your place, in

case you change your mind about being together tonight."

"I won't change my mind, but you can drop me off at my hotel."

We exited the restaurant, the doorman signaled for a cab, and once we were seated, the driver turned to us and asked, "Where to?"

Pam quickly replied, "Hotel Gramercy Park."

I couldn't believe what I heard. What a break. Her hotel is just a couple of blocks from the college. This is going to be better than I expected.

We got to her hotel in no time at all, and after leaning over and giving me a kiss - nothing passionate – said, "Twelve noon tomorrow."

"I'm looking forward to it," I replied.

"So am I," she said, and then she entered the hotel.

The next day, I got to the New Yorker about twenty to twelve and found a comfortable chair in the lobby where I could see the front doors. I daydreamed about her and the coming events, and when I next looked at my watch, it read twelve-ten. Where the hell could she be? Was this all a put on?

I fidgeted in my chair and glanced at my watch again. It was twelve-thirty-five. Now I was sure something was wrong. I wanted to phone the hotel, but I didn't know her last name. Then I got an idea. I left the New Yorker and stopped off at one of the closeout stores on 34$^{th}$ Street and bought a pocket book for three dollars. I grabbed a bus and got off at 23$^{rd}$ Street and walked over to the Gramercy Park Hotel. When I got up to the front desk, the clerk said: "Can I help you, sir?"

"I don't know," I replied. "I found this pocket book on the floor of the cab and wanted to return it. The only thing in it was a piece of torn postcard with the name Pamela on it and the name of this hotel."

"Oh," the clerk replied. "It must belong to our guest Pamela Winfield in Room 634. I think she is still in her room. I'll phone her and tell her that her bag has been found. What's your name?"

"Marco Falcone," I answered.

"You can go right up. Miss Winfield will be glad to see you."

I took the elevator up to the sixth floor, walked to 634 and knocked.

"Come on in, it's unlocked," called Pamela from inside. "Close the door behind you and lock it."

Once I did this, I glanced around the room and saw Pam sitting on the couch, her legs crossed showing her sexy thighs. As I approached her, I didn't know if it was passion or anger, but I blurted out, "What the fuck is going on? You stood me up. I haven't figured it out whether I should chase you down to get even or to get fucked, or both."

Pam then stood up, and the filmy gown she was wearing showed every part of her luscious body. It was plain to see that she wasn't wearing any underwear. She moved slowly to me, grabbed me and thrust her tongue into my mouth, flicking it in different directions and moving it with different tempos. When she stopped, she stepped back a pace or two and before I could say anything, she said, "Sweet thing, you passed the test. I knew you would. I, as you say, stood you up on purpose, just to find out how important I am to you and how hard you would try to find me. I don't know how you thought of the pocket book ploy and I don't care. It worked, and that's all that matters. Is this worth your effort to find me?" And with that she opened her gown and it slid to the floor. She was standing before me completely nude, statuesque as a goddess.

"You are so right, it was worth it," I said.

"Good," she said. She picked up her gown and put it on. "I was counting on you finding me, so I ordered up a light lunch and tea."

While eating she asked me about my personal life, and I told her a little but not much, just enough to satisfy her curiosity. I then asked, for some unknown reason, what her maiden name was, and she replied, "Winfield. My married name is Thomas. I use my family name in the airline business, because my pilot's license is in the name of Pamela Winfield and it was more convenient to just leave things as they were." She paused and grinned at me. "My time for a few questions, since we are going to be fuckmates, I'd like to ask about any sexual preferences or inhibitions and also about your experience. By being candid with each other, we can bring on the optimum degree of pleasure. The great part of good sex is pleasing one's partner to the utmost. So, my dear Marco, are you sexually mature? Really mature? Are you up to trying different things?"

"I sure am," I said, not knowing what else to say.

"Any positions or techniques that you particularly enjoy?"

"With me, anything and everything goes." Thinking fast, I added, "Let's experiment and see what pleases us the most."

"I'd like that. I think we will do very well together. Good sex to me is very important. I feel my life is not complete without it. Without the satisfaction, I'm not whole, and I need this feeling of wholeness, especially when I'm piloting the planes across the Atlantic. So in a way, making me feel 100% content is your contribution to the war effort. By the way, Marco, you do have condoms with you, don't you?"

Good thing I had picked some up at the drug store the previous day. "I brought some with me."

"How many, may I ask?"

"Six," I replied. "You think that's enough for this afternoon?"

"You are very cute." With that she got up, took me by the hand, and led me into the bathroom. "Let's take a shower together. This is a good way to get acquainted." She dropped the gown and then proceeded to help me get undressed.

Once I was naked, she looked me over, carefully remarking, "You have a great body, and I know you'll make a good lover."

During the shower, we soaped each other, swapped spit, fondled each other, and then we toweled each other dry. What an experience.

Once we were somewhat dry, Pam said, "Take your condoms." And I reached down and took the package out of my pants. She then took me by the hand and led me to the inviting bed. Once we were both in, we turned to each other and the real fun started. We explored each other's bodies from head to toe, using our both hands and mouths. I took my cues from her. I can remember how exciting it was. I reached out to grab a condom when she whispered, "Not yet."

And then she went down on me and a few seconds later, I exploded. I could hardly catch my breath, I was so consumed with pleasure. Pam then took my head and gently pushed it down to where she wanted it, and I did her. I know she must have loved it, because she moaned and groaned with pleasure every few seconds. A short while later; she reached down and pulled me off her. "Now it's time to put on the rubber," she said. And I did.

We fucked at first like two animals in heat, rested a bit, and then made sharing and caring love. Pam taught me positions I never heard of. We must have continued this great, great sex for about three hours. I used four out of the six rubbers I bought. I guess Pam had an effect on me that I had never experienced before. She made me want to please her more and more. It was thrilling for me to be able to do this.

I guess we both must have dosed off for a couple of hours, and the next thing I felt was being gently shaken awake. "Time to get up Marco, it's getting late," she said. "We have to shower, get dressed, and I'll let you take me to dinner."

"I'd love to take you to dinner. Any preferences?"

"Yes, a big juicy steak."

We both got up, sort of drained but happy, went to the bathroom, showered, dried up and got dressed. Once outside the hotel, I hailed a cab and directed him to Al and Dick's Steakhouse on 54th Street. On the way there, we didn't say very much, but her hand said a lot by rubbing my thigh all the way up to my crotch, and it worked.

"I was trying to see if you have anything left," she said. "I'm proud of you Marco. We'll be great together."

The cab pulled up in front of the restaurant. I paid the driver and we entered. The maitre d' seated us at a very nice table and we enjoyed a wonderful steak dinner with all the trimmings. Pam had a glass of wine and I had a club soda. Our conversation during dinner was light and humorous, and we laughed a lot. Pam lit a cigarette over coffee and desert, and asked me if I wanted one. I answered, "No, I don't smoke."

"That's strange," she said. "I thought everybody in America smoked."

And I laughingly replied, "I heard smoking interferes with the ability to perform."

"Well, I'm glad you never took up smoking." Pam then got serious and said, "I don't know when I will get a call and will have to go to work, and moreover, I won't know till I get the call where to report. I can't tell you or anyone anything about where and when I have to report. But I would like to see you again."

"Are you kidding?" I said. "I'd love to see you again."

"Let's leave love out of it," she said. "I'll tell you what, give me a phone number where you can be reached, or where I can leave a message for you." I gave her the phone number at the store, and she continued, "If I cannot talk to you in person I'll just say 'Ask Marco if we could go to the movies on Saturday.' This will tell you that I'm on the move. When I get back into town, I'll call and leave the message asking you to get me the record of "Home on the Range." Once you get this message, you can call the hotel and they'll connect you.

"One more thing, when we make up to meet, I think it best for you to book a room for the night at the hotel, same floor if possible. Hotel clerks have a habit of being nosy and talkative and it's best for us to keep things low key. Is this ok with you? In my line of work a security breach can be very dangerous."

"I understand," I said. "No problem. It's a done deal."

A few moments later she said, "It's time to go, lover boy, but I do believe you knocked me out. I'm going to sleep good tonight, except for the times I'll wake up thinking of how good you made me feel."

I signaled the waiter, paid the check, and hailed a cab that took us back to her hotel. On the way back, we said little, but I remember her resting her head on my shoulder and holding my hand. When we got to the hotel, she said, "Don't get out, we'll say goodbye here. It's better that way."

She then gave me a kiss on the cheek, a hug, then got out and entered the hotel.

"Where to?" the driver asked me, and I gave him the address at the store. Normally I would have paid the fare and taken the subway home, but tonight, it was cab all the way.

The next day it was back to college. I admit I was a little sore all over because of the hectic activity the day before, but it was well worth it.

I waited until my classes for the day were over and phoned the hotel. I was a little disappointed when the clerk informed me that Miss Winfield was not taking any calls. I was going to walk over to the Gramercy to look for her, but changed my mind. There must be a good reason for her not taking calls, and I let it go at that. Besides that, I had to get over to the club and deliver the vig money I had collected the past week.

After dropping the vig off, I went home. Upon entering the store, Papa greeted me by saying, "Some girl called for you about an hour ago and left a message for you something about going to the movies on Saturday."

Before Papa could say anything more, I said, "Thanks," and went to my room.

Over dinner that night, the conversation was casual, mostly about school, and when Papa again mentioned the phone call, Mama's ear perked up.

"So, who's the girl?" Mama asked.

"Believe it or not, Mama, I met a girl in the Automat, and we started to talk and I invited her to go to the movies on Saturday."

"So what does she do?" Mama asked.

"She works for a transportation company," I said.

"Doing what?"

"I don't know, I never asked. I'll let you know as soon as I know."

Mama was about to ask me more questions when I stopped her by saying, "Mama, after we go to the movies I'll know more about her and I'll give you the full history."

"I'm sure she's a nice girl," said Mama, "but remember you have a lot of college work and you cannot let anything interfere with it."

Papa interrupted by saying, "He's nineteen years old, leave the boy alone. I should say leave the man alone. Other boys his age are in the Army fighting overseas."

With that I finished my coffee and cake, I kissed Mama and Papa and went to my room where I hit the books for a couple of hours. Then I showered and went to bed.

The following weeks went by so fast. School, collections, Octet meetings, quizzes and final exams. I think it was during the last week of the second summer semester when I got the message I was waiting for. It was Pam and she left word to see if I could get her the record "Home on the Range."

I was thrilled. I wasted no time and raced to a phone, called the hotel and was connected. The sound of her voice excited me all over.

"Welcome back," I said. "I can't wait to see you."

"Me too," she replied. "Phone me when you check in. I think check in time is around twelve noon. You might want to order some lunch for us. I have to go now. See you Sunday, my sweet chap."

I called the Gramercy and booked a room. Luck was with me, because they had one available on Pam's floor, pretty close to her room, and I was even able to get the student rate. As I left the store, I waived to Mama and Papa who fortunately for me were waiting on customers.

I told them, "We have a big test tomorrow and we are going to have to study all night, so we took a hotel room near the college. This is an important test and we need to do very good. I'll call you after the test is over and let you know how I made out."

Mama and Papa, it seemed in unison, yelled out as I went out the door, "Good luck. We will be praying for you."

At about ten to twelve on Sunday, I checked in carrying a small suitcase that I bought at a second hand store in my neighborhood and went up to the room. I immediately phoned Pam, who answered on the first ring. After greeting each other warmly - very warmly - she said, "Why not call down and order lunch for the two of us. Sandwiches and tea would be great."

When the food arrived, I phoned Pam, gave her my room number, and a couple of minutes later there was a knock on my door.

"It's open," I said, and as she came in I added, "Close the door and lock it behind you."

"Copycat," she said, laughing as she locked it behind her.

We embraced and started to get heated up when she stopped me. "Let's eat first and then have fun," she said.

We both gobbled our food down, and then the rest of the afternoon was a blur. Our previous sexual encounters were amateurish compared to this afternoon's event. Later on, close to six, we dragged ourselves out of bed, went to dinner and came back to the hotel. We got up to my room and she said, "I think I'll call it a night and go to my room. I never know when I will get a phone call regarding my job. Besides, you have school tomorrow. What time do you have to be there?"

"Eight-thirty," I replied.

"You better get a good night sleep. If I get into bed with you, I might be keeping you up all night doing what we both like to do."

"Come on, let's spend the night together," I laughingly suggested. "Besides, I got the room booked until twelve tomorrow. I'll tell you what, let's just try to get some sleep. If we can't, you can always go back to your room. Waddya say?"

She thought for a moment and said, "Ok, let's see what happens. I'll be back in a moment. Leave the door open, and you, darling boy, get ready for bed and sleep, and I mean sleep."

I washed up, brushed my teeth, and then, keeping my undershorts on, climbed into bed. Good thing I took my books with me. Pam came in a couple of minutes later and undressed in the bathroom. Couldn't understand why she chose to undress in the bathroom, since we had both been naked just a few short hours ago. I guessed I had a lot to learn about women. While she was in the bathroom, I called the front desk and left a wakeup call for seven in the morning. Just as I finished, Pam came out in a pajama outfit, climbed into bed next to me, gave me a big hug and a little non-sexy kiss, said goodnight, and turned on her side with her back toward me.

"What time are you getting up in the morning?" she asked.

"I left a wakeup call for seven."

"Good. If I'm asleep, be sure to wake me up. Maybe we'll have time for a cup of coffee before you leave for school and I go back to my room. Besides, I have a zillion things to get started on tomorrow."

I was smart enough not to ask what they were. Before I knew it I was fast asleep.

I was suddenly awoken by the phone ringing.

I reached over and picked it up and heard, "Good morning, it's seven a.m."

When I turned towards Pam, she was up and heading for the bathroom. A few minutes later, I heard the flushing of the toilet, then silence. When the bathroom door opened, I saw that Pam was fully clothed. She approached the bed and said, "No coffee this morning. I'm going back to my room and get started on things that need to be done and you, my lover man, get ready for school."

As she reached the door, she turned and said, "It was so

nice sleeping with you. Let's do it again soon. Be in touch." And then she left.

As I mulled over a muffin and cup of coffee, I couldn't help but thinking, I am the luckiest nineteen-year-old guy in the world. I'm getting a paid for education, will get an M.D. in about two and a half years, have a car, am making good money working for the shylocks, and just had the best fucking imaginable without any entanglements. What a great life.

Also, the overnight test preparation excuse for the hotel room seemed to satisfy Mama and Papa's questions. In my mind, I was not lying to them when I called them the next morning after spending the night with Pam. When asked how I did, I told them, "I passed with flying colors." I was just quoting Pam.

Pam and I kept seeing each other every chance we could. But as time passed, the frequency of our being together was less and less often. The supply of planes to be delivered increased substantially and the supply of pilots was limited.

College also became very demanding. Our Octet study group was a life saver, and I don't think I could have done it without them.

# XXVIII

1942 came and went.

I saw Joe when I could but it was not as often as before. I did manage to have dinner at his house about once every two months or so, and it was nice seeing Uncle Vito and the Mancuso family again. Questions about my progress in college took up a good portion of the conversations. Uncle Vito said little but nodded in approval when I answered the questions the family asked.

Paulie and Vinnie continued to sit in the chairs we originally sat in, adjacent to Uncle Vito, and I caught Paulie looking at me with the crappy smirk that he reserved for me. I just smiled back at him, which pissed him off more.

A couple of weeks later, I phoned Joe. "What say we have dinner Monday night," I said. "Right after I drop the package off."

"Sounds good," said Joe. "Monday night it is."

"How about Gallagers for a steak? Seven o'clock?"

"Seven it is."

We met, hugged each other, and ate some great steaks and all the trimmings. We had small talk, much to do about nothing. But then over coffee, Joe whispered to me, "I have a little news that might be of interest to you."

"What's it about?" I asked.

"Paulie got the letter from the draft board. They are going to re-examine him, and once they find out he's ok, he's going to be 1A, and off to the war he goes."

"He got away with it once," I said. "What makes you think he won't come up with another scheme?"

"He already has one. He's going to join the Merchant Marine, get a couple of months training and then through our connection with the Long Shoreman's Union get a no-show job somewhere around the docks."

"No shit, he has all the luck."

"Let's see what happens."

Sure enough a couple of weeks later, Joe told me that Paulie had signed up with the Merchant Marine and was told to report the following week for the three-month training period some place in upstate New York. Joe further added with a smile, "You'll be glad to hear, he left yesterday. And now Donald took over."

Things were sure going to be better without Paulie around. I went back to my regular college classes and collection routes, and was looking forward to the next session with Pam, but no such luck. The phone call about going to the movies came in later on that week, but as it turned out, it was for the best.

Because of an anticipated shortage of food, gasoline, and especially automobile tires, the U.S. established a mandatory rationing program. The focus on tires was strong because the Japanese had captured the major countries producing natural rubber. The U.S. strove to develop synthetic rubber plants and it would take some time for these plants to become functional. Tires were in high demand, and good money could be made by supplying them within or even bypassing the rationing system.

It was near the end of the second semester of the summer session when Papa gave me a message to call Joe.

"Be outside your store this Sunday at two o'clock and I'll pick you up," said Joe. "Don't wear your Sunday clothes or shoes." Joe's tone was so matter-of-fact that I just said ok. At two, Joe picked me up and we drove over the Manhattan Bridge to a warehouse section in Masbeth, and Joe parked behind a large warehouse that had a loading dock. On the way over, I asked Joe, "What's going on?"

"We're on a pickup caper," he said.

"What the hell are you talking about?"

"We're going to get a trailer truck here at three o'clock loaded with brand new tires and were going to help unload the truck and then reload it on to our own trucks. When we are finished loading our trucks, they'll take off and so will the trailer and then we'll get out of there. That's all you need to know about this operation."

For the first time, I felt my anger towards Joe really rising and getting heated and I said, "Bull Shit. I want to know what's going on and what am I getting into."

"Ok, I'll tell you," said Joe with a sigh. "We got a guy driving this trailer from Ohio loaded with new tires that he's supposed to deliver to a distribution place in Long Island. He's going to stop off at a diner near here and while he's in there eating, we take the truck, drive it over here and unload it. And then, we load the tires onto our trucks. Once the trailer is unloaded, it'll be ditched far from here.

"It's a sweet deal 'cause the driver is in on it and we even got a set of keys from him. The driver takes his time eating and when he comes out, he goes into his act when he sees the truck gone and calls the cops. By the time the cops come to the diner and take the information and start the search, the trailer has already been ditched and our trucks are on their way to our warehouses in other parts of the city."

"I don't want to get involved with this," I said. "I ain't gonna be part of this. I want out."

I didn't like the look on Joe's face when he turned to me and said, "Listen and listen good. You're in and you can't get out. This is our crew affair and we all have to do what we are told, no matter what we think or say, and especially you, Marco. You're taking the dough for school, have a tailor-made money making collection route to fit in with your schedule, and you're telling me you want out. I'm telling you, you're in and we'll be in until you're told different. Capiche?"

I didn't answer for a moment or two. I let Joe's words

sink in, and once I realized he was telling like it was and maybe dropping some sort of a threat hint, I decided I had no choice, so I turned to him and said, "Capisco."

"No more talk or bullshit about not being part of our crew, and when you're called to help out, you do as you're told. Let's not talk about this again."

We pulled up to a warehouse that was guarded by two guys who nodded hello to Joe. We walked through a metal door into a small office and through another door into the warehouse itself, where we were greeted by some of the guys I had seen at the club, and others I had never met before. In all, there were about twenty of them. They all seemed to know Joe and gave him the glad Hello. He introduced me by just saying, "Meet Marco." They nodded hello, and I nodded back.

Joe then led me to a small group where greetings and small talk took place. About ten minutes later, one of the guys from outside, a big guy with narrow eyes, came in and said, "The truck is here. It's going to back into the loading dock in a couple of minutes, and I'll raise the overhead doors. Once this is done you all got to move fast to unload, and I mean fast. There are plenty of dollies and hand trucks, so some of you load up and bring the tires in, and the rest of you stack them. Once the trailer is unloaded and out of here, our delivery trucks will come in and we'll load them. I'm gonna tell you once, and that should be enough. Work together and work fast, and don't fuck up."

I could hear the sound of the truck getting close and a few minutes later the overhead doors were raised and two of our guys opened the back doors of the trailer. It was loaded with tires that smelled of fresh rubber.

A group of us grabbed hand trucks and with the help of four other guys loaded up and quickly moved into the warehouse, where the guys who did the unloading directed us where to leave the loaded hand trucks. We then grabbed empty ones and ran back to the trailer to pick up another load.

Once we got the system down pat, it worked like a charm, and the entire truck was empty of tires in about an hour and a half. Once we were finished, the overhead door was closed and the empty trailer truck took off. When we could no longer hear the sound of the truck's motor, it seemed that all the guys went around hugging and congratulating each other. I remember them saying, "This was a piece of cake, what a score, this beats the other small time cowboying gas stations for a couple of bucks." Then one of the guys who were guarding the outside came in and everybody all of a sudden became quiet.

"Listen you guys," he said. "You did good, but the job is half done. Our trucks will be here in ten minutes. There's room on the loading dock for two trucks to back in at a time. As soon as they do, we'll raise the door and you'll load the trucks by stacking the tires. Once the two trucks are loaded, they'll leave and two more will take their place. And you'll keep on loading until all the tires are out of here. Then you'll look around and make sure you don't leave anything, and I mean anything. That means no cigarette butts, cigar butts, or their packages. If you took a piss or even a shit, take some toilet paper and wash the seat and use some more to rub the sink and any other place you put your hands and take the rest of the toilet paper with you and dump it some place." We all heard engines outside. "I think the trucks are here so let's get going. One more thing, when you get your share of the score, we want you to bury the money until we tell you it's safe."

The overhead door opened and we loaded up using the same system. Before I knew it the trucks were loaded and they disappeared, with the exception of one large truck.

"Ok," the main guy said, "now load all of the dollies and hand trucks and throw your gloves in the truck outside. Load them right so that they all fit in."
We did and the truck took off. By this time, the guys were wiped out and they left after saying goodbye. And Joe and I left too. While driving home, we didn't say too much, but I had a question and decided to ask it.

"Is it ok for me to ask who those two guys were that sort of ran things?" I asked.

"These two were sent from one of the other branches of our family," Joe replied. "We're the soldiers, and they're the captains. It's as simple as that. They are in charge of this job."

"How did they get to be captains?"

"They got promoted because they learned how to take charge and earned big for the crew and especially for the Padrone. Like I told you before, it's all about earning. And the bigger the earner you are the more you move up." Joe hesitated for a second, then broke into his great smile and said, "That's enough schooling from me to you today, especially since you are a college boy."

As he dropped me off at the store he continued, "You did ok today, and it didn't go unnoticed. Now go back to do what you have to do. Let's get together this week if you have time."

As I got out of the car, I said, "Thanks, Joe, for giving me the score. I'm not too happy about it, but I guess I'll have to live with it."

"Who said you have to be happy with it? If and when you're called, you go and do the right thing."

"Ok," I said, "We're still brothers, ain't we?"

"Sure are," Joe answered as he drove off.

As I walked through the store, I said hello to Mama, Papa and Sol, and told them I was going to take a shower. Then it was time to eat dinner with only Mama and Papa. Sol had again been invited to dinner, Papa told me, by a rich Italian woman who lost a husband about a year before. I kidded with Sol about it before he left, saying, "Be careful. If you don't do right by her the whole family will come after you, and they mean business."

Sol answered, "She seems like a very nice lady, and she knows I'm Jewish and she told me she likes Jewish men because they know how to treat a lady right."

"So go and have a good time," I said.

As we ate, Mama and Papa asked me about school and I told them my schedule and the kind of classes I was taking. Mama then took up the subject of what she called 'The Girl.'

"Did you see her lately?" she asked.

"No, Mama," I replied.

"What does she do? Tell me again."

"She works for a big transportation company."

"But what does she do?" Mama asked again.

"She has something to do with moving equipment," I said.

"So she works for a moving company?"

"Something like that."

"Is she Jewish?"

"I don't know, I never asked her," I said, and it struck me that I never had.

"Well, is she at least Italian?" Mama asked.

"No, Mama, she's English."

"I'll bet she's not Jewish."

"There's a lot of Jews in England," I said.

"I'll still bet you she's not Jewish."

"Mama, when the time is right, I'll ask her," I said. I changed the subject by asking Papa how business was going.

"We have plenty of customers," Papa replied, "but we can't get enough merchandise to sell them all they want, because they don't have enough ration stamps. I can't order more because my suppliers will only give me merchandise equal to the number of stamps we have. The more stamps we have the more we can order."

Mama added, "So we all have to sacrifice, but that's nothing compared to what the boys are doing fighting those German *Momsers*."

Papa then asked, "Do you have a lot of studying to do tonight?"

"Yes, a lot," I replied.

"Ok, you better get started."

I kissed Mama and Papa goodnight, then went to my room and studied for about three hours before turning in.

Final exams came and went, and our group did well. We were primed to do the second and last year of college and then it was on to med school. The workload that semester was very heavy, and coupled with the collection work it all kept me very busy.

This one night I actually had a decent night's sleep, but it was interrupted by my thinking of Pam. I hadn't heard from her for close to a month. I kept on thinking about her flying alone over the ocean and imagining all the bad things that could happen. *No*, I thought to myself. *She's a great pilot and will call me soon.*

About a week later I got the message I was hoping for and I met her the following Sunday. We made up for lost time, over and over again.

Later on, as we finishing dinner, Pam looked at me and said, "I need to tell you this because I truly trust you, and I know whatever I tell you now will go no further. There is a rumor going around that a group of us are going to be transferred, maybe to cities closer to where the planes are made. These new planes now have larger fuel capacities and can reach our given destination from all parts of the U.S. and Canada without having to refuel. We can now get more planes over in a lot less time. The scuttlebutt is that I will be picked as the new group leader of the transferees."

"How good is the rumor?" I asked.

"From what I heard, pretty damned good."

"When?"

"No way to tell," she said. "In any event, no matter where I'll be as group leader, I should have more time off and I'll have the privilege of catching planes going each way, especially to New York. I'll make sure we'll keep our fuck fest alive and kicking for a long time." She leaned closer to me "You are so good in bed, Marco. You make me feel like a woman again."

I really didn't know how to answer that one, so I just smiled.

"Let's play this by ear for now," she said, "and I'll let you know somehow where I am once I am transferred. For now let's just have fun. Let's go back to the hotel and go to bed, and

I don't mean sleep." She paused. "That's if you're up to it? I promise to let you get a couple of hours of slumber before we get at it again."

When the phone rang at seven the next day, this time I had a problem getting out of bed. I was sore all over due to the sexual gymnastics Pam and I performed, but mentally, I was feeling terrific. I eased out of bed, washed up, got dressed and left Pam sleeping. She looked so calm, peaceful and beautiful laying there. I scribbled a note telling her to call me and then I left. I just made it to class.

When I got home that night, Sol told me, "You got a message from some girl saying something about the movies. I'm sorry, Marco, I didn't get the whole message, because we were very busy when the phone rang."

I guessed Pam was on her way.

I went back to study, collections, study, collections, tests, collections, and it seemed I had no time for anything else.

It was about a month after the tire caper and as I was dropping off the vig money one day, Phil said to me, "Come into the club. Sallie wants to see you."

I said ok and followed Phil as Sallie waved to me. Sallie motioned for me to sit down at his table. After the usual greetings were made, he said, "You did good on the tire thing. The report came back that you pitched in real good." He took an envelope from his back pocket and handed it to me. "Here is your end. Bury it for at least two to three months and even then don't make a show that you got sudden cash."

"No problem," I said.

"Two of the jerkoffs that worked with you, even though you were all warned to keep a low profile, went out and splurged. One idiot got his *amante* a fur coat and the other moron bought his wife showy jewelry. It's lucky for us that they came to a little celebration party we had and we spotted what they were wearing. These two could've gotten us into a lot of trouble. The local cops and even the feds are looking for anything that might give them an idea where to look further." He looked hard at me. "So what would you do college boy?"

"I don't know," I said.

"Well, we took the mink coat and the jewelry away from them and told them they could have it back in three months once we could get both insured. This seemed to satisfy the women. Remember, women who get pissed have a habit of sharing their anger with their friends, and that could lead to us having a headache. Also, we didn't want to make small of these guys in front of their dames. This could lead to a headache too. We took care of that later. Ok, kid, beat it."

"Thanks and Goodnight," I said, and left.

Once I got in the car, I opened the envelope and counted out five hundred dollar bills. I could hardly believe my eyes Five hundred dollars for just a few hours' work. This dough went right into my stash and would help me pay off my loan sooner. In the back of my mind the thought sneaked through that I could make a lot more money loansharking and hijacking than I could possibly make as a doctor. I quickly chased this idea out of my head and replaced it with, *You always wanted to be a doctor and you are on your way and you will be a doctor.*

After I got done berating myself, I smiled and thought, *I'm proud of you, Marco,* and let it go at that.

# XXIX

College was still a grind, and our Octet meetings were more and more important, but our tempers and patience got shorter and shorter as the class schedule became harder and more intense. Good thing we had the "Brain" as the chair, because he was able to keep us from blowing up and breaking up the group.

Final exams came and so did Christmas and New Year's. 1943 was here. We got our final grades and we all did well. We had two semesters left before starting med school; the spring semester and the summer one.

All this time I didn't hear from Pam, but I didn't have but a few moments now and then to even think about her and us. Even couldn't spare much time to see Joe or his family. I made sure, however, to make a meet with Joe once a week and with Uncle Vito and the family about once a month.

A few weeks into the semester, I met Phil as usual to deliver the package. "Sallie wants to see you," he said to me. "So come on in."

"Sure," I said, and I followed him in and waved to the guys as Phil and I walked over to the table where Sallie was sitting.

"Have a seat college boy," Sallie said to me. "How're you doing?"

"Ok, so far," I said.

"We got a little problem and it needs to be solved."

I decided to say nothing and just sat there and listened.

"The problem is," Sallie continued, "a lot of our street guys got drafted, and so we're kinda shorthanded. We were counting on you to fill in when we need you but I got the word you ain't able to help us out, except maybe on a Saturday or a Sunday. Understand we can't do the things we have to do to fit in with when you can make it. Now you tell me how we can solve this situation."

"I don't know," I said. "As it is I have to squeeze the collections somehow during the week. I'm lucky I don't have any problems on that end. The customers pay the vig off and then most of them renew. I get finished with college this August and start medical school in September. From now to then, I am jammed up. Maybe medical school will be easier than what I'm doing now and I'll have more time to do what I'm asked once I start med school."

"Good answer," Sallie said with a grin. "Just what I expected from you. We like you, Marco. You proved yourself to be stand-up. You know that there is a lot riding on you, so it came down from the boss that we use you for now when you can help out and if it don't interfere with your schooling. Stay in touch." And that signaled the meet was over.

As I left the club, I got the feeling that if called, I better not refuse too often, but I decided not to worry about it.

It was about two weeks after the meet with Sallie that I got a phone call from Joe who told me, "We're going on a little treasure hunt on Sunday. Put on your old clothes and shoes and take along a heavy sweater and warm jacket. I'll pick you up at ten." And he did just that.

Once I got in the car, I said, "What's up?"

Joe came back with, "We're getting a big truckload of sides of beef and the idea is to cut them up and sell the front end to the kosher butchers and the ass end to regular butchers. We get a lot more money from the kosher guys."

"But this meet has to be approved by a special Rabbi for it to be kosher," I said, "otherwise the kosher butchers won't buy it."

"Don't worry, we got the kosher stamps and metal tags to put on the meat we cut for them."

"Who's gonna cut the meet?" I asked.

"Our crew is, and this includes you and me."

"Listen," I said again, "These kosher butchers know which cut of meat they can use and we got to be very careful that they are only those cuts."

"We got it all worked out," said Joe. "One of the guys has a good friend that's a kosher butcher someplace upstate. I think it is in Monticello or near there. And this friend is going to come down and show us how to cut the meet into kosher pieces and non-kosher pieces."

"Where are we going to do this?"

"Leave it to our captains," Joe replied. "They found a place in Long Island that was a meat packing plant and went out of business with all the equipment left in it. The owner was glad to rent it to us. He got paid good, and was told to stay away for a couple of weeks. We told him we were doing some secret work for the government. This satisfied him and he swore that he wouldn't even come around or say anything to anybody."

Joe and I got to the plant, walked in, said hi to the guys and a few moments later we heard a truck coming in and then we watched it backing into the loading dock. The plant overhead doors were opened and a group of us were told to push a big revolving oval meat rack up to the truck's open end. While we were doing this, some of the other guys opened the back of the trailer and hopped in. The truck was jammed full of meat hanging on hooks and on revolving oval tracks. Once our rack was in place, the hooks holding the sides of beef were lifted off the truck rack and placed in the hook opening on our rack. The racks looked like vertical conveyer belts. Once we had about twenty sides on the rack, we pushed it into the main room of the plant. It was cold in there and I was glad I had listened to Joe and had brought the heavy sweater and warm jacket with me.

One of the captains hopped up on a table and shouted out, "All you guys get around here. You gonna get a lesson on how to cut meet so it's kosher. Listen close and do as you're told. This here guy Moish is going to show you what to do and you better listen good. So come up here, Moish, and show these grease balls how to cut kosher."

A short middle-aged heavy round-faced man with a goatee beard climbed up on the table. "This won't be hard for you if you follow what I tell you," he said. "Now go over to a side of beef and look at the inner part."

We did what we were told.

"Now," he continued, "look for the first rib starting from the top. This is important. You must count from the first rib. Now count down seven ribs. Once you locate the seventh rib, you just cut forward of the seventh rib. This is very important. In order for the meet to be kosher, it can't have the *seventh* rib. So remember to cut just above the *seventh* rib. That's all there is to it. Now watch me." We all looked as he counted the ribs from the first one over to the seventh. "Did you all see what I did? Any questions? No, that's good. Now watch me cut the meat." He picked up the meat that was lying on the table. "I find it easier to leave the beef side on the hook while cutting."

He then took the saw and started cutting. When he got to the backbone, he told two of the guys to wheel a big canvas basket and place it beneath the side where he was cutting.

Moish continued, "When I cut through all the way, the meat will fall into the basket. The meat left on the hook will pass as kosher once I put the kosher stamp and the metal ring on it. I brought enough stamps and rings to take care of all the meat you have. I see that there are plenty of saws to go around. This is not a hard job, but I'll stick around for a while to answer any questions and see how you are doing."

At first things went very slow, and a few mistakes were made. I started to think that some of our crew couldn't count up to seven. After a while the pace picked up and we buzzed along pretty good. All of a sudden, Moish was not around. He just took off. We finished cutting, then loaded the trucks and cleaned up in about four hours. I was so glad to get out of there, it was so freaking cold.

Once Joe and I were heading home, Joe said, "That wasn't too bad, was it? Now that you got experience cutting up a cow, cutting up on a person will be a snap."

I didn't want to answer him, but I blurted out, "That's some fucking comparison."

The conversation after that centered on Joe's sex life and his new conquest. He bragged that he was scoring big time and none of them were dogs.

"How are you fixed for next Saturday night?" Joe asked me. "Maybe we can go to Roseland, or I'm pretty sure I can fix you up with one of my girlfriends' friends. All the ones I met are good lookers. If I fix you up, you might not get laid the first time out. If you're lucky you might get a hand job. In any case, we take two cars, because my girl doesn't want her friend to know that I'm fucking her and we sort of worked it out good in the back seat. Also want you to know all my girls are not jailbait, and her friends ain't either."

"Sounds like a plan," I said. "But I have to see if I have any quizzes coming up in that following week. I'll let you know by Wednesday."

"That's time enough," said Joe. "With the shortage of guys around, a lot of girls are sitting at home on Saturday nights."

"I'll call you as soon as I find out."

"We decide then if it's dance or dates," Joe said.

"Sounds like a plan."

I called Joe on Wednesday and he asked, "Well, is Saturday a go?"

"Yep," I answered.

"Good. Let's go to Roseland. We haven't been out dancing for a long time and I don't want to become rusty. I know you feel the same. Besides, there are some new dances out and we can get them taught over there."

"What happened to the dates?"

"I ain't lucky," said Joe. "Two of my dolls got their periods and it don't make sense to go out with them if I can't get laid by either one."

"Ok, Roseland it is."

Joe and I met, went to Roseland, and had a great time. A lot of the good girl dancers were Puerto Rican and some actually taught us the new dances. I tried to make a move on one of them who seemed very interested, especially when I told her that I was going be a doctor.

Joe heard this and grabbed me aside and said, "Don't even think about anything but dancing with her. You are liable to get the shit kicked out of you or a shiv in your back if you screw around with any of the Puerto Rican broads. The same would happen to one of their guys if they tried to get close to one of the girls from our neighborhood."

"Ok, ok," I said. "I gotcha."

# XXX

During the next several months, I got calls to pitch in. I remember one was a load of liquor, another was women's silk stockings, and we had another capture of meat. This time it was pork sides so we didn't have to bother with the kosher business.

I heard that Paulie had to sign on for a ship out of Savannah. The "No Show" job that he was counting on had fallen through. It seemed that the Maritime Union had some sort of beef with the Long Shoreman's Union, and because of this no favors were done for anyone.

June rolled around and we all survived through the finals. Seven weeks to go until we were finished with college, got a week off, and then we would start med school right after Labor Day.

It was around the end of July that I got a letter postmarked San Diego, California, with no return address. When I opened it, there was another envelope enclosed with my name on it. I could hardly wait until I opened it. It was from Pam, who wrote:

> "Dear Loverboy, I asked one of my group to forward this onto you. She was on her way to another assignment and had a stop-over in San Diego.
> How are you, my darling doctor to be? The memory of you and the luscious hours we had together has helped keep me sane through some trying hours. I am ok, and quite frankly miss you. Hope this damn war will be over soon so

*that we can renew our fuck fest for as long as it can last. Hope you miss me as much as I miss you. I'll try to keep in touch as often as possible. Your fucking partner,*
*Pam"*

I read this letter over and over, and started to wonder whether Pam was now getting interested in maybe developing a real relationship. I too had been thinking that there might to be something more. But only time would tell.

Since the Fourth of July came out on a Sunday, I thought Uncle Vito might hold another Fourth Bash as he did in the past, but under the circumstances I couldn't see how it could happen.

Tom Dewey, who became governor of New York, picked Frank Hogan to take over as the New York D.A. Dewey got his reputation for being a crime fighter by focusing on organized crime. He got convictions and sent many of the Mafia bosses to prison. It was clear that Hogan was looking to beat Dewey's conviction record and his main target was the Amatto family, headed by Uncle Vito. Word came down from him not to discuss any crew business in the club. It might be bugged. Do it outside and make sure that there was nobody near you that could hear what you're talking about. Don't use your cars unless you have to, because the dicks maybe taking down license plate numbers. Use payphones to call on business. Take subways, busses, and taxis. They were safer for the time being.

Joe and I had planned to go to the beach on the Fourth and see if we could line up some girls to fool around with. I got a call on that Friday before the Fourth from him, telling me to dress up in holiday clothes and shoes and meet him at the usual subway stop at ten-thirty on Sunday. Hearing Joe's tone, I knew from experience not to ask why.

I met Joe at ten-thirty and we took the subway to someplace in Brooklyn. When we got out, we walked a couple of blocks to a big church.

"What the hell are we doing here?" I asked.

"We're going in," Joe replied. "And make it look like we are attending the twelve o'clock mass."

"Hey, did you forget I'm Jewish, not Catholic?"

"Don't worry about it. We ain't going to try to convert you. Once we get in, just follow what I do and where I go. Capishe?"

As we started to walk up the steps to the church entrance, I glanced around and saw certain key members of our crew and their families also heading in our direction towards the church's entry doors. Joe, in a low voice, cautioned me, "Don't say hello or nod toward any of the family. Just don't recognize anybody."

I looked at my watch. It was about a quarter to twelve when we walked in. I followed Joe up to the steps before the altar where Joe bowed and crossed himself. I then bowed but didn't cross myself. I followed Joe around a small partition - which I later found out was the confession box - to a door behind it and through the door we went. It led into a pretty big house where the priest lived and also had his office. We went past the kitchen and into a large living room. It even had a fire place. Pictures and little statues of Jesus were hanging all over. Folding chairs were set like a meeting was going to take place. Since we were the only ones there, I whispered to Joe, "What the hell is going on?" Then I thought, *Maybe I shouldn't use that word in here.*

Joe responded with a smile. "Don't be cute, it ain't funny. Uncle Vito is going to get the reports here. It's safe."

"How come the priest is allowing the meet?"

"Uncle Vito and Father Simone grew up together and their families go back a long way in Sicily," Joe explained. "Besides, Uncle Vito has donated a lot of money to the church and has done the Father a lot of good and favors. He didn't have to ask to use this place. The Father knows the situation and insisted that Uncle Vito can use this Rectory any time he wants."

"So what?" I asked, feeling stupid.

"Our guys will come in with their families before the Mass and work their way little by little over to where we are and then we take care of business. When we're finished, we'll go back into the church and out the front door. Simple, ain't it?"

"You betcha."

Little by little the room filled up with our crew, who took seats and said little other than hello. I checked my watch. It was ten after twelve when Uncle Vito came in, nodded hello and sat down behind a table that was set up facing the chairs.

He then said, "I want to thank you all for coming and we'll make this as short and fast as possible so that you could spend the rest of the day with your loved ones. You start, Benny."

"Padrone, we got a new load of ration stamps right off da press," said Benny. "You can't tell them from the legit. When you give the word, we'll give them to our guys and they'll get rid of them. They'll sell like hot cakes, for big money. I ask your permission to go ahead with moving them."

Once Uncle Vito nodded ok, Benny walked over to the table and put an envelope on it. He bent over and kissed Uncle Vito's ring, then returned to his seat and sat down.

"Ok, Charlie," said Uncle Vito. "What do you have to tell us?"

"Padrone, our chop shops are doing ok," said Charlie. "We got twenty swiped cars in the past two weeks. It took us a little longer than usual to cut them up because a lot of the guys working for us were drafted. Besides that, the idiots that stole the cars swiped Mercedes and it ain't good to drive a German made car today, so the price for parts dropped down a lot. But all in all we did good." And he too placed an envelope on Uncle Vito's desk and kissed his hand, reaffirming allegiance.

And so it went with reports from Alanzo on gambling joints, Basilio on protection and strong arming, Sonny on burglary and highjacking, Andy on loan sharking, Carmine on the whorehouses, and Luigi on payola. Luigi's report was not as positive as the others.

"The judges and cops," Luigi reported, "were sort of afraid of taking their monthly end, so I had to increase it. These bastards would sell their mothers if the price was right. The good news is that I'm working on getting some advance information from the D.A.'s office. One of Hogan's married assistants is fucking around with one of our putanas. He doesn't know that she's a pro. He thinks it's a legit love affair. We haven't put the pressure on him yet. We gonna catch him in the sack with her. We'll have pictures in a week or two."

"Ok, Carmine, you're up." Uncle Vito said.

"Padrone, our cat houses are doing real good," said Carmine. "The ones near the Navy yard and the other docks are busy seven days and seven nights. The sailors come off with hard-ons and hard cash. It's a win-win situation. Too bad we don't have more places."

Uncle Vito then offered, "Did you think about opening maybe four or five more places around the Navy yard and maybe also around the Time Square area? Sailors and soldiers always want to visit Time Square, and they are always looking to get laid."

"That's a great idea about spreading out," said Carmine.

"Reach out for Big Eddie the Pimp and offer him a deal for him to supply the girls," said Uncle Vito. "I think we should start with six or eight girls in each house. Maybe put a high yellow in each one in case some of the customers want to change their luck. Big Eddie will stock our places with especially young putanas, know how to handle them, and keep them happy. Tell him his end is forty percent and he takes care of the girls. This should make everyone happy. Carmine, you and Louie set up these houses nice, like high class joints. We will pay for the setup and also take care of the cops."

Then pointing to Donnie, Uncle Vito said, "Call Nick the Greek. He owns a lot of checker cabs. And tell him that once the houses are ready for business, his cabbies will get a 'fin; from us on top of the fare for taking customers over to our places. We can keep the cabbies honest by making them take the Johns to the door and giving whoever you got guarding the joints, their hack number. Straighten out with the cabbies every week and let Nick know who got what. This way Nick can get his piece. Also keep the rates for the military cheap enough so that they can come back and more importantly spread the word that we have bargain basement whore houses."

Everyone laughed.

Carmine replied quickly, "Consider it done Padrone." He walked up and put an envelope on the table like all the others, except his was a little fatter than the others. He followed the ring kissing protocol.

"How are the Casino's doing, Alanzo?" Uncle Vito asked.

"Terrific!" replied Alanzo. "Our ten joints are doing real good. We got our places running five nights a week and since we get filled up early, we now open at eight and run it till three. We're now at the point where no new players can come in except when they're vouched for by another regular. Also we got a couple of good watchers in all our places, looking to nail scumbags that try to rip us off." Alanzo then brought his envelope up to the table, placed it on the pile and like all the others bent and kissed Uncle Vito's ring.

"Anything else, Alanzo?" Uncle Vito asked.

"Yeah, Padrone, we have a little problem with one of our dealers. This kid Jimmy, that's what I need to talk to you about. We got asked a favor from your friends in Brooklyn asking us to give this kid a job. Because your friend asked, we put the kid to work as a dealer. We caught him skimming off the top the last couple of weeks."

"Are you positive he's ripping us off?"

"Yes, Padrone, and we need your permission for us to deal with him and make him an example for anyone else who might even think of fucking us. Can we have your permission to teach him a lesson he'll never forget?"

"How much did he beat us for?" asked Uncle Vito.

"At least a hundred dollars a night for the last two weeks."

Uncle Vito paused for a moment then replied, "Thanks

for the low down. You did right by not doing anything until now. What's this punk's name?"

"Jimmy Mastriano."

"Ok, I'll make a call over to Brooklyn and ask them to handle it. You'll get a call to make a meet with them to give us our money back. If we are not satisfied with their solution, we'll handle it ourselves."

"You are very wise, Padrone." And with that Alanzo walked over to the table, dropped his envelope on top of the pile, kissed Uncle Vito's ring, and returned to his seat.

Uncle Vito then looked at me and surprised me by saying, "Stand up, Marco."

I did so immediately.

"This here is Marco," Uncle Vito said to the others. "And if anyone don't know him, in a couple of years he's going to be a doctor. Our private doctor." Then he jokingly added, "So make sure you and your family don't get sick until then. Ok, Marco, you can sit down now."

He addressed the whole crowd. "Thank you for your loyalty and good work and pass this along to the rest of our family. The waters are getting muddy out there so be careful what you do or what you say." And with that the Padrone headed for the door leading to the main body of the church, taking the envelopes with him.

A few of the guys then left one at a time. Joe and I stayed back along with just a couple of the others that I remember meeting before at Joe's house. It came to me like a flash that the guys who were here today were actually the representatives of the Amatto family crews.

The mass must have been over because Father Simone walked through the door from the church into the room where we were waiting. He greeted us with a big smile and said, "We celebrated a wonderful, meaningful mass. I hope that your meeting went real good also."

We all nodded in agreement and the Father added, "Since this mass is over, you don't need to go out through the church. I'll open the Rectory side door and you can leave that way." And we did, after thanking the Father for his help.

We just had small talk on the subway ride home. Joe kept telling me about his recent sex life experiences, and even if his tales were one half true, he was doing great in that department. He could be so fucking descriptive. I was starting to get jealous, but kept the feeling to myself.
When we reached our stop, I suggested we stop off at Patsy's Pizza Joint, which was right by where we got off the subway, and grab something to eat and drink. There were a few tables in the back of the store since most of Patsy's business was take out. While eating I asked Joe, "How come I got an invite to go with you today?"

"I got no idea," said Joe. "I wasn't asked, but I bet you figured out that all of the guys there were blood relatives except you. Uncle Vito, I think, now considers you part of the blood family as well as a crew member. I never heard or saw anything like that before. You're a lucky son of a bitch. He declared himself when he said you're going to be our private doctor. You see, all the relatives there today were the messengers who brought reports from all of our businesses as well as the appreciation envelopes.

"You didn't see everything that might happen at one of the meetings. It didn't happen today, but if there was a real big score in the works, Uncle Vito needs to ok or reject it. If he gives his ok, the deal goes forward and he stands behind it no matter what happens, good or bad. If he says no, then the move is dead and nobody better go around him or behind his back. It becomes very unhealthy to do that. Also, Uncle Vito once in a while gives a suggestion like he did with Carmine and Alanzo. I never saw it work out a loser. Any more questions?"

"Yeah, I got one," I said. "Let's say we get out of these church clothes and put on something sporty. Grab our bathing suits and go to Coney Island. We could have some fun, maybe hook up with some good lookers and maybe stay for the fireworks."

"I gotta think about this for a minute," said Joe. "I got a

date with a sure lay tonight, but what the hell, let's go to the beach. I can fuck her some other time this week."

We had a good time, met a few girls that weren't interested in screwing right away but suggested that we call them again. The fireworks were better than ever, even though it was wartime.

I guess that special permission was given because it was the Fourth of July.

# XXXI

    Back at college, we started counting the week and then the days until graduation. But first we had to get through the finals, and the Octet meetings paid off again. We all passed with flying colors.
    The graduation ceremony was short and simple, no long speeches or guest speakers, no special awards since all in our group made Phi Beta Kappa. We were allowed to invite only immediate family as guests. We had a touch of the pomp since the school band played the customary procession music as we marched to our seats in the auditorium. We were requested to remain standing as the rest of the audience was asked to rise and recite the Pledge of Allegiance. Once we were seated, our mentor, Professor Kramer, came to the podium and congratulated us as having pioneered the accelerated college-medical school program. He further added that because of our success in completing this project in the competent way it was done, it would serve as a model for many other institutions of higher learning. You are to be congratulated for your efforts, and I have no doubt that you'll be a credit to the medical profession."
    With that he called upon the head of the science department, Dr. Murray, to hand out the diplomas. As our names were called by Professor Kramer, we came up to the podium to receive the diploma from Dr. Murray.
    Since there were only sixty of us, it didn't take very long before the last name was read. We then marched out of the auditorium and photographers took all kinds of pictures.
    I had a lot of them taken with Mama and Papa. Mama

had on a new dress she had bought just for this, and Papa looked big and handsome in his navy blue suit, white shirt, and striped red tie. I bet Mama picked out the tie for him. They were so proud and kept hugging and kissing me. Mama kept saying, "My son is now a college graduate with a degree, Papa. Did you ever think in your born days you would live to have a college graduate for a son and soon a doctor?" She wiped a tear from her eye. "God has been so good to us that he gave us this *groiser mitzvah.*"

I jumped in at that point and said to both of them, "Come, I want to introduce you to my group that helped me get through up to now."

Mama being Mama came back immediately with, "I'm sure you helped them too." She then started to call me endearing terms in Yiddish, English and Italian.

"Mama," I said sweetly, "I want you and Papa to meet my friends before they leave."

"Aren't they coming to your party tomorrow?" Mama asked.

"No, Mama, they are having their own parties."

"Too bad," Mama said. "Yours will be the best."

"They'll just have to suffer that," I said jokingly.

I introduced Mama and Papa to our group and their parents and to a few of the other classmates and their folks. Then I went to the locker room, retrieved my suit jacket, put my cap and gown into the box it came in, and rejoined my parents.

"Let's go home," I said. "This college graduate wants a big bowl of your chicken soup with matzo balls."

Papa said, "Mama's bowl of soup will be so big you'll be able to swim in it." He grinned. "We'll take a cab home."

When we got back to the store, and after Papa unlocked the front door, I saw they had a big sign on it reading:

"We will close tomorrow at twelve o'clock in honor of our son Marco's graduation from college, so we can't have any customers but all our friends and neighbors who have been our customers are invited to celebrate with us. So come one and all."

While I was feasting on the chicken soup and Mama's famous lightweight matzo balls, Mama and Papa kept telling me again about my graduation party the following day. This was about the tenth time I had heard about it this past week alone, but I knew it was their *nachos,* so for the tenth time I appeared as excited as the first time I heard it.

The party was fantastic. The store was jammed. Mama and Sol had been cooking for about a week and even our competitors brought big trays of food. The Ling family, owners of the biggest restaurant in Chinatown, had their son Lee bring in all sorts of Dim Sum. Even the local Boar's Head distributor had his driver bring in cheeses, sausages, and other items we normally didn't carry in the store.

It was about three o'clock when Joe and his family came by, and Joe's mother brought in trays of Italian homemade delicacies. Even Tony sent over gelato and pastries.

Papa hired David, the photographer, to take pictures of me in my cap and gown. It seemed that everybody also wanted to have their picture taken with me wearing them.

Some of the girls from the neighborhood who I knew in high school came by to wish me well and sort of flirted, smiled, and gave me a come-on. A lot of them had sure grown up since I had seen them last. I made a mental note of who I would ask out. I kept looking for Joe in the crowd and found him as usual surrounded by the prettiest girls. He was pitching with his going overseas on a secret mission, too secret to talk about, or said that he was doing high security work in Jersey but couldn't talk about it either. The more secretive he was, the more the girls lapped it up. I would lay odds that Joe would have them in the sack before they knew it. I bet two weeks would be all that it would take. Little did Joe know that his make-believe story would become a reality.

At about eight o'clock, Papa got up on one of the tables and said, "Thanks so much for coming. There is a lot of food left over and it would be a *shanda* to let it go to waste.

"Besides," he said with a smile, "it's free, so please

help yourselves. There are plenty of bags on the counter. Once again, Marco, my wife, and me want to thank you all for coming to honor my son. Maybe his graduation from college will prove that in America, a kid from our neighborhood can make it. Only in America could this be done." He then quickly added, "The store will be open regular time tomorrow morning."

After filling up the bags with food, the people left saying goodnight, kissing, hugging and even shedding a few tears.

Joe's mother and sisters and Mama's cousins from Philadelphia and Papa's relatives from Brooklyn stayed behind to help clean up. Papa and Joe's father disappeared somewhere outside, probably to grab a smoke.

I finally came across Joe, who was smiling from ear to ear. "I made a hit with some of those Jew broads," he said. "I'm sorry, I really meant some of the *Jewish girls*. I hope they don't compare notes on what I was doing but I can get around that. I heard that Jew... er, Jewish girls are something special in bed."

"I don't know Joe," I said. "I've only been screwing *Dago broads*...er, I'm sorry Joe, I meant Italian girls." We both started to laugh hysterically.

# XXXII

    Come Thursday, all medical first-year students were required to attend orientation, which required a physical exam and a tour of the school, including the anatomy lab. I had never seen a dead body before, and here was a room full of them. One of the guys in our group turned white and I thought he was going to puke or pass out. Luckily I was standing nearby and grabbed him and walked him out. Our guide - I think he was a senior - came out and said, "Don't worry, it happens to a lot of our first year students."

    Hearing this, the guy I was holding took off towards the bathroom, and a few moments later I heard the sound of puking. When he came out, he was green and said, "I don't know if I can do this."

    "Tour's over," said the guide. "Go home and come back tomorrow as listed in your orientation letter." With that he took off laughing as he left the lab.

    The following day at one, the first year med students assembled in one of the big lecture rooms. There were about two hundred of us and we all stood up as a gray haired man wearing a white lab coat I guess he was about sixty entered the room and went up to the podium and said, "Please be seated. I'm Doctor Samsky and I want to congratulate you on your acceptance here and welcome you to our school. Since this class is the first in the government-endorsed three-year program, I want to tell you there will be a lot of pressure and long hours on you until you graduate. To be frank, we have accepted two hundred ten students this year, and our experience has proven that at least one half of you will not be around for the second year. Contrary to undergraduate school, there are no electives here. You have no choices. For your further information, our library is open from two p.m. to eleven p.m. Monday through Friday, and from ten a.m. to eight p.m. Saturday and Sunday. Since it is an accelerated program, there are no holidays. On your way out, you will get a list of books and manuals you will need for the first semester. You will also need to purchase at least one lab coat. Put them on when you come to school. You will also be given name tags which you will attach to your lab coat.

"I would suggest searching for good used books. You can save a lot of money by doing so. A word of caution: try not to get sick. If you fall behind, you're out. One other thing: if your tuition is not paid in full the first day of classes, you won't be admitted.

"Pick up your locker key on the way out. If you have any questions, stop by my office and make an appointment. My secretary's name is Mrs. Breyer. Good day. Have a great Labor Day weekend, and we look forward to seeing you on Tuesday." And with that he left.

*Holy shit*, I thought to myself. *I never thought of getting in touch with the Union for the tuition money or books.* As soon as I left the school, I ran to a phone booth, dialed the Union and asked for Ray. The guy who answered said, "Who wants him?"

I gave my name.

"Hold on," was the response.

A moment later I heard, "Hello Doc, what's new?" It was Ray.

"I forgot to tell you about tuition and money for books," I said. "School starts on Tuesday and they won't let me in if the tuition isn't paid, and I'll also need the books."

"Marco, *nonja* worry, it's been taken care of," said Ray. "We paid the tuition a week ago, and your books are waiting for you at the book store. We do the right ting, and we know you'll do the same. Anything else?"

"No," I said.

"Ciao. If you see our friend, make sure you say hello."

"I will, and *grazie por tutti*." I hung up the phone.

I hurried over to the book store, and sure enough all of my books, brand new, were waiting for me. I had to show my driver's license to prove it was me. They were also two brand new lab coats included. I kept wondering how the hell these guys knew when and what to order for me. I got the feeling once again *the family* had connections way beyond what I had once thought. I had a little trouble going over what I said to myself. I said, *the family*, but could I say *my family* without the feeling of being insecure and troubled? Once again, I rationalized that I wouldn't be in medical school if it wasn't for their help and decided to let it go at that.

On Tuesday the first class was at nine o'clock, and was held in the same lecture room as the orientation. I couldn't believe I was here. I was sure all of the other students felt the excitement and the positive energy that filled the room, especially when the professor entered the room, strode up to the podium and said, "Good morning Doctors."

The classes at med school were great and entirely different from college. First came the lectures and then the labs. After two to three weeks dissecting the human cadavers, it did not bother us anymore. All of the lab instructors were very helpful, answering questions and then asking us hands-on questions relating to the subject we were studying.

Our Octet group continued to meet two to three times a week, depending on the subject we were studying. Anatomy was usually three times. One night, during our anatomy study, the suggestion was put forward that some of us, if not all, take rooms close by the school itself and the library, so that we would have some much-needed time for additional study and use of the library. I suggested the Gramercy Park Hotel. It was close to the school, the library, and had a special discount program for undergraduate students and a bigger discount for graduate students like us. After some discussion we all agreed it was a good idea, and they chose me to find out what the cost would be. Once I reported back, individual decisions could be made.

Next day after class I went over to the Gramercy, spoke to the manager, and got the rate of fifty dollars per month for a single room and sixty-five dollars for a double. An Octet meeting was called for that night, and after studying I gave my report. All agreed it was a very good deal, but parents would have to be consulted before any commitment could be made. We decided to hold off a day or two before notifying the hotel of the number of single and/or double rooms that would be needed. We all agreed to meet two nights later for study and answers about the rooms.

When I got home, Mama and Papa were still up, and Mama as usual started to heat up some food for us to eat. When I told her I had already grabbed a bite in the school cafeteria, she seemed insulted and said, "What's the matter, my food isn't good enough for you, my doctor-to-be? You couldn't come home to eat a decent dinner and then go back to do your studying?"

"No Mama, I know your food is terrific."

Before I could continue, Mama said, "Maybe you should know that a nice plate of good food is what the body needs and wants in order for a person to be healthy and wise. I never went to medical school, but I know more than you think. I made dinner for you and Papa and you are not here to eat and enjoy it? Maybe you don't like my cooking anymore?"

"Mama, I love your cooking," I said. "And I'll try to come and eat with you at least twice a week. Please understand that school and studying takes up most of my time and there is just not much left to sit down at your dinner table and enjoy - really enjoy - what you make. We were told at the beginning that half of my class will be thrown out at the end of the first year."

"Can they do that?" asked Papa.

"Yes they could and would," I said. "They have a long

history of taking in two hundred and at the end of the first year asking only about one hundred to return for the second year."

"That's terrible," said Papa.

"That's the way it is. I have to tell you, medical school is much harder than I expected. College was nothing compared to what we need to learn and learn perfectly. Remember I'm in an accelerated program and am scheduled to graduate in three instead of four years."

Hearing this seemed to calm Mama down and she said, "All right, I guess Papa and I will have to settle for two nights a week, hopefully Friday and Saturday. Sometimes two nights are better than nothing."

I then broke the news that I needed to take a room near the school and library, maybe just for the first year.

For a moment there was absolute silence, and Mama and Papa just looked at each other and then at me. Then to my surprise, Mama said to Papa, "Remember when we told our parents that we are moving to America? Remember what they said? They told us that they will miss us and they understood. They realized we had the chance to make a better life, better than the one they had, and that we could do things in America that could never be done there. There we would have always been Jewish Italians. Here we are American Jews. *Gay in gesunta height* and follow your dreams." She smiled at me. "You have our blessing. If you need to take the room, do it." She looked to Papa. "Do you have anything to say, Ivan?"

"Yes, Mama is right," said Papa. "You have our blessing. The name sounds so good. Marco Falcone, M.D."

Mama then said to me, "Now that this is settled, have something to eat. A little chopped liver, tea and homemade strudel."

After eating, while Mama was cleaning up, Papa asked me in detail about my classes, and particularly about the work in the labs. I was frankly surprised how much technical and anatomical things he seemed to know. Then I remembered that he was a butcher in Italy, experienced in cutting up meat. As soon as Mama finished her kitchen work, we kissed each other goodnight and went to bed.

Papa woke me up early like I asked and I was off to school. As planned, our group met that night at the library. We were really lucky that the head librarian let us use a small reading room for our study workshop, and the time we had there was put to good use. Once we went over and digested the work assigned to us that day, we turned our attention to the room situation.
We took a vote and I was pleasantly surprised that all eight of us were in favor of taking up residency at the Gramercy Hotel. The Brain and I chose singles and the rest decided to double up, so we wound up with three doubles and two singles. I was then asked to make the final arrangements and to schedule a move on the 1st of October, sooner if possible. I was told to try to get rooms next to each other or at least on the same floor. I told them I would reconfirm that we could use one of their meeting or banquet rooms for our study get-togethers.

"I'll see the manager tomorrow after classes are over and get the full details," I said to the group. I turned to the Brain. "When do we meet again?"

"Wednesday night, here at the library at six," the Brain replied.

Wednesday night, before we started to review, I gave the report that the rooms were reserved for us as we wanted. Two single rooms and three doubles on the same floor with the ok to use one of the small conference rooms. Otherwise the breakfast room would be substituted since the breakfast hours were mornings from six-thirty to nine-thirty.

I still tried to get the manager to give us a better rate, but he wouldn't budge, claiming that this rate was worked out with the school and was the best that could be offered. He told me that he would, however, throw in room cleaning and changes of linen once a week. He added that the first month's rent plus a one-month security deposit would be required before moving in, and that the rents for the following months would be due no later than the fifth of that month.

    Everybody agreed that the terms were fair and that they were going to take the deal. The guys that were going to share the doubles said they would work it out by themselves. The whole group thanked me for the good job that I had done and it was further agreed that each of us would come up with the money due and pay it directly to the hotel. And we did just that.

My immediate problem was to contact my Union sponsor and ask for the rent money. I didn't know how it would sit with them and I didn't want to take a chance that I would get turned down. The best thing to do, I decided, was to pay my rent out of the vig money since I was still collecting it.

    October 1st fell out on a Friday, so I went over to the hotel during lunch break and paid the rent and security. Some of our group had already done this before going to the first class. The rest, I was told, were going to drop off their money right after their last class. Saturday, October 2nd, was our moving day. I packed a small suitcase and left the bulk of my clothes in my closet. I had hoped that by doing this, I gave the impression that my move was just temporary. I made sure to give my phone number to Mama and Papa on my way out.

    On the way back to the hotel, I stopped off at a couple of the department stores and bought new replacements for the clothes I had left and made my way back to the hotel. When I got there, I noticed that some of the guys were moving in at the same time and I got a call from the Brain that everyone was checked in at six o'clock.

    My room was small but nice. The bed looked comfortable. The closet was large enough to hold all of my clothes, as was the dresser. There was also a small table that could serve nicely as a desk and above it were enough shelves to hold all my books. The bathroom was just a bathroom but it had a stall shower instead of a tub, which made me very happy. A medicine cabinet above the sink was just right to hold all my toiletries. Next to my bed was even a night table with a telephone and a radio on it.

"I am gonna be very happy here," I said to myself.

# XXXIII

The next Monday morning, we got to school and began our class work. Since our group was really on top of things, we decided to take a night off from group studying. I called Joe and arranged with him to meet for dinner on Wednesday night.

Over dinner, I gave him the news that I had moved and asked him to pass my contact information onto Phil. Joe told me that he thought my moving out was the right thing to do since it more or less moved my folks out of the scene of what was going on.

"The D.A.'s office is really leaning hard on our enterprises," said Joe. "They are pinching a lot of guys and sweating them out to become rats and wear wires. As far as we know, nobody has turned. They know what will happen if they break the *Omerta*."

"So far we are lucky," Joe added, "'cause the cops seem to be concentrating on the Brooklyn Italian bunch and the Jews out of Brownsville. Nobody knows when things will change. Just keep this to yourself and be extra careful with your collections. I have a meet with Tony A on some other business and I'll see how that goes. If it goes good and he sees that it can earn good, I'll talk to him about asking Uncle Vito's permission to let you off the hook as far as the collecting the *vig* is concerned. Uncle Vito knows that if you take a pinch for shylocking, you can get thrown out of med school, and all the money laid out for you will be in the toilet. Besides, your being a doctor is more important to the family than a six for five shy."

"That's good of you, Joe," I said. "But I need the

money. Now I have rent to pay, gotta buy food or eat out, clothes and maybe go out once in a while. I count on my end of the collections to do these things."

"Don't worry," said Joe, waving his hand. "If Tony A goes for it and Uncle Vito gives the ok - and I have no doubt that he will, you know how he feels about you - the green will come through. It's for the family's benefit that you graduate."

"I don't know what to say."

"Say we'll go out whenever you get a free night," said Joe with a smile. "I know a lot of girls that want to meet a Jew doctor-to-be. I'll bet they'll all lay down for you, one-two-three. You need some fun and a lot of humping. It clears the mind. By the way, if I can get Tony A to swing the deal, you might have to turn in the car."

"I don't care," I said. "I really don't need it if I don't have to make the stops."

"Let's see what happens, just go about your business like usual. As soon as I know anything I'll let you know. In the meantime, call me and let me know when we can go out and leave the rest to me." He paused for a moment. "One more thing."

"What's that?" I asked.

"This time, you pick up the check," Joe said laughingly.

As the days passed by, medical school became more and more intense. We all agreed that our group study paid off big time again, and our move to the hotel proved to be the icing on the cake. We were now meeting on the average of three nights a week, four if we voted to do it. For me it was tough because I still needed to make my collections, and sometimes I got to the meet late and needed to make up excuses that once in a while seemed sort of lame. But they were accepted.

It was about three weeks later, when I met Phil to deliver the collection money, that Phil told me that Tony A wanted to see me at the Mini Pub on 36th Street, and told me to ask for Whitey when I get there. And if Whitey wasn't there, I was to ask for Freddy. "You'll be told what to do," Phil said.

"Be there at nine o'clock on Thursday."

"I'll be there," I replied.

"Ok, ciao," Phil said.

Thursday night I got to the restaurant a little before nine. It was a nice looking place, small but elegant. The bar took up a good portion of the room and there were ten or twelve small cocktail tables along the outer wall. When I got there, the bar was jammed and the two bartenders were really hustling to serve both the people sitting there and attend to the service bar, which in turn took care of the customers at the tables. As I walked in, I looked around for someone to approach but no one came up to me, so I just stood to the side of the front door and waited for something to happen. It was almost nine and I had to make a move, so I approached one of the girl servers and asked for Whitey.

"He's not here right now," said the server, and she started to walk back to the service bar with empty glasses.

Following her, I asked, "Is Freddy here?"

"Yeah, he's here," she said.

"Where can I find him? I was told to ask for him if Whitey wasn't here."

"What's your name?" she asked as she put her tray on the service bar. She then grabbed the phone on the wall and dialed the number.

"Marco Falcone," I said.

"Freddy," she said into the phone, "there is a guy by the name of Marco Falcone here asking for you or Whitey. Watta ya want him to do?" A pause. "No, he don't look like a cop. He's too good looking." Another pause. "Ok, I'll tell him. Thanks, Freddy." Turning to me, she said, "At the end of the hall, past the bathrooms, there's a staircase going upstairs. Find your way up and Freddy will be waiting for you."

"Thanks a lot," I said. "Mind giving me your name?"

"It's Christy. Why?"

"I'd like to get to know you better, if it's ok with you."

"I'm married, and don't fool around," she answered, but with a big grin.

I walked down the hall and up the steps to the next level. A swarthy, short, curly haired guy dressed in a tuxedo greeted me and said, "I'm Freddy," as he extended his hand and shook mine.

"I'm Marco and I'm here to meet somebody," I replied.

"Your party is here in our private room, so just follow me."

I looked around and saw that contrary to the bar downstairs, this upper unit was a fine-looking restaurant with seating for about a hundred people, and the place was full. Each seat seemed to be taken.

I followed Freddy to a door at the end of the dining room and he opened it with a key and ushered me into a small, private, secluded dining room. Seated at the sole table were Tony A and Ray, the president of the Cement Mason's Union. Seeing me, they waved me over and told me to sit down.

"Ray and I are going to have a little dinner, just some arugula salad and pasta," said Tony A. "We're also gonna have some wine. You take some Pellegrino water. Ok?"

"Sounds great," I answered.

During dinner we just had small talk, mainly with them asking me questions about med school.

Over espresso, Tony A said, "Think the move to the hotel was a good one. It's closer to your school and it keeps eyes and ears off your mother and father, especially with all the heat that's on. We don't like to dig into your money situation, but we want you not to have any distraction having to earn a buck that could screw up the schoolwork. Ray here is going to ask you a few questions and then we'll see what we can do."

Ray took over and asked me what I need each month to get along. After I told him about my rent and incidentals, he asked about food money and I told him that I was going to eat with my folks Friday and Saturday nights and I would take food back to the hotel with me but that was a problem cause I had no refrigerator in my room and hotel wouldn't let me keep food in theirs.

"No problem," said Ray. "What do you think you'll

need for rent, food, and a little extra for the month for some fun? You gotta get your whistle wet once in a while. We don't want our doctor to be in dry dock, it dulls the mind." Ray grinned. And then Tony and Ray started to laugh and I felt I had to join in.

Freddy brought second rounds of espresso and two shot glasses of what I guessed were Anisette. Ray lit up a cigarette while Tony A bit off the end of a cigar and then lit it.

"Good fucking cigar," Tony A said. "Real Cuban."

"I think two hundred dollars a month should cover everything, including the taking care of the whistle," said Ray. Both he and Tony laughed again.

Once they stopped laughing, Ray continued, "This's the way it's gonna be handled. You gonna be elected one of our delegates and once a week you'll go to a job site and say hello to our main man there. We'll give you his name. That's all, no more, no less. If anybody else approaches you with a question or a beef, just tell them to call the office. You'll be doing your delegate job by just showing your face. Once a month around the 5th, you can pick up your check at the office, or it could be mailed to you. Work that out with Angelo, our bookkeeper. You do what I'm telling you and everything will be good."

"I'll do exactly what you say," I said, "and I want you to know how much I appreciate what you're doing for me. I'll never forget it. I promise that every cent will be paid back." Once I said this, I saw Ray look at Tony A. with a questioning look on his face, and at the time I couldn't figure it out.

"You finish out the route this week," said Tony A. "Phil will call you and make the meet on Sunday, and then you're through."

"What about the car?" I asked.

"Keep it for the time being," Tony A answered. "Ray and I have some things to talk about, so you can take off."

I got up, thanked them both again and left, thinking to myself, *My money problems are solved and I still have a stash in my homemade safe. Should I open a bank account? Yeah, it's a good idea.*

# XXXIV

The weeks ran by and the fall semester was over. All of the Octet members did well on the finals. The new semester started right after New Year's and the work really piled on. I noticed the empty seats in the lecture halls and knew they were an indication that some of the students that started had dropped out or were asked to leave.

The arrangement with the Union worked out well. Checks from the Union were mailed to me at the hotel around the 1st of each month, and I immediately deposited them into an account I opened at a local bank, and the room rent was paid out of that account.

It was a big relief not to have to pick up *vig.* The weekly stop over to the job site as a delegate was no problem. The workers started at eight in the morning, and my classes began at nine, and the construction site was just a couple of blocks from the school. The foreman on the job must have gotten the word about me, and he was all friendly and cooperative. I had plenty of time to make the stop and get to my first class. The spring semester went like this and I found myself settling into the flow of medical school, difficult as it was.

Before I knew it, it was the end of June and once more our group fared well on all the lecture material and lab exams.

During this time I managed to average one night a week eating dinner with my folks. I think they finally realized that med school demanded an awful lot of my time. Once in a while I even slept over in my own room and couldn't imagine how I had slept on that old worn out mattress for so many years.

    When I would leave the next morning, after seeing the hustle and bustle of the customers and Mama and Papa and Sol waiting on them, I had memories - some good, some bad - of all the years I was a part of it, and I was more thankful than ever for my parents' courage coming to America and striving to realize the American dream.

    I then made a promise to myself that as soon as I could I would see that they retired and enjoyed an easier life.

    We were given the July 4th weekend off and I thought about going to the beach, but the luxury of sleeping till noon, seeing movies, and going to a dance was a better priority.
It was back to school again and we had to do six months' work in eight weeks. Our group was now meeting at least four nights a week, sometimes five. We started to get on each other's nerves. It was a good thing the "Brain" was able to placate everyone.

    It was around the 15th of December when I got a call from Joe. He was talking gibberish.

    "Slow down, Joe," I said.

    It took about a minute and then he said, "I got the letter from the draft board to report for a physical next week."

    "What are you going to do," I asked.

    "Gonna do?" said Joe. "I got to go down and take a physical and hope I don't pass. You're in med school, tell me how I can fail the exam. I heard putting brown laundry soap under the arm pits will give me a high fever. Is this true?"

    "I don't know, never heard of it," I said. "Take it easy, you'll have a heart attack and die. That'll solve all your problems."

    "Thanks a lot," he said. "I gotta reach out and see if there is a way out of this. I'll talk to you. Goodbye."

    Tests were coming up and I didn't have time to worry about Joe. I felt sure he would come up with some angle to beat the draft.

But I was wrong. So wrong.

I called him several times the following week and couldn't reach him. I left word for him to call me. I guess he was trying to find a way of getting rejected. It was the following Thursday that I got his call.

"I passed the physical and have to go in," he said. "I gotta report in two weeks, right after Christmas. This is gonna fuck my life up. Good thing you're in med school and your ass is safe."

"I don't know what to tell you, Joe," I said. "Knowing you, you'll come up with some scheme and probably get a cushiony job with a lot of good looking girls around. I hear some of the WAC's and nurses are real good looking. Besides that, a lot of civilian broads just love guys in uniform. In a way I'm jealous of you. I'm here studying day and night, have no social life, while you will be living it up."

"You think so?" he asked, his voice starting to perk up a bit.

"I know so."

"Talking to you always made me feel better," said Joe. "I got a lot of things to do the next couple of days. I'll call you and let you know what's gonna be."

"Ok, soldier."

"Don't be so fucking cute," he said. "Bye."

Christmas came and went but school was still on for us. The night before he had to report in for induction, Joe had a going away open house party. Because we had finals, I didn't have a lot of time to spend with him, but I did run by to see him at the party. I hoped he understood why we couldn't hook up before then. We had a brief moment to talk in between people coming and going. We promised each other to stay in contact as much as we could and as soon as possible. We hugged each other and reaffirmed that we were brothers, and that we would always be. More people were coming in and I left after saying goodbye.

Joe left me a message at the hotel a couple of days later.

He was in the Army and was at Camp Yapank in Long Island, and he said it wasn't too bad. A week later he left another message saying he was at Fort Dix and that was the last I heard from him. I kept calling his house and they didn't hear anything either.

# XXXV

    June went by and so did August and our entire group was told to report for the fall semester. We had made it so far. We had a day's break for Labor Day and I slept until two o'clock and had dinner at my parents. It was back to the grind the following day and it continued day after day through the first of the new year. The spring semester was a breeze compared to the ones before. Our main courses included making hospital rounds with some of the professors and residents. I started to feel like a doctor wearing my white jacket, actually seeing patients and observing surgery. It was a far cry from working on cadavers. I really liked being in the E.R. with their emergency situations and variety of cases.
    It was on a Saturday night three weeks later when my phone rang. Looking at my watch while I picked up the receiver, I saw it was ten after three in the morning.
    "Hello, who's this?" I asked.
    "It's Phil. Get dressed. Be in front of the hotel in twenty minutes." And with that he hung up.
    I had no idea why he called, but I knew I had to do what he told me.
    He drove by to pick me up. "Climb in," he said. And once I did, we drove off.
    There was no conversation until we stopped in the driveway of a house in Staten Island. "We're here," he said. "So let's go." As we approached the front door, I saw Carmine and Louie guarding it.
    When they saw me, Louie said, "Hello Marco," and Carmine nodded in agreement.

When we entered what must have been a living room, I couldn't believe my eyes. It was set up like an E.R. room, and on the table lay one of the guys I recognized from our crew. I saw that he was stripped to the waist and had blood-soaked cotton wadding over his right shoulder. He was asleep and I could hear breathing and groaning.

Phil then motioned for me to follow him out of the room into the foyer. "This guy is stand up, and needs to be taken care of good," he said. "He was shot twice and you're gonna help patch him up."

I felt my knees buckling. "I'm only a student," I said. "We haven't learned how to do anything like this. I don't even know where to start."

"We think you know enough," Phil answered. "And beside that, Doc Volpe is going to walk you through step by step."

"Then why do you need me?"

"The old doc is a drunk, he has the shakes," said Phil. "It's hard for him to even hold an instrument. In his day he saved a lot of our guys. He'll tell you what to do and you do it. Let's go back in and get started before my friend bleeds to death."

When I got back in the room, Phil told one of the guys, "Call Volpe and tell him to get his ass down here right away."

A moment or two later, a wizened little old man came shuffling in wearing a white coat that had seen better days. When he saw me he straightened up a little and said, "I'm Dr. Volpe, and I understand you are here to assist me."

"Yes sir," I replied.

"Just listen to what I tell you and everything will go ok," he said. "I sedated the patient and he'll be under for another couple of hours. Let's scrub up and get started. Then put on the rubber gloves."

While we were scrubbing, he stood next to me and he reeked of alcohol. I was silently praying that he was sober enough to walk me through the procedure.

Following his instructions, I was able to remove the two

slugs, close the wounds, and bandage them. My work really looked professional.

Once we were finished Dr. Volpe said, "The patient here has to be watched carefully for the next twenty-four hours."

"Do you want me to stay?" I asked Phil.

"Not unless you want to," he said. "We'll keep Volpe sober enough to take care of him. If there is a problem, we'll let you know. Just tell me where I can reach you."

"I'll either be at the hotel sleeping or visiting my parents," I said.

On the way back to Manhattan, Phil loosened up and we had a chance to talk.

"You did good tonight," he said. "Nicki is a good friend of mine and has had my back since we were kids, just like you and Joe. He could have died if it wasn't for you."

"I did just what Dr. Volpe told me," I said.

"Yeah, but you did it good."

It was around seven in the morning when I got dropped off at the hotel. On the way there Phil asked me if I wanted to stop off and have breakfast. I told him no, I just wanted to get some sleep. I got up around four and looked in the mirror while shaving and thought to myself, *you did your first hands-on surgical procedure. And the guy is pulling through.*

I knew that Nicki wasn't taken to the hospital because the hospital has to report all bullet wound treatments to the cops. Having guys around like Volpe solved the problem. I then got the premonition that this wouldn't be the last time I saw Volpe or guys like him, and little did I know how many I would see. Now I was really scared that if caught I would get thrown out of school or worse. I then rationalized that I wasn't a doctor yet, so what could they do to me? And besides that, I saved a guy's life.

A couple of days later the hotel desk clerk called out, "Marco, there is a package here for you."

"From who?" I asked.

"I don't know. Some delivery company brought it in this morning."

He gave it to me and it was addressed to me but there was no name of the sender anywhere on the outside. When I opened the package in my room, I couldn't believe my eyes. There was a black leather medical bag staring right at me. I quickly pulled the bag out and put in on the bed. It was beautiful. I was nearly bowled over when I opened the case and saw it was loaded with what I could now recognize as top-of-the-line medical and even surgical instruments. I grabbed the stethoscope and put it around my neck like the hospital medical staff wore theirs. It felt so good.

When I got finished admiring myself, I looked through the bag again and found a card at the bottom, on which was written, *Thanks*, and signed *Friends of a friend*.

I was so overwhelmed that I sat down on my bed and thought to myself, *you are so lucky, see what your crew has done for you. And when they call you for help, you help them. Your family deserves your loyalty.*

Since I was told to stay away and not contact anyone, I would wait until I was contacted and then give them my thanks.

# XXXVI

As the months rolled by, our class got more and more into "hands on doctoring," which meant seeing real live patients and then being tested for making the right diagnosis. I loved it. Our group continued to meet but not as often because the textbook and lab classes gave way to making rounds and observing medical and surgical procedures including the births of babies.

I kept on going back to the E.R. every chance I had. I got to know the doctors there, who after a while let me observe and once in a while, especially when the E.R. was jammed, let me assist. The joy of doing this was beyond comprehension.

There was still no word about Joe. I phoned his mother at least once a week and was sadly and tearfully told, "No, Marco, no word. "Carlo and I go to church every Sunday and pray that my Joey will come home soon, safe."

I always told her that Joe was also in my parents' prayers every Friday night as they lit the Sabbath candles. I tried to assure Mrs. Mancuso that Joe would come back safe and sound.

I hadn't heard from Phil in quite a while, but I had a premonition that he would be calling me if needed, no matter when.

For some time there were rumors of a friction building up between the Family and the West Side Irish Mob, known as "The Westies." It was over long respected territorial boundaries that were beginning to be violated. This was happening on both sides. Each side blamed the other and neither side stopped.

Several meets between the parties proved nothing but empty promises. And then it went from bad to worse. A couple of guys tried to hijack one of the Family trucks carrying loot swiped off the docks. It was usual for the loaders to take a walk after putting a mark on the containers holding easy sale merchandise, once our trucks came in sight. It seems that the driver's helper had a piece on him and shot the two guys trying to rip them off. They were identified as members of the Westies.

It didn't take two weeks before the Westies retaliated against the Amatto family members. Johnny Cheech and Sammy Fingers were shot dead coming out of an East Side restaurant. If they hadn't been whacked, I had the feeling that I would have been called upon to work with Volpe again. I kept my fingers crossed that if the shooting continued it would happen over the weekend, so if called to help, I wouldn't miss school.

As time went by and the violence continued, the public outcry caused the D.A. to set up a special detail to see that the carnage stopped. They started pinching anyone they thought was connected to both the Westies and the Amattos. Then they began busting up the cat houses and gambling joints as well as putting pressure on the shylocks and chop shops. The cops who were on the pad were now afraid to protect both groups. To make matters worse, the Feds and the I.R.S. were called in to help. From what I was later told, the local police and the D.A.'s office could be dealt with after a while, but there was no way to handle the F.B.I. taskforce and neither group wanted the I.R.S. checking on them. All remembered what the I.R.S. did to Al Capone, who sat ten years for tax evasion in federal prison. So a sit-down was arranged by the five-family commission and the top guys from the Irish bunch. The result was a truce, and boundaries were re-established. Each group promised to keep their guys in check and deal with them themselves if the rules were broken. Things seemed to calm down after the meet, but neither side trusted the other, and a couple of the young bloods on either side were chomping at the bit to get even for the killings. From what I heard, it took a lot of talking and pressure by the Amatto family captains to keep these guys in check. I guessed that the Irish captains had the same problem. By hook or crook the peace was kept with very few exceptions, but everyone wondered how long it would last.

# XXXVII

School continued to be great. It was more and more clinical with a lot of on-the-job training. I spent every spare moment I could in the E.R. and really started to feel like a doctor. The semester was spent sharing hospital time in the various medical specialties including the O.R.

One month ran into another and the time arrived for us to apply for internship positions and take the National Boards. Our Octet group got together to review, and it was more social than academic because we were so up to speed academically.

We discussed the hospitals where we would be applying and the reasons why certain hospitals were chosen. It came down to basically the reputation certain hospitals had for specific specialties and the residency programs for those specialties. When my turn came, I told the group I was going to apply to both Bellevue and King's County Hospital, primarily because of my interest in getting certification as an E.R. physician.

It was the last time the Octet met officially.

Two weeks before graduation, I received notification that I had passed the National Boards, granting me the privilege to obtain a license to practice in several states and a letter of acceptance to the internship program at Bellevue. The letter also advised me to make an appointment to see Dr. Cronin, Belleview's Chief of Staff.

At this meeting, the Doctor outlined the duties of the incoming interns and the hours they had to put in, which were thirty-six hours on, twelve hours off. Rooms would be furnished and discounts for meals would be available at the hospital cafeteria. Official white name jackets would also be provided at no cost. The pay was just about enough to cover the cost of food.

As I left Dr. Cronin's office, I saw the Brain, Lenny Brandt, and Chris Welsh from our group sitting in the waiting room.

"Don't tell me you also got accepted?" I asked.

Lenny answered right away, "Do you think we would let you do this alone? We are here to protect you from screwing up." He laughed and then looked at the secretary sitting at the desk in front of Cronin's office, and seeing that she obviously heard his remark, quickly added, "I was just kidding. This guy here," he said pointing to me, "is one of the best students NYU Med School ever had and will make a great doctor."

After hearing that the secretary dropped the frown and said to the Brain, "You can go in now."

Figuring there was no sense in waiting around, I left after telling Lenny that someday his perverted sense of humor would get him into real trouble. And I let it go at that, feeling that I might need his help in the future.

Graduation came and went. It was not a spectacular ceremony, partly due to the fact that our class was the experimental accelerated medical program pioneers and out of the sixty that started, only forty-eight remained to graduate. Only two guest tickets were allocated to each graduate and the graduation ceremony was held in a small lecture room without much fanfare.

My parents, of course, attended.

My name was called and as I walked up to the podium in my cap and gown to receive my diploma, I glanced up to where my folks were sitting. I could not help but notice my father sitting on the edge of his seat, chest expanded, with an expression of both awe and great love on his face, and my dear mother wiping her joy filled eyes.

Once all of the candidates received their diplomas, Colonel John Elder of the Army Medical Corps was introduced as the guest speaker.

"Congratulations, Doctors and guests," he said in a strong, booming voice. "No doubt you all have worked very hard and sacrificed a lot to be here today. Representing the U.S. Army Medical Corps, I want you to learn of the opportunities offered to you as doctors while serving your country in the time of war. Those who sign up will receive commissions as second lieutenants, receive the same pay and benefits as the other officers of this rank, and what's most important, our Army Intern Program is accredited by every state medical board. Information officers, located outside of the main office, will be on hand for the next week to answer questions you may have." He looked upon us proudly. "Good luck, congratulations, and God Bless America"

After the graduation, Papa, Mama and I went out and had a festive dinner. Mama and Papa were so proud. Papa kept telling me that my becoming a doctor that day was the greatest day of his life. As he was saying this, Mama kept crying. People at some of the other tables glanced over as Mama was doing this and Papa, with a big smile on his face, pointed to me and said, "My son here graduated a doctor today!"

I'll never forget that people actually got up from their tables and applauded. I was sort of embarrassed, so I just nodded my head in recognition. When my folks dropped me off at the hotel, Mama made me promise to come over for dinner the following night at eight and when I got there the store was closed. Sol let me in.

"Hello and congratulation, Dr. Falcone," Sol said. "Mama wants to get started with dinner so let's go back to the apartment."

When I opened to door, there was a group of friends and relatives who shouted, "Surprise! Surprise, Dr. Falcone!" I was shocked and tears welled up in my eyes. Everyone started to shake my hand and kiss me on my cheek. I saw Sol go out to the front door of the store. He put up a sign saying, *Come on in and congratulate Ivan and Sarah's son the new Dr. Falcone.* Among the people that were there were Joe's mother, father, and two sisters. I was so happy to see them. Many gifts were given. I remember a box of business cards, each card inscribed with gold raised letters reading *Dr. Marco Falcone*. This was from Isaac Goldman, the printer. Moishe, who had the novelty shop, brought a beautiful frame for my diploma.

The first chance I got, I went over to Joe's family, who wished me well again.

"Any news about Joe?" I asked them.

"Not a word," Joe's father replied.

"I can't tell you not to worry," I said, "but my mother has a saying she learned from her mother, 'no news is good news.' I know that Joe will come back safe and sound."

Joe's mother began to cry and then after wiping her tears said, "I pray every day that he will be ok and come back to us soon." She placed a hand on my shoulder. "Marco, you have been like a brother to Joe and a son to us. I know Joe, wherever he is, is so proud of you like we are. Come, Marco, I want to give you a big hug and a kiss." As she hugged me she whispered in my ear, "My brother asked me to give you a message. He congratulates you and is sorry that he could not come tonight. He knows you'll understand why and will be in touch when the time is right."

The party seemed to go on forever. It was around eleven when the last of the guests left. We were all exhausted. I chipped in helping in the cleanup and felt it would be the right thing to sleep over in my old room, in my old bed. This made Mama so happy.

I slept until about ten, being awakened by the noise of the customers ordering and the ringing of the cash registers. These sounds brought back many pleasant memories, although at the time, I thought they weren't that enjoyable.

After eating some leftovers for breakfast and saying goodbye to my folks, I went back to my hotel room and stretched out on the bed, clothes and shoes on, and placed my hands behind my head and smiled, saying to myself, "You made it, Marco. You did it. You are now really a doctor and you will save lives." I then fell back asleep and dreamed wonderful dreams of me doing miraculous things in my practice of medicine.

    I got up again around three in the afternoon and decided to bring a few things over to the hospital. I received my room assignment through the mail. I found out I was to share this room with Eric Jensen, a resident in surgery who would be around for two or three more years.

He was sleeping when I started to move some of my stuff in and I guess the noise woke him up. He jumped out of bed looking bleary eyed and said, "I'm Eric Jensen." He extended his hand and said, "You must be the new kid on the block and I guess I'll be stuck with you for the next year or two." Eric looked about five-foot-ten, a typical Swede; blonde haired, blue eyes and a great smile. I felt sure that he made a very comforting impression on all his patients.

    I started to unpack and put my stuff away in one of the only empty closets. The room was small; just two beds, two dressers, two closets, and a small desk with a mirror over the desk. As I looked around, Eric said, "You're lucky. We have one of the better rooms. We got a toilet." He pointed to a door. "Most of the other rooms don't have that and a lot of times, the guys have to wait in line to use the crapper on the floor. Go down to Cronin's office and let them know you are here and pick up an ID badge and room key. If you have the time, I suggest you start to get familiar with which is what in the hospital. Might be a good idea to introduce yourself to the on-duty floor and charge nurses on each floor. If you have the time today, stop in and say hello to the techs in radiology and hematology. Don't go into any patient's rooms. Check out the library and cafeteria."

    He sure had a lot of advice to give, and he wasn't done.

    "And one more thing," he added. "After you're finished, don't come back here. I'm off until twelve tonight and I need to get back to sleep. Besides you don't have to be back here until Monday morning at six so go and have a good time because for the next year at least, after doing thirty-six on and twelve off, you'll be too tired to do anything but sleep. Forgot to ask, are you married?"

"No," I replied.

"Got a steady girl friend?"

"No."

"Well, you better catch up and get your fill of getting laid between now and Monday morning. After that, unless you're some sort of Tarzan, you won't even be able to just get it up. Now scram. I need my sleep and get back to dreaming of having a ménage e' trois with Dorothy Lamour and Betty Grabel."

The first thing I did when I got back to the hospital was to call Ray at the Union and let him know that I wouldn't be able to continue to serve as a delegate because of my schedule, and I let it go at that. He didn't seem surprised and told me that my resignation was accepted and told me to stay in touch. He then asked for a number where I could be contacted and I felt I had no choice but to give it to him. He further added, as a favor to me, that he would pass the number on to certain friends of his. I felt I had no choice but to say thanks.

"Anything else?" Ray asked.

"No, not right now," I replied. "But I would like to make an appointment to come by to see you once I get settled."

"Anytime," said Ray. "So long." And he hung up.

Deciding to take Eric's advice about having a fun weekend, I started to make phone calls to see if I could wrestle up some of the girls, especially those who had put out for me in the past, but I struck out. Couldn't find even one that was available or even interested in seeing me.

Then it came to me in a flash. Belleview had a school of nursing and there were a lot of girls attending. These future R.N.'s were in several houses around the hospital. One of the E.R. techs clued me in that a lot of them hung out at the Chelsea Coffee Shop and those old enough to drink patronized the Blarney Stone Pub. I was also told that sometimes the nursing school held dances. When I checked it out, I saw that a dance was on for Saturday night.

I decided the best thing was to go hunting and get the lay of the land. So around eight that night, I dropped in at the coffee house, had a cup of coffee, and stayed around for a about an hour. I saw that nothing much was happening so I went over to the Blarney Stone. The place was jammed. I counted at least two girls for every guy there, maybe more. I looked around and spotted three girls - all good lookers - sitting at the bar. There was one empty stool next to them and I grabbed it. I picked on three girls sitting together rather than two because, according to Joe's theory of conquest, two girls that come together don't like to split up. But with three, if one of them wants to stay, it wouldn't break up the pair.

As I sat down I said, "Good evening ladies. Can I buy you a drink?" And they accepted. Their interest in me seemed to increase tenfold after I told them I was starting by internship Monday. I then learned that all were completing their last year of nursing school. After a while, it became evident that I was devoting my attention to Linda, the girl sitting next to me. She was a knockout, about five-foot-six, a hundred and twenty pounds, black hair, sexy brown eyes and with a body to die for. Shortly after and another round of drinks, the other two caught on and left.

Once again, going off a page from Joe's book of getting a girl into the sack, I let Linda do most of the talking.

I sensed there was good energy flowing between us. Then all of a sudden, after glancing at her watch, Linda said, "I got to go. It's almost midnight."

I quickly came back with, "I'd like to walk you home." And she readily agreed.

On the way back to her nursing student housing building, I asked if I could see her the next night.

"I'd love to," she said.

When we got to the front door, she turned to me and started to tell me how nice it was meet me, and before she could finish the sentence she was in my arms, our tongues finding each other in a sensual embrace, the rest of our bodies clinging to each other. All of a sudden she broke away and said, "I've got to go. I'll see you tomorrow at seven." And she disappeared through the front door.

    The following evening I picked her up at seven as planned. She looked great and I noticed that she had a little suitcase with her.
    The evening went fantastic. We dinned, danced, and wound up back at the Gramercy where we spent the night and all the next day. Linda was tremendous in bed and I felt like a love-starved lion let out of a cage. She reminded me of Pam.
    I wondered what had happened to her.
    Linda and I didn't take time to even go out for food. We just ordered stuff in and then went back to bed. I saw the only time she opened the suitcase was to take out a tooth brush and a change of underwear.
    We left the hotel around six-thirty, grabbed a bite to eat, and then went back to her quarters. When we got to her front door, she turned to me and said, "I know that from here on you'll be working you ass off. Little sleep and lousy food. I understand that. I'd really like you to call me when you can. Just leave word what time and where I can call you back. If you want to reach me, call the reception desk and leave a message." She handed me a piece of paper with a phone number on it. "I had a great time being with you, Marco. You made me feel like a woman again and I hope I pleased you as much as you satisfied me. You turned me on the minute I laid eyes on you and it hasn't stopped yet. I got to go now and with that she gave me a big lingering wet kiss and grabbed my crotch. "Save all this good stuff for me."
    Before I could answer, she was through the door.
I then headed back to the hospital. It took a few minutes on the way for the bulge in my pants to subside.
    When I got to my room Eric's bed was empty. Maybe, I thought, he was off or had a call. Frankly, at that moment I didn't care either way. I was so spent that I crawled into bed after leaving a five a.m. wakeup call. Before I knew it the phone was ringing, giving me the wakeup call.

As I grabbed my clothes I glanced over at Eric's bed. It was still empty.

At five-thirty, I went into the intern's lounge and had some coffee and oily stale donuts and then reported to the designated area for the specialty rotation assignments. These major rotations - Surgery, Medicine, OBGyn, and E.R. - were structured to give the interns intensive "hands-on" experience by putting into practice what was learned in medical school, under the watchful eyes of residents and the attending physicians. These tough task masters did not take errors in judgment lightly. But they didn't berate us in front of patients. They did it instead at the daily meetings held with the other first year interns.

Sure, I made mistakes. But I also learned from them.

Eric Jensen eventually did return to the room, and he proved to be a great roommate, and subsequently a friend. When available, he was willing to answer medical and surgical questions and soon allowed me to observe his procedures in the O.R. After a couple of weeks of doing this, I was allowed to perform surgical procedures myself with Eric or other residents standing right by me.

# XXXVIII

As time raced by and I was eight months into my internship, I started to feel complacent. The peace between the Irish mob and the Amatto family seemed to be holding, for the most part. If there was a problem, I never heard about it.

My peace of mind came to a halt, however, when I got a message to phone Phil. He asked when I had my next day off and I told him it was the coming Friday.

"Be in front of the hospital at ten in the morning," said Phil.

"I don't get off duty until twelve," I told him.

"Ok, be in front at twelve-thirty," said Phil. "Take your medical bag and also bring some blank prescription forms. Ciao."

"I don't know if I can get any," I replied.

"Find a way," said Phil. And he hung up.

I felt a bead of sweat running down my face. My heart raced and my knees buckled. When I calmed down, I tried to think about how I could get out of whatever it was that they wanted me to do. I had no answer. *This is the last time I'm going to be at their beck and call*, I thought to myself, *I'll call Ray at the Union and make arrangements to pay back the loan with as much vig as they want. Yes. That's what I'm going to do.*

I went back on call as scheduled and was kept busy throughout the thirty-six hour shift. With practically no sleep, I was waiting in front of the hospital at twelve-thirty when Phil came by and picked me up.

"Whattaya say, Doc?" Phil said to me.

I got in and put my medical bag in the back seat. "I say, I'm dog tired and can't really see straight," I replied. "I got only two hours' sleep during the past twelve hours."

"Well, you better pull yourself together," said Phil. "You gotta do a little favor for us."

I didn't say anything, but noticed that we were not heading toward the Staten Island ferry and Dr. Volpe. Instead, Phil drove uptown to around 108$^{th}$ Street and parked in front of a brownstone building. "We're here," he said. "Take your bag."

On the way to the steps of the door, there was a bronze sign attached to the stone wall reading, "West Side Veterinary Clinic."

"What the hell is going on," I said, sort of yelling.

"Shut the fuck up," Phil snapped. "I'll tell you when we get in there." He rang the bell and the door was then opened by a guy wearing a white jacket, similar to the one I wore at the hospital.

"Come on in," said the guy at the door. "I'm Gary Durago, one of the few dago veterinarians in New York. And you're?"

"Marco Falcone," I answered.

Gary nodded. "I got the patient all prepped and put under. You can go to work any time." He walked me downstairs to the first floor and into a room that was a miniature version of an O.R. On the table was a young lady dressed in a hospital gown with a screen covering her body from the hips up. Her feet were already placed in the O.R. table stirrups. At her side was a guy dressed in a nurse's uniform, monitoring the patient.

I turned to Phil, who was taking up the rear. "I gotta talk to you now," I said.

He saw I was shaking, and I guessed he didn't know whether it was from pain or fear. If he would've asked, I would've told him both.

"What am I doing here?" I asked. "I'm not going to do anything until you tell me. You can do what you want to me, but I ain't doing nothing until I know what's up."

"Ok, ok. Shut up and listen," Phil said. "One of our captains knocked up his amante. He's married to another captain's niece, and if she found out it wouldn't be good. Our guy, who is a gumba of Tony A, reached out and you're it to do the job."

"Are you crazy?" I exclaimed.

"Don't worry," said Phil. "We know you'll do good. Besides, the vet here could help."

"Since when do vets do abortions on dogs and cats?"

"Yeah, but we know he fixes them so they can't have kids, so he must know something. Now enough of this bullshit. Go in there and do what you have to do. If she dies, she dies. We got to get our guy out of this situation. Capishe? I'll wait upstairs. Let me know when it's over. And one more thing; you *got* to do this, so get started."

As Phil walked away, Gary approached me. "We got her out for another twenty to twenty-five minutes," he said, "so we better get on with it." Gary scrubbed up with me. I started to open my medical bag, but then realized I would have to sterilize the instruments. Gary caught on and in a flash said he had sterilizers on all the time. It would take less than five minutes.

I thanked God that I just finished OB-Gyn rotation and had actually performed a couple of D.C. procedures that was the protocol for this, and other types of uterine problems. Once the instruments were sterilized, I did the D and C and all went well. To my relief, there was very little bleeding. A few minutes later, the patient woke up.

"Is it all over?" she asked.

"Yes it is," I told her. "And you're gonna be ok."

She nodded and went back to sleep.

"We can take care of her from here on out," Gary then told me. "We have her blood, in case she needs some, and I have some pain pills that I give the animals that are better and safer than you can get for people at the drugstore." He looked me over. "Hate to say this, but you look terrible, Marco. When's the last time you slept?"

"I can't remember," I replied. "It seems like years ago."

"It's safe for you to go," said Gary, Pattyng me on the back. "But give me your phone number, just in case."

And I did. I collected my instruments, put them in the medical bag, and left the basement and up the steps into the foyer. I looked around for Phil, but he was nowhere to be seen.

"Where's Phil?" I asked Gary, who trailed along behind me.

"He's gone, but he left five bucks for cab fare for you and said he'd be in touch." I didn't want to take the money, but Gary pressed it into my hand. "Don't be stupid," he said. "Refusing it wouldn't be a smart thing to do."

So I took it and left, saying goodbye to Gary.

"I think we might be seeing more of each other," he said with a wry grin.

I hailed a passing cab and while riding back to the hospital, I had the time to think about what I was doing, what I had done, and what I might be told to do next. I was scared shitless. How could I get out of this? Should I join up with the Army Medical Corps? Could I run away? Should I tell them 'no' the next time they called? I felt I was in a maze with no way out.

I got back to the hotel and collapsed into bed. It seemed that as soon as my head hit the pillow, I was asleep. And then the phone rang. And rang. And rang. I picked it up and was reminded I was back on duty in a half hour.

Fortunately, the following thirty-six hour shift was not too bad. I was able to get a couple of hours sleep during it, and the ten cups of coffee daily helped.

It took about two shifts and two days off before I got back to myself and I had my fingers crossed that I wouldn't get any phone calls like the one I recently had. Every time the phone in the room rang, I started to shake. And the phone did ring more often, many times with messages from Phil telling me to call Gary, now referred to as Dr. G. When I did, Dr. G, after asking for and receiving my days off for the following week, attempted to make his conversation social by asking me to lunch on specific days or saying for me to come up and look at a couple of dogs he had up for adoption that might interest my parents.

I knew what he meant. The two dogs were actually two patients that needed abortions and Gary was told to schedule them with me.

I felt I had no choice but to go over to Gary's office and do the procedures. I hated myself for having to do this but was afraid to say 'no,' and the calls kept coming and I kept obeying. After a while I started to wonder where the hell these pregnant women were coming from. I knew there was a rubber shortage due to the war so maybe there was a shortage of condoms. I later found out that I was also being leased out to guys from the other New York families who got their *amantes* knocked up. Some of the girls were more than three months pregnant. I then told Gary that I wouldn't do the procedure on patients this far gone. He then told me he had to make a phone call and after speaking to someone on the other end, he motioned for me to pick up. When I did, I heard someone's voice on the other end telling me in a cold quiet voice - one that sent shivers throughout my body – "Doc, I don't want to hear that you won't do the job you were sent in to do. You go and do it and that's all I'm going to say. You don't want a problem with us. Your friends vouched for you. Capishe?"

"But at this stage the procedure is dangerous," I protested. "The patient could die."

"Make sure she don't," said the voice, and the phone went dead.

I thought I was going into shock as I hung up. The room was swirling around and I was about to lose my balance. This is when Gary grabbed me and dragged me over to a nearby chair and pushed my head and upper body towards my legs. Once this was done, he quickly bought me a glass of water and made me drink it.

After about fifteen minutes, I regained my composure. "I don't know if I can do this anymore," I told Gary.

"You gotta do these two today," Gary told me. "Your

people ok'd this and it won't look good for them to have you back out. It'll embarrass them."

"Gary, what do you think I should do?" I asked. "I can't do this anymore."

"You have to do the two procedures today. Then set up a meet with whoever - I don't want to know - and see what you can work out. Maybe they'll let you off the hook. You have no other choice. Just finish up today and see what happens."

I pulled myself together, drank some more water, wiped the sweat off my face, scrubbed up and did the two procedures. Gary was there to help. The guy in the nurse's outfit left the room as soon as we walked in.

When I got finished and both patients were stable, I thanked Gary and started to leave when he said, "It was good meeting you, Marco, and I hope you and I can stay in touch with each other, just socially, unless you get a dog or cat and need my help. Hope things work out ok for you."

"Thanks again," I said. "And yeah, let's stay in touch."

Gary handed me five dollars. "Here's for your Taxi," he said.

"I don't want it, do whatever you want with it."

And I left for the hospital.

I lay on my bed tossing and turning, trying to sleep but couldn't. I kept having nightmares about what I had just been through. I needed an answer and found it. I would call Ray and set up a meeting and workout a repayment program. I figured I owed the union for all the money they'd laid out; about fifteen thousand dollars. I still had about three thousand hidden away in my basement safe that I had accumulated from the monies I earned from the book making, shylocking routes, and the hijacking capers. I figured I could use this as a down payment and pay off the balance in three to five years, maybe sooner once I got into private practice. To sweeten up the deal, I would tell them I was willing to pay the customary vig for a loan of this type. I learned from all my years with the Amatto family that they and all the other families' creed was greed, nothing else. Money - lots of money - was the goal, from the lowest soldier up to the Don himself.

I called Ray and made an appointment on Thursday, my next scheduled day off, at two o'clock, my shift being over at nine o'clock that morning. This would give me enough time to get over to the store, pick up the money, and visit with my parents. Even if all went well, I could come back and have dinner with them before going back to the hospital.

On Thursday, the day of the appointment, I arrived at the store around noon. Mama had prepared a wonderful lunch of everything I'd like. While I was eating, Mama and Papa kept asking me questions about what I did at the hospital, how I liked it, how many people did I save, what kind of roommate did I have, how was the food, and many more questions that came so fast and furious that I had trouble eating while answering. I put a stop to the questions by telling my parents that I would answer the rest of the questions that night when I would come back for dinner around six. Mama was so happy to hear me say these words. She actually came over to me and kept hugging and kissing me.

"Let the boy eat!" Papa exclaimed. "He looks like he hasn't had a good meal in weeks."

Over coffee, I had a chance to look closely at Papa. He didn't look too good, and when he got up to take some dishes to the sink, he was unsteady on his feet.

"Are you feeling ok, Papa?" I asked.

"I feel great, better than ever," he replied. He looked at me and this time he was not smiling. "You're a doctor, not even for a year, and now you have X-ray eyes. I feel good, doctor. When I need you, I'll call you." Turning to Mama, Papa said, "Let's get back to work. Sol needs our help out there. The doctor here can finish his coffee."

When both of them left, I went down to the basement and picked up the money I had hidden there.

As I prepared to leave, I was able to get Mama aside without Papa hearing and told her, "You gotta get Papa to see Dr. Rabinowitz. There's something going on with him that I don't like."

"I tried to make an appointment for two weeks now," Mama replied, "but Papa said he doesn't need to go. You didn't see his feet or legs. Marco, they're swollen and I'm worried."

"When I come back tonight, we'll talk about it," I said. "I've got to run now."

I then went off to my meeting with Ray, the three grand tucked in my pocket. When I arrived at the union executive offices, I gave my name to a guy at the desk, who then directed me to the conference room in the back.

Sitting at the table was Ray, who greeted me with a big smile saying, "Hello doc, glad to see you. Understand you're doin'the right ting by our friends and doin' it good. How can I help you? Running a little short on cash?"

"No, nothing like that" I said. "I'm getting by."

"Doc, I got a busy schedule," said Ray. "I don't have time for a social visit if that's what it is."

"No, no social visit," I said. "I want to start paying off what I owe on the scholarship loan. I think my balance is around fifteen large. I got three big ones as a starter and I want to make up a payment plan with you."

"Whoa, hold up," Ray answered. "I can't take any deposit or any money from you. The ok has to come from Tony A. So to get things straightened out, I'll do you a favor and reach out to Tony and set up a meet for us to have a sit down and go over tings. Ok?"

"Ok," I said. "I'll give you my day off schedule for the next two or three weeks. Could you set the meet up pretty quick once I call to set things up?"

"Call me, and you'll hear back before you know it," said Ray. "On your way out, tell the guy at the desk to come in."

"Sure, thanks," I said, and I left.

In the elevator, I couldn't help but think that my meeting with Ray was a wash up, and I now had to assume that Tony A was calling the shots. If this were true, this might put me in a position that I wouldn't like to be in. No sense worrying about it, though. I further consoled myself with the thought that if push came to shove, I could approach Uncle Vito. I felt confident that he would work things out for me so that I could finish my internship and go from there on to my residency. After all, he was the Capo of the family and could call the shots.

My main concern now was what was happening to Papa, so I decided to head back to the hospital and pick up my blood pressure cuff and stethoscope and then see if I could get Papa to let me look him over. It wouldn't be easy, but with Mama's help, he might come around.

And after much persuasion, he did. My findings were not good. Papa had signs of high blood pressure, an irregular heartbeat, and edema in his ankles and legs. There was a potential high risk of stroke, heart attack, or the formation of blood clots in his legs or heart, or a combination of all three. I didn't want to scare Papa, who kept on insisting that he was as strong as a bull. The best I could get from him was that when he had some time, he would see Dr. Rabinowitz.

Papa claimed that Rabinowitz had been his doctor for nearly twenty years and knew his body better than he did. I told Papa to make his appointment on the same day I was off, so that I could go with him. "Maybe I can learn something from him," I told Papa.

"You certainly could," Papa said. "He doesn't go around telling his patients that they can get a stroke, heart attack, or blood clots."

I know Papa's remarks were a little curt, but they were telling me that he was actually concerned, if not scared, and didn't want us to know it.

The dinner meal itself was wonderful, but the conversation was stilted. Mama kept it going by picking up where she left off at lunch, still asking more and more questions about my work. After a while, Papa started to join in and the rest of the evening went fairly well.

When it was time for me to leave and when Papa was

making up the deposit, I got Mama on the side and told her, "You need to make an appointment for Papa to see Rabinowitz. The sooner the better. Don't take no for an answer, promise me. I'll meet you at his office. Here's my schedule for the next week. I'll call you every day to see when you got the appointment."

"Don't worry, I'll get the appointment," said Mama. "But it'll be nice to hear from you every day."

I kissed Mama good bye, hugged Papa, and made my way back to the hospital.

I called Mama when I had a chance the next day. She told me an appointment for Papa was made for the following Monday at two o'clock. This fit in with my schedule and even allowed for some sleep because my shift ended at eight that morning. I was kept busy with patients all weekend and before I knew it, my shift was over. I got some sleep until around twelve, ate some of the lousy cafeteria food, and met Mama and Papa at the doctor's office.

Rabinowitz was a short, rotund, ruddy faced man, who was nearly bald and still wore his mustache, even though it was grey. We had to wait a few minutes in the waiting room, now showing signs of wear.

"Come in," he said, after an elderly lady left thanking him.

Once we walked into the office, he said, "So nice to see you, Ivan and Sarah. And especially you, Marco. I hear you're finishing up your year of internship. Are you going to stay for residency?"

"I don't know yet," I replied.

"There's plenty of opportunity to practice good, old fashioned family medicine," he said. "When you have a chance, come talk to me. You won't make as much money and you'll work a lot harder than being a specialist, but I know you'll really love what you do."

"Ok, I'll do that."

"Now Ivan," said the doctor, "let's see what's going on with you. Even though you are a doctor, Marco, why don't you take your mother into the waiting room and keep her company. I'll call you in as soon as I look this shtarka over." He smiled and pointed at my father.

Mama and I then went into the waiting room, and Mama's barrage of questions continued. First it was a repetition of describing my living quarters, my roommate, what kind of food I ate, the type of work I was doing, and then came the advice that I needed more sleep and nourishing food. To my surprise the subject of my social life came next. "Do you go dancing, or even out on one date?" she asked me.

"No time, no time," I replied.

Then she asked, "Did you hear anything about Joe?"

"Not a word," I murmured. "I speak to Joe's mother at least once a week, and she hasn't heard anything from him or about him."

Just then, the door opened and Rabinowitz waved us into his office, pointing for the two of us to take a seat while he took a seat behind his old desk, loaded with charts. Out of the corner of my eye, I could see Papa buttoning his shirt in the examining room. Papa then came in and set down next to Mama.

"Ivan, I've got some good news and some not so good," said Rabinowitz. "The good news is that you're going to live to a ripe old age.

Papa said, "See, I told you there was nothing wrong with me. Let's get out of here and go back to the store. We have things to do."

Rabinowitz then cut in with, "Wait a minute, Ivan. I've got to give you the other side of the coin. You have high blood pressure, an enlarged heart, and you're bordering on Diabetes. This can all be controlled by medicine and diet, but you can't live in the lifestyle you've been living all these years. My advice to you is to sell the store and move to a warm climate, like Miami, and enjoy life. You've earned it. You got Marco here, who became a doctor, and he's on his way. You could get a good price for the store, so go and enjoy the fruits of your labor. If you don't take my advice, I would have very big concerns about your health and longevity. In a nutshell, Ivan, if you want a long healthy life, my advice is to quit and move to a warm climate away from the winters here. I'm going to give you some scripts for medicine I want you to take. You need to get more sleep, and I want you to sleep with a pillow under your legs. Ok? I'll see you in two weeks. Good to see you, Sarah." He then turned to me and asked, "Could you stay for a few minutes after your folks leave, Marco?"

"Sure," I said. I turned to my parents and told them, "You go on home. I'll talk to you later. Papa, everything will be ok. Just listen to the doctor."

Papa gave me a grunt answer and left the room followed by Mama. I heard the arguing as they left the office.

Rabinowitz sat down with me. "Marco, I'm really worried about your fathe'rs condition, from one doctor to another," he said. "Put pressure on him to quit." Before I could say anything else, he continued, "I've been in practice here for over forty years and I too have health problems. Between my making hospital rounds in the morning and then office hours most of the day, and house calls at night, I'm worn out. I'm getting too old for this. It calls for a young man like yourself. Would you consider taking over my practice? I own the building. There is a beautiful two-bedroom apartment upstairs, and I would work with you on the money. You're from the neighborhood and that's a big advantage. Don't give me an answer now, just consider my offer." With that, he gave me his hand and I shook it.

"Thanks for laying it on the line with Papa, and thanks for the offer," I said. "I'll definitely consider it."

"One more thing," he added. "Make sure your father takes his meds and come back in two weeks. He needs to be monitored."

"I will, and thanks again." I left the office and made my way back to the hospital.

The next few days were a blur. Between being swamped with work, my concern for Papa's health, and my efforts to reassure Mama that he would be ok, I was dog-tired. In addition, the anticipation of receiving phone calls from Gary or Phil also took its toll. I couldn't sleep too well, had no appetite, was moody, and it had an effect on my work.

After a short time, Eric began to pick this up and one night after we both got off, he said, "Let's go over to the coffee shop and talk."

While drinking a decent cup of coffee, he asked, "What's going on? You look like shit and aren't up to par on your work."

I went into detail and was pretty sure I convinced Eric that my concern for my father was the problem. Now that Papa saw his own doctor and was on meds, this would take a load off my mind and I would now be able to get back to my old self again, I told Eric. I avoided any mention of the sessions I had at Gary's.

Eric seemed satisfied. We finished our coffee and went back to our room at the hospital, washed up and crawled into bed. I think I was asleep as soon as my head hit the pillow. It was the first day of my shift as I was making rounds when one of the candy stripers came up to me and said, "Dr. Falcone, you have an emergency call. I think it's your mother. You can take it at the nurses' station."

Hearing this, I rushed over and the charge nurse pointed to a phone with a receiver lying on its side. I grabbed it and heard Mama's hysterical voice.

"Marco, your father was just taken to Beth Israel Hospital!" she exclaimed.

"What happened?" I asked.

"He was schlepping a bag of onions up from the basement and when he got to the top of the steps, he collapsed. I don't know if he fainted, had a heart attack, or something else. Sol came over with cold towels, which sort of revived him. Papa tried to get up on his feet, but couldn't. Sol called and got the ambulance. They came and took him out on a stretcher. Can you come right away?"

"As soon as I can, I'll call a cab and pick you up," I said. "If you didn't already do it, I'll call Dr. Rabinowitz and tell him what happened. Or better still, ask Sol to do it. Don't worry, Mama. Papa will be ok. I promise you. I'll see you soon."

As soon as I hung up, I thanked the charge nurse, hunted down the chief resident, told him what happened and got the ok to take off.

I flagged down a cab, picked mama up, and went to the hospital E.R. The place was crowded with people in the waiting room, both patients and visitors. I sort of elbowed my way to one of the admitting cubby holes, showed proof that I was a doctor and got what I guessed was professional courtesy because they told me that Papa was in bed number four and to go in. I took Mama by the hand, located bed four, and we saw Papa lying there with an oxygen mask covering his face. His eyes were closed but when he heard us come in, he opened them and waved us to come closer to him. I left Mama by his side and went to find the E.R. doctor who was on duty and responsible for treating my father.

I caught up with him as he came out of another cubicle. Dr. Samsky was no youngster. He had the appearance that he knew what he was doing and had everything under control. After introducing myself, I asked if any diagnosis of Papa's condition was made as of yet.

"I haven't really examined him fully yet," he replied. "We put him on oxygen as a precaution when they brought him in. I'm on my way to look at him now."

I followed him back to where Papa was lying and motioned to Mama. "This is my mother, Doctor."

"Why don't you go back to the waiting room and you'll be called once I finish in here," the doctor said to us. "You have a choice; go back with your mother, or, because you're a doctor, you can stay here and observe. By the way, we got your father to tell us who his G.P. was and we got word that he'll be on his way shortly."

I decided to stay. Mama left after kissing Papa on his forehead.

Dr. Samsky' examination was extremely thorough.

Blood was drawn and EKG, X-rays, and urine samples were taken as well as examination by stethoscope. The techs in the E.R. were terrific and had all the results back in less than an hour. By this time, Dr. Rabinowitz arrived and I was allowed to be a party to the diagnosis and prognosis.

Papa had had a slight heart attack with a little damage to the heart, but nothing life-threatening. It was thought best for Papa to be admitted and checked for at least three days. Mama was called in and Doctor Samsky explained the situation. She was so relieved hearing that Papa would be alright that she grabbed Dr. Samsky and hugged him.

"Ok, I have other patients to see," said the doctor. "Dr. Rabinowitz will tell you what will be going on. Nice meeting you. Keep an eye on your father and tell him to behave himself. We'll take your father up in a few minutes. Let me see if I can get him a private room as a professional courtesy to you. Why don't you take your mother home? You can call me in a couple hours." He handed me a phone number with his extension listed on it.

Mama and I took a cab back to the store and when we went in, we saw a strange guy behind the counter waiting on customers along with Sol. Mama whispered to me, "Who's he?"

"I'll find out," I said, and I motioned to Sol, who came from behind the counter.

"Before you ask me," said Sol, "I ask you, how's your papa?"

"He had a slight heart attack but will be ok," I said. "Who's the guy behind the counter?"

"He's Stephen, the Polack," Sol replied. "He got laid off from Trunz Pork Store two weeks ago. I got a hold of him and he was glad to fill in. He's honest and knows the business. I've known him for years. Between he and me, we can do the ordering and I can help your mother make up the deposit and take it over to the bank. Now tell me more about your father."

"Like I told you, he had a minor heart attack," I said. "They'll keep him in the hospital for a few days then send him home. He has to take it easy. Thanks a lot for taking over like this. Mama can go and stay with Papa instead of her having to be here."

Mama and I went back to the apartment where she fixed us something to eat. She kept asking me to call Dr. Samsky and ask him when we could come see Papa. I told her we had to wait a while because they have to take him upstairs into a room and get him settled. Every ten minutes, Mama kept asking me 'Can we call now?' and I kept answering 'Let's wait a little while longer, I don't want to nag the ER doctor.'

"Then please, call Rabinowitz," said Mama. "He'll know when we could go see Papa."

Reluctantly, I phoned Rabinowitz, and when he answered he said, "I just got off the phone with the hospital. Your father is in Room 613, a private room, resting comfortably and you can go over now. I'll see him later. Marco, you can call me any time for a report. He'll be ok, but he has to quit working. He was lucky this time. Maybe he won't be the next. Tell you what, call me tomorrow around ten."

"Thanks for everything, Doctor," I said. "I'll call you tomorrow."

I called Belleview and got a hold of my senior resident. I told him my story and asked if it was ok to take the rest of the day off. I told him that I'd make the time up by working on my days off.

"Don't worry about that now," said the senior resident. "Just take care of what you have to do. Just keep in touch, so I know how to make out the schedules."

"Thank you, it's appreciated." And I hung up.

Mama and I went back to the hospital and up to Papa's room. Despite the IVs coming out of his arm and the oxygen mask, Papa looked ok. He motioned us in when he saw us and grabbed Mamas hand and then mine. I left Mama at his bedside and walked over to the nurses' station. I showed them my intern ID and asked to look at Papa's chart.

"Not without the ok in writing from the attending," the head nurse answered. "I can only tell you that we have him stabilized and we'll keep our eye on him. Dr. Rabinowitz is one of our favorite doctors and we give his patients a little extra special care. Not that we don't take good care of all of our patients. You talk to him about getting permission."

They kept Papa at Beth Israel for a total of ten days. I didn't want to get in touch with anybody from the "Family" directly, so I called Gary and told him the situation with Papa and that I was going to spend every minute of my free time with him and my mother at the hospital. I couldn't and wouldn't do anything else, and explained that with all my due respect. I had to do this.

"I'll pass on the message and get back to you," said Gary. "I think you'll get the ok on this, for the time being."

Papa seemed to be getting better every day. The EKG, however, showed heart damaged and validated Dr. Rabinowitz' initial diagnosis. I kept going to see him every chance I got. One afternoon, I bumped into the chief resident at Beth Israel, who told me that Rabinowitz' specialty was cardiology, but he loved to practice as a G.P. He also told me that other doctors consulted him on their own patients.

After receiving after-care instruction, Mama and I took Papa home in a cab and Papa received a warm welcome when we got back to the store. Papa, after thanking everyone, went back to the apartment and immediately into bed.

I had to leave shortly thereafter to go back to the hospital and back to work. I called at least twice a day, and when my shift was over, I went over to the store to see him. He was looking better and better each time I visited.

"I had a lot of time to think about things when I was lying there with tubes stuck all over me and an oxygen mask on my face," said Papa, "and I realized I'm too young to leave your Mama. So, I'll do what Rabinowitz told me, and the store is going up for sale. This has to be done quietly, without too much commotion, and I know you're very busy, but I'm going to need your help."

"Don't worry, Papa," I said. "I'll take care of things."

The war in Europe was winding down. The Russians were just a few miles from Berlin and the Allies had taken all of their assigned objectives. American GIs who had wounds or broken bones that would take months to heal were sent back to the States for treatment and then discharged. One of them was Robbie "The Fat Boy" Fano. He was fat from the day he was born. In the Army, he was a cook and somehow a piece of his foot was blown off when he stepped on a mine. His father Tony was the local shoe maker. Once Robbie got discharged and sent home, he started to nose around the store a couple of times a week, then a couple of times a day, making little purchases every time he came in.

After a couple of weeks, Robbie asked Sol how he could get in touch with me. Sol told him I would be visiting Papa the following Tuesday afternoon and Robbie said he'd stop by around three. At three, Robbie came by and I invited him into the apartment. It was the first time I had seen him since high school. He was fatter than ever.

"I hear your father isn't well and the store is up for sale," he said.

"Papa had a little heart attack, but is recovering nicely," I replied. "He might consider selling if the price is right, and if he's sure whoever buys it will do right by the customers."

"How much are you asking for?"

"You'll have to talk to my father about that," I said. "If you're serious about buying, come back tonight."

"Ok if I bring my father with me?" Robbie asked. "He closes his shop around six, and we can be here by six-thirty."

"That's fine. Let your father and mine discuss the money end of it. That's the way they did it in the old country."

"See you at six-thirty," he said. Then he left.

I passed Robbie's message onto my parents, and Papa looked sad but relieved.

"Ok, we'll meet," said Papa. "I've known Robbie's father, Tony, for a lot of years. He's a good shoe maker and a good man. Robbie takes after him. What should we ask for the store? Don't forget, it comes with the apartment and we have fifteen more years to go on the lease. Also, Mama and I want to live nice."

"How about asking sixty-five thousand?" I suggested.

"That's a lot of money, Marco," said Papa. "Do you think they'll go that high?"

"It doesn't hurt to ask."

"One more thing," Papa added. "Sol has to stay with the store for at least two years, but if he wants to leave sooner, he can. I don't care about the Polack."

At six-thirty, Robbie showed up and our fathers gave each other a hug and a kiss. Seemed that this old Italian custom was still alive here on the lower East Side.

"Ivan, I was sorry to hear that you have had a little health problem," said Tony. "I want you to know you are in our prayers every Sunday. Robbie wants the store. He can get a loan from the government. If he is short, I can help out."

My father turned to me and Robbie and said, "Why don't you two go into the store, have a cup of coffee and keep Mama company? Tony and I are going to talk alone."

Robbie and I complied.

About fifteen minutes later, Papa stuck his head out the door, motioned to us, and said, "You two, come back in and bring Mama."

When we returned, Papa told Mama to make some espresso and bring out the anisette. Nothing much was said until the espresso cups and pony glasses were filled. "Salute!" Papa said as he raised his cup, and we all answered, "Salute!" We drank the coffee and then the anisette. After we finished doing this, he, as usual, wiped his mouth and his moustache. He said, "Tony and I have reached a deal, and the deal is this. We will sell Robbie the store for sixty-five thousand dollars. Tony said there's no problem with the money, right. Tony?"

"Ivan, there will be no problem," Tony said.

"I told Tony we'll need three months until we get settled somewhere else, but Robbie can take over the store once we get all the money. We agreed that there's no payout. All the money has to come in at one time. I told Tony we would pay one hundred and fifty a month rent for the apartment until the time we leave and that's the agreement as I understand it." Papa turned to Tony and asked, "Is that how you capishe, nostro accordo?"

"Si," Tony replied.

Tony and Robbie then got up and shook hands with Mama and I. Then he and my father hugged, kissed each other, and left.

"Let's eat something, not too much," said Papa. "Then I'm going to lie down and try to sleep. I'm tired. We'll talk tomorrow."

Before he could get up, I asked, "Don't you think we should talk to Mo Weinberg, the lawyer, about drawing up papers about the sale?"

"We don't need papers," said Papa. "We shook hands and that's enough. That's better than any lawyer's written stuff."

With that, Papa kissed Mama and me goodnight and went into the bedroom.

About three weeks later, I had my day off and went to see my folks. Papa was sitting in his usual armchair reading. Mama ran over to hug me and give me a big kiss. She was smiling from ear to ear. Before I could say anything, she said, "Boy, do I have news for you. We are moving to Miami Beach, Florida, four blocks from the ocean. Isn't that great?"

"How did you do this?" I asked. "How do you know where you're going to live?"

"Easy," said Mama with a smile. "I remembered my cousin, Helena, the one from Philadelphia. Her husband's the dentist. She has a sister, Rosalie, who moved to Miami Beach two years ago, so I got her number from Helena and called her. She told me there was a beautiful one bedroom furnished apartment that just became available, and the rent is only one hundred and twenty-five dollars a month! The apartment is on the first floor, so Papa doesn't have to walk the steps. She even sent us pictures of the apartment, and Papa agreed that it was a beautiful apartment, so I called Rosalie and told her we'd take it. She told me that she'd talk to the landlord and get the lease in the mail right away."

My folks got the lease a few days later. They signed and returned it with the required deposits. Once I found out all of the details, I told Mama, "You deserve a metal."

"A medal for what?" asked Mama.

"Being a good wife," I said.

"I've loved your Papa always, from the first day I laid eyes on him, and I know he loves me, and I'm positive we will love Miami Beach. I can't wait, and although he didn't say it, Papa can't wait also."

All that was holding them up was the money for the store. Papa told me to stop by Tony's and ask him to come by and see me. When I did, I let Papa know that Tony asked me to tell him that he would come to the store right after he closed his shop that night.

I couldn't stay for their meeting. I had to go back to work. I found out later that Tony told Papa that Robbie's G.I. loan had been approved but it would take about sixty more days before the money came through.

"I can get the money much sooner and not have to wait on the government," said Tony. "Can you give me a week or ten days at the latest and we'll straighten out?"

"That's ok, Tony," said Papa. "We need that time to get ready to move to Florida."

About a week later Tony came by with the money. Papa told me it was about half in money orders and the rest in cash.

Robbie came in the next morning when the store opened. When the morning rush was over, Papa gave him a list of suppliers and other information that would be helpful. Sol had been clued in as to what was happening and he had assured Papa that he would give Robbie his cooperation.

I took the next few days off from the hospital, having made arrangements with Lenny Brandt to cover for me. I promised him that I would cover for him when he wanted to take off, even if it meant weekends. During this time, I accumulated cartons, newspapers, wrapping paper, and cord and then packed all of the things my folks wanted to take to Florida.

I remember the packing of Papa's clothes resembled a vaudeville skit. Whatever Papa wanted packed, Mama said "You don't need it. It's hot in Florida. You'll never need gloves, heavy sweaters, or goulashes." This was followed by the back and forth discussion regarding mufflers, earmuffs, stocking hats and flannel pajamas.

When it came to a heavy jacket and wool overcoat, Papa put his foot down. "I'm wearing the overcoat to Florida and I'm keeping my heavy jacket. You never know when it'll be cold down there."

After this heated conversation when on for about half hour, an armistice was reached.

Papa could keep the jacket and coat. All the rest I bundled up and earmarked for charity. Railway Express picked up the cartons a couple of days later, promising a seven day delivery date.

The next day I went over to Grand Central Station and bought two tickets for Miami.

I didn't tell my folks that I bought them a compartment where they would have more comfort, privacy, and their own toilet.

Two days later, I picked them up in a cab, and without turning their heads to take a last look at the store and where they had lived for many years, they got into the cab and we were off to the station. On the way there, Papa turned to me and said, "Mama and I want you to pay off the loan. We have plenty of money to live real good for a lot of years and have enough left over for you to give back what you owe. We would like to see you free of any debt while we are still alive because the money will someday be yours anyway."

"Thank you, Mama and Papa," I said. "Let's wait until you get settled and we'll talk about it."

I helped them onto the train and kissed them goodbye. There were tears in both Mama and Papa's eyes. Tears began running down my cheeks.

"We'll talk every week," Mama said.

"On Sunday, when it's cheaper," Papa added.

"I promise to write at least twice a week," I said.

With that, I heard the conductor call out, "All aboard!" and I got off the train. I didn't look back, and went back to the hospital.

It didn't take me very long to realize that an important chapter in my life had just closed.

# XXXIX

It was about three weeks later that I got a message to phone Phil. *Oh shit*, I thought to myself. *I wonder what's up now.* I made the call, left my number with the guy that answered, and in about five minutes the phone rang.

"Hello Doc, when is your next day off?" said Phil.

"Day after tomorrow at eight in the morning," I replied.

"Well, Dr. Volpe is not doing good. We think he's on his way out. Doc, we think you should see him."

"What if he's dying?" I asked.

"Doc, we think you need to see him and bring along a blank death certificate," Phil reiterated.

"What?" I exclaimed.

"You heard me."

"I don't know if I can get one."

"Figure out how to get one," said Phil. "We're counting on you. Be in front of the hospital at nine." And he hung up.

I knew I had to do what he said, and after searching around I found out where a supply of death certificates were kept and grabbed one. I also promised myself that I wouldn't do this anymore. I'd take Papa up on his offer, pay off the loan, and get out from under the Family.

Phil drove up at nine as I paced in front of the hospital, and we drove out to Volpe's place. We didn't talk too much on the trip out there.

When we walked into the living room, I recognized a couple of guys from my crew, including Rocky, the captain. After greetings were made, Rocky motioned for me to follow him upstairs to Volpe's bedroom. When we entered, I saw

Volpe lying motionless on the bed. I ran over, took one look, and knew that he was dead. To check, I looked for a pulse, heartbeat, and to see if there was any respiration, but there was none. He was definitely dead.

"How long has he been like this?" I asked

"I don't know Doc," said Rocky. "He was breathing last night."

"You got the death certificate on you?" Phil asked me.

"Yeah, I have it," I replied.

"All you have to do is just fill it out and sign the doctor shit. Disobeying could mean death. We found him like this in the morning."

I didn't have the guts to refuse, so I did it. When finished, Phil drove me back to the hospital.

Back in my room at the hospital, though lying in bed and exhausted, I couldn't sleep. Something was in the back of my mind that was bothering me and suddenly, it came to me and I nearly jumped out of bed scared out of my wits. Rocco told me Volpe was breathing last night. I hopped out of bed, threw on some clothes and hurried over to the hospital's medical library, where I looked up Rigor Mortis chronology. As I read the data, it reinforced my semi-conscious alert that something about Volpe's death didn't add up. There were signs of Rigor when I examined him and Rigor comes about usually forty-eight hours after death. Yet Rocco told me Volpe was alive last night and was found dead early this morning. *So, I was lied to*, I thought. But why? And if Volpe was dead at least two days ago, why were questions I asked left unanswered? The 'why' kept plaguing me until I couldn't think straight, so I took the shot and phoned the number Phil had previously given me. I left word with the person answering the phone to have Phil call me, and he did a few minutes later.

"We need to talk and to do it today before I go back on shift tonight," I said. "When can you pick me up?"

"Hold your horses, Doc," said Phil. "I got things to do. Maybe around seven. Be outside."

"Ok, see you then."

At about seven-fifteen, Phil showed up. I got in the car and we drove off.

"Will this take long?" Phil asked in an unfriendly voice. "I'm busy tonight."

"Let's go someplace safe where we can talk," I said.

It didn't take more than five minutes before Phil pulled up behind a meatpacking houses' loading dock on the West Side.

"We can talk here," he said. "Now, what the fuck is so important?"

I told him my conclusion that Volpe died at least two days ago, and my signing the death certificate - which probably listed a phony cause of death - if discovered, could cause me to lose my license and probably go to jail.

Once I told Phil this, he looked me square in the eye and said, "Sometimes you gotta do whatchya gotta do. Volpe knew he was dying and he started calling for a priest. Certain people were concerned what he would say in confession. They wanted to make sure no secrets were told. In a way, this might have included you also. The bosses decided it would be best for Volpe to pass away, maybe just a little while sooner."

"That's murder!" I blurted out.

"You better keep your fucking mouth shut about anything you just heard," Phil snapped, "or you and me will be in a lot of trouble. Volpe is out of his misery, and he'll have a nice big wake. Don't you show up. Did you see one of the Mancuso's meat wagons coming up to Volpe's house as we left? He came to pick up the body and death certificate, so everything is now up and up. Any more questions?"

I was in shock, but was able to mutter, "No." And Phil drove me back to the hospital.

As I got out of the car, Phil leaned over. "Remember to forget what happened today and what we spoke about just before," he said. "Our lives depend on it."

There's no way I could continue leading two types of life. I made up my mind once and for all, no backing down no matter what the consequences. So I decided to call Ray and set up a meet.

"What's the purpose this time?" he asked.

"I want to make out arrangements to pay off my loan," I replied.

"When could you meet with us?" he asked. "we'll talk about it."

I gave him my days off schedule and we set up a meeting at Tepperstein's office the following Tuesday at one.

When I hung up, I felt better. Meeting at the lawyer's office, I thought, meant that once the financial details of the loan repayment were worked out, Tepperstein would draw up the papers. Finally, I would be out from under the gun and away from the mob way of life. For the first time in years, I was actually happy.

On Tuesday, I got to Tepperstein's and was immediately ushered into his private office. Upon entry, J.T. arose from his desk and shook my hand and said, "It's been a long time since we've seen each other and I'm so pleased that you made it out of med school and became a doctor."

"Yep, it's been quite a few years," I said. "As I grow older, time seems to run by faster and faster." I then asked, "Is Ray here?"

"He's here in the conference room, where you met before," J.T. answered with a smile on his face. "Do you remember those circumstances?"

"I sure do," I said. "They're hard to forget."

J.T. then walked me over to the conference room door and unlocked it. Once I was in, I heard the door close behind me and my heart nearly stopped. Sitting around the conference table in addition to Ray were Tony A, Rocco, and Phil.

"Have a seat, Doc," Tony A said. "What's this I hear? You want to pay off the loan and leave us?"

"Not exactly," I said. "I'm applying for a residency so I can become a specialist, and board certification could take three years. I won't have any time to do anything else. Besides, my father will give me enough money to start paying off my loan."

"You hear that?" Tony A said, facing Ray and Rocco. "He won't have time to help out the family, because he wants to be a specialist and leave us with no help in case we need it."

Before I could answer, there was a knock on the door and when it opened my heart practically jumped into my mouth. As Paulie walked in, he said hello to everyone, but just nodded to me as he took a seat around the table. Paulie looked real fit. He had slimmed down a lot and was more muscular, but still had that grim look on his face, which got grimmer when he looked my way.

"Our friend Paul here just got out of the Merchant Marine," said Tony A. "And he doesn't have to go back on the ship if he doesn't want to. So, welcome back Paulie. Let me bring you up to date. The Doc here, after we were so good by getting him financed all through college and medical school, wants to pay back the money we laid out and say 'arrivederci' to us. Is that right, Doc?"

"Tony, that's not the way it is," I said. "I want to make arrangements to start repaying what I borrowed, and as I start making more money, I'll pay more. I want to become an emergency room specialist and that's going to take two or three more years and I'll have less time off than I do now. I won't be able to leave the hospital even if I wanted to."

"Am I hearing straight?" Rocco asked Tony. "The Doc here, is he doing ball four, and wants to leave us after all that was done for him?"

Paulie then chimed in, "I could have told you this years ago. That's the way his people operate."

The only one who came to my defense was Phil. "I know the Doc here, for years," he said. "He's honorable and he'll do the right 'ting. Am I right, Doc?" He directed his attention at me.

I had no choice but to nod yes.

Turning to Ray, Tony A asked, "How much total was laid out for Marco here to become a doc?"

"Fifteen big ones, without any vig," Ray answered.

"That's a lot of wood, even without the vig," said Tony. "How much do you figure with as little as two points?"

"I'd say around a hundred large," Ray replied.

Turning to me, Tony asked, "Can you come up with a hundred big ones in one lump sum?"

"No, I can't," I said. "The most I could scrape up would be around twenty-five thousand."

"Twenty-five thousand, are you kidding?" said Tony. "That's an insult. Let me tell you what the score is. We don't want your fucking money. I was just playing with you. We made an investment in you and now you've got to pay us the dividends. Not money, but your service. For our family, you are the Doc. You gotta be ready when we call and no matter why we call. We'll let you know when you're debt is paid. Capishe? And don't try to disappear or avoid us. It ain't healthy. By the way, how are your folks enjoying life in Miami Beach?"

The sentence sent chills down my spine. I answered, "They're fine."

"Send them our best."

Phil interjected, "Doc here is honorable, and he'll continue to do the right thing."

"One more thing," Tony A said. "When will you be finished working at the hospital?"

"In about three, maybe four months," I replied.

"Do you want Volpe's office? You can live upstairs."

"No, I don't want it," I said. I thought real quick about my reasoning. "Besides, he might have hidden some records or information there that might be dangerous."

"I think that Doc here is right," Tony replied. "You look around, and we'll put out the word than an office is needed and something will come up. In the meantime," he said to the guys sitting around the table, "tell your crews not to get stabbed, shot, or whacked or get any of the *amantes* knocked up until the Doc gets the office." He started cracking up and the rest of the crew joined in. "Any questions, Doc?"

"No, Tony," I replied.

"Meeting over," he said. "Stay in touch, Doc. Caio."

On the way back to the hospital, I felt like a rat caught in a maze with no way out. I saw myself stepping in Volpe's footsteps and winding up like him; a beaten alcoholic old man, looking forward to death.

Then it came to me; Uncle Vito could be my way out. Since I was told not to contact him, I hadn't. But now, I had to take the shot and do it. The best way, I thought, was to get a message to him through his sister, Joe's mother. I called her every week to ask for news about Joe, and in case anyone was listening, the call wouldn't seem out of the ordinary.

As soon as I got to a phone, I called Joe's house and before I could say a word, Joe's mother told me, "Marco, I've been trying to get in touch with you. I called the store looking for you. I didn't know your father sold it. I was told you were working in some hospital but didn't know which one." Her voice perked up. "I got some good news. I got a letter from my Joe. He's coming home in about three weeks, maybe sooner! I'm so happy, I can't wait to see him. We're going to make a big party for him when he gets here, and all the family will be invited including you to see my Joe finally back home. Give me a number where you can be reached and I'll have him call you as soon as he gets here."

I gave her the number and before she said goodbye, she again promised to contact me as soon as Joe got home. After she hung up, I heaved two sighs of relief. The first one was that Joe was coming home, and the second was that Uncle Vito was sure to be at the party no matter what. Once I saw him there, maybe I could get him on the side and tell him about my problem. I knew that he would help me.

I counted the days waiting to get a call from Mrs. Mancuso. So about three weeks later, I phoned her.

"No news yet, but there should be soon," she told me.

I'll never forget it. I just got into bed after an eighteen hour shift and was fast asleep when I was awoken by the phone constantly ringing off the hook. I tried putting the pillow over my ears but it didn't drown out the sound. Finally I grabbed the phone, and without even asking who was on the other end, yelled, "You asshole!"

The response was, "Hi Marco, if I'm an asshole you're one too. You taught me how to be one."

"Joe!" I blurted out. "Is it really you?"

"It's me in the flesh!" said Joe.

"When'd you get home? Are you there now?"

"I'm at a debriefing camp in Virginia and should be out of here and home in a couple of weeks. I'll let you know when I'm a civilian again and we can start having some fun. Just wanted to tell you, I'm back and rearing to go. I was told you're really working your butt off without a lot of free time, so give me your schedule for the next couple of weeks and I'll call you. Especially when you're sleeping." And he gave me that old familiar laugh.

"You haven't changed your lousy sense of humor," I replied.

"No, it got worse! Gotta go now. Ciao."

I was so glad to get this phone call. My chances of a meet with uncle Vito were getting better. Over the next couple of weeks, Joe kept his word and phoned during the times we previously agreed on and old times were revisited.

"I'm getting out of here a week from this coming Wednesday and arriving at Grand Central at about two o'clock," he told me. "I looked at the schedule you gave me. It looks like you're open, so how about meeting me before I head home around two-thirty at the Oyster Bar in the station. I haven't had clams, oysters, or calamari since I left New York."

"That's a go," I said. "Put on a rose in your left ear so I can recognize you."

"That's a shitty joke," said Joe. "It's just like all the rest I remember you telling. But what am I gonna do, I still love you like a brother."

"Same here," I said. "I can't wait to see you."

"Double for me. Ciao."

On Wednesday I got to Grand Central early, found the track that Joe was arriving on, and waited there for him. The train arrived and I kept looking at the incoming passengers. Finally I spotted him carrying a duffle bag on his shoulder. When he saw me, he reached into his breast pocket and put a rose into his ear. The son of a bitch upstaged me again. Once he was clear of the gate, we ran over to each other and actually kissed each other on the cheek in the customary Sicilian manner. I didn't understand why people were staring at us. Here were two young guys, hugging and kissing with one having a red rose in his ear. We both got the picture at the same time and started to laugh hysterically.

Between our peals of laughter, Joe said, "If that's the way they want to think, let's not make liars out of them." So he started to swish as he walked to the restaurant, still with the rose in his ear. I followed behind him with his bag. I didn't have the guts to walk his walk, but it felt just like old times.

As we approached the Oyster Bar, Joe took the flower off his ear and we got a table in the rear. The place wasn't crowded and there were empty tables surrounding us, so we hoped we could talk without being heard. Joe looked really fit and trim, but his face had aged considerably. The boyish eyes I knew were now steel and hard looking. I noticed he now carried himself like a guy who was all together. The boy I knew was now a man. The waitress came over and I heard Joe ordering two dozen oysters, a platter of little neck clams, fried calamari, and a pitcher of beer. I forget what I ordered, but I know it was nothing like what he did.

Once the food arrived, Joe dug into it, sucking up both the oysters and clams in great gulps, each followed by gulps from a stein of beer. When the shellfish were consumed, Joe attacked the calamari. Only when the food and beer were finished did we have a chance to talk.

"Where's your uniform?" I asked.

"I wasn't in the Army," said Joe. "What I say now is just between you and me, nobody else. I want your word on this."

"Ok, ok. You got it."

"I was picked for the O.S.S. and sent to a special training camp in Virginia. There I spent three months training in communications and the various ways of taking out the enemy, especially the Germans. Our group got dropped just behind the German Gustav line, where we hooked up with the Italian partisans. Our mission was to gather intelligence about German troop movements, their supply routes, and everything else to help our troops kick the shit out of the krauts and chase them out of Italy. We also helped in sabotaging anything we could to screw their troops up. In between, we were able to knock out some of their convoys and whack a lot of those Nazi bastards.

"When the Germans retreated to their Gothic line, we dropped behind them again and did our job better. I'm proud to say that I helped kick their fucking armies out of Italy. Once they were out of Italy and the new Italian government took over, we weren't needed anymore and the O.S.S. sent us home. And here I am."

I started asking more questions about his doings in Italy and was a little surprised to hear him tell me he didn't want to say anything more just yet, and that I should hold my questions until he was ready to talk about it.

"Ok, no problem," I answered.

"I gotta go home now," he said. "I can't wait to see my folks and my sisters. Have you got the phone number of the house, in case they changed it?"

"Are you kidding? I called at least once a week all the time you were away. Here's my schedule for the next two weeks."

"Good enough," he said. "I'll get in touch with you as soon as I get settled. It's going to be like old times again, you and me together. If I remember right, it's your turn to pick up the tab. I did it the last time, which seems a long, long time ago."

"You haven't changed," I said with a big grin on my

face. "You always were two steps ahead of me, so I guess I'm stuck for it."

Joe then got up, picked up his duffle bag, and dug the rose out of his pocket and laid it on the table. "Here's something to remember me by, Sweetheart," he said loud enough for other people to overhear him, and then he left.

I didn't hear a word from Joe for the next week or so. I figured he was busy, probably saying hello and shaking hands with dozens and dozens of relatives. I was just about to phone his house when I got a call from Joe's mother telling me there was going to be a party for Joe's homecoming. It was this coming Sunday at two and it would last until who knows when. I told her I'd be there. When I hung up and checked my schedule, I realized I was on duty that day. I hunted down Lenny Brandt and fortunately got him to cover for me. Of course, it came with the price of covering two for one.

I hadn't been to Joe's house or seen his parents and sisters since he left. But everything seemed to be the same, except his parents had aged and his sisters had grown up. The house was jammed with friends and lots of relatives that came and stayed. Food - mostly Italian - and drink was laid out in every possible place. To make things easier, Joe's sisters were able to hire some of their high school friends to help with the food serving and the dirty dishes.

I'll never forget when I got there. Those relatives who I'd met before gave me great recognition. 'Hello, Doc' and 'Como sta Doctore' were some of the greetings, followed by, 'How ya doin'?' and 'Got a card?' Some of them cornered me a little later and asked me about their aches and pains and what to do about it. I avoided definite answers to all of the questions by telling them that I didn't have a stethoscope, blood pressure cup, or other instruments with me and couldn't give an opinion. This seemed to satisfy most of them, but a few - mostly the elderly - just wouldn't give up. So I told them to call our clinic, make an appointment, and I'd try to see them as patients. This seemed to satisfy them and I let it go with that.

Joe saw me and pushed his way through the crowd. We hugged each other and made believe this was the first time we had met since his return. This was what we made up once we actually saw each other so that Joe's parents wouldn't be hurt that he didn't come home first.

"This is some home coming party," I told him. "You must be a very popular guy, or maybe all the people here are just looking for free food and booze."

"Very funny," said Joe.

Before this went any further, the door opened and Uncle Vito came through with all of his family. It took about ten minutes before all the kissing and hand shaking from his relatives and friends was over.

Joe motioned for me to stay back with him and wait until Uncle Vito spotted us. When he did, he made a bee line over to us and hugged Joe, saying in Italian, "Welcome home, welcome home. Our family is so proud of you and we are so glad that you came back to us safe and sound."

He turned to me and said hello and kissed me on both cheeks. "We are also proud of you, Marco," he said. "I will have a little time to talk later. Now we celebrate Joe's coming home." And with that, he rejoined his family and was immediately surrounded by other guests while his wife and Joe's mother brought over food that they knew Uncle Vito liked.

I then said to Joe, "Where's Paulie? I don't see him around."

"He's over there in the corner," Joe replied, "scheming with some of our cousins who think that because they're related to the Capo, they can get away with anything, and I mean anything." He leaned closer to me. "Paulie, I found out, is also pissed at me."

"Why? What did you do to him?"

"Nothing," said Joe. "When he came back nobody made a party for him. Our people felt that going into the Merchant Marine was nothing, so when he came out, it was no big deal. Besides, he was earning when he was in. I got a sneaking suspicion that he's not on the up and up. I don't know what it is just yet, but I'll find out sooner or later. In the meantime, stay away from him. He's still out to get you." He patted me on the shoulder. "Now, I got to mingle. Stick around if you can. Otherwise, I'll call you or you call me, not before twelve. I got lots of sleep to catch up on."

It was about an hour later when Vinnie came over to me. "The Capo wants you to come into the big bedroom now," he said. "Make sure you close the door behind you. I'll be right outside to see that nobody bothers you."

I did what Vinnie told me and entered Joe's parents' bedroom and shut the door. Uncle Vito was sitting on the edge of the bed.

"How're you doin?" Vito asked.

"Doin' good," I said.

"Hear ya havin' a little problem with your loan."

"I just want to make arrangements to pay it off," I said. "I guess you heard my folks sold the store and moved to Florida, and love living there. They offered to help me pay the money back."

"That's good," he continued. "I understand you work on a schedule. Give it to Vinnie and he'll call with an appointment for us to meet and we'll see what can be done with payback of the money you borrowed. Ok?"

"Thank you, thank you so much," I said. "I applied for a residency so that I could become an emergency room specialist, and now maybe I can do this."

"Don't do anything until after we meet and everything is straightened out," said Uncle Vito. As he arose from the bed, he continued, "Send my regards to your folks. Hope they're well." And he walked out of the room.

After he left, I felt a big load taken off my shoulders. I had nothing to worry about now. After all, Uncle Vito was the Capo and he said things would be straightened out. I left the room, got a hold of Joe, and told him I had to leave but would be in touch. I said good-bye to Joe's folks and sisters and a multitude of people and hopped it back to the hospital.

Joe and I met a few times during the next couple of weeks when I was off. We had either lunch or dinner together and mainly reminisced about old times, and even tried to relive some of them. We made plans to go back on the Staten Island ferry - this time paying the fares both ways - and of course to visit Roseland. We wanted to see if we could still pick up some girls and do some dancing, although we were both stale. We also tried the single dance routine and met a lot of girls, but we just couldn't capture the old time comradary. Maybe we just grew up and out of it. Joe's experience in the war and my going through med school also might have had something to do with it. In spite of it all, we felt like we still were brothers, each following a different path, and that was ok.

The call I was waiting for came in about two weeks after Joe's party. I remember I had just finished a very busy shift in the E.R. and was just about to hop into bed.

"Doc Falcone, is that you?" asked a voice I recognized as Donald Lugano..

"Yeah, what can I do for you?" I asked.

"I got a message from your Uncle. He wants you to meet him at the club tomorrow at four o'clock, providing you are free. You know where the club is?"

"Yeah," I said. "I can make it."

"One more ting," Donald said. "Bring your medical bag, in case anyone asks you what you're doing there. Just tell 'em that you got a call and was going to see a patient who's not feeling good. Got it?"

"Got it," I replied.

# XL

At precisely four o'clock the next day, bag in hand, I rang the doorbell of the Sicilian-American Club, which was immediately opened by Dino, one of the crew I had previously met.

"Hi Marco," he said. "Or should I say, Doc Marco. You're expected. Go up the stairs."

"I remember where to go," I said. "And Marco or just Doc is ok."

I climbed up the steps and went to the door that I remembered was the entrance to Uncle Vito's office. I knocked and heard him to tell me come in. The room looked pretty much the same as I had last seen it and Uncle Vito was seated behind his old big beautiful desk. He rose to greet me and reached to shake my extended hand.

"So glad you can come and visit with me," Uncle Vito said. He motioned for me to take a seat opposite him. "It's good you brought your medical bag with you, like you were told. What's your problem, Marco?"

"Like I told you at the party, I want to pay back the money that was loaned to me," I said. "Papa said he would help me do this, with the money he got from selling the store."

"I understand that you owe about a hundred thousand dollars," said Uncle Vito. "Do you have that kind of cash on hand?"

"No, I don't," I said. "I can raise about thirty-five thousand and pay out the rest, once I get into practice, after I finish my residency."

"How long would that take?" asked Uncle Vito.

"About three years," I replied.

"That ain't gonna work," he said, shaking his head. "Let me give you the bottom line. We don't want your money. We want your service as a doctor when we need you."

"You mean I'm to take Volpe's place?"

"Yeah. You take Volpe's place. We thought we had another guy to do it, but things didn't work out. So you're the man. Marco, we've known each other a long time and I always considered you as family and being family helped you. Now it's your turn to help us when we need it. Capishe?"

"Uncle Vito, I appreciated everything you did for me and my folks, and I mean everything," I said. "But I thought the money I got from the union was really just a loan that could be paid back."

"It was a loan," he said. "We gave you money, and you pay back by keeping our family alive and healthy. The money we gave you, if we put it out on the street, even at two points a week, would come back maybe ten or fifteen times more than what we gave you. It was figured that you would owe about a hundred big ones. So here's what we can do for you, because you are considered "familia." The loan will be cut to fifty thousand dollars and every time you treat anyone we recommend as a regular patient - and you know what I mean - we'll knock off twenty-five dollars from the loan. If you need to take care of special people, like Volpe did, it's a hundred dollars off what you owe. This way, Marco, you have a way out. When you're finished with the obligation, you're free to do anything you want. Again, this is being done for you, because we like you, and this wouldn't be done for anyone else. Understand?"

"I understand," I said.

"Agreed?"

I had no choice but to nod my head in agreement, but underneath I was shattered.

"When are you going to be finished working at the hospital?" he asked me.

"In September," I replied.

"Can you get out earlier?"

"I don't know. I'll have to inquire."

"I understand you turned down working out of Volpe's."

"I did," I said. "I didn't think it was a good idea, for all concerned."

"Nobody has to worry about that now," said Uncle Vito. "About two weeks ago, Volpe's office and house burnt to the ground. If you have a problem getting an office, reach out for Tony A. He'll find you one. The only thing is there may be a cost to you for doing this, which will be added on to what you owe. Do you have a car, Marco?"

"No, I don't."

"We still have the car you used when you were on the routes sitting in a garage. You're free to use it when you need it. I'll put the word out for you to get the keys and registration. Anything else, Marco?"

"No, nothing else," I replied

"Any problem with our agreement?"

"No, Uncle Vito and thanks for your help." I forced those words from my lips and then shook his hand while leaning over and kissing him on both cheeks. I then left, my knees shaking as I exited the building.

Spotting a coffee shop, I went in, ordered a coffee and sat down in the rear. I must've looked ashen-faced because an older lady at the next table asked me, "Are you ok, young man? You don't look too good."

"I'm alright," I replied. "Thanks." I forced myself to give her a little smile. I finished the coffee and ordered a second one, just sipped it, sat there and tried to figure out what to do next. I started to review my life up to this point, and I tried to be objective about what had brought me to the position I now found myself in. How could I have been so naïve to believe the scholarship loan money didn't have strings attached? I think I made myself believe that I got it because Uncle Vito was in my corner and I could repay it from the monies I made practicing medicine. I was suddenly struck with the realization that he was right. I'm going to have to repay it from the monies earned from the practice of medicine, only it was the "familia" way of repayment. This was their plan all the time and I realized that I had to do what I was told and when I was told.

I thought of running away, but was scared that they would reach out, find me and fit me with a pair of cement shoes. The families had contacts with other organized crime families all over the country and even in some foreign countries. More important, they knew where Mama and Papa lived. I was afraid what would happen to them if I disappeared. The thought of getting into them deeper by letting them get me an office was a no brainer. If I did this, I was sure I would wind up like Volpe. Maybe I could join the Army. Maybe they wouldn't come after me there. That idea was no good, because the war in Europe was over and a lot of military doctors were getting discharged, and again, the safety of my folks was at risk. I accidentally glanced at my watch and saw that I just might make it back to the hospital, so I grabbed a cab and went on duty just in time.

During all this time as an intern, I bumped into Linda an average of three to four times a month. She was now doing ward duty as part of her R.N. training. When she had some free time that coincided with mine, we had coffee in the cafeteria and enjoyed ourselves by just talking and feasting our eyes on each other. When we could arrange it, we had sex in one of the store rooms or large linen closets. This helped keep both our sanities and it was understood that there was to be no romantic entanglements, but just plain raw sex that she said was great, and I agreed.

There was a message waiting for me a couple of days after the Uncle Vito meeting, asking me to call Dr. Rabinowitz. When I reached him on the phone, after exchanging greetings, he told me the reason for the call was to get my parents' Florida address. "I somehow misplaced it," he said. "I want to tell your father to see a certain doctor near him, who had privileges at Jackson Memorial Hospital. I've known this doctor for a long time, and he's the right man for your Papa to have as a doctor. He can also take care of your Mama if she needs treatment."

Once I gave him the information he requested, he continued by asking, "Marco, did you ever give some thought to the proposition I offered to you? You told me you were going to seek a residency. Did you get set up with one yet?"

"Not yet," I replied. "But I would be interested in at least talking to you again."

"When will you have time off?" he asked.

"This Friday, from six in the morning on."

"How about coming over to the office about noon? We can have lunch and talk freely."

"Sounds good," I said. "Twelve it is."

"Look forward to seeing you, Marco."

"Same here, Doctor."

I got to Rabinowitz's office a little before twelve and there were still patients waiting to see him.

"I'm running a little late," he advised as he stuck his head out of the inner-office door. "Can you wait? I need to see these next two patients."

"Ok, doctor."

It took about forty minutes before the last patient left.

"Marco, let's go upstairs," he said coming out of the office. "I took the liberty of picking up something to eat for each of us. I hope you like tuna on rye and I make a good cup of coffee. Besides, I want to show you where I live."

So up the stairs we went. His two bedroom apartment included a spacious living room, a dining room, and a fully equipped kitchen. The bathroom was tiled throughout and had a large bathtub, shower, as well as a commode.

"This is some apartment," I commented.

"My wife and I lived here for many happy years, and she deserved a metal for putting up with my lifestyle, up until the day she died. Making early morning hospital rounds seven days a week, office hours from nine to twelve o'clock, five days a week, but I never turned a patient away, like you saw today. Then back to seeing patients from two to five, eat dinner around six or six-thirty, and then make house calls until I was finished, maybe around ten or so. Then of course, in case of an emergency, no matter what day or time, I had to respond. But I loved it. I still love it. I don't know how she put up with me all this time. Is the tuna sandwich ok?"

"Yeah, it's great," I replied.

"How about the coffee?"

"It tastes nearly as good as the sandwich. I think I'll have another cup."

As the doctor poured the coffee, he said, "Funny thing, I always believed in first impressions and when I met you, I felt some very good vibes and that's why I asked you to stay in touch."

He then sat down and, facing me, said, "To tell you the truth, I'm reaching the stage in my life where I don't have the strength to make early hospital rounds and evening house calls. Would you be interested in doing this for me? I'll also work it out so you can have your own patients and treat them here. I'll even throw in a place to live. You can have one of the upstairs bedrooms and we can share the rest of the apartment. I got to warn you, I snore." He grinned. "But I was told, if you keep both bedroom doors closed, you won't hear anything. To be honest, I have angina and was told I have to start taking it easy. I expect all my patients to follow my advice, and I'm going to listen to my doctor. If things work the way I expect they will, I'll probably retire in about a year or so and we'll talk about you taking over the whole practice and maybe buying this building. I own it free and clear. I have no brothers, sisters or kids, and the Holocaust took all of my other relatives. I'm very seriously thinking about moving to Florida once I retire. The cold weather up here is not good for me. What do you say, Marco?"

I hesitated to answer right away.

"Tell you what," he said, "don't give me an answer

now. Think it over. I know you were considering a residency that would take three years, then you'll have to open an office and depend on other doctors to refer patients, or stay on a staff at a hospital, put up with hospital politics and work for a lot less money than you could earn in a private practice as a G.P." Rabinowitz then looked at his watch and said, "Whoops! It's nearly two. I gotta open the door and let patients in and go back to work. Let the dishes and cups stay on the table, I'll take care of them later."

We walked down the steps, opened the door, and five people were already waiting to come in. As I exited, I turned to Rabinowitz. "Thanks for the lunch," I said. "I'll be in touch by the end of the week."

"Good, look forward to it." He then motioned to the patients, telling them to take seats in the waiting room as I left.

"I need to think," I said to myself while sitting in the hospital's medical library after leaving Rabinowitz's office. What choice did I have other than taking Rabinowitz's offer? Bucking the mob could be a death sentence. Running away might put my parents in danger and sooner or later, I'd be found anyway. That's the way business was taken care of by the so-called familia. On the other hand, I considered myself lucky. Rabinowitz's office was a sweet one. A built-in practice. Time to develop my own. No explaining my making night and emergency day calls, and a nice place to live. In the back of my mind was the thought of me eventually paying off the loan and getting into the residency program, or just staying, buying out Rabinowitz and becoming the best G.P. on the lower East Side. I then decided the right thing to do was to accept Rabinowitz's proposition and back off any other ideas.

Three days later, I called him and said, "Doctor, I thought it over very carefully and I'm happy to say I'll accept your proposal."

"I'm so glad," he said. "I was hoping you would agree. I think it now necessary for us to sit down and work out all the details and commit them to writing so that there is no misunderstanding at a later date. I want you to know, Marco, how pleased I am. You made the right decision."

During the next few weeks, I met with Rabinowitz and went over the details of our business arrangement. There were no real differences in our discussions as to terms. Rabinowitz was very fair, and I walked away satisfied that I was on the brink of a great opportunity.

Joe and I met for dinner the following week and I clued him in on the details of my meetings with both Uncle Vito and Rabinowitz.

"Look, Marco," Joe said, "I think you've got the break of a lifetime from Uncle Vito. It could have been a lot worse if he didn't step into the picture, and from what you've told me about the deal with Rabinowitz, you're gonna be ok. So let's move on and start having some fun."

When I was off shift, I spent as much time with Rabinowitz as possible, but only as an observer because I wasn't, as yet, licensed to practice. I had to finish my internship and then apply for a New York license.

Rabinowitz set up an appointment for us to meet with Sam Cohen, the lawyer, and the contracts were signed. On the way out of Cohen's office, Rabinowitz turned to me and said, "Now that that's over, we can go about our business of practicing medicine. Until you get your license, you look and I'll do."

"I got you, Doctor," I said.

"One more thing, when we're with patients, you can refer to me as Doctor. Otherwise, my name is Irving. When will you be finished at Belleview?"

"In eight weeks," I said. "Then I'd like to take a week off to maybe visit my parents and catch up on some sleep."

"I can understand that, but in the meantime, I'd like it if you would come into the office as often as you can and also start making night house calls with me. This way, you can meet my patients. It's important that they get to know you. Once you get licensed, you'll have to apply to hospitals for privileges. I am associated with both Beth Israel and Beekman Downtown. I want you to apply there. That's where I send my patients if they need to be hospitalized."

"Will do, Doc—I mean, Irving."

And so it went.

I received my diploma, applied for my license, got it, and soon after, privileges at both hospitals were granted. I remember as I took the last of my belongings out of my room, Eric Johnson walked in.

"So you're really deserting the ship?" he said. "I hate to say this, but I'm going to miss you. Now I'll have to break in another roommate." He smiled. "All kidding aside, I really thought you would stay on for a residency in surgery or E.R."

"Sometimes things don't work out the way they're expected," I said. "I think I made the right choice. If I don't like doing general practice, I can always look for a residency opening. After all, I'm still a young kid, not like some of the married old farts around here."

Eric picked up a pillow off the bed and threw it at me in a playful manner. "Stay in touch. You're a good guy."

"That's a promise," I replied as I exited the door.

It felt strange leaving the building where I had spent the last year working my ass off, eating lousy food, and getting little sleep or time off. But in spite of all, I loved it. I could not help but feel let down.

*Let's look at it another way*, I thought to myself, *I have the beginnings of a readymade practice and a nice place to live. I know I'm going to learn a lot from Rabinowitz.*

Once I got settled in my new quarters, I reminded Rabinowitz that I wanted to take a week off, and he readily agreed.

"Why don't you grab a plane and go visit your folks for a few days?" he said. "The sun, the beach, and the ocean will do you a lot of good. You'll come back a new man, ready for action."

"Great idea, Irving," I said, using the doctor's first name. "Think I'll do it."

That night I met Joe and over dinner I told him of my

thinking of going down to Miami Beach for a weekend. To my surprise, he said, "This idea is so good, I think I'll join you. I hear there are a lot of hot chicks down there - and I don't mean hot from the sun - who are just waiting to meet two young handsome studs like us."

"I don't know if my folks have room for us," I said. "They only have a one-bedroom apartment."

"Don't worry Marco, or should I say, Doctor?" Joe said as he bowed down from his chair. "Arrangements will be made for us to be treated first class. Let's plan to leave this Thursday and come back Sunday. I want us to come back with tans that look like we've been there a month. Just bring a toothbrush. We'll buy everything down there."

"Let me at least get the tickets," I said.

"No way," Joe said. "You gave me the idea to partner with you, and that alone is worth the price of the tickets. I'll get everything set between now and Thursday and I'll give you a call and give you all the details. Do me a favor and bring along your stethoscope. Ladies get so impressed when they see a guy with a stethoscope, and I'm looking forward to doing some complete physicals on as many of them as I can. Don't forget to bring it with you."

The flight down was good. As soon as we took off, I fell asleep, but couldn't help hearing Joe try to get real friendly with the blonde stewardess who didn't seem to mind. Her co-worker was working the rear section of the plane, a pretty redhead. After I woke up, they both stopped by on several occasions, offering both Joe and me soft drinks and food.

"We seemed to be getting special treatment," I whispered to Joe.

"Yeah, once I told them we were bachelor doctors going down to Miami Beach for a long weekend, their interest perked up. I asked the blonde if she knew anyone who could show us the town and she volunteered. She said she was based in Miami and had time off coming. Then she added that she and the redhead share an apartment." Joe leaned closer to me.

"She whispered that her friend, the redhead, wants to get to know you better. And then she added that they don't have to make a trip until the middle of next week."

"You haven't lost your touch," I said. "What's their names?"

"My girl is Lorie," said Joe. "And Peggy is your doll. Lorie worked it out with Peggy, who is hot to trot and gave me her phone number. I told them we would take them out to dinner tonight and get acquainted and we would call at seven."

"How do you know this is on the up and up and they're not just playing with us?" I asked.

"I'll bet you two to one that they want to touch base with us."

We landed and just nodded to the girls as we left the plane. We didn't want to make it obvious that there was more to it than a passenger saying goodbye to the stewardesses. Outside the airport, we grabbed a cab and my jaw nearly dropped when Joe told the driver to take us to the Fountain Bleu Hotel. Hearing this, I turned to Joe with an expression that said 'Are you crazy?'

Joe caught this and came back with, "Don't worry, I got everything covered."

After we arrived at the hotel and Joe paid the driver, we went up to the desk and checked in. I smiled when I saw Joe write "Drs. Joe Mancuso and Marco Falcone" on the registration form. When the clerk saw what was written, he broke into a big smile and said, "Welcome to the Fountaine Bleu. Your rooms are ready. If there's anything you need, call the front desk. Our manager, Bill Martin, is looking forward to meeting you in person and will be in touch. He's off premises now but will be back later this afternoon. Don, here, will show you to your accommodations."

We really didn't have any luggage, just some small carry-ons, but Don the bell hop grabbed what we had. "Follow me, gentlemen," he said, and into a waiting elevator we went and got off, to my surprise, at the pent house floor. "This way, please. It's the second suite on the right. If you don't mind, I'll go in first to check and see if everything is in proper order. It will only take about a minute or so."

Once the door was unlocked, Don disappeared inside, and he was right. He was back in less than a minute. He ushered us in and proceeded to show us around. The suite was magnificent, two large bedrooms with adjoining walk-in closets and bathrooms on either side of a gigantic living room. The kitchen could compare with that of a fine intimate restaurant. The panoramic view of the ocean, white beaches and the city was unbelievable. I pinched myself to see if I was dreaming.

"Not bad," Joe mused after he finished walking through the suite again. "What's say we grab an hour of shuteye and then we go shopping for Miami Beach duds?"

I started to ask about the room but was interrupted when Joe said, "I'll answer all your questions once we get the hour nap. I gotta plan out how I'm going to get Lorie to beg me to get her into the sack.

I hit the bed and it was just what the doctor ordered - and I'm the doctor. It seemed like I hit the bed for just a moment when I heard Joe knocking on my door, "Up and at'em, Marco! We've got to grab something to eat and go shopping."

While grabbing a bite to eat at the hotel sandwich shop, I asked Joe, "Where do we pick up what we need?"

"Right here in the hotel," he replied. "They got everything we need from soup to nuts, including hookers, if our dates don't work out."

"This ain't a cheap hotel. The suite must go for super bucks and I'll bet the clothes aren't cheap either."

"Don't worry about a thing," Joe said. "I told you I got everything covered, thanks to you. Don't ask questions, just enjoy. When it's time, I'll tell you. This weekend, the sky's the limit."

We finished eating and walked down to the lower level, where there was a shopping arcade with all kinds of shops. Joe and I picked out a complete wardrobe and when I looked at the prices, I winced and nudged Joe.

"I could live a month for what this sport coat and a pair of pants cost," I said.

"Do you like them?" he asked.

"I do, but…"

Before I could continue, Joe said to the salesman, "We'll take it." The same story went for all the items of clothing - including beach wear and even toiletries - that Joe said we should have. I was sort of flabbergasted when I caught a glimpse of the bill. Joe nonchalantly looked it over and just signed it, telling the salesman, "Just have these sent up to Penthouse A."

"Very good sir, and thank you," was the reply.

Once we got back into the upper lobby, I said to Joe, "What's going on? It doesn't make sense. Where the hell is the money to pay for all this gonna come from?"

Joe steered me over to a seat in the gorgeous lobby facing the beach and ocean. "I want to know now what's what," I said. "Well, my brother, this whole trip and all the costs is a gift to us by our friends. They feel that they owe me for something I did for them overseas and they want to show their gratitude for the favors you've done for them, if you get what I mean. We just sign and everything will be taken care of. Marco, you still have friends and are a part of the *familia*. Enough of this bullshit. Let's go up, change, and go down to the beach. Maybe we'll even take a dip in the ocean. I'm sure our stuff is waiting for us."

And so it was, hanging in closets and laid out on the bed. We quickly changed into our cabana suits and hopped down to the beach. Beach attendants, after asking our names, ushered us over to two lounge chairs and supplied us with towels. After trying out the chairs for a few minutes, we looked at each other and, having the same idea, took off for the ocean, which was warm and calm as glass. Joe and I had a great time goofing around in the water and must have stayed in for about a half hour, just having fun like old times.

"Let's get out and grab some sun," Joe suggested. "I

told Lorie I would call her around five. I guess it's about three-thirty now, so we got about an hour to soak up the Miami Beach sun." As we lay in our lounge chairs, Joe commented, "This is not a bad way to live. I dreamed of doing this when I was overseas working with the Resistance."

Before I could say anything, he changed the subject by pointing at a couple of girls coming out of the water, "Look at those two beauties," he said. "I bet they're just a sample of the dolls wanting to meet us. In case things don't work out with Lorie and Peggy, we'll just latch on to two others tomorrow, no problem."

"You sure about that?" I asked.
"I'm not sure…I'm positive our beds will be occupied every night we're here. We can't miss." With that, Joe leaned over to the girl on the lounge next to him and said politely, "Excuse me, I'm sorry if I'm disturbing you, but could you give me the time? Foolishly, I left my watch up in the suite. I'm a doctor and have to call and see how some of my patients are doing."

Hearing that the guy requesting the time was a doctor, the girl actually sat up and turned her body towards us, showing off her best features. "It's ten past four, doctor," she said. "You're staying here at the hotel aren't you?"

Joe replied, "My colleague and I are here for a long weekend. It's our first time here in Miami and we want to see the town and have some fun. Are you staying here also?"

"Yes, I'll be here another week and then it's back to Boston."

"I'm Dr. Joe Mancuso, and my friend here is Dr. Marco Falcone, and you are?"

"Joan Wray," the girl replied.

"If I'm not being too forward," Joe said, "maybe we can get together for breakfast or lunch and get to know each other better. We're in Penthouse Suite A, and you are in?"

"1804," Joan replied.

"We really have to run now. These calls must be made. So nice to meet you, Joan. We'll be in touch."

"That would be nice," was the reply.

Joe and I got up, said goodbye, and headed up to our suite.

"You ain't lost your touch."

"I know," Joe replied.

Once we got back to the suite, we just had enough time to shower and shave. Those terrycloth bathrobes the hotel furnished were real nice. At five o'clock, Joe called the number Lorie gave him and when she answered, Joe gave me the high sign.

After the hellos and small talk was over, I heard Joe say, "You and Peggy grab a cab and meet us, say, at seven-thirty in the lobby of the Fountainbleu. Or if you want, we could meet you outside." A pause. "Ok, outside it is, see you at seven-thirty."

Sure enough, around seven-thirty a cab came up and the two girls got out dressed to the nine yards. They nearly took my breath away.

"Pay the cabby," Joe whispered to me. "I'll meet you inside." He escorted the ladies in.

I paid the cabby real well and joined Joe and the ladies in the lobby.

"Let's go upstairs and have a drink," I said. 'We have a beautiful penthouse suite. We're up so high, you'll think you're up in the sky again."

I saw that they were a little hesitant for about a minute, but then Peggy said, "I've never seen a penthouse suite before, so let's go."

So up the elevator we went. The girls didn't say much, so Joe was carrying on most of the conversation, keeping it very light and laughable. This kind of banter seemed to relax the girls and when we reached the door of the suite, there was no appearance of apprehension on their part. Once they entered, they were really impressed.

"This is stunning," Lorie declared. "I never saw anything like this. Did you, Peggy?"

"Yeah, I did once in a movie," Peggy replied.

"It must cost you a fortune to stay here!" said Lorie.

Before I could say anything, Joe replied, "We're doctors and have some wealthy patients that will let us use this place if available. Have some champagne. The hors d'oeuvres are on their way up and we'll have a chance to chat before we go to dinner. Is that ok?"

"Sounds good to me," Peggy replied, and Lorie nodded in accord. The food arrived and the champagne in the suite was chilled, compliments of the manager. We opened it and the party started. We put on some dance music records and both girls turned out to be pretty good dancers. They, in turn, were surprised that Joe and I were that good on the dance floor.

The suite, the top of the line champagne, the food, and the service must have helped create a little more interest in Joe and me and they seemed to be a lot more receptive to some of our suggestions after a while.

Joe came out with, "I heard that the women's shop here in the hotel just got in a shipment of real silk stockings."

"Are you kidding?" Lorie asked, "I haven't had a pair of silk stockings for years."

"And me too," chimed in Peggy.

"Whaddya say we go down and buy you some," Joe said. "The only restriction is that my friend Marco and I want to see you both put them on."

"You're naughty, but nice," said Lorie. "And I want to get those silk stockings."

"I'll go along with that," said Peggy. "I'm as anxious to get those silk stockings as she is."

The girls then left for the bathroom to freshen up.

While they were at it, I got a moment to ask Joe, "Where did you get the crazy idea of the silk stocking story? How do you know the store here even has them? And if they do, they gotta be sky high! I don't have a lot of cash with me. I might not be able to foot my share of the bill."

"Don't worry," said Joe. "Like I told you before, this weekend anything we want is on the cuff. I checked before and they have the silk stockings. I can't wait until we come up with the girls and help them put them on."

I remember clearly that not only did Joe and I buy Lorie and Peggy the stockings, but he insisted that they pick out silk pajamas and other intimate items. As they were trying them on in the dressing room, Joe turned to me and said, "Don't even ask the question. We're making an investment and I'll lay you ten to one it'll pay off."

Then the girls reappeared with big smiles on their faces. "I don't know how to thank you enough," said Peggy.

Joe told the sales lady after signing the bill, "Please have all these things sent up to our suite, Penthouse A."

Once we left the shop, Joe said, "You ladies must be starving," and before they could answer Joe added, "I made reservations at the restaurant here in the hotel. They tell me it's one of the best on Miami Beach."

When we walked in and Joe whispered a name to the maitre'd, who smiled broadly and led us to a table behind a red corded off table section of the restaurant. Joe told me later that this section was reserved for celebrities, politicians, and other important patrons.

The food and service was excellent. Champagne came - and plenty of it - and our waiter advised us that it was complimentary. After dinner, Joe suggested we go into the Boom Boom Room to dance, and dance we did. The girls were very good followers. I guess after the gifts and a lot of champagne, they loosened up a lot. It was about one-thirty when we decided it was time to leave and without any resistance, Lorie and Peggy went up to the suite with us. When we walked in, the packages were on the table in the foyer.

"I don't want to do any unpacking now," said Lorie. "I just want to go to bed. Come on, Joe." She actively led him off to his bedroom. Before she closed the door, she leaned out and said, "I hope you two are going to have as good a time as I expect Joe and me to have. See you in the morning, and not too early." She closed the door.

When she did this, I didn't know what to do or say, but just looked at Peggy and finally said, "Look Peggy, if you think you owe me something for the gifts and the evening, you don't. I really love being with you and can't think of anything else I'd rather do than have you in bed next to me, making love. Not just raw sex, although that's not bad. The truth is, I really like you and want to see more of you."

Before I could say anything more, Peggy put her finger over my lips as if to shush me and said lovingly, "Marco, I was waiting to hear something from you like you just said, and I really, really want to make love to you. So let's get our asses into the bedroom and make love."

And we did.

The following morning, it was about ten when I heard a knocking on the door and Joe loudly saying, "Get up, you lovers! I ordered breakfast for the four of us and it's here, so rise and shine."

Reluctantly Peggy and I got up, washed up, brushed our teeth, put on our robes and went inside to the dining room.

There were all sorts of goodies on the table and we all ate ferociously. Over our second cup of coffee, Joe and I suggested possible plans for the day. Then Lorie gave us the news that both she and Peggy had to be back at the airport that afternoon. It was mandatory that they attend and no excuses were acceptable. A new plane was being put into service and all stewardesses needed to learn their jobs when working on it.

Peg then added, "We should be through no later than six and could be back here by eight. Keep the champagne chilled. We don't have to report to work until Sunday afternoon at two. We could still have a hell of a good time. We're gonna leave all that sexy stuff you bought us right here, so that we can model it for you."

Lorie then broke in, saying, "And you, Joey, lover man, I'm looking forward to your helping me get in and out of the stockings and lingerie you bought. But now, we've got to hurry and get back to the apartment near the airport, shower, get ready, get into uniform and report in."

As soon as they left, I told Joe I had to call my folks and let them know I was in town.

"Absolutely," said Joe. "Call them and see them and send them my regards."

"What are you gonna do?" I asked.

"I'm gonna hang out at the beach. Maybe I'll go for a swim and get reacquainted with Joan in 1804. I'm thinking of staying over for a couple days more, and it gets lonely sleeping by myself."

"My money's on you to come out on top," I said. "I'm sure you will."

And we both laughed.

When I phoned Mama and Papa and told them I was here on Miami Beach, they were ecstatic. They were further thrilled when I said I would come for lunch and would be at their apartment in about a half hour. Questions from them kept flying at me, and I remember saying only that I would answer their questions when I saw them in person. As I was getting ready to leave, Joe told me to stop off at the hotel flower shop and pick up the flowers he had ordered for my mother and, from the tobacco shop, a box of Cuban cigars for my father.

"Tell them these are from the both of us," he said. "They're being held in your name. It's part of our honeymoon package." He did a little dance and ducked as I threw a couch pillow at him.

"See you later," I said as I left. "I should be back here by seven-thirty or so. If there's a problem, I'll call here."

"Don't you fret. If you get delayed I'll have no problem entertaining both those lovelies. Maybe I'll invite them to have a threesome until you get here." He then quickly added, "I'm just kidding. I need my strength for Lorie. She's a big user and I also need the reserve for Joan, the doll in 1804. She doesn't know what a great lover I am, but she'll definitely find out. Now go, and once again, give your parents my best. Tell them I'll try to see them before I leave."

"Will do," I said. "Ciao."

It was only a fifteen minute cab ride over to the place where Mama and Papa lived. I noticed while paying the cab that there seemed to be an assembly of people on the porch in and around their door. As I came up the steps, one of the men standing around yelled inside, "He's here! He's here!" and Mama and Papa came out just as I got to the porch landing.

Mama and Papa took turns hugging and kissing me for at least five minutes, and then the introductions to the neighbors started, always with Mama and Papa, proudly saying, "This is my son, Marco, the doctor." Or, "This is Dr. Falcon, our son." I must have greeted and shook hands with at least twenty or more people on the porch that day.

Papa then announced, "Friends and neighbors, thanks for welcoming our doctor son. Now it's time for us to go inside and let my wife fatten up her son with lunch. I'll tell you the truth, I never saw a woman put together food for a king or a son so quick as my Sarah did when she heard Marco was coming. Now we go inside to eat." Turning to Mama, he added, "Put those flowers in the water right away. They must have cost a fortune. I'll take in the other package he brought."

Mama was always a great cook, and after having to eat all that medical school and cafeteria garbage that they called food, what she served tasted even better than ever. I kept on eating and eating and as soon as I emptied out my plate, she filled it up again, despite my telling her that I couldn't eat anymore. During all this time, both Papa and Mama kept asking me questions and questions and questions and I kept answering between chewing and swallowing. I finally said I would answer the rest of their questions once we finished our meal.

"Let the boy eat," said Papa. "No more questions until he's finished. You want him to choke? God forbid."

After that all was sort of quiet, except for Mama asking, "More cake? Another cup of espresso?"

Once we finished, we went into their living room. It was small but certainly adequate for the two of them.

"Let me show you around," Papa said to me. "It's not a big apartment, but it's comfortable and large enough for us." Pointing to the couch, Papa said like he was telling a big joke, "If I have an argument with your mama, she can sleep on the couch. It opens up to a big double bed. We haven't opened it yet because we haven't anything to fight about." And he started to laugh.

As Mama looked at him with a smile, she said, "Ivan, you shouldn't talk like that in front of Marco. Tell him the reason we have the sleeper is because we thought he would have a place to sleep when he came down."

I then had a quick tour. Nice sized bedroom, two big closets, two chifferobes, and the bathroom with both tub and shower. The kitchen was all that Mama wanted. I think this unit was picked because Mama liked the kitchen.

We then returned to the living room where the question and answer period started and kept on going. After about a half hour of constant loving grilling, I had a chance to ask my folks a question. The first one was to Mama. "Did you read the card attached to the flowers I brought?" I asked her.

"I didn't see any card," she said. "I'll go now and look for one." A few minutes later she returned and gave me a big hug and kiss. Thank you so much and thank Joe also. I feel very proud and will keep this card forever."

"What does it say that makes you so emotional?" Papa asked.

"I'll read it," Mama said, "'Enjoy these flowers and may your lives continue to be as beautiful as they are.' And Papa, this card is sent from your two sons Marco and Joe. That's so beautiful. Thank Joe for me and tell him I've always considered him as a son."

"I will," I said. I turned to Papa. "How about opening your package?"

And when he did, he exclaimed, "This is so good! This is so wonderful! I've always dreamed of having one and now I have a whole box full of them. Look Mama, it's a box of Monte Christo hand rolled Cuban cigars. They must have cost a fortune. They're the best in the world. I can't wait to start smoking one."

"Well, don't do it in here," said Mama. "This is a small apartment and the smoke will stink up the whole place and probably kill the flowers."

"Alright, alright," said Papa. "I'll smoke one outside on the porch. I got an idea, I'll wait to light up when I see that momser Schwartz sitting near me. He has a son that is a city commissioner or something like that, and he keeps on bragging how important his son is and what the son does for him. He doesn't have a son who's a doctor that saves lives. Only one that's a politician who probably takes a lot of graft."

Turning to me, Papa continued, "Schwartz is also a cigar smoker and probably plotz when he sees me light up and he smells the smoke. In fact, I'll bring the box up and show him what my son, the doctor, brought me."

After Papa finished his cigar, spending half the time blowing smoke in Schwartz's face, we went back into the apartment. That's when the knocking on the doors started. Visits were being paid to look me over by mothers of single daughters. They wanted to meet Ivan and Sarah's son the doctor and then to whisper to Mama that they had a single daughter or granddaughter or niece that would be just perfect for Marco. Each one stated positively that the ones they spoke about were beautiful, had hourglass figures, were well educated, and were good housekeepers as well as cooks, and all stressed the fact that each girl came from a wonderful family.

When they asked for my phone number, I caught Mama's face signaling no, so I said I was in the process of moving and would give the new number to my mother once I got it. After a while, the visits stopped and we had time to reminisce and just enjoy being a family together again.

"When are you going back?" Mama asked

"Sunday, the flight leaves at five."

"Good, you'll come for breakfast on Sunday morning and I'll make lunch also."

"Mama, I'm here in Miami Beach and I need to get some sun. What am I going to tell my friends and patients? That I was in Miami and didn't get a sun tan?"

"Alright, get your sun tan," she said. "I got some Coppertone for you to put on. It'll help give you the tan without a real burn." She gave me a bottle of the lotion. At five o clock, we celebrated the coming of the Sabbath and ate the traditional meal that was so good. At seven o'clock, the cab I called was waiting outside. After kissing Mama and Papa goodbye, I headed back to the hotel.

As I entered the suite, I heard Joe on the phone saying, "Miss you too, so get over here." And he hung up. Seeing me, he said, "Hey, Brother, how was everything?"

"The best," I said. "I had a wonderful time with the folks. What did you do?"

"I had a great day," he said. "Did the beach scene, took a lot of dips in the ocean, got lucky, and connected with 1804. We had lunch and drinks at the pool, and I'm going to get together with her Sunday night. Once I saw her in a bathing suit, I decided she looked too good to pass up, so I'll get another flight sometime during the week."

"Where the hell do you get all the energy?" I asked.

"I didn't have the time to use it up going to college and medical school like you. It's all on deposit like a bank, waiting to be drawn out. Marco, you better change into your Miami Beach night duds. The girls will be here soon and we're gonna do something great."

Once Lorie and Peggy arrived, we ordered up some drinks and a platter of finger food and did some small talk. When the phone rang Joe picked it up. I heard him say, "Ok, twenty minutes it is." As he hung up, he turned to us and said, "Grab some overnight things. We'll have a limo waiting for us downstairs in twenty minutes."

"Where are we going that we'll need overnight things?" Peggy asked.

"A surprise, because we like you so much and know you like to fly," said Joe. "We're going to Cuba, and we'll be back tomorrow night. I hear the beaches, the restaurants, the food and the shows are sensational. And the casinos let you win once in a while. There's an empty suitcase on my bed. You can deposit your stuff in there." He looked at Peggy and Lorie. "I know there are nude beaches there so don't take too much stuff, maybe just the silk stockings."

"Don't count on it Joey," said Lorie. "I save the good stuff for you in the bedroom."

And with that, we brought the things we thought we needed and filled up Joe's valise. The limo was waiting outside as we exited the hotel and off we were to a private airport where a plane was already warmed up and waiting. Peggy recognized the twenty-passenger plane and told me it was owned by an exclusive Havana hotel used to transport special guests to and from Miami.

The plane took off and about fifty-five minutes later, we landed in Cuba. A limo was waiting and off to the hotel we went. The reception and the accommodations were unbelievable. We quickly unpacked, washed up, and went out around town. We ate, drank, danced, saw star-studded shows. It was said that nudity was accepted in Cuban night clubs, and the people that said that weren't misrepresenting. We were back in our hotel suite around three in the morning and went to bed. It was a nice feeling having Peggy bare ass naked cuddled up next to me.

Joe left a ten o'clock wakeup call and the four of us had breakfast in the suite. We then spent the rest of the day at the hotel's private beach complex, which included a spa, and we made time to try every amenity that was offered. A couple of times, Joe and Lorie disappeared for about an hour or so. I assumed that they went to the suite to get laid. This seemed like a good idea to me, so I nudged Peggy and we went back to the suite and we got laid. It was around five when we left the spa after getting their complete five-star treatment and went back to our rooms.   We got dressed, had dinner at six-thirty and caught the plane back to Miami at eight. We were back at the Fountain Bleu a little after ten and went to bed. I think that the Cuban sun and water plus the screwing knocked me out. The wakeup call at nine-thirty sounded like someone was playing a loud siren right in my inner ear. Peggy heard it also, and she jumped out of bed and hit the shower.

By ten-thirty the four of us were down in the restaurant

having breakfast and I noticed that both of them were glancing at their watches.

"Don't worry, we'll have you outta here by noon so you'll have plenty of time to get to work," said Joe.

It was shortly before noon when we helped them into a cab, kissed them goodbye, and saw the cab take off.

I immediately called my parents and told them I would be a little late and would be at their place by one-thirty.

"Let's talk," I said to Joe. "Do you think we'll ever see Peg and Lorie again?"

"Maybe yes, maybe no," he replied. "Don't forget, they travel all over the country most of the time and not together. I left a number where they can leave a message for either one of us. If Lorie calls me and I want to get together with her, I'll follow it up. But I'll let you know about Peggy."

"Peggy gave me her number in Atlanta and told me she would get back to me when she could, if I called. I left her my office number."

"If they call they call," said Joe. "If not, it's been a great weekend."

"You were always good at words, my brother. I've got to ask you again, how come I got to tag along with you on this extravaganza?"

"Look, Marco, I don't ask questions. I was offered this deal and they told me to invite you. That's all I know, all I wanted to know. The bosses know that you and I always, since we were kids, did the right thing and are expected to continue to do what we're told. There maybe are things that they tell us to do that we don't like doing, but we do them. For that, there are rewards and favors and these will continue as long as we obey the rules. There are consequences if they are ignored or broken. We've been honorable all these years, and that's why we had all of the goodies so far, with maybe more to come.

"When you see your folks, send them my best. Tell them I'll try to visit them before I leave. Marco, I'll call them if I can't see them. Leave all the Florida stuff we bought here. I'll either have it shipped up to us, or have the hotel store it. I got a feeling we'll be back soon. Miami Beach and Cuba are fun and I'm sure we're gonna have good times in both places."

"I forgot to ask, how come we shot over to Havana the other night when we could have stayed here in Miami?"

"To tell the truth, " said Joe, "I didn't want to take the chance of 1804 seeing me with another girl. Coulda screwed up my chance of fucking her."

"You are a genius," I said. "No wonder they put you in the O.S.S. I'm still waiting to hear the stories."

"You better step on it," Joe said. "Get over to your folks' place. I got a date to meet Joan in a couple of minutes."

"Who's Joan?" I asked.

"You forgot so soon? She's 1804 and my next jump. And this time, I don't need a parachute. See you in New York." He blew a kiss as he flew out the door.

The lunch with my parents was so good. Thank goodness there were no neighborly visits. I remember Papa telling me that Schwartz the Monser stopped bragging a lot when our neighbors told him about me and when Papa showed him the box of Monte Cristo cigars, and he said the best was when he blew a little smoke in his direction.

Time just flew by and soon it was time to leave for the airport. The cab was already outside waiting for me and I had just finished hugging and kissing my beloved parents goodbye when Mama said, "Wait a minute." She handed me a paper bag. "There are two good sandwiches in it. Eat them on the plane. I guarantee they're better than the junk they give you on the airlines. Our neighbor Molly got sick from eating the plane food when she flew down last week. Call us when you get in and then every week."

"It's cheaper on Sundays," Papa added.

"I will, I will," I said. "I promise." As I entered the cab, I turned around and yelled as loud as I could, "I love you Mama and Papa!" As the cab drove off, I could see Papa putting his arm around Mama. I knew in my heart that Mama and Papa were still very much in love.

The flight back to New York was uneventful and the sandwiches were delicious. So were the half-sour pickles Mama included.

By the time I got back to my house, it was past nine and all was quiet, except I heard Rabinowitz snoring, so I closed his door and mine and went to bed.

The constant ringing of the phone woke me up. While picking up the phone, I was able to turn on the night light next to the bed and I glanced at the clock next to it. It read 2:30. As soon as I said hello the party on the other end answered, "Doc, is that you?"

"Yes, it's me," I replied.

"Listen, your friend Gary isn't feeling good," said the voice on the other end. "You need to come over right away and see what you can do for him. There'll be a cab waiting for you, outside your office in about ten minutes. Don't keep the cab waiting, ok?"

"Ok."

I threw on some clothes in a hurry, grabbed my medical bag, and walked out to the curb just as a cab drove up. I got into the cab and the driver took off. I noticed the driver didn't put the flag down, and there was no hack license or picture of the driver on the bracket provided for that purpose.

There was virtually no traffic and we arrived at Gary's place quickly. As I got out of the cab, I leaned over through the open window and asked, "How much do I owe you?"

The fast response was, "Nothin', it's taken care of. One more thing, forget everything about the ride up here, including me."

"No problem," I responded, and the cab took off.

The door to Gary's place was opened immediately after I knocked. I was sure the peephole showed it was me.

Once I entered what was Gary's waiting room, Gary greeted me and said, "They're in there," and on the way over to the treatment rooms, Gary added, "If you weren't here, I don't know what I'd do."

"What's going on?" I asked.

"Come inside and see for yourself. It isn't pretty."

I followed him into one of his treatment rooms and saw two guys lying side by side on gurneys grimacing with pain. One had a bloody bandage on his hand, and the other had a big gauge pad - also bloody - over his right ear.

"Give me a rundown of what these injuries are," I said.

"The guy over there on the left with the hand bandaged is missing at least half of his index finger. The guy on the right is now without an ear."

"How the hell did this happen?"

"Phil and Rocco are here and maybe they'll tell you later," Gary said. "You better start working on them right away. You better not let them check out. They lost a lot of blood."

There was no time to start IVs on the two wounded, so I gave them shots of Demerol to kill the pain and treated the finger first. There was enough skin for me to suture the stub closed. The ear presented a more difficult problem. The entire external ear was sliced off and nowhere to be found. The one that did this job knew what he was doing when he sliced the ear off. I was able to pull and tug and suture together all of the loose skin remaining. After I finished the actual procedures and had the patients bandaged, I gave them each mega doses of penicillin to prevent infections.

I gave Gary post-operative instructions and where he could reach me in case of any problems. When Gary got into the waiting room, Rocco asked, "How are they doing?"

"I think they'll pull through," I said. Then he and Philly left.

Once they were gone, Gary turned to me and said, "I'm reaching the end of my rope. I don't know what to do. These guys think I owe my life to them, and maybe I do."

"How'd you get involved with them?" I asked.

"My brother-in-law helped me pay my way through college and vet school," he said. "I graduated, got licensed, and looked around and found this building for sale. I showed it to my brother-in-law and he liked it and said he would come across with the down payments for the building and the office equipment. Before he could do this, he was whacked on the job for the "family." It was at the wake when I was approached by what I thought was just his friend Albie, who I later found out was his captain. He told me, 'Your brother-in-law was a stand-up guy. He said some good things about you. We know he was going to help you. He can't now, but out of respect for him, we will. Write out a list of what you need and how much it'll cost. When you got it down pat, call me at this number and we'll set up a meet.'

"Two weeks later, I sat in an attorney's office for the closing on the building and the title was in my name without any mortgage. It was mine, I thought, free and clear. All of the equipment I asked for was delivered, including for the x-ray and fluoroscope, within the next month. Albie dropped around every so often to see how things were going and when I asked him about making arrangements to pay back the monies that were spent on my behalf, he repeatedly said 'Don't worry about it now, first get your practice going then we'll talk.'

"For the first three or four months, everything went good. The practice started off with a bang and I was busy making money. I started to get the rich Fifth and Park Avenue trade. They all seemed to have dogs and cats as pets. I think it was about six months later, about one-thirty in the morning, when I got a call from Albie saying 'We have an emergency for you Doc, and we'll be there in fifteen minutes. No need to turn on the stoop lights. We don't want to disturb your neighbors.' Well, a large wrapped object was brought in and laid on my biggest examining table and it wasn't a dog or a cat, and it was dead.

"'Do your thing Doc, and make it the size of a big dog, or a lot of little ones,' they told me. 'We'll be back in three or four hours. Doc, one more thing, don't get any foolish ideas like making unnecessary phone calls. Capishe?'"

"I was so scared that I almost shit in my pants. I don't know how I did what I was told. I remember vomiting three or four times. It was about three hours later that there was a knock at the door and Albie and three other guys with bags loaded them and took them out. 'Good job, Gary,' Albie said as he pinched both of my cheeks. 'This counts a little toward your payback.' And he left. It took me at least a couple of hours to clean up and it was close to six in the morning when I finished.

"This was how it started and it hasn't stopped. It even got worse. But I don't want you to know. What you don't know you can't tell."

"I can't believe this," I said, shaking my head. I glanced at my watch. It was close to six and I had to run in order to meet Rabinowitz at the hospital and make rounds with him. I didn't even have time to fret too much over what Gary had told me. "Try to take care of yourself, Gary."

He managed a nod. "Yeah, you too, Marco."

Luckily, I found a cab right away and just made it on time. The penicillin must have done the job, because two days after the procedure, Gary told me, a limo came by and picked up the two patients and I never heard anything about them again.

As time passed by, my association with Rabinowitz became stronger and stronger as he became weaker and weaker. He now had problems walking steps and grew tired more and more often. In spite of all this, he managed to still see patients, but only at the office. I took over and made the hospital rounds and night house calls in his place. When I got called out for emergencies during the day, Rabinowitz took over for me, as sick as he was. When I got called out at all hours of the night, he never questioned me as to where I was going and for what purpose.

Since I was now his doctor, I monitored him on a regular basis. I saw that what was previously a slow rate of circulatory degeneration had increased to a rapid one. It finally reached where Rabinowitz, himself realized he was a very sick man and it was time to quit. So one morning over coffee he turned to me and said, "I spoke to my wife last night and from the grave she told me 'Irving, it's time to quit. If you don't, I'll see you before I want to. Don't worry, I'll be waiting for you whenever you get here, so don't rush. You got lots of time left on earth.' Marco, I always listened to my wife so I'm going to quit and maybe move to Florida."

"I think as your doctor and your friend, you are making the right decision," I said.

We made the financial arrangements and Rabinowitz agreed to take thirty-thousand dollars for both the practice and the house. He also threw in the car as part of the deal. In my mind, Rabinowitz was being more than fair on the terms.

I phoned Papa and explained the situation and the money was wired in to my bank the next day. I also received a wire from Papa and Mama reading "We are so happy for you and for ourselves for being able to do this for you while we are still alive."

A week later, Rabinowitz and I went to the lawyer's office where the papers were signed and the money changed hands. I was the new owner of the property, the practice, and the car. On our way back to the office after the closing, Irving said little but what he did say stuck with me the rest of my life.

"As a doctor, you are just a healer," he told me. "Only God makes the supreme decision and it's beyond man's comprehension to understand his motivation and decisions."

"I understand, Irving," I said. "From the beginning you started out as my mentor and this has grown into a firm friendship. I want you to stay and practice medicine for as long as you wish. Take as much time to decide what you want to do and where you want to go. Is that a deal?" And I followed up jokingly, "If you don't take my advice, as your doctor, I'll tell you to leave what was once your office and house.

"Irving," I continued, "I really need your help and I know you'll be there for me when asked. You could start by reading the latest medical journals and then keep me up to date with the latest advances in medicine. Besides that, I love your cooking but I'll do the shopping. Just make out a list. One more thing as your doctor; I want you to take it easy for the next week or two and no more diagnosing yourself. I'm your doctor and you are my patient. Understood?"

"Understood."

When we got back to the property and as I prepared to help Irving up the stairs to the front door to the building, he turned to me and said, "Follow me, I got something to show you." And he walked slowly while taking a key from his pocket to unlock the street level door of the building. Once we got inside, the hallway led to a large room. I was in awe. The room was dusty but contained three hospital beds in addition to enough medical equipment that would meet the standards of a small hospital emergency room.

"I haven't used this room for a lot of years," he said. "When I first went into practice, I had destitute patients with so many mouths to feed, and when the wife became pregnant again, I did what was needed to be done, if you get my drift. I also delivered many babies here if the parents didn't have the money to go to a regular hospital delivery room. Between you and me, I also delivered badly deformed babies and I did what I thought was the right thing to do.

"As time went on, my practice got bigger and bigger and I was fortunate that I had several policeman's families as patients and always gave them a big discount on my fees. I got tipped off by one of them that I was under investigation and that I needed to immediately stop what I was doing down here or risk the probability of losing my license or even going to jail. So I closed this part of the practice and the office down here. The nice part of it was that the patients understood."

"Thanks, Irving, for taking me into your confidence," I told him as I helped him up the steps to our living quarters, and then I went downstairs to start treating the waiting patients.

While we were having dinner a couple of weeks later, Irving asked me if I thought, as his doctor, that he was well enough to take the train to Miami. I told him that he needed to spend the next three days resting with no climbing steps during that period and if he followed my instructions to the letter, he was good to go. And he did.

It was exactly a week later that Irving told me he was leaving the next day. He made arrangements to stay with a doctor friend in Miami until he could find a place for himself on the Beach. He then asked me to send the three cartons he had packed to him via Railway Express once he got settled, and I assured him I would. He then told me that he had ordered a cab to take him to the station and turned down my offer to drive him there.

When we heard the honking of the cab horn the following afternoon, I picked up the valise and walked Irving out to the waiting taxi. We hugged each other and shook hands several times before he got in.

"Let me know where you are staying and how you can be reached," I said as he got into the cab. "We need to stay in touch."

Irving then rolled down the window and loudly responded, "Good luck and be careful. I'll miss you. You were like a son to me."

That was the last time I saw Dr. Irving Rabinowitz.

# XLI

When I got a break from seeing patients, I went down to the basement and took another look at the potential mini emergency room. I found that there was actually more equipment than I had seen the first time. I also found two other unoccupied rooms that could be adapted to examination and treatment rooms. I also discovered large storage closets that held additional medical equipment, many in their original carton. I then looked around and found three neighborhood kids and hired them to do a real good cleanup of the entire downstairs, and they did an A-1 job.

During the next month, there seemed to be a lull in the battle for the control of the streets. I thought maybe things were worked out and would remain quiet. How mistaken I was.

One day soon after, I got a message from Phil that Rocco wanted me to meet him at the Mini Pub the following Sunday night at eight. I got there a little before eight and after giving my name to the bartender, I was directed to the private dining room on the second floor, where I found Rocco and also Tony A seated at a table. I noticed that there was no one else in the room except the waiter.

After appropriate greetings were made and acknowledged, Rocco motioned for me to take a seat. "Have some dinner, Doc," he said. "We already had Sunday dinner with our families."

The waiter took my order, served me, and left the room. As I was eating, Tony A started the conversation by asking me, "Do you read the papers, listen to the radio, or watch TV?"

"I don't have the time," I replied.

"Well, I'll clue you in," he said. "After we won the war, thousands of Spics from Puerto Rico came to this country and most of them settled here in New York, a lot of them in the Irish areas and then in our neighborhood. They opened their own stores and businesses, which was alright with us. A lot of them became greedy. They musta thought that kindness on our part by letting them do this was weakness. Thinking we were pussies, moves were made first into the Irish territory, then they had the balls to start in on what we controlled for the last twenty-five years and we earned good all this time. The PRs even tried to take over the Jew section, so we had a meet with the captains of the Jew group, the Micks, and our guys, and worked out plans to keep these PRs in check, but the more we pushed them, the bigger their crews got and the more problems we had with them.

"They began by shaking down our storekeepers and trying to take over our other businesses. These poor bastard shopkeepers were told they didn't care who else they have to pay for protection, they gotta pay their PR crew for their business safety ever week and were told the number. If the storekeeper wouldn't or couldn't come up with the money, stores were broken into and showcases destroyed along with the merchandise in them. Stink bombs were thrown and store fronts were smashed. These storekeepers came crying to us, telling us they couldn't afford to pay us and the PRs, so we had to do something about it."

Tony A thumbed his nose in disgust at the story he was telling.

"The decision," he continued, "was to grab as many PRs as we could and give them just beatings as a warning. These fuckin' PRs came back at us, not only with baseball bats but also with ice picks and even pieces. I think you've seen some of their work. We couldn't take this shit lying down, so we go after them to even up the score, but we do one better. For every one of our guys that gets clipped, we take out two of them. For every one of our crew that gets a beating or the ice pick, we give back the same treatment to three of their people.

Maybe they'll get the message. If they don't, there's gonna be an all-out war. These PRs are like bedbugs; you kill one and two take its place."

"That sounds terrible," I said.

"And that ain't the worst of it," said Tony A. "These PRs *bastardos* got into the drug business. We didn't care a fuck if they just sold it in their own neighborhood, but their pushing the weed and we found out also heroin in our area and getting our people hooked on it. On top of it, some of our younger guys found out how much money there is in dealing, they disregarded the order from the bosses that our familias do not get involved in the drug business. These young punks come up with the excuse that they only wholesale to the *Mollies* in Harlem and not in our neighborhoods, and further claim that more money could be earned in a week dealing drugs than all our other businesses can earn in a month. These kids don't want to understand what loyalty to the familia is and are willing to take the chance to earn big. They are waiving around a lot of cash and try to convince other young familia newbies to join them. These scumbags refer to the bosses as old mustaches and that the only way to get a win-win situation is to get rid of the bosses and take over the family.

"We got some idea who these low-life's are, but we want to settle the PR problem first and then take care of our problem. Meantime, our eyes and ears are open. We want to find out who's involved and who's the head troublemaker. Marco, if you hear anything, you let us know. Ok?"

"Ok," I said.

Tony A nodded. "The bosses are staying firm. Getting caught selling or dealing in drugs is a death sentence and it don't matter who it is or how high up in the familia they are. Sell drugs, you get whacked. This is the policy."

Rocco then broke in, "If we nab a PR who's dealing in our neighborhood, we gotta find out who his supplier is. Depending on how cooperative the guy is, the more fingers on his hand he can keep. If the guy is stubborn and won't at all help us, then the decision has to be made to cut off his balls or take his eyes out one at a time. There ain't be no problem getting the information we want. Once we found out before, we scouted around and found the scumbag PR dealers and they were whacked. This didn't stop the trade, the money was so good."

I listened to Rocco and Tony A very carefully as they each took turns talking, and wondered why they were telling me all this. So I took the shot and asked, "What has this got to do with me?"

"That's just the point," Rocco responded. "You're our Doc. In every war, there's guys that get wounded and guys that get killed. Our guys that get killed deserve a real good send off and we don't need the cops involved. You helped out before with death certificates and we count on you to continue to do the right thing. Now if we bring you one of our crew that has been worked over, cut up, or shot, you fix him up."

"But," I replied, "I don't have the facilities or equipment that a hospital has, and I can only do so much with what I have."

"You do what you can do, Doc," said Rocco. "And so far your record is pretty good."

"With all due respect," I answered, "if I get a patient with a vital area wound or puncture, unless that patient receives major surgery, which I don't have the equipment to do, that patient will die."

"Doc, let me level wid you," said Rocco. "We got a war on our hands and the cops are doing nothing but just sitting on their asses. They figure that every one of our guys that turns up dead is one less street guy they have to deal with. Now the Feds are looking down our noses because of all the drug shit. It's funny that the Feds and us are on the same side. We both want to get rid of the drug dealers in our neighborhood. The difference is that we deal differently with the dealers we catch than they do, capishe?"

"I understand," I said. "I understand what you're saying. But again, with respect, what does it got to do with me?"

Tony A then took over, looking me square in the eyes. "Hey, Doc, are you stupid or something? Maybe I have to spell it out for you." He then lowered his voice. "Listen and listen good, if you get someone in that you can't save, put him out of his misery and put him to sleep permanently. If he is one of ours, fill out the death certificate with a legitimate cause of death and then call Mancuso's. If the dead guy was a PR, call Phil and he'll take care of it."

Rocco then added, "Good thing you have a back door to your downstairs office."

Tony A again said, "Now do you capishe?" He then softened his tone and continued, "Marco, we known each other a lotta years and sometimes when I don't feel too good, I always get a laugh when I remember the caper that you and Joe pulled by taking out two of our top earning hookers and using my name to get the best table at the Copa. Some balls you and Joe had." Then Tony A leaned over and gave me a hug. "We brought you a long way from then. I think you owe us. Am I right, Marco?"

"You're right, Tony," I said. "I didn't forget."

"By the way," said Tony A, "I heard that you and Joe had a great time in Miami and Havana. There'll always be rewards for doing the right thing. So let's have some espresso and Sambuca and drink on it."

Once we did, good-byes were made and the meeting was over.

As the weeks passed the battle for control of the streets continued, but with greater intensity. The storekeepers in our neighborhood kept being hounded for protection money by the PR gangs. Drive-by shootings became more and more common place, while at the same time the stabbings and beatings continued at a more rapid pace. People were afraid to go out at night. The situation was so bad, but the cops still didn't do anything about it.

My legitimate practice was growing and because of the gang wars, so was my mini emergency room practice. There were many nights that the three hospital beds and four camp cots I had purchased from an Army/Navy surplus store were full of patients. Others with minor wounds had to sit on the floor until I could take care of them. I was working on the average of fifteen hours a day, seven days a week. I was on the brink of a nervous breakdown. It took a few phone calls to reach Phil and I told him I needed help and needed it fast. I felt I was slipping into a deep dark hole with no way out.

"Take it easy, Doc," said Phil over the phone. "Give me a day or two and the problem will be solved. We don't want a nut job on our hands, or see the guys in the white coats come to get you. You're important to us."

Two days after my conversation with Phil, he phoned and told me he would stop by about twelve that afternoon and he was bringing someone along with him. And he did; a fat squinty eyed balding ruddy faced guy. Phil introduced him as Pino, but told me everyone referred to him as Tubbs.

"Tubbs here is from Bari," said Phil. "He was a medic in the Italian Army and deserted when the Allies landed in Italy, and was a POW till we chased the Germans out. He has no papers, and understands he has to do what he's told otherwise we send him back. We know he's done something over there that will get him whacked if he is sent back. He speaks a little English and with you knowing enough Italian, you'll be able to understand each other. If you can't bed him down here, get him a room nearby. Also, get him some new clothes and shoes so that he looks medical. Any problems with him, call me. Meantime, we're on the lookout for a replacement, if this guy doesn't work out." And then Phil left.

Tubbs and I went shopping. I bought him new clothes, shoes and toiletries. We found a uniform shop and I outfitted him with a couple of male nurse uniforms. Now he sure looked the part. When we got back to the office, I told him I would look around for a room for him. He told me he'd rather stay in the lower unit - as we now referred to as the lower facility - and sleep in one of the hospital beds or cots if not occupied. When I showed him the unpacked equipment that was in one of the store rooms, he helped me set them up in the examination and treatment rooms. While we were doing this, he kept on saying, "Bene, molto bene." Once the large storeroom was empty, Tubbs said he could move one of the old couches into it and use it as a bed. He further told me he could fix the store room up real nice. He was especially pleased when he discovered there was a toilet and shower next to this room.

I was very glad to hear Tubbs tell me that the main reason for his staying in the basement facility was that he wanted to be close to and watch over the patients. Tubbs wouldn't take any money from me other than money for food. Where he purchased the food, I didn't ask, but for a grown man, it was very little. Over the next few months, I began to depend on Tubbs more and more. I didn't know where he had gotten his medical training and I didn't care. He had excellent skills in suturing and in treating the results of beatings that some of our patients received. He was also a good diagnostician. It got to the point that when patients were delivered with bullet holes or other wounds we couldn't treat, I just walked out of the room and Tubbs did the rest. All I had to do was to write out a death certificate and phone the funeral parlor.

As time went by, I began to trust Tubbs. And not only that, I liked him. He was like a big teddy bear, kind and helpful, but dangerous if he thought anyone was trying to take advantage of him.

It was sometime during the week when I got a call from one of our newbie crew guys, Pete Zino, asking me if he could come over and see me. I thought it was for a legitimate medical reason. Because he was a member of our crew, I made it for a time after I was to see my last patient. He arrived on time, way after my last patient left. I wondered why he brought along Ralph Cortello, another young turk from our crew. I soon found out. They were there to offer me big money for writing out prescriptions for medical narcotics. I could either write them out for them, leaving the patient's name space blank, or they would give me names that I was sure were bogus.

"Doc, there's a fortune to be made with no risk and everything is in green, small bills," Pete told me. "You could retire just from writing on pieces of paper in less than two years and live the life you want to live and go where you wanna go. This is a big opportunity, so don't pass it by. We got some other Docs working with us and they're earning big." As they started to leave, Pete turned back to me. "Think it over," he said. "We'll be in touch, Doc."

A few hours later, I heard the front door bell ring and to my surprise when I opened the door, I saw Joe standing there big as life holding a gift of French aftershave lotion.

Joe grinned and said, "I thought I'd surprise you." He entered the foyer and he looked at me. "You look like hell. When's the last time you had a good night's sleep?"

"I don't remember," I said.

"Well, I'm taking you outta here tonight for a good steak dinner at Kenny's Steak House. I haven't had a good steak for months. Maybe afterwards I can talk you into staying overnight at my hotel where you can get that good night's sleep. I might even send up a hooker to make you get a better night's sleep.

"Joe, I ain't got enough strength. I'm so tired I don't even think I could get it up."

"We'll see after you get the prime rib or filet mignon in you and a couple of glasses of champagne."

The dinner was fantastic and so was the champagne. We didn't say too much over dinner, just joked around. Over coffee he asked and I told him about the street war, and then I brought up the recent visit and proposition made to me by Pete Zino and Ralph Cortelloo.

"Son of a bitch," Joe whispered after hearing their names. "These two little fuckups were starving to death and begging us to give them some way of earning and we gave them a shot because they got cousins through marriage that were part of our crew and got iced by the PRs." With that, Joe got up. "I'll be right back."

I saw him go up to one of the managers, who then escorted him to the kitchen and then to what I later found out was the head manager's office. When Joe returned, he told me the word came down to accept the offer when either Pete or Ralph called. "Ask them for a number where you can reach them to discuss details and use a payphone to call and tell them that the deal is on. Then tell them the terms: a hundred dollars for a thirty day supply, and a hundred and fifty dollars for a sixty day supply, for a starter. If they start to negotiate terms, tell them to take it or leave it and that they got fifteen minutes to call you back, and they will call and agree to the price. When they do, settle on a date and time, the later in the afternoon or early evening the better. Make them meet in your office and tell them to bring small bills. Once this is set up, call this number." He handed me a piece of paper. "If the person answers the phone and says anything other than 'yeah,' hang up and get outta there fast. Capishe?"

"Capisco," I replied. "Do you wanna tell me where you've been and what you've been doing?"

"Not yet, my brother. I'll let you know when it's time."

"Any hints?"

"No hints as I said before," said Joe. "I should be around for a month or so, so let's make plans when you think you can get away and have some fun and relaxation."

"It's not as easy as that," I said. "Maybe things will quiet down for a while, but it don't look like that. It's been like a jungle out there and there seems to be no end in sight. I've been working night and day."

Joe thought for a moment. "Call me at my mother's and leave word for me to get in touch with you when you think you can take off for lunch or dinner. Roseland is still in business and we should go there for old times' sake."

"Sounds good."

"It's time for you to go romancing and get laid," Joe said with a smile. "How about me getting you fixed up with a hooker who knows how to take care of a worn out but horny guy like you? No sense telling them you're a doctor, in case she asks. Tell her you sell insurance. I won't take no for an answer. Just listen to your brother; go and have some fun. It's a freebie, on me, but you can leave a tip." Then Joe started to laugh. "You're Jewish and maybe you don't have a tip left."

"Very funny," I smirked.

We had more espresso and small talk. When I looked at my watch, I said, "It's late and the wounded parade is about to get started, if it hasn't already."

Joe grabbed the check and hailed a cab and dropped me off at my office. Before I left the taxi, Joe and I hugged each other and we promised to stay in touch. I went back into the building and down the stairs to the lower facility. There were five patients waiting there for treatment, and fortunately none of their issues were too serious. Tubbs did the prep work and removed a flesh wound bullet from one patient, put casts for broken arms and legs for two others, and sutured a knife slash to the face on another.

I prayed that these were the only patients I would get that night so that both Tubbs and I could get some sleep. I guess my prayers were answered because we had no more patients that evening and were able to get the well-earned rest we deserved. To tell the truth, I had a dream about a hooker climbing in bed with me and making nice all night.

Joe was right; sure enough I got the call a week later. It was Pete. The message was short and sweet. "Ok, Doc," he said. "We'll have the prescriptions filled out just like you said." I guess he was trying to be careful in case anyone was listening in. The appointment was made for them to come to my office the following Tuesday at six when all of my patients would be gone.

I also guardedly told them, "Bring my fee in small bills."

As soon as Pete hung up, I went to a public payphone and called the number Joe gave me and when the guy answered, I gave him the information about the meet. The rest of the week passed quickly; nothing unusual with my legitimate patient load and a little less time spent treating the lower facility patients.

That entire week Tubbs and I only saw two bullet holes, one ice pick puncture, two stabbings, and three beatings. It was an easy week compared to what we'd had in the past.

Joe and I were in touch but only by phone. He thought it best for us to stay away from each other until the meet with Pete and Ralph was over.

It was around a quarter to five the day of the meet when I started looking out the window facing the street. Time seemed to just crawl by as I kept glancing at my watch. It was exactly five minutes to five when a car pulled up in front of my building and I was able to see Pete and Ralph get out and start walking toward my office. Just as they got to the bottom of my steps, two guys suddenly appeared out of nowhere. They approached Pete and Ralph, said something to them I couldn't hear, and then the four of them turned around and walked backed to the car and drove off. I could see Pete at the wheel and Ralph in the passenger seat, with the other two guys sitting in the backseat.

This was the last time I either saw or heard from any of them.

After this event passed, I waited a week before I left word for Joe to call me. We had a series of lunches, dinners, and even dates with girls he had met while he was back. He never failed to fix me up with one of their friends on blind dates. These blind dates were always with good looking and nicely built girls, but Joe's were always better looking and had figures that made my dates look like young boys. Joe was the same old Joe. He'd never change.

Every time I brought up the subject of Pete and Ralph, Joe changed the subject. After several weeks of partying, Joe called and said, "Let's go to dinner tonight, just the two of us. You pick the time. If you don't have emergencies, make it as early as possible. If you do, take care of them first and then call me no matter what time."

I called Joe at eight and told him so far so good, and

that I would phone Tubbs every hour to see if I was needed back.

"Let's go to Ruby Foo's," Joe said. "I like their food."

We went, ordered dinner and did some small talk. Joe then told me, "I gotta leave tomorrow early and I'll be gone for a month, maybe longer."

"Can you tell me why, what, and where?" I asked.

"No can do, my brother. It's for your protection as well as mine. Just leave it set for the time being. I'll let you know when the melon is ripe. Capishe?"

"Capisco."

"Marco," Joe continued, "you did a good job in following the instructions I passed on to you involving Ralph and Pete."

"Can you at least tell me about what happened?"

"I'm taking a chance but you're my brother and also a trusted member of the familia, so you've earned the right to be in the know. The two guys we imported from our friends in Chicago met Pete and Ralph by your building and after sticking a piece in their ribs, persuaded them to go back to their car. They were told to drive to a certain place - where is not important to you - and after being worked over for a couple of hours by our Chicago friends, they decided it was in their best interest to talk. They were then taken to separate rooms and checked to see if what they told matched up. It would be their ass if their stories were different.

"The bottom line is that these two punks are tied up in the drug trade and deal in weed, heroin, and prescription dope. They also help to recruit guys from our family, especially newbies, despite the bosses' orders. It came out that a couple of our captains were involved, and they'll be done with when the bosses say the word. First they got to give us the lowdown on who is running the operation. The scumbags Ralph and Pete know only who they take orders from and told us two of their captains were involved. I bet these gabbanos doing the drug shit will start singing like songbirds after we reach out to the guys from Chicago to come and have a talk with them.

"This way, if any of these lowlife's go to the cops and rat us out so that they can work out a deal for themselves, the out of town muscle will be long gone. No identity. No evidence." Joe then told me, "I gotta leave tomorrow for two or three weeks, maybe longer. Don't ask me why or where. Like I told you before, when it's the right time, I'll let you in on everything. Just go back to your business like nothing happened. Also, you might start getting visitors. The ruckus is caused by the PRs and the word getting around about the familias getting involved, although not true, has brought a lot of bad publicity and is causing no end of trouble. Now the federal government is looking how we and the other familias all over the country are doing and earning. This Kefauver Committee is even calling some of the top people from all over the country to come before them and testify. The newspapers say we are part of a national organized crime conspiracy."

He shook his head. "All this problem because the PRs started fucking with the drug shit. Marco, just be careful of what you say and to whom you say it. Don't talk our business over the phone. Use different pay phones all the time. Call my father's funeral home as seldom as possible. Just keep the stiffs as long as you can. I know you're smart enough to call Tepperstein in case there's a problem. Clue Tubbs in to keep his mouth shut. The only thing he can say is, 'I want a lawyer,' and then contact Tepperstein for him too. I'm sure this will all die down after the election. These bastards are raking up all this bullshit just to get votes and get reelected."

Joe again grabbed the check, hailed the cab, dropped me off at my office, said "Ciao" and continued on

The constant ranting and ravings about what the media now called "La Cosa Nostra" and their control of the unions and all of the vice in the country continued to be the media's top focus. This in a way was good for me. My lower level facility patient load was drastically reduced and all my calls to Mancuso's were substantially cut down. Now I had time to read the medical journals and get the best new techniques, treatments, and medications developed during the war. I also had time to catch up on some sleep. Tubbs was also very helpful in my regular patient practice and was very liked by all.

    Time has a habit of running by when one is busy and doing the things one really enjoys, and this was the case with me. I loved practicing medicine and I was so thankful that my lower facility was doing poorly. I was hoping that the time would come when I could shut it down altogether and put the past there away forever.

# XLII

I'll never forget the phone call I got several weeks later. It was about three in the morning and the phone kept on ringing. I thought it would never stop. I tried putting the pillow over my ears but it didn't help. The calls interrupted my wonderful dream that Marilyn Monroe and Betty Grable were fighting over who was to climb into bed with me, and the damn phone wouldn't stop ringing. I reluctantly crawled out of bed and answered it. It was Phil speaking in a very agitated manner, saying, "Don Amatto had a stroke in his club and is in Lenox Hill Hospital. Get right over there and find out what's going on and get back to me. They won't tell us shit."

"I don't have privileges there," I said. "So I can't just walk in and ask questions like I could in one of my own hospitals."

"We don't give a crap about that," said Phil. "You're our Doc, so get your medical ass over there and see what the hell is going on. Then call me back."

I remember Phil's voice as he delivered the message. It was cold, calculating and somber. After he hung up, I was in a cold sweat. As I got dressed, I woke Tubbs up and told him to stabilize any lower level facility patients that came in during my absence, and in case of an emergency with one of my other patients, for him to call an ambulance.

It took me about fifteen minutes to find a cab and while on the way to the hospital I tried to figure out how I could get in to see the Don and find out what was going on. Then it hit me. My classmate Chris Welsh was doing his residency at Lenox Hill. Lucky for me, he was on call when I got there and

I was so relieved when I saw him coming out of the elevator into the lobby. He greeted me by saying, "What the hell are you doing here at four in the morning? I didn't think you missed me that much."

I told him as little as I could about my relationship with Vito Amatto, other than that he was my boyhood friend's uncle and as such was so close to me.

"Follow me," Chris said. We went into the E.R. Chris went to the nurses' station and got the Amatto chart once he got the name from me. "He's lucky. He's John Cantore's patient. Cantore is one of the best neurologists in the business and I'm his chief resident."

"Which bed is he in down here?" I asked. "I'd like to see him."

"They took him up to the Neurology floor a few minutes ago. They're gonna need some time to get him settled and start doing what they need to do, so let's grab a cup of coffee. I need the caffeine. I was on duty for the last eighteen hours."

We chatted for about fifteen minutes when Chris said, "Let me call upstairs and see if they finished settling him in. What did you say your uncle's name was?"

"Vito Amatto."

"I think I heard that name," said Chris. "He's a top dog." He then went to a wall phone, dialed a number and came back with a report. "We can go up now. You can see him while I get a hold of his updated chart."

When Chris and I entered the room, I saw Uncle Vito lying in a hospital bed with an IV attached to one arm, an oxygen mask over his face, and a BP cuff wound around his other arm. His breathing seemed labored. Chris then handed me his chart, which I quickly but thoroughly scanned. It was evident that Uncle Vito had suffered a stroke, but how massive it was was yet to be determined. The diagnosis was confirmed. Many tests, however, needed to be done before treatment was ordered and prognosis followed.

I looked at Uncle Vito. His eyes were opened but there

was a vacant stare in them. Chris took a pencil light, shone it across both eyes, and he confirmed that there was no reaction to the light.

"Marco," Chris said, "this is a waiting game now. We need to evaluate the test results before we can make any decisions as to treatment." He further added, "If the patient is close to you, why not apply for privileges here at Lenox Hill? I'll sponsor you and you should have no problem getting them in about four to six weeks. I'll try to push it because I don't want to have to get you in here when I'm on call, and also have a problem getting you onto the floor when I'm off. There's nothing more that can be done now. Cantore will see him later on, about two, I guess, so you gain nothing by hanging around. I'll get what's left of my beauty sleep. I'll call you around four this afternoon and give you a heads up."

"Thanks Chris," I said. "I owe you one." I took one more glance over at Uncle Vito as I left with Chris. We separated at the elevator with Chris telling me that he had other patients to see and he was going to make rounds a lot earlier than usual, thanks to me. I knew him long enough to know that this was said in jest.

As the elevator door opened, Donald "Duck" stepped out. How he was able to get in, I didn't ask. He acknowledged me with, "Comme Sta, Doc? How's the Don doing?"

"Too early to tell," I replied.

"Well, I'm gonna be here outside the Don's door during the day and Phil will take over for me during the night thing."

Rather than question him further, I said, "That's good. I'll stay in touch." I rang for the elevator. I then made my own hospital rounds first and went back to the office and saw patients. For the following week or two, there was another lull in the number of lower facility patients. I had my fingers crossed it would continue this way, but this was not to be.

Chris and I were in touch at least once a day and he told me there wasn't too much to report. "Time will only tell when and if progress was being made," he kept repeating over and over. "So far, there hasn't been much, if any."

Rocco called me about two weeks after the Don was admitted and told me to meet him at Tepperstein's office at one o'clock the following day.

"No problem," I replied, and appeared there as told. I went through the now old routine of going through Tepperstein's private office and then into the conference room where Rocco, Tony A, and another guy were waiting.

"Sit down, Doc," said Tony A. "Say hello to Frank."

"What's going to be with Don Vito?" asked Rocco.

Turning to Frank, Tony A said, "The Doc here is going to level with us."

I then explained in layman terms that the stroke affected various parts of the Don's body, but the vital organs were not involved, like the heart, lungs, liver and kidneys. He had paralysis in both arms and legs and had also lost the ability to speak, see, or hear.

"Holy shit," Tony A blurted out. "It means that Don's a vegetable?"

"In a nutshell, for the time being, yes," I answered. "He has the best neurologist in the country as his doctor, who is pretty sure, but not positive, that there will be some if not all regaining of the affected organs. I'm in touch with Cantore's chief resident every day and I expect to get privileges at the Don's hospital in a few weeks so I can go and see him and find out what's happening any time of the day."

"That's good, Doc," said Tony A. "Thanks for coming by, stay in touch if there's any change either way."

I took this as a dismissal and so I shook hands all around and left.

Chris Welsh and I were in touch with each other daily while I was waiting to hear from Lenox Hill as to whether privileges would be granted to me.

It was exactly three weeks from the date I applied that I received notification that I was granted full physician privileges. I think Chris must have gone to bat 100% in getting this for me in three short weeks. I visited the hospital and went through the necessary registration paperwork and received the physician's ID. I could now come and go as I pleased. After completing this process, I went up to the neurology floor and introduced myself to the charge nurse, who looked at my quizzically, even after I showed her my ID.

When I asked to see the Amatto chart, she said, "Just a moment, Doctor." She picked up the phone to call someone, evidentially to check on my credentials. When she finished, she turned to me and said, "Sorry, Dr. Falcone, it is a rule here at the hospital that all physicians that we don't know need to be checked out by the Physicians' Registration Department. You're ok, so how can I help you?"

"I'd like to see Vito Amatto's chart, please," I said.

She handed it to me and said, "He's stable and there has been little or no change."

I looked it over carefully and she was right. No neurological change was indicated either up or down. I gave the chart back to her and asked her for the room number and walked over to it. Sure enough, Donald was sitting on a chair next to the door of Uncle Vito's room. I said hello to him and he answered hello back, and I opened the door to the room. I approached the bed and saw Uncle Vito lying there, still comatose. I examined him and found there was still no reaction to light, and no response to neurological stimuli in his arms and legs.

As I exited the room, Donald said, "Any changes, Doc?"

"Not as yet," I replied. "We just have to wait. Tell me, Donald, were you there when it happened?"

"I was right outside his office door when I heard a big noise like something fell," said Donald. "I thought at first maybe a picture or some of the trophies dropped so I came in and saw the Don lying on the floor next to his chair. There was spit coming out of his mouth. I tried to pick him up but he was dead weight so I yelled for help and a couple of the guys came running up the stairs. We tried to lift the Don off the floor but decided instead to straighten out his legs, put him on his back and call for an ambulance. They came and took him to the hospital. You know the rest."

"Has he been getting a lot of visitors?" I asked.

"The word is out, no visitors. Of course, the Padron's wife and kids come in every day."

"How are you and Phil holding up?"

"We're doing ok," said Donald with a nod. "Thanks for asking, Doc. I'll say hello for you to Phil when he gets here at nine tonight."

"You do that," I said, and then I left.

Uncle Vito's condition did not radically improve during the next three months, so Doctor Cantore called a conference to discuss the case. Chris and I were the only ones invited. During this meeting, we went over the medication and treatment. Cantore then told us that the patient would be better served by being transferred to a rehab center. Turning to me, Cantore said, "Doctor, this center is associated with the hospital and has a very good physical therapy department. He will receive physical therapy at least twice daily. This will stop muscular deterioration and could possibly increase his libido. I visit the center twice a day and will be able to keep a closer watch on him than I can here. Any disagreement, Doctor?"

"None whatsoever," I replied. "I want to thank you for what you've done so far."

"Very frankly, this is a very interesting case," said Cantore. "We don't see too many that have functional vital organs after having a massive stroke. Most of them die, not basically from the brain damage itself, but from the vital organs that shut down as a result of the stroke. In this case, we have something to work with, so we'll try different approaches and see what happens." He then addressed Chris. "Speak to the wife and get her permission to move the patient. If there's a problem with getting the wife's approval, maybe Dr. Falcone here can talk to her. I understand that they are in some way related. Anything else, gentlemen? If not, we'll meet again next week." He looked at me. "Goodbye, Doctor." He then turned to

Chris. "Come with me. We have a new patient I need to see and I'd like you to be there."

Uncle Vito's wife signed the consent forms and he was moved to the rehab center. He was assigned to a room much larger than the one he had at Lenox Hill. The physiotherapy twice daily started to bring back some of the muscle tone in both his arms and legs, but there was little if any improvement in the sight, hearing, and voice. "It's a waiting game," Cantore continued to say. "As long as he's alive there's always a good chance for him to recover at least some functions."

The situations in the street didn't get much better. Crime commissions started to spring up in the major cities. Some of the bosses were even arrested based on testimony given by lower echelon rats that made deals, and some of the top guys were convicted and sent to jail. This was the opportunity the younger soldiers that were pushing drugs were looking for. If a boss went to prison, these guys were in a position to take over the reins of power. If they could recruit enough of their crew, then plans were made and most of the time carried out to whack anyone that stood in their way in taking over the family.

The case with the Amatto familia was, for the time being, quiet. Tony A, with the permission of the other four New York mafia families, got the go-ahead to temporarily take over as Capo of the family. Tony A knew he had a loyal group around him, but he was still on his guard and took no chances. He kept the no-drug rule and at times orders were given to take out any of our own guys that were caught dealing. They just disappeared and nothing was heard of them again. But the business, in spite of everything, continued to get bigger. Tony A held off questioning the three of our captains that were ratted out as being traitors, but there came a time when things started to get out of hand, especially with the news of bosses getting iced in nearby Jersey, Philadelphia, and Boston. The suspected captains had their phones tapped and pictures taken of their actions. During a chance meet, Phil told me when I was came to see Uncle Vito at the rehab facility that Tony A jokingly remarked he felt like the Italian J. Edgar Hoover, investigating the bad guys. It didn't take much convincing for the captains to tell everything they knew to the Chicago guys that were brought back to town. The three captains were questioned separately and confessed that they had broken the rule.

They named Paulie as the main supplier and gave up full details including transport, storage, and customers of the operation.

"I should have known better that it was that fuckin' Paulie running the operation," said Tony A. "But he's a nephew of the Don. How could that piece of shit do that to his uncle who has been so good to him? I'll never be able to figure it out. The next problem was what to do with the three captains."

Tony A, after speaking it over with Rocco and Phil, sat the captains down and told them, "Now, you're back working for us again. Continue what you did before with Paulie and the street guys under you. You'll be told when, how, and to whom you'll tell everything that's going on. You're rats, but you won't be dead rats if you do what we tell you. Also, don't try a fade out. We'll find you and your family will never see you again. You've got a chance to see your kids grow up if you work with us on this." The three rats then got on their knees, kissed Tony A's ring, and swore their allegiance to him.

It was during this time that Joe reappeared and was brought up to date by Tony A. Joe was the one who filled me in on all the details.

"You should be happy," Joe said to me. "It looks like Paulie is the main guy in the drug business and is supplying half of Harlem in addition to our own neighborhood. I'm sure Tony A will have to make a move to get him out of the picture, but he has a problem. Paulie is still Uncle Vito's blood nephew, and needs some sort of ok from him, but Uncle Vito can't do it. Tony A is smart and shrewd. He'll work something out to take care of the problem."

And he did.

In the ensuing weeks, Tony A didn't let on that he knew what Paulie was doing. He obeyed the old Mafia code, 'keep your friends close and your enemies closer.'

I continued to worry about how the situation with Paulie was unfolding. Later on, Joe sat me down and let me know all about what Tony A was doing to deal with the issue.

"One day," Joe told me, "Tony A had a sit down with Paulie, Rocco, and Frank. I sat in also because I was told to."

"I met Frank at Teppersteins," I said. "Who is he?"

Joe replied, "He's the representative of the four New York families. Tony A could have won the Academy Award for his performance. He told Paulie that it was found out that Pinky Barone was the drug lord and had to be iced and that Paulie was chosen to do this himself. As a reward, Paulie would be "made" and could not come to harm unless permission was given by the Capo. Paulie then left, and when it was certain that he was off the premises, I heard Frank saying to Tony A, 'You done good. We got Paulie boxed in. He has to whack his main man, who does the buying, oversees the shipping, storage and largest distribution of the weed and heroine coming in. If he makes the hit, the operation is gonna be shut down until he can get a replacement. If he doesn't whack this guy, Paulie's no fool—he knows we'll get suspicious. I'm sure the other Capos will be very pleased the way you handled this.' Then Tony A said, 'One thing about Paulie, he has the patience and lots of it. He's like the lion in the grass, waiting as long as it takes to grab his prey. He waits until the time is right, then he makes the move.'

"About six months later," Joe continued, "the press reported:

> Three men entered the Casa Mia restaurant and shot to death mobsters John 'Pinky' Barone and Santo 'Sonny' Muzzio and walked out. None of the other patrons or help could identify the shooters when questioned by the police. Paul

Sabatino, the nephew of crime boss Vito Amatto, admitted he was having dinner with the other two but claimed he had left the table just prior to the shooting and was in fact in the toilet when he heard the shots.

"The media kept on with follow up stories of what it labeled as a 'mob hit' and even expanded with columns reporting that the violence was an example of the war for control of the Amatto mafia family by some of the younger members involved in the drug business."

True to their word, Paulie was 'made' by the familia several months after the shooting incident, according to the old Sicilian custom. He now could not be harmed but he had to pay the price of his whole operation having to be shut down. The three informers kept feeding information to Tony A, particularly about Paulie trying to make deals to restart the flow of drugs.

Joe was back in town more and more often and he filled me in on what was going on. It was about a year after the shooting that our informers reported that Paulie had found a new partner with better connections, and larger quantities of drugs than before started to flow into the city. In order to stem this tide, many of the low level street guys were whacked and had to be replaced by Paulie. This wasn't a real problem for him, but he had to be careful once reports of investigation and arrests by undercover cops and the F.B.I. came out. Conviction of a federal crime could mean a lot of years in the joint. The best way to solve a problem, Paulie confided in one of our former captains, was to take out the Capo.

"But he's your uncle," the captain said to Paulie.

"Relatives are relatives, business is business," Paulie replied. "Besides, he's a vegetable and he's gonna die soon."

"What about Tony A?"

"He has to go also," Paulie said. "Once they're both out of the picture, I'll step in and take over the family. Everybody will be earning big. Who's going to touch me? I'm made. This has to be planned real good. You and me, let's sound out some of the crew quietly and see if they want to join us. Tell them over and over that the time of the old mustaches is over. They made their score. Now it's our time for us to earn, and we will. Real big. But don't push it, just feel it out slow-like and get an idea if there's any interest."

"Will do," the captain said. "I'll be in touch as soon as I get someone that looks good."

Soon after, I heard the details of this conversation. The captain Paulie took into his confidence was one of the three that we had turned, and all the information was relayed back to Tony A, then he told me.

"So what is Tony A going to do about Paulie's plans to whack him and Uncle Vito?" I asked Joe.

His answer surprised me. "Nothing right now," he said. "Tony knows Paulie inside out. He knows that Paulie is a very patient guy and won't make any moves until he's sure the time is right. Tony A will be one step ahead of him and before Paulie can make his move, Tony will make his, and my money's on Tony A."

Time has a habit of moving on. I was kept busy treating my regular patients. The lower facility patient load was shrinking down to maybe two or three a week. Some weeks, there was no one to treat, probably because there were guys who got the contract who were good at what they did.

I made it my business to stop by and see Uncle Vito at least twice a week. He was still in a coma, but there were some positive signs of improvement. His fingers and toes reacted somewhat to stimuli. It was hard to believe that two years had passed since the stroke. Cantore was overjoyed and kept telling Chris and me, "Mr. Amatto's recovery will now continue at a much faster rate. Just you wait and see. I think the brain edema has lessened and the cranial hemorrhaging has been stopped and the clots are being to some extent absorbed. Unless something radical happens, he has an excellent chance of making it, but let's be conservative about his condition with his family." Both Chris and I concurred.

Word must have gotten out that Uncle Vito had signs of improvement. According to our informant, who was both Paulie's confidant and our man on the inside, Paulie faced a dilemma. Who should he take out first; Tony A or Vito Amatto? After thinking this over for about a week, our source told us that Paulie had placed Tony A first on the hit list. Upon hearing this, Tony A took extra precautions as to where he went and where he ate. He also doubled his normal two-bodyguard team. He felt pretty safe and started to make plans to take out Paulie.

It was on a spur of the moment that I decided to pay Uncle Vito a visit and see how he was doing, although I had already stopped in two times earlier in the week. He seemed to be a little more alert every week I saw him.

When I approached the door to Uncle Vito's room, I saw that Donald was not at his usual guard station. His chair was empty, but I thought nothing more of it at the time. Maybe he had gone out for a smoke or to take a leak, so I opened the door.

And I was shocked.

There was Paulie, standing over Uncle Vito's bed with a pillow in both hands, just about to take him out.

I yelled, "What the hell are you doing, you son of a bitch?!"

Hearing that and seeing me, Paulie threw the pillow in my direction and I was able to duck it. He then lunged at me and reached into his jacket for the gun that he always carried in a shoulder holster. I was able to get to him before he could get his piece out of the holster, and with all the strength I could muster, I smacked him square in the nose. The blow must have broken his nose, because blood came pouring out. As he put one hand up to his nose to stop the bleeding, I reached into his coat and grabbed the hand still trying to get his piece from the holster. We struggled over ownership of the piece and with my free hand I smacked Paulie a second time in the nose. He then stepped back, writhing in pain, and I was able to get control of the gun. Paulie kept grappling for the gun so I had to shoot him, trying just to wound him, but he kept coming at me, so I shot him again and he went down.

The next thing I knew, Donald came running into the room, gun in hand, followed by a couple of the rehab security people and a staff physician. When Donald saw me standing there with a gun still in my hand and Paulie lying on the floor, he screamed, "Lay the gun down on the floor and kick it over towards me, Doc!"

I did just what he told me.

"Is the Padrone ok?" Donald asked.

"I guess so," I said. "I stopped Paulie from killing him. He was just about to smother him with a pillow when I walked in. Is it ok if I see how bad Paulie is?"

Before Donald could answer, the staff physician looked at me and told him, "I don't think he should go near the guy on the floor. He might screw up some evidence. I'll see if he's still alive."

"Ok," Donald replied. He turned to me and said, "Doc, you just stay put until we can figure things out."

The staff doctor went over, took a look, checked for pulse and breath, and then said, "This guy is dead."

By this time someone had called the police and when they arrived it was again determined that Paulie was indeed dead. One of the cops picked up the gun by the trigger guard. He then placed it into a cellophane bag.

Staff and attendants from the coroner's office came into the room a short time later as well as a group of crime scene people. As soon as they arrived I was asked to accompany the two cops that were first on the scene to an unoccupied waiting room where we were joined by two other men who introduced themselves as detectives, and the two uniform cops left. The detectives started to question me about who I was and about my relationship to the decedent and to the patient. Before I would answer I asked if I was under arrest, and they replied no. One of the detectives then left the room and returned fifteen minutes later. "Let's continue our discussion at the station house," he said. "From what I heard from witnesses, you'll not have any problems. Ok?"

"No, it's not ok," I said. "If I'm not under arrest I don't have to go back with you. I'm going back to my office. I have patients to see. If you need me, you know where to get a hold of me."

"Hey Doc, don't be a wise ass," said the detective. "We're only doing our job and looking to help you."

"Thanks a lot but no thanks. I don't need your help. Can I go now?"

Both of them nodded yes and as I left, one of them handed me his card. I left the rehab center really shook up and went home. As soon as I got there I called Tepperstein's law office and left word with his service to have him call me. I said it was an emergency. It wasn't more than ten minutes before the phone rang. It was Tepperstein returning my call and I told him what had happened.

"Be in my office at ten o'clock tomorrow morning" he told me.

"I have patients to see," I said.

"Cancel them," said Tepperstein, and he hung up.

I contacted the G.P. chief residents in each of my hospitals to make my patients rounds for me that morning and called Tubbs to call and reschedule my patients for the following day.

At ten I entered Tepperstein's main office and was immediately ushered into his private one. Once I entered he motioned for me to take a seat facing his large desk. There were no formal greetings this time.

"Marco," he said, "tell me everything that happened from the time you walked into the rehab center until now."

And I did, not leaving out any details that I could remember.

"How many times did you see your patient Amatto this past week other than last night?"

"Twice not including last night," I replied.

"How many times do you usually see this patient each

week?"

"Twice."

"So last night was the third time this week?"

"Yes," I said.

"Did you ever see this patient three times during the week?" Tepperstein asked.

"Yes, but it was a long time ago."

"So it was not usual to see him three times during the week."

"No, it was not usual."

"Tell me, Marco, what made you decide to visit Mr. Amatto for the third time last night."

"I don't know," I said. "I had some free time and I wanted to see how he was progressing since the last time I saw him."

"And how long ago did you see him other than last night?"

"Three nights ago," I said.

"You're telling me you saw Amatto three nights ago and went back last night to check up on his progress? Does that make any sense to you?"

"Since you put it that way, it doesn't."

"Any other reason you went back?" Tepperstein asked. "Maybe to kill him?"

I balked. "No, I would never do that. He was family to me and if it wasn't for him, I wouldn't be a doctor today."

"Tell me," Tepperstein continued, "how did you and Paul meet?"

"We met in Joe Mancuso's house."

"How did you two get along?"

I was starting to get annoyed at Tepperstein's line of questioning. "Not too good," I said. "From the time we met, Paul disliked me and I could never figure out why. Maybe it was because I was Jewish. He was also jealous since Uncle Vito took a liking to me."

"Anything else you want to tell me?" Tepperstein asked.

"Yeah, I went up to see Uncle Vito not only because I was his doctor but also because I like and respect the man. He has done a lot for me. I would never do anything to harm him. If I wasn't there last night, Vito Amatto would be lying dead in the morgue right now. I saw Paul trying to smother him and I did what I did to save my uncle and also to save my own life and I would do it again if I had to."

"Good ," Tepperstein said. "I asked you all these questions because you will be asked the same ones even more when you're called in for questioning. Who were the two detectives that first interviewed you? Did you get their names?"

"One of them gave me his card on my way out," I said. "I just stuck it in my jacket pocket. I still have it on me." I handed the card to Tepperstein.

"Ed Feeny," Tepperstein said. "I think I know him. He has a partner, Pat Raffety, a red headed guy. They're both Irish."

"Yeah that sounds like them," I said.

"Listen and listen carefully," said Tepperstein. "If the cops contact you and ask you to come in, tell them that you will as long as you can bring your attorney. If they tell you that you don't need one if you don't have anything to hide, just tell them again,' I'll come in voluntarily as long as I can bring my attorney along.' And if they continue to say that you don't need one since this it's going to be a friendly chat, hang up. Be careful who you meet, where you meet them, and what you say, especially over the phone. If it is anything other than your medical business, use different pay phones. Your regular phones will be tapped. The cops also could put a tail on you. Just go about your business liked nothing happened, including your visits to see your patient Amatto. He is still your patient isn't he?"

"He is."

"One more thing. Don' talk to reporters."

"Is it ok if I speak or meet with my friend Joe?" I asked.

"That's ok. But don't have dinner at his house. If you

go to a restaurant with him, don't discuss the case or anything else, only innocent social things. Use your head, Marco. Always be on guard. I'll be in touch with you and you can call me day and night if anything comes up about the case.

"One more thing and then you can go." J.T. then handed me a paper. "Sign this retainer where it is marked X and also make out a check to J.T. Tepperstein Esquire for twenty-five hundred dollars. Mark 'Retainers' in the lower left hand corner of the check. We'll need this in case the cops want to know who's your lawyer and where the money came from."

"I don't have my check book with me," I said. "It'll take me a day or two to scrape up the money, but I'll have the check in the mail to you in three or four days. In fact, I'll send it out certified."

"Marco, just make sure the source of the money is legit and you can prove where you got it. Now go. I got other things to do."

"Thanks J.T."

He shook his head. "Don't thank me yet."

Things got back to somewhere near normal; making rounds, seeing patients, and visiting the rehab center. Whenever I got there and entered Uncle Vito's room, whoever was guarding his door - be it the Duck or Phil - came into the room with me and stayed with me until I left.

I didn't hear from the cops until about a month after the shooting. It broke up my hopes that the incident would be closed as a self-defense act.

"Hi, Doc. This is Detective Ed Feeny. How you doing?"

"Ok," I replied. "What can I do for you?"

"Listen, it's not too late to come in and just have a talk with my partner and me," said Feeny. "We just want some more information so that we can close this case."

"That's great news," I said. "When can I come in?"

"How about tomorrow at one o'clock? You know where our precinct is?"

"Yeah, sure do."

"Come up the steps to the second floor and you'll see the sign 'Detective Bureau.' We'll be waiting."

"One more thing," I said. "I come with my attorney or I don't come."

"Go fuck yourself," said Feeny. And he hung up.

I took J.T.'s advice and was extra careful.

Joe came into town more and more often and we were able to get together a lot. We made sure that the places where we met were safe from prying eyes and ears. But in spite all of our security precautions, we had a great time. We even went over to Roseland and danced several times. Even some Broadway shows and great restaurants were on our agenda. I was glad we didn't discuss my case a lot, but Joe filled me in on some of the latest details. He was told that the cops pulled Donald in a couple of times for questioning, and he had to tell them what he saw. The cops also took statements from the two security guards and the doctor.

"No telling when the cops will be after your ass," said Joe as we sat at a coffee house. "No sense worrying about it now. We take one step at a time.

"Look, Marco, plans have to be made to cover every contingency. You know damn well the newspapers are not letting up on the storyline about the shooting. What makes matters worse is that this is an election year and the fucking politicians all of a sudden become knights on white horses coming to save the people. Their hands will be out the day after election."

"What should I do?" I asked.

"First thing, you gotta protect your practice in case there's a trial. You need someone to take over for you while you're tied up with the law shit."

"You're right. I'll put out feelers. But it won't be easy and it'll take time."

"Marco, I think I got the right guy for you. He's a Filipino who went to med school here and got a license to practice in New York. He's down on his luck. He got no job, no money, and no place to live. It wouldn't hurt for you to talk to him. I also was told he's a pretty good doctor."

"So when can I meet with him?"

"I'll give you a call and we'll set the meet." Joe then looked around the room. "We better go now. You go first."

As I prepared, I turned to Joe and said, "I really don't know how to thank you. And I want you to know what I told you happened that led up to my shooting Paulie was the God's honest truth."

"We've be like brothers for many, many years, and I know you're on the level with me."

We hugged and both left.

True to his word, Joe phoned me a couple of days later and said the other doctor was very excited about meeting with me, so we set up an appointment at my office at two o'clock the next day. I asked Joe if he was planning to also come along, and he said if I wanted him to join in and I answered, "Of course. Tell him to bring all his credentials with him."

At about two o'clock the next day Joe and another guy entered the waiting room. I came out and shook hands with both of them and invited them into my office. Joe then introduced the guy with him as Doctor Tala Adapon, and I asked them both to take a seat.

"Joe tells me that you are licensed to practice medicine here in New York," I said. "Can I see a copy of the license?"

Tala took it out of the small suitcase he had at his side. It was in order. I then went through his college, medical school, and intern history, and I was satisfied that he was competent on paper to be a G.P.

After the preliminary discussion was over and Tala and I started to go over medical specifics, Joe turned to me and asked, "Do you guys need me any longer?"

Tala and I looked at each other and we both shook our heads, and Joe left.

The next couple of hours, Tala worked alongside me seeing patients, and I was very satisfied with the way he handled them and with his method of treatment. After we saw the last patient, we went back to my office and worked out the details of his coming into the practice, including compensation. It was also agreed that he would move in and use one of the rooms in the lower facility as living quarters. Once we agreed on all these issues, I invited Tala back that night to join me in making my night house calls. He said he would be back at seven and left. Once he was gone, I sat down with Tubbs and filled him in on what was happening. I got the idea that he knew the position I was in and what I might be facing. I assured Tubbs that his job was secure as long as I owned the practice. I remember he listened to every word I said without emotion, and when I finished he just nodded his head and said, "Bene Grazia."

    Tala returned on time and we made the house calls. I was impressed with the way he conducted himself with all of the patients, asking questions and making observations. He reserved the medical treatment suggestions only after we left the patients' homes. Some of them were valid, most of them not, but I appreciated his comments.

    Tala moved in the next day, bringing with him his medical bag and a small suitcase, and he was ready to join me in seeing patients in less than a half hour. He was wearing a white lab coat, and I smiled when I saw 'St. Albans Naval Hospital' embroidered on it. Tale was a good practitioner, and I was very satisfied with his work and his attitude with the patients. After a couple of weeks I thought enough of him and his work to have him apply for privileges at Beekman and Beth Israel, and Tala received privileges at both - it was not a good idea at that time for him to apply to Lenox Hill. Having Tala as part of the office medical staff allowed me to free up some time for myself. I took advantage of this and caught up on sleep and even went out on some blind dates that Joe and some of my patients arranged for me.

    The months rolled by and I heard nothing more about the shooting. Maybe the cops decided it was self-defense after all and I was off the hook.

That dream came to an end when I got a call from Tepperstein telling me to come to his office the following day at three. He told me that the cops would meet me there to arrest me and take me in. They had a warrant issued in my name for the murder of Paul Sabatino.

"I called in a favor to have you arrested at my office rather than at yours," said Tapperstein. "This will save you a lot of embarrassment and loss of face. I advise you to let as few people know as possible, but alert the people working for you. Destroy any papers that might be helpful to the prosecutor. Don't take anything of value with you. Marco, don't panic. I think we can present a very good argument that you shot Paul in self-defense while saving Vito Amatto's life. I'll find out where they'll be holding you and we'll see you tomorrow. Good luck and don't worry. Everything will turn out ok."

I did what Tepperstein told me and informed Tala and Tubbs. They gave me assurances that they would carry on the practice as before. Patients, if they asked where I was, would be told I had to go away for a short while.

It was a little before three the following day when Feeny and Raffity entered J.T.'s main office and were rushed into his private office, where I was waiting nervously. After greeting J.T., they turned to me and Feeny said, "Marco Falcone, stand up. We have a warrant for your arrest for the murder of Paul Sabatino. Empty your pockets and place the contents on the desk."

Once I did this, handcuffs were put on me and I was taken down and put into the back seat of a car that was parked in front of the building. I was driven to the police station, where I was put in a holding cell. The handcuffs were removed.

"You still have a chance to talk to us," Raffity said. "If you just explain what happened, maybe we can hold you here instead of moving you downtown for processing. And if it sounds logical, we can call the D.A.'s office and see if he would drop the charges, and you could walk out of here today."

"I'll be glad to tell you as long as my attorney is present," said Marco.

"Have it your way," said Raffity. "Hope you can enjoy Rikers." And he walked away.

I remember just sitting on the wobbly chair, it seemed like for hours, and I was going over and over what had happened and why I was there, sitting in a cell awaiting who knows what.

I guess it was about four o'clock when two cops in uniform came to my cell and opened it. They put me in cuffs again and escorted me out to an armored car. They opened the back door and helped me get in and sat me down on a bench seat. They then exited and I heard them lock the door. The vehicle took off and about twenty minutes later stopped and the back door was opened and I was escorted out.

"Where am I?" I asked one of the cops.

"You're at Center Street Police Headquarters," he replied. "You're gonna get processed here, and then you'll have a nice ride to Riker's Island, where you'll find a hotel like you never saw before. It's a jail for scumbags like you waiting for trial, if you live that long. There are guys in there that will chew you up like peanuts just for fun."

True to his word, I was taken in, fingerprinted, had photos taken, was told to strip down, and was body-searched, including all orifices. Prison attire was then issued, including shoes. A bag was given to me and I was told to put my regular clothes into it. The bag was then tagged with my name and date of arrest, and I was told, "The bag will be sent with you to Rikers, and you'll get the contents if you need them for court."

Following the processing I was led back to a cell, where I just sat down and waited. I guess it was about two hours later that a food tray was given to me. The contents looked terrible and smelled worse.

Noticing the distasteful look on my face, a guy who looked like a trustee said, "The food here is like the Ritz compared to Rikers, so you'd better get used to it." He then took a closer look at me and said, "You're Falcone, the doc for the Amatto family. You're the guy that shot Paulie."

I remembered what I was told and just replied that it was his life or mine, and I changed the subject.

Evidently this must have satisfied him, because he followed with, "Don't eat this shit. I'll stop by a little later when I mop the floors and I'll bring you some fruit. My name is Mitchell, but everybody calls me Mickey. I'm a trustee here. Slide the tray through the door slot."

I did as I was told and he took the tray.

"See ya later, Doc," he said.

Sure enough, he returned a couple hours later with two oranges and an apple that he had hidden in his shirt. If the Screws would have stopped and found this stuff on us, we would be in deep shit.

"Thanks a lot, Mickey, I'm starving," I said. "How come you're helping me?"

"I don't know myself," he said with a soft chuckle. "It's just my gut reaction that you're a good guy. They're gonna come to get you and take you over to Riker's pretty soon. Just a word of advice; stay by yourself. Don't get friendly with anyone, even if you've known them on the outside. There are a lot of stoolies and they're looking to get brownie points for ratting you out. Don't get friendly with the prison hacks. They'll also rat you out, 'cause it might mean a promotion. If any one of the prisoners gets you on the side and asks you what you're in for, look him or even them straight in the eyes and tell them, 'I'm in for Murder One for killing a guy that asked too many questions,' then turn your back and walk away with a little swagger. Once you do this, the word will get around and you'll be respected and left alone." And with that, Mickey turned around, looked back, and said, 'I gotta go now. Wish you the best, Doc."

"Thanks, Mickey," I said.

It was later that afternoon that two jail guards came to my cell. While one opened the cell door, the other said, 'Step back and stick your hands out." And the other one came right into the cell and put the cuffs on me. "You're gonna take a little bus ride over to Rikers. That'll be your new home for a while." They walked me down a corridor leading to a large garage where there was a bus waiting. Except this bus was different from any other bus I had ever seen. All the windows were covered with iron grating, and as I entered the vehicle from the rear door, I saw there was an iron grating separating the driver and front seat passenger section from the rear portion. A bench lined each side of the bus, and after I was seated, three other guys in prison garb like mine came onboard. After the rear door was locked, the bus took off.

    On the ride over, the other three prisoners huddled together and talked and ignored me. From what I could hear, all three were not newcomers to Rikers and it seemed like a sort of class reunion that was being held.

    I tried closing my eyes and was just about to dose off when I heard one of the guys say to the other two, "We got a celeb riding with us." And pointing at me he said, "This is the guy that took out Paul Sabatino. It takes balls to whack the nephew of a boss."

    I just sat there and said nothing.

    Then the guy continued, "I knew that fucking Paul. If anyone deserved getting whacked, he stood first in line, and this should have happened a long time ago. But the word came down to leave him alone." Pointing to me, he continued, "You did the right ting, and a lot of other guys in some of the other families agree that he had it coming."

    After a while we arrived at Rikers and were ushered into the administration building and addressed by what I later learned was a deputy warden, who stated all of the rules. Disobeying any of the rules, he told us, would result in loss of privileges.

    Our names were then called out and cells were assigned. When I looked around, I saw there were at least fifty of us listening to the deputy warden, and I subsequently found out that Rikers serviced the entire five boroughs of New York, and not just Manhattan. I was assigned a cell just for myself. I later found out from one of the guards that this was common practice for those arrested for murder and awaiting trial, and especially for killing a connected guy, where retaliation - even in Rikers - might be ordered.

I knew it was in my interest to obey every rule to the letter. I was able to get books from the library and spent most of my time reading and exercising in my cell. Time went by slow, but it went by.

It must have been three or four days after arriving at Rikers that a guard came to my cell door and said, "Falcone, you have a visitor. Your attorney is here." He opened the cell door and told me to follow him. He led me back to the administration building, up to a door marked 'Attorney Conference Room.' When I entered the room, I was glad to see JT Tepperstein seated at a little table and he motioned for me to sit down on a chair opposite him.

"How you doing, Marco?" he asked.

"Doing the best I can under the circumstance," I replied.

"Tell you one thing, Doc. I think it's harder to get into here than it is to escape out. They really give you a thorough going over before they pass you through."

"JT, that's all well and good. My nerves are worn to a frazzle. I want to know what the hell goes on from here with me."

"Look, Marco," he said. "This is the way the system works. The court has already been advised that I am now your attorney of record. You and I will both be notified of an arraignment date with the court, at which time the charges on the indictment will be read to you. And I will waive the reading of these. You will then be asked how you plead, whether guilty or not guilty, and you will plead not guilty. I will then ask the judge to consider bail, and I will present an argument for a money bail release, which will in all probability be turned down, and you will be remanded back into custody at Rikers. The judge will then set a date for trial, and you'll go back to jail to just sit and wait.

"In the meantime, I will have my people do the

investigation and see if we can dig up some additional evidence that you acted in self-defense. My hope is that your Uncle Vito will be well enough to tell the D.A. and the court what really happened. Unless there is something urgent that comes up, since the trial date is four to six months down the pike, I'll be by to see you in about four to six weeks. Just try to stay calm and go with the flow. I know it's not easy, but this is the only sane thing you can do. Now just knock on the door and the guard will open it and take you back to your cell."

He stood up and started to walk to the door then turned around. "Before I go, I want you to know that we are doing everything possible to see you get a fair trial." Then he left.

As I sat in jail day after day, I thought, *How can anything get worse?* But it did.

Newspaper headlines in many major papers kept repeating over and over, "Mob Doc Indicted for Murdering a Fellow Mafia Member." Another read, "Mobster Paul Sabatino Killed, Mob Doc Indicted for the Murder." Another read, "Doc for the Mob, Alleged Killer, To Go on Trial."

These and other similar headlines kept appearing and reappearing over and over the months following my appearance in court.

It was six weeks later that I was given my bag of clothes, told to dress, and was advised that my arraignment date was set for that afternoon. I was subsequently led down to a waiting area and then escorted to a bus - similar to the one that had taken me to Rikers - back to the courthouse.

I entered it and saw JT Tepperstein waiting for me. Greeting me, he said, "Don't answer anything other than what the judge asks you. When he gets to the part as to whether you plead guilty or not guilty, just reply in your normal tone of voice, 'not guilty, your honor.'"

The arraignment came and went, just as JT had earlier explained to me. I was denied bail. The best part of it was the bus ride to the courthouse and back to Rikers. At least I could see people riding back and forth and observe some activity.

Also, the lunch served at the courthouse holding cell was a lot better than the food at Rikers. Trial was set four months from my arraignment appearance.

It was thirty days after the day I was in court that JT came to visit me.

"I have had my investigators look over every piece of evidence, and they came up with nothing new," said JT. "In my opinion, your case is a toss-up. It'll depend on how the jury feels about you rather than if you actually did this in self-defense. The fact that you're Amatto's doctor gives you some credibility. So it's going to be your word against Vinnie's and the two security guards'. The good thing is that they can't testify they saw you doing any part of the crime. They can only testify that they saw you with the gun in your hand after they came into the room. This should be the basis for a verdict of not guilty based on reasonable doubt, but you never know what a jury does.

"One good thing I can tell you is that you got a good judge assigned to the case. Arthur Brandon is a fair guy, and runs a good courtroom. He doesn't have to take any pressure or bullshit from the D.A.'s office or the prosecutor because he was just reelected for another twelve-year term. I don't know who's going to appear for the prosecution, but we'll find out soon." He paused for a moment. "The most important thing is that I cannot continue to represent you as your attorney."

"But why?" I asked. "Did I do anything wrong? How can you back out now? I was depending on you to get me off." I thought I would burst into tears.

"Take it easy, Marco," said JT. "I had to withdraw as your attorney because I feel there's a conflict of interest here. Over the years I have represented defendants that had ties to the decedent and it was strongly suggested that I get replaced by another counsel that is independent of any of my connections. I have spoken to a guy that I have known for years. He's one of the best criminal attorneys out there, and he agreed to take your case pro bono, no cost, after he read the file. Lucky for you, he has a vendetta against the New York

D.A.'s office and many of its prosecutors, and gets his gun off if he can beat them in court."

"What's his name?" I asked, sort of loudly.

"Calm down, Marco. This is a top guy with more wins in court than me. You're in great hands."

"What's his name?" I asked again.

"William Duggan," JT replied. "He's the senior partner in Duggan, Fowler, Houser, and Levine. You couldn't get better."

I let all this sink in and quietly told JT, "I trust you, and I'm trusting you with my life. I think you believed me when I told you I shot Paul in self-defense when I stopped him from murdering Uncle Vito."

"I believe you, Marco. Otherwise I wouldn't help you. You've got to realize that I have other clients and obligations going back many years, and I owe loyalty to these clients also."

I thought for a while and replied, "I see where you're coming from, and I have to respect your decision."

"Look," JT said, "I filed notice with the court regarding change of attorney, and once that's approved, Willie Duggan will be in touch."

With that, JT got up and so did I, and rather than shake hands, we hugged each other.

"Keep calm and keep your mouth shut around the other prisoners and guards," JT said. He then knocked on the door. The guard opened it, let JT out, and took me back to my cell.

Over the next couple of weeks, I became more and more despondent, and kept on going over and over again, *What am I doing here?* and *Why did I get here?* Although I was not particularly religious, I started to think that this was God's way of getting retribution for all my past transgressions. I kept on thinking, *I am nearly thirty-two years old, have no wife, no kids, and no future.* My dream of becoming a doctor had been realized, but look at the price I had to pay for it. Was it worth it? Even my social activities were limited to having one-night stands or getting laid in empty hospital rooms or even linen closets, with nursing students and nurses. Although I had met some nice compatible girls on blind dates or by introduction, I had to drop them. I was afraid that no decent girl would want to get involved with a rogue doctor who was at the beck and call of mob bosses. It's no wonder that no lasting relationship was in the cards for me.

It was about six weeks before trial when one of the guards came to my cell and announced, "Hey, Falcone, you have a visitor. Your attorney is here."

After he took the cuffs off, he let me into the conference room. Standing there before me was a guy about sixty with a full head of red hair just starting to turn gray at the sideburns. He was over six feet tall, slim, with grayish steel eyes, and was impeccably dressed in a black silk suit, white shirt, and coordinating tie. He advanced his hand to shake mine and as he did he said, "Hello, Marco. I'll Bill Duggan, and I'm here to help you and hopefully get you off." His voice and demeanor commanded respect, and I could understand why he was so successful in the courtroom. "Now, Marco, sit down and start from the beginning. And I mean from the very beginning. Every facet of your life. Whatever you tell me is privileged and stays right here in this room."

I started to describe my life from the moment I met Joe until now. I tried to trust this guy, but I also remembered the Omerta oath I had taken, and left out anything that could get anyone else in the familia in trouble.

When I got finished, Bill Duggan looked me straight in the eye and said, "You've got a good defense here. There were no witnesses to the actual act, except Amatto, and he can't testify. The prosecution's case is weak, and if we get a decent jury, you walk out a free man. Let me talk to the prosecutor and see if he'll offer a plea."

"With all due respect, I don't want any pleas." I said. "I acted in self-defense. Paulie was going to kill me because I caught him trying to smother Vito Amatto."

"Ok, Marco," Duggan replied as he stood up and shook my hand. "I have some background from what you've told me.

I'm going to put my people to work right away to see what we can come up with. Take it easy, I know it's tough in here. And I'll be back a week or so before the trial to go over our defense." He then knocked on the cell door and left, and I was led back to my cell.

Time at Rikers was a horror. There were all sorts of inmates housed there, but there was one thing in common amongst most of them; they were tough. There was a great diversity of inmates; those awaiting arraignment and bond hearings, those awaiting trial, those convicted and awaiting sentencing, and those already sentenced awaiting transfer to another prison. The diversity of inmates ran the gamut from the petty thief to those in Rikers, like me, for Murder One. I found out after being there just a few days that Rikers was really run by the House Guys - the trustees. The guards seemed to be there just to keep order. The inmates got three meals a day and the rest of the time was spent doing nothing. Some lucky inmates were allowed to play cards, listen to the radio, or watch T.V. Others could use the gym, depending on what they were in for. For me, it was boredom and more boredom, which turned into self-pity and bitterness. I kept on going over and over again, *Why am I here? I only tried to do the right thing.* And the story of my life became a sad tale that I kept repeating in my mind over and over again.

The only thing that saved my sanity was the phone calls I was allowed to make. All the calls had to be made collect. There were a limited amount of phones and a lot of inmates trying to make calls, so there was always a long line waiting from early morning to late at night. Tempers flared easily and fights broke out all the time. I didn't join in on any of the fracases and stood my ground in line, and my position was somehow respected. I later found out the brawls were mostly gang related.

I was pleased that my collect calls were always accepted and for the next few months this was the highlight of my day. Each time I called the office, Tubbs answered and filled me in on how the practice was going and how Dr. Tala was doing. Both reports were great. Tubbs said that Dr. Tala was a very good doctor - not as good as me - and that all the patients seemed to like him, and the practice is growing. Although I was happy to hear this, in a way my melancholy increased and I was jealous that Tala was there and I was here.

Like a lot of the other inmates, I was allowed to have a calendar in my cell and it was common practice to X out the proceeding day. It wasn't really mentally helpful, but it was done anyway just to count off the days. And the days just dragged by. I read most of the books in the library, and new ones were hard to come by. The most enjoyable reading matter was the letters I received from my folks. I wrote to them twice a week and they promptly answered. They kept on writing that they wanted to come and visit me, but my letters kept reassuring them that I would be visiting them in Miami shortly. Besides, it would not be good for Papa to travel because of his heart condition.

And then the rug was again pulled from underneath me. It was all over T.V. and radio that Vito Amatto had died in his sleep. I was stunned, shocked and saddened. During the following days, details of the wake, religious service, and internment were the media's main topic. I asked to see the warden to request my being allowed to attend the funeral, but this was denied.

Sitting in my cell, I felt a real sense of sorrow and loss. It also came to me that the only one who could testify and prove my innocence was gone.

The major T.V. stations had graphic coverage of the actual internment and shots were taken of many of the mourners that attended. All of the capos from the other New York and Jersey families were there, including the wives and children. It was reported that there were also representatives from all of the major Mafia families from throughout the U.S. in attendance.

I caught a glimpse of Joe and his mother, father, and sisters, as well as a large contingent of both the Amatto and Mancuso families. The funeral looked very impressive. It was more like a burial service for a king or emperor. I saw that Tony A, Rocco, Phil, Ray, Donald, and Joe were all pall bearers.

A couple of days later, after standing in the Rikers phone line for close to two hours, I was able to put a call into Joe at his home and was lucky enough to reach him. I extended my condolences to him and his family and asked him to have my words spread around to the other crew members, and Joe said he would do that for me.

"Look", he said, "there is gonna be a lot of changes made in the next three to four weeks, maybe sooner. Once they settle down, I'll try to arrange getting in to see you. It won't be easy but I'll think of some way. Just sit tight and I'll work it out, ok?"

"Ok," I said.

"Got to run now and see how the cards are being played out," Joe said. "Caio".

"Caio."

For first time since I got there, I went back to my cell with a smile on my face.

I counted the days, sitting on pins and needles waiting to hear from or see Joe. It was standard operating procedure that all prisoners at Rikers were notified of forthcoming visitation by approved relatives and friends. I was elated when I was notified through the warden's office that Joe Mancuso was approved to visit me the following Wednesday at a specified time slot.

Sure enough he showed and we had a chance to talk for the first time in a real long time.

"Marco, how's it going?" he asked.

"This ain't the Fountainbleu," I replied, and I even managed to get a smile on my face.

"I know Marco, it ain't easy but hang in there," said Joe. "You've had some real shitty luck. Things will work out and this will wind up as a bad dream."

"Joe, I don't know how long I can remain sane in here."

"Like I said before, you gotta think positive," he said.

"We're doing everything we can to get you outta here. Everything is gonna turn out all right."

I felt it would serve no purpose to keep talking about my problem, and because there was a time limit on visitations I continued by saying, "I was really very sorry to hear about Uncle Vito's passing. I think his body just couldn't take it anymore and just shut down. He didn't suffer any pain. I read in all the newspapers I could get ahold of about the funeral that Uncle Vito was given the right send off. You gave my condolences to the family, didn't you?"

"I sure did," Joe replied. "I gotta bring you up to what has been going on since Uncle Vito died. There have been moves made by a lot of our captains hoping to take Uncle Vito's place as the capo. These guys couldn't fill Uncle Vito's shoes but they're scheming. The bosses of the other families got together last week. It wasn't easy because the cops and feds were watching all of them like hawks. The decision came down that Tony A was their choice as the new head of the Amatto family. He'll stay as capo as long as other factions in the family don't decide to take him out and put their guy in as capo. You already know that Tony A is no slouch. He knows which end is up and will cover his ass in any way he can. You can bet that anyone he thinks is disloyal or a threat will be fitted with a pair of cement shoes. Also anyone Tony A thinks knows too much will also be on the list to be whacked. Besides that, when the decision was made to make Tony A the boss, it also included an order to make sure all loose ends were tied up that could implicate any of the other bosses. The feds have been on their asses to put them away for life. Anyone getting pinched could be on the bosses' hit list because of their fear that these guys could turn rat and spill out their guts in order to make deals with the D.A. or the Fed attorneys. The Fed Witness Protection Program is giving these rats a way out once they squeal."

Joe looked around and leaned real close to me. "That's why I want you to be extra careful in here," he said in a soft voice. "I know you heard this before, but it's more important now than ever."

Inmates, especially at a place like Rikers, had a way of getting news that was not even printed or broadcast on radio or T.V. A lot of the prisoners here were crew-related and those that had visitors had them bring the latest goings on and then the word was passed on to the family-connected ones on the inside. It was no surprise to me when I heard through the grapevine that certain guys in the five New York families were getting hit or had just disappeared, probably fitted with cement shoes. Quite a few of the soldiers and even some captains in the Amatto family paid the price for not proving their loyalty and obedience to Tony A. Like Joe told me, Tony A was taking no chances on having any competition or being in the position to have any problems, be they legal or otherwise. The rule prohibiting drugs stayed in effect and those suspected of being involved were whacked.

True to his word, one week before my trial I met Bill Duggin at the client attorney conference room and he discussed the selection of the jury and trial procedure. He told me, "I have a list of witnesses the prosecution will be calling and you and I will review what they possible might testify to. I want you to think back and tell me again every little detail of what you saw, did, and remember. Just picture yourself getting off the elevator and walking towards Mr. Amatto's room and relate everything."

And I did.

Duggan was particularly interested in the details of what happened immediately after the shooting and I told him everything I could remember, including the moment that Vinnie entered the room followed by the two security guards, the staff doctor, and then the uniformed police and detectives.

When I got finished reliving the agonizing details, I was wiped out.

"When you are in the courtroom there are certain things I advise you not to do," said Duggan. "Don't look at the jury. The fact that you are a doctor is advantageous. People innately have a lot of respect for members of your profession. Look alert and give the impression that you are listening to every word spoken by the judge, the prosecutor, and the witnesses. Don't grimace or shake your head nay or yay, no matter what they say. Don't act sad or sorry or happy. Just act interested. No fidgeting, hand clasping, or negative body language. If you have anything to tell me relating to the case while we are in the courtroom, there will be a pad and pen on our table. Write the message down and hand it to Jason, our second chair, and he will get it to me. Understood?"

"Understood," I replied.

# XLIII

The trial started on a Monday at ten o'clock. The courtroom was packed with reporters from both the newspapers and T.V. stations. No cameras were allowed.

A lot of motions were made by Bill Duggan or one of his assistants, and they were promptly denied by the judge. This included the motion to dismiss the proceedings because of lack of evidence, arguing that the prosecution did not have a prima fascia case. After about a half hour of this, the jury was brought in and seated. The trial started when the prosecutor Robert Berstein was called upon by the judge to make the prosecution's opening statement. Berstein then addressed the jury, laying out the case for the prosecution step by step. He seemed to have the ability to turn what might have happened into what did happen.

Berstein was about five-foot-eight, in his middle fifties with a dark complexion, and walked with a distinct limp. He was a career prosecutor, having worked in the D.A.'s office for over twenty years. He held the record for the most convictions of any prosecutor in the New York five boroughs over the past ten years and had won cases defended by top defense teams. Berstein had no political ambitions so no one was able to get to him. When he was finished with the opening statement and was seated at the table provided for the prosecution, the judge called upon Bill Duggan for the defense to make his opening statement.

Duggan's focus on the case was that there was absolutely no positive proof whatsoever that this was a premeditated murder and there was no evidence by any witness as to what occurred. "It will be established that there were no witnesses to the shooting," he said. "Therefore, this leaves an unanswered question as to what happened and if this is so, reasonable doubt prevails and under the law reasonable doubt demands a verdict of not guilty."

When Duggan was finished, the judge called for a two-hour lunch break and Duggan and I had a chance to sit down and talk.

Before I could say anything, Duggan said, "In spite of what Berstein said to the jury, I think the reasonable doubt situation had a positive effect on them. Also you came off real well. Just keep doing what you are doing. Believe it or not, it has an effect on the jury." He handed me some papers. "Here's a list of prosecution witnesses that will be called to testify against you. I noticed that the two security guards, Charles Manning and Gilbert Bailey, as well as Donald Lugano, were also listed as witnesses for the prosecution. Look these over and if you have any information that could shake up their credibility or make them look foolish let me know. Use the pad as I told you before. I'll see you back in court." Then he got up and left.

Back in my holding cell, I ate the cruddy lunch that was left for me. After a period of time I was led back to the court room.

Once the judge called the court to order, the prosecution started to call their witnesses. The first one called was the staff doctor Rodriquez who had pronounced Paulie dead, and over the next four days, the uniform cops, detectives, crime scene investigators, and representatives from the medical examiner and coroner's offices were put on the stand. They could only testify as to what happened after the shooting. Upon cross examination, Duggan had all of them reiterate that they did had not seen the shooting and had arrived at the scene only to see a body on the floor of the room and a gun lying on the floor with Vito Amatto's bodyguard pointing his gun at the defendant.

There was no consensus as to my demeanor when they arrived at the scene, and Duggan informed me later that this was a plus for me, adding to the reasonable doubt defense argument.

The case was adjourned for the weekend and resumed again on the following Monday.

Security Guard Gilbert Bailey was called first that day and the usual questions were asked that were asked of all witnesses, such as name, age, occupation, length of time at that occupation, length of time employed at the current job and relationship, if any, to the defendant.

When these preliminary questions were answered to the satisfaction of the prosecutor, the questioning of the witness began.

"I didn't see the shooting," said Bailey. "But I heard gunshots and me and my coworker Charlie Manning ran to the room where we thought the shots were coming from. When we entered the room, we saw Donald, gun in hand pointed at Dr. Falcone, telling him to kick a gun on the floor over to him a couple of feet away from a guy lying in a pool of blood. I saw Dr. Falcone kick it over as told and then Dr. Rodriquez, the staff doctor, came in and soon after the cops arrived and took over."

"Thank you, Mr. Bailey," said the prosecutor. "One more thing. Does the person you referred to as Donald Duck have the legal name of Donald Lugano?"

"I believe so," Bailey replied.

"No more questions. Your witness."

Duggan then arose and approached the witness. "Did you see Dr. Falcone at the Rehab Center visiting Vito Amatto?" he asked.

"Yeah, I did," Bailey replied.

"How often?" Duggan asked.

"At least twice a week."

"Any set time that he would come to see his patient Vito Amatto?"

Bailey shrugged. "No set time that I could remember. Sometimes it was late afternoon, sometimes it was around eight at night and sometimes it was early morning."

"So it wasn't out of the ordinary that Dr. Falcone saw his patient at night?" Duggan asked.

"No it wasn't."

"Tell the court, was Dr. Falcone considered a good doctor?"

Bailey nodded. "He was considered one of the best not only at the rehab center but also at Lenox Hill main. I worked there for eight years before coming over to the rehab center and saw good ones, bad ones, and very bad ones. Dr. Falcone was one of the best. The staff respected him and the patients loved him. He was a damn good doctor."

"I have no more questions of this witness," said Duggan with a smile.

"You may step down," the judge ordered.

The next witness was Charles Manning, who basically repeated the same testimony as Bailey for both the prosecution and the defense and was subsequently dismissed by the judge. Since it was on Friday around two when Manning left the stand, Judge Brandon called a recess until Monday, when Vinnie was scheduled to appear as the state's final listed witness.

I met with Bill Duggan that Monday morning at nine, an hour before the trial was to start. He felt confident that if Donald would give similar evidence as Bailey and Manning, he would ask the judge to dismiss the case based upon the prosecution not being able to prove its case. He felt confident that the odds were in our favor, that the judge would grant the motion, and that I would be able to walk out of the courtroom a free man and put all of this behind me.

I couldn't wait to get into the court. I was so happy.

The trial started again at ten and Berstein called Donald Lugano to the stand. As he passed by where I was sitting, he just ignored me and looked the other way. I thought this was strange, but pushed it out of my mind.

After being sworn in and answering the perfunctory

questions, Berstein began what he later referred to as the meat of the case.

"Tell me, Mr. Lugano," said Berstein, "how long did you know Mr. Vito Amatto?"

"Objection, relevance!" cried Duggan.

"Overruled," replied the judge.

"Since I was ten years old," said Donald.

"And were you employed by Vito Amatto?" asked Berstein.

"Yes, I was."

"And what were your duties of employment?"

"I was his chauffeur," said Donald.

"Was that your only duty?" asked Berstein.

"No, I also looked after him."

"So, you were also his bodyguard?"

"You could say that," said Donald with a shrug.

"And did you know the decedent, Paul Sabatino?"

"Yeah, I knew him for seven, eight years. He was Mr. Amatto's nephew, being he was Vito's sister's son."

"And do you know if he also worked for Mr. Amatto, and if so, in what capacity?"

"Well, he was sort of a gopher for his uncle," said Donald.

"Do you know the defendant, Marco Falcone?" asked Berstein.

"Yeah, I know him."

"Is he here in the courtroom, and if so, would you point him out?"

Donald pointed to me.

"How long did you know the defendant?" asked Berstein.

"I know him for almost twenty years."

"How did you come to meet him?"

"He was good friends with Vito's other nephew, Joe Mancuso."

"How did the defendant first come in contact with Paul Sabatino?"

"I think they met at Joe's house when Marco was invited for dinner."

"And did they come in contact thereafter?"

Donald nodded. "Yes they did, on many occasions."

"Did Dr. Falcone and Mr. Sabatino get along?"

"Objection!" Duggan spoke out. "Calls for conclusion by the witness."

"I'll allow the witness to answer," the judge said.

"To tell the truth, from the start, Paulie, I mean Paul, didn't like Marco," said Donald. "He was jealous of his friendship with Joe and the fact that Vito Amatto took a liking to Marco and started to treat him as one of the family, even though he wasn't real Italian."

"What do you mean he wasn't Italian?"

"Well, even though his family came from Venice, they weren't real Italian. They were Jews."

"You are telling this court that Paul Sabatino didn't like Marco because not only was he jealous of Marco getting accepted as family by Vito Amatto, but also because he considered Marco a Jew and not really Italian?"

Donald nodded. "Yeah."

"Any other reason you can think of that Paul had it in for Marco?" asked Berstein.

"Yeah. Mr. Amatto ok'd the money for Marco to go to college and medical school and become a doctor."

"How did Paul feel about this?"

"He was really mad. He told me that if it wasn't for his uncle's protection order on Marco, Paul would have probably had him whacked."

"Do you know if Marco knew about Paul's utter dislike, maybe even hate, for him?" asked Berstein.

"Yeah."

"So Paul really had it in for Marco, huh?"

"Absolutely. Marco must have felt this, because Paul became vocal about this, especially after Vito had the stroke."

"Can you tell the court what happened the night of the shooting?"

"I left my post outside of Mr. Amatto's door in order to go and take a leak - I mean use the toilet - and afterwards I started to walk back to the room."

"How far is the toilet from Mr. Amatto's room?" asked Berstein.

"Eh, maybe fifteen to twenty feet away," said Donald.

"What happened then?"

"I heard a shot coming from the inside of the room, so I pulled my gun and ran into the room."

"What did you see?"

"I saw Paulie trying to get up off of the floor. He had blood coming from his nose and also running down the sleeve of his jacket. As he sort of pulled himself up, I saw Marco, with a gun in his hand, shoot Paul and down he went."

"You are telling this court that you observed the defendant Falcone shoot Paul Sabatino in cold blood?" asked Berstein.

Donald nodded. "Yes, I saw Marco Falcone shoot Paul Sabatino as he was trying to get up off the floor."

"And you saw blood coming out of his nose and down his arm as he was struggling to get up off the floor?"

"Objection!" cried Duggan. "There's no evidence of Sabatino struggling to get off the floor."

"Overruled," said the judge.

With that, Berstein told the judge, "I have no further questions of this witness," and then he turned to the defense table, looked at Duggan, and added, "Your witness."

Duggan then asked the judge for a recess to consult with his client, and the judge responded by saying, "It's nearly twelve o'clock. Let's say we take a lunch break until two." Since there was no objection, the judge slammed his gavel. "Court will resume at two. We are in recess."

I just sat there frozen, my mind whirling, my heart racing, and my fingers tingling. When the two deputies came to cuff me and take me back to the holding cell, they literally had to lift me up from the chair while putting handcuffs on, and they had to hold me up under my arms so that I could be halfway dragged out of the courtroom.

"Are you ok?" they kept asking. "Do you need to see the doctor?"

I was so stunned that I couldn't answer verbally, but I managed to get the strength to shake my head no. When we reached the holding cell and the cuffs were removed, they sat me down on the cot. They then left after locking the cell door. One of them said through the bars, "You don't look too good. Maybe you should see the doctor here."

I again shook my head no.

"If you are up to it, just bang on the bars and ask the trustee for your lunch. Don't wait too long, otherwise you won't get it. See you a little before two. Don't do anything stupid. You know what I mean."

I looked up and nodded yes.

When they were gone, I tried to pull myself together but couldn't. I had to bury my head in the pillow so that the other inmates wouldn't hear my sobbing. I vomited several times, had the dry heaves, and avoided shitting in my pants by making the toilet just in time.

It was a few minutes later when a trustee came to the cell door and told me, "This is the last chance for you to get something to eat until late in the afternoon. That's if you're still here."

I was about to tell him that I didn't want it, but suddenly changed my mind. "Ok, I'll take it," I said. The tray was sent through the slot in the bars. I don't remember what I ate, and the coffee was cold and lousy. I had to get a grip on myself. I was forced to realize and further ponder how the jury could be convinced that Donald was lying. I had no answer, and was racking my brain when one of the guards came to my cell and told me that my attorney was waiting for me in the conference room, and subsequently led me there.

Once I was seated opposite Duggan, he said, "We have a problem here. Lugano's testimony was damaging, and he has to be discredited. And he, as a witness, has to be proven a liar. You need to help me establish this. I don't have the ammunition right now to do this. Tell me everything about him, what he's been up to, and don't hold anything back. We have to destroy his credibility and you need to give me tools to do it. Your life depends on how badly I can destroy this guy's testimony."

I spent the next forty minutes telling Duggan everything I know about Donald. Duggan made some notes on a little pad he kept in his coat breast pocket.

One of the guards came to the door ."You're due back in court in ten minutes, so we gotta go back now," he said. "This judge don't like anyone coming in late."

Judge Brandon called the court to order and told the bailiff to bring in the jury.

Once they were seated, he looked at Duggan and said, "Is the defense ready to begin cross-examining the witness Lugano?"

"We are, your Honor," said Duggan.

"Take the stand, Mr. Lugano," said the judge. "You are still under oath. Understand?"

"Yes, Judge," said Donald.

Duggan approached the witness stand. "How long have you known Vito Amatto and what you did for him?" he asked.

Berstein jumped up. "Objection!" he shouted. "Asked and answered."

"I'll allow it," the judge replied.

Duggan continued, "You were basically his bodyguard, weren't you?"

"I was also his chauffeur," said Donald.

"But basically you were his bodyguard?"

"You could say that."

"Why would Vito Amatto require a bodyguard?" Duggan asked.

"Relevance!" Berstein objected.

"Overruled," said the judge.

"He was an important man and had enemies," said Donald.

"Is it true that Vito Amatto was the head of one of New

York's five mafia crime families?"

"No," said Donald. "As far as I know, Mr. Amatto was in the investment business."

"By the way, Mr. Lugano, have you ever been convicted of a crime?"

"When I was a kid, I did some stupid things."

With that, Duggan returned to the defense desk, picked up a folder, and announced, "Your Honor, defense wishes to offer into evidence Exhibit marked #12." Once accepted, Duggan began reading from the folder to Donald. "You just said when you were a kid, you did some stupid things. How old were you, and what were those stupid things?"

"Objection!" burst out Berstein. "Relevance!"

"Goes to credibility of the witness, your Honor," said Duggan.

"Overruled," said the judge. "You may answer the question, Mr. Lugano."

"I was around fifteen and got caught once for stealing fruit off a pushcart," said Donald.

"Anything else?" asked Duggan.

"Yeah, about a year later, I got busted for breaking into a candy store."

"Did you serve any time?"

"No, I got probation."

"Any more problems with the law?" Duggan asked.

"Well, I was grabbed for trying to steal a car, and my probation was revoked, and I served a year at an upstate juvie place, and got out when I was eighteen. I forget the name."

"And then what happened?" asked Duggan

"That's about all I can remember."

"Let me refresh your memory. You served three years at Sing Sing for extortion, and two years later you were convicted for armed robbery, and you were put away for eight years back at Sing Sing, but got out on parole after four years. Does that refresh your memory?"

"Sort of," said Donald. "I try to forget all the bad things I did when I was young."

"When did you become a soldier in the Amatto crime family?" Duggan asked.

"I don't know what you're talking about."

"Come on, Mr. Lugano," said Duggan. "Do you deny that you were the bodyguard for the boss of the Amatto mafia family?"

"I don't have to answer that."

"Yes you do," said the judge. "Unless you exercise your right prohibiting self-incrimination."

"I wanna do that," said Donald.

"By the way, Mr. Lugano," continued Duggan, "are you a citizen of the United States, and if so, when did you acquire citizenship?"

"You bet I am a citizen," said Donald. "I was made one over ten years ago."

"Let's get back to the night of the shooting," said Duggan. "You say were in the toilet when you heard a shot. Are you sure it was only one shot and not more?"

"I heard only one shot, ran into the room, and saw Marco pointing a gun at Paulie and then shoot him."

"What did you do then?"

"I pulled my piece, pointed it at Marco, told him to drop his gun, and then the security guards ran in and then the staff doctor. After that, the cops came in."

"Tell me, Mr. Lugano, where did you purchase the gun you pointed at Dr. Falcone?"

With that question, Donald seemed to grow a little nervous, and he squirmed on the witness seat and looked as if he was trying to think of an answer.

Duggan wouldn't let up. "Tell me, Mr. Lugano, where did you get the gun you pointed at Dr. Falcone?"

"I don't remember," Donald answered.

"You mean to tell this court that you don't remember who gave you a lethal weapon? What make and caliber was the gun?"

"It was a Colt .38 caliber Detective Special."

"It's funny you can answer the make, model, and

caliber of the gun you own but can't remember who gave it to you." With that, Duggan turned with a questioning expression to the jury. He then returned, facing the witness, and asked, "Do you have a concealed weapons permit?"

"No, I don't have one," said Donald.

"You know that a convicted felon can't get a gun permit? Do you know it is a felony to carry a concealed weapon without a permit? Remember that you are under oath, Mr. Lugano."

"Objection!" shouted Berstein. "Mr. Lugano is not on trial here!"

"Sustained," replied the judge.

With a look of disgust at the witness, Duggan turned to the jury and said, "I have no more questions for this witness." And he walked back to the defense table and sat down. He leaned over to me and whispered, "I don't care if the objection was sustained. The jury heard that Lugano was a convicted felon and was carrying a gun in violation of the law."

Berstein rose and addressed the jury. "The prosecution rests."

Judge Brandon then called a recess until the following day.

After leaving the court room, I was again led to the attorney-client conference room, and upon entering I saw Duggan pacing back and forth. He had his suit jacket off, tie loosened, and shirt collar unbuttoned. Once I sat down, he faced me and put both hands on the table. "Lugano hurt us in there today," he said. "Why didn't you tell me he was there when you shot Sabatino?"

"I swear to you he wasn't in the room," I said. "He came in after I shot Paulie the second time. Paulie was lying on the floor when he came in."

"How do you know this for sure? Your back was turned to him, wasn't it?"

"I don't know," I said. "You got me confused. All I know - and I'll say over and over, and I'll swear on the lives of my mother and father – is I saw Paulie trying to smother Uncle

Vito. We fought for his gun. I got control and shot him, first in his shoulder. I didn't want to kill him, but when he got up and lunged at me, in self-defense I shot him again and he went down."

Duggan, without expression, replied, "I believe you. But it's up to a jury to decide."

"Look, I'd like to tell what happened to the jury, and once I tell them, they'll believe me, and find me not guilty."

"Just a minute," said Duggan. "I'm not putting you on the witness stand."

"You're not? Why not? Once they hear what I have to say, I'll be cleared."

"I strongly advise you not to be a witness."

"Please tell me why," I said.

"Berstein can ask you questions about your entire life. Who you knew and what you were involved in. Don't think Berstein's investigators haven't dug into your past, and don't think he doesn't have potential witnesses on call to refute what you might say. I advise you again not to get up on the stand and testify. Berstein will crucify you."

"You mean to tell me I'm sunk?" I said.

"Not necessarily," said Duggan. "Listen to what I'm going to tell the jury when I begin my closing argument.

"I'll start out by impugning Lugano character, saying that he was and is a big shot mafia figure, has a long list of felonies, and has spent a considerable part of his life in prison. He had on his person an unregistered firearm whose serial numbers were filed off, couldn't remember who sold it to him, but remembered the make, model, and caliber. At the time of the incident, Lugano committed another crime. It's a felony to carry a gun in New York without a license. I will also inform them that Lugano is an out-and-out liar. He lied on his application for citizenship, swearing that he had no criminal record, when he in fact, at that time, was a twice-convicted felon. How can a jury believe anything he said?

"It makes sense that Paul entered his uncle's room when neither Lugano or the other guard was not on duty outside the room. Sabatino's intent was to smother Vito Amatto to death and take his place as the Capo of the Amatto mafia family. If this wasn't Sabatino's purpose, why was a pillow found on the floor next to the bed? It's because Dr. Falcone entered the room and saw Sabatino in the process of killing his uncle. Sabatino, upon seeing this, dropped the pillow, came toward Dr. Falcone, and attempted to draw his gun and kill Dr. Falcone. Fortunately, Dr. Falcone was able to wrest the gun from Sabatino and in order to protect himself, shot Sabatino in the shoulder. He didn't want to kill him, just stop him. But Sabatino, so filled with long-stirring hatred for Dr. Falcone and frustrated by the inability to carry out his murder scheme, felt the adrenaline flowing through his veins, and mustered the strength to again attempt to kill Dr. Falcone. So he rushed him, and fearing for his life, Dr. Falcone had no other choice but to shoot Sabatino. Dr. Falcone had no motive - no motive whatsoever - to cause harm to his beloved mentor, Vito Amatto. This is a case of self-defense, and since the state has not proved its case, we ask that you, the jury, bring in a verdict of Not Guilty."

The next day, after the court was called to order and the jury was again seated, the judge asked Duggan, "Is the defense ready?"

"We are, your Honor," replied Duggan.

"You may call your next witness."

"Your Honor," Duggan replied, "the defense rests. However, I'd like to make a motion to have this matter dismissed because the state has not proved its case."

"Motion denied," stated the judge. "I'll let the jury decide on whether the state has proven its case. Are you ready for closing, Mr. Duggan?"

"I am, your Honor." And with that, Duggan strode, faced the jury, and told them essentially what he'd told me the day before, but now he used body language, hand motions, and voice modulation to bring what he considered were salient points of my defense.

After he finished, the judge declared a two-hour lunch

break and ordered that the proceedings would resume at two-thirty. It was around two-forty-five when the judge called on the State for its closing argument.

Berstein walked toward the jury box, then turned, pointed his finger at me, and said, "Ladies and gentlemen of the jury, what you see sitting here is a cold-blooded murderer. The defense has tried to confuse you by putting road blocks up, but I know, ladies and gentlemen, this will not deter you from finding a just verdict, that of Guilty. What defense was put forth? Only a vicious, meaningless attack on the only witness that saw the killing. This tactic was cleverly used by the defense to belie the facts of what actually happened, and I am sure that you will see through the defense's sole plan to take you down a path that has no relevance to your reaching a verdict based upon sworn evidence given in this case. The defense seems to hang their hat on the witness Donald Lugan's past history, as they try to have you discount his testimony. But remember one thing; Lugano is not on trial here. Marco Falcone is. And notwithstanding Lugano's previous transgressions, he swore under oath that he, Donald Lugano, saw Marco Falcone shoot and fatally wound Paul Sabatino. We ask you therefore to bring back a verdict of Murder in the First Degree. Let justice be served." And with that, Berstein returned to his seat.

The judge gave the charge to the jury, outlining the legal criteria for finding a verdict or not being able to find a verdict. He then told the jury to retire to the jury room and select a foreman and start deliberations.

I was taken back to the attorney-client conference room, where I met Duggan. He seemed in a happier mood than before he made his closing argument. "I think we have a good chance of getting one or maybe two of the jurors to get on our side. There can be no conviction unless there is a unanimous vote by the jury. If they can't reach one after several tries, the judge must call a mistrial, and you could possibly walk out of here. The State has the opportunity of trying the case again, but I would doubt it. So all we can do now is sweat it out and see what happens."

"How long does it usually take for a jury to reach a verdict?" I asked.

"In my experience, with a Felony One case, the longer it takes the jury to reach a verdict, the better chance a defendant has in getting a favorable one. So just keep a cool head about you and hope for the best."

As he left, he turned to me and said, "We both will be informed when the jury reaches their verdict and that's when we will be summoned back to the court."

The wait was the most agonizing time I had ever spent. I couldn't eat or sleep. I had bouts of depression, diarrhea, and then nausea and the dry heaves. I must have lost ten pounds during the six days from the end of the trial until I was informed that the jury had reached a verdict.

The courtroom was crowded. The feelings of anticipation were evident in the expressions and body language of all that were there. For some reason I was suddenly calm and just sat quietly in my seat.

Before the judge called the jury in, he warned the attendees not to make any disturbance of any kind once the verdict was read. He added further, "I see representatives of the media are here, and I order you not to leave the courtroom until I adjourn the proceedings. Now bailiff, please bring in the jury."

Once the jury was seated, the judge looked over to them and said, "Mr. Foreman, would you please rise." Once the foreman did this, the judge continued, "Has the jury reached a verdict?"

"We have your Honor," said the foreman.

"Would you hand it to the bailiff?"

And he did, and the bailiff brought it over to the judge, who glanced at it, and upon handing it back to the bailiff said, "Please return this to the foreman."

Once this was done, the judge, looking at me, directed, "Will the defendant please rise." And I did. Bill Duggan also got up and stood next to me.

"Mr. Foreman, will you please read the verdict?" asked the judge.

The foreman started to read the preamble to the actual verdict. State of New York vs. Marco Falcone, case number, docket number, and description of the charges. I couldn't wait. The anticipation was causing me to hyperventilate and sweat. I was tingling all over. *Get to the fucking verdict*, I kept saying to myself over and over. And then I heard the foreman read it out loud.

"We the jury find the defendant, Marco Falcone, guilty of Murder in the First Degree."

The judge then asked the jury, "Say you one? Say you all?" And I saw the jurors all nod their head in the affirmative. There was an eerie hush over the courtroom as the judge continued, "Marco Falcone, you have been found guilty of Murder in the First Degree by a jury of your peers." Glancing down at his desk, he added, "The date of sentencing will be in sixty days, on April 4, at ten a.m." Addressing the jury, the judge said, "The court wishes to thank you for your deliberation and verdict. While I can't order you, I strongly suggest that you do not discuss anything that went on in the jury room that led to your verdict." And with that, he dismissed the members of the jury.

The two guards came, cuffed me, and told me stand up. I heard them, but I was frozen in my seat, drained of any mental capacity. "Stand up, Falcone," one of the guards said to me. I tried to but couldn't move any part of my body. I was like a stone. The two guards had to physically lift me off of my chair, each one holding me by my arm, and drag me out of the courtroom to the cell area. I was about halfway there when my entire body started to shake and shutter. I couldn't stop. I heard one guard commenting to the other, "Maybe we should take this guy to the infirmary."

"No," answered the other. "It's way over on the other side of the building, and it's nearly time for lunch. This guy could be faking it. I've seen it before."

I don't know how I got the strength to whisper, "Slap me hard across my face a couple of times." And they did, which abated the convulsions. One of them took a paper napkin from his back pocket and wiped the white foam from around my lips and face. Once they brought me to my cell, I was uncuffed. Then they left, locking the cell door behind them.

I lay down on the cot and tried to get some sleep but couldn't. I tried to use the toilet, but couldn't. All I could manage to do was lie on the cot and reflect upon where I was, where I could have been, and where I might be going.

"Don't worry, Doc," the lunch trustee told me. "Even if you get the sentence to sit in the hot seat, it's gonna take years and years before that can happen. You got a lot of time from all the appeals you can make. In fact, I was told that by a jailhouse lawyer that an appeal must be made for you on a Murder One death sentence, even if you don't want it."

During the next sixty days, I had to go through all of the presentence procedures with some hope of possible vindication, but that didn't happen.

It was about nine o'clock on the day of sentencing when a guard came and left my civilian clothes on the bed, telling me, "Get dressed, and be ready for court in an hour."

I was happy to get out of my prison garb, even though I was heading to a courtroom that would decide whether I would live or die. I hadn't really thought of what had physically happened to me since I was arrested. Putting on my clothes was a visual reminder of what I once was, and what I was now. My pants were so loose that the last buckle notch wasn't even tight enough. I had to twist one end of the belt around the other and hope that this would hold. My shirt hung like it was ten sizes too big and my jacket, once I put it on, also looked ten sizes too big. I looked like a little boy dressed up in his big father's clothes, or an overdressed scarecrow.

The court was not as crowded as it was during the trial.

Duggan was already seated at the defense table when I got there. It seemed to me that he was a little shocked at my appearance, but he just said hello.

All in the courtroom were called to rise as the judge strode out. Once seated in his chair, he said, "You may be seated." He then looked at me and asked me to stand up, and once I did, he proceeded to state, "Marco Falcone, you have been found guilty by a jury of your peers of murdering Paul Sabatino, and you now stand before me to be sentenced for this crime. As a medical doctor who has taken the Hippocratic Oath to save lives, you have violated this oath by taking one." The judge glanced out at the courtroom. "I see that there is no one here that wishes to address the court on behalf of the defendant. If there is, please raise your hand and the court will recognize you." He looked around, and there was no one, and he said, "Do you wish to address the court, Mr. Falcone?"

I shook my head no, as I was literally in shock.

"All right, we shall proceed. After careful consideration of all the facts in this case, I am hereby sentencing you, Marco Falcone, to death by electrocution on a date determined by the Department of Corrections. You will be remanded to Sing Sing Prison, where you will be housed until the time of your execution. May God have mercy on your soul." He then adjourned the court.

Before the guards came to get me, Duggan leaned over to tell me, "Marco, this is just Phase One. I'm going to file an appeal in a couple of days, and have had success in a lot of cases similar to yours over the years. Don't worry, our firm won't abandon you. We believe you, and we'll work our asses off to get you a new trial. One thing more; keep a low profile while you're in the joint. Stay a loner, but don't back down. Once you are respected, your life will be easier. We'll be in touch."

The guards then came up to me, cuffed me, brought me back to my cell and told me to get back in my prison garb.

"You might get moved tonight or tomorrow morning," one of the guards said to me. "You'll know when they come to get you."

# XLIV

    Upon arrival at Sing Sing, I underwent a physical exam and was issued new prison clothes and an inmate number that was stenciled on my prison shirt, shoes, and toilet items. I was taken to a large room where other new inmates were assembled. I later found out that the new ones were referred to as 'fish.' We were addressed by one of the prison guard officers, who spelled out the rules and the penalty for infraction of any of them. Once he finished the orientation, we were separated into groups according to inmate numbers and led out. My group, much smaller than the other groups, was marched over to the wing occupied by prisoners sentenced to death, and once I was locked in a cell, I sadly realized that I was now one of them.

    A few minutes later one of the guards came over and said, "You're the first one here. We've never had a doctor before on your side of the bars. I want to tell you, doctor, that you are no better than the lowest scumbag in here, and if you expect special treatment, forget it." And with that, he walked away.

    Time had a way of going by. Some days and nights slow, and others slower. I was summoned to the deputy warden's office and was told that an appeal had been filed on my behalf as mandated by the law. Once I was told this, I was escorted back to my cell.

    The only breaks in my cell life were the two showers a week and the two daily visits to the large bare old room where I could walk, jog, or run. I learned to do isometric exercise in my cell so that my body wouldn't fall apart.

After a week or so, I began to talk to the two guys on either side of me. This was one way I hoped to keep my sanity. The guy in the cell on the right side of me was a black guy who was convicted of killing his wife and her lover after he caught them both in the sack. The guy to the left of me was an old-time Irish hood who had shot and killed a liquor store owner during a stick-up. The guy he was with testified against him and he got away with twenty years.

It was a little over three years when the decision regarding my appeal came through. It was turned down. At the same time I got a letter from Duggan's office saying that they were going to file another appeal to a higher court, and to not lose hope. I had nothing else left but hope, and like a robot, I went through each day methodically. The news from the outside regarding the activities of the five families indicated that the power struggle for control continued at a faster and more violent pace. More and more of the older guys were getting whacked. I heard that guys who I knew that were part of the old Amatto crew were being knocked off and younger guys were taking their places. The drug business was the prize. Tony A was still the boss, but even he knew he was on shaky ground. He realized he might be a target and guys he knew that were loyal to him acted as his advisors and bodyguards. His standing order was if one of our crew gets it, take out two of them.

Even on Death Row, prisoners were permitted to send and receive mail. This mail was censored and subject to being blacked out if the material was not deemed appropriate.

Duggan, I found out, had another client in the general population section of the prison, and had occasion to visit him, and when he did he somehow managed to see me. Outside of the niceties of his visit, the talk about what was going on with my case was dismal. Duggan told me, "Maybe this appeal to the higher court will be positive, and the case would then be sent back to the lower court for retrial. You just have to wait it out."

"How long do I have to wait it out?" I asked. "I've already been here for three years."

Duggan looked me straight in the eyes and said, "Maybe two years more before the court comes to a conclusion."

"I don't know if I can hold out that long before I go completely nuts."

"As I told you before," said Duggan, "appeals are a process, and it takes time for this process to go through the various steps. Meantime, bide your time as best as you can. We are still working very hard to get you out of here. You have no other choice."

And with that, Duggan left.

Hours ran into days, days into weeks, and weeks into months, and finally, into years. So many things had changed during the five years I'd been here. I felt like the world has passed me by, and felt that I was alone on a small desert island.

I got a notice from Duggan that my appeal was coming up before the court in about three weeks. This raised my spirit and I finally had something to hope for.

I remember it was about ten days before the appeal was to be heard when one of the guards, Joe Simpson, came to my cell and announced, "Falcone, you got a visitor. I don't know why and I don't care how you were able to get one. Somebody in the system must like you. Let's go." He cuffed me and led me to the visitor's room, where there were booths on either side of a thick glass partition running the entire length of the room. Telephone receivers were hanging on the booth wall on either side of the glass. This was the standard means of communication between inmates and visitors.

"Who the hell is coming to see me?" I asked. The hack wouldn't tell me as he took my cuffs off, so I just sat there and watched other inmates come in, be seated, and watched their visitors sit down opposite them and start conversing over the phones.

I said to myself that it couldn't be Duggan because he

recently had been here and said he wouldn't be back until the appeal verdict was declared.

     Looking through the glass partition, my eyes opened wide and my jaw actually dropped. It was Joe, dressed in a shirt, suit, and tie, a lot different from the Joe I knew. He looked haggard and drawn, a lot older, but still had the striking blue eyes and the smile that captivated a lot of girls.

     He sat down opposite me, placed his palm on the glass, and pointed to the phone receiver on the wall, and we picked up our respective receivers.

     "How you doing, Sliding Marco?" he asked, palms stilled pressed against the glass.

     Seeing him and listening to his voice opened a pent-up flow of emotion. Tears of joy, happiness, loneliness, and anger that had been under my mental lock and key for nearly five years came out. I felt I was in a maze and helpless, with uncontrollable tears running down my face. Me, the convicted so-called murderer, crying like a baby.

     Joe, seeing my pain, continued to tap on the window, and after a minute or two, I put my palm up on the glass to meet his. I even managed to answer his greeting, asking, "How are you, Twinkle Toes?"

     "Ok," he nodded. "They just gave me a few minutes to meet with you. I know you got fucked up, so there's nothing that can be done about that. Now listen to what I'm going to say, and it should help explain things.

     "There's a new breed of guys running things out there. They got no honor or loyalty. Respect is a word they never heard of. They know they can stay on top as long as they can eliminate anyone they think is a threat to them. This guy, Frankie Pumero, came out of Attica about two years ago after doing ten. You might remember word getting around about him before he went away. He was also known as Red, and he was one rough tough son of a bitch. He's a fucking animal who enjoyed doing whatever his contract called for. Only he did it more, and don't ask me what I mean by more. Well, when he got back, he got into the drug business and moved up real fast, and got a lot of the young Turks to follow him. Anyone who got in his way was hit by his soldiers, or by him doing it himself. Red had his aim on one thing, and that was becoming the boss of the Amatto family. When he felt he had enough loyal guys behind him, he ordered hits on the top guys in the family. I'm sorry to tell you that the first they took out was Phil and Donald, and about three weeks ago, Tony A was clipped. This guy Red is now the boss and you are number one on his hit list."

I thought over this shocking information for a moment. "I feel real sorry for Tony A and Phil," I said, "but in a way I'm glad Donald got his. He got me convicted by lying on the stand about what happened. He's the reason I'm here. I hope he fucking rots in hell."

"Marco, you are so fucking wrong," said Joe. "The Duck did you the biggest favor you ever got. He saved your life."

"What the hell are you saying?" I asked.

"I'm saying he lied to save your ass. Let me clue you in. When the news got out about Paulie's shooting and your involvement, Tony A was positive you didn't kill him on purpose, but only to save Uncle Vito's life, and yours too. You, my brother, got put on the top of the hit list. Tony A really liked you, and knew that you were honorable. So did Donald. They then had a meet with a guy who we first met when Tony A called us in after we took out the girls. After talking to him and getting the low-down, Tony A decided not to take any chance you would get acquitted or have a mistrial so that you could possibly walk or be jailed until you get a new trial. This would be a death sentence. If you went back to Rikers, there were guys in there that would score big if they took you down. If you copped the walk, you would be dead in no time, no matter where you tried to hide. One of Red's hit list guys ran to Costa Rica, and he was found there with his throat cut and his cock in his mouth. This Red is vicious and don't just whack. He leaves examples of what could happen if he's crossed. So the safest place in the world, Tony A decided, was on Death

Row, where even the general population here at Sing Sing can't get you. So Donald did what he had to do."

"Why do they want me so badly?" I asked, trying to understand all this.

"You know too much." Joe then looked at his watch. "I got less than ten minutes left before they kick me out of here. You got no choice. Call Duggan and tell him to withdraw the appeal."

"Are you crazy?" I exclaimed. "It's supposed to come down in ten days."

"Marco, if you win you lose. Withdraw the appeal or you're a dead man."

"If I get the chair I'll be dead anyway. You gave me all the whys, now tell me what's gonna happen when I do what you tell me."

"I can only tell you this," said Joe. "You ain't gonna sit in that chair. Just trust me. Now cancel the fucking appeal and do it right away."

I couldn't look at him, and started to put the phone back on the wall. But before I could do this, I turned to Joe and put my palm on the glass, and he did the same. Then I said to him, "Brother, I will always love you."

"I have always loved you as a brother," said Joe. And with that, he got up and left the room.

The guard then came, cuffed me, and took me back to the cell, where once again I was uncuffed. I then asked the guard if I could speak to the warden, and said it was an emergency situation.

I was on pins and needles waiting for a reply when the guard came and escorted me to the warden's office. As I stood before him, he asked me, "What's the emergency? It had better be good."

"I want to withdraw my appeal," I said.

"You what?"

"I want to withdraw my appeal."

"I've been warden here for twenty years, and this is the first time I've had a request like this. Are you sure?"

"I am sure," I said.

"Take a seat, Falcone," said the warden. He pressed on an intercom and I heard the him direct one of the office clerks to bring my file into him. He then opened the file and asked, "Is William Duggan still your attorney?"

"Yes," I replied.

And with that, the warden picked up the phone and called Duggan's office. Once Duggan was on the phone, the warden motioned for me to pick up the extension that was sitting on the table next to where I was seated.

"Listen, Mr. Duggan," said the warden, "the only reason I'm letting your client Falcone make this call is because I've never heard a request like this before." The warden then looked up at me and said, "You got five minutes, Falcone." And I nodded ok.

"Look Bill, you heard the warden," I said to Duggan over the phone. "I have only five minutes, so listen good. Don't ask me why, and no back talk either. I want you to withdraw my appeal before it's handed down."

"Are you crazy?" said Duggan. "I can't do that. It's unheard of."

"You've got to figure out a way to do it," I said.

"I have to warn you as your attorney, you are going against my advice. I strongly advise you not to do this."

"But I am telling you to get this done."

There was a silent pause on Duggan's end. "I'll see what I can do," he said with a sigh.

I don't know what came over me, and I replied, "That's not good enough. My request as your client has to be followed."

"Ok, Marco. I'll need your request in writing."

The warden got into the conversation and said to Duggan, "I was a witness to this conversation and will confirm the details of Falcone's instructions to you."

"Ok, warden, that's good enough for me," Duggan said. "Marco, you'll get notice from the Court of Appeals regarding your request."

The warden then broke in and said, "Time's up. I will now ask you to conclude this conversation." And we did.

About a week later, I got a letter from Duggan stating that my request had been granted by the appeal court, and he further added that he had notified the court to withdraw his name as my attorney of record. I thought to myself that he just have gotten pissed because I didn't listen to him. I now had no other choice but to believe what Joe had promised me.

During the time I was on Death Row, I didn't see too many guys walk the walk to the death chamber. This was mainly due to the slow length of time the appeals process worked. I learned some guys had been sitting in my cell block for as long as twenty years. The ones I did see had to pass my cell on their way to the door at the end of the walkway. Each man that had to take this walk behaved differently. Some just walked slowly. Others shuffled their feet. The worst were those that were screaming 'I don't wanna die! I don't wanna die!' at the top of their lungs as the guards physically dragged and sometime partially carried the prisoners into the death chamber. It was a horrible sight. I had nightmares for a long time after an execution was carried out. As this was happening, the remaining prisoners pressed their bodies against their cell doors and yelled out words of comfort and sorrow as the guy walked his last walk. A few even broke down and cried. A little while later the lights in the cell block began to flicker. That lasted about five minutes, and then stopped, signifying that the State of New York had carried out the death sentence. Complete silence then permeated the cell block - except for the ticking of the wall clock - for the rest of the night.

Months passed I didn't hear from anyone, even Joe. To make matters worse, the new governor, Nelson Rockefeller, was intent on speeding up the rate of electrocutions because of the growing popular demand to eliminate the death penalty. Supposedly the governor wanted to get as many in before the law could be changed, and therefore the process was sped up at the fastest pace possible within the law.

I was informed just two weeks before the start of my sixth year of incarceration that my sentence would be carried out one hundred days from the date of notification. Reality hit me like a ton of bricks. I hadn't heard a word from Joe. Did he hand me a fairy tale, or would I really not have to sit in Old Sparky? I didn't know what to believe. As the days ran by and the time raced to the faithful date, I began to think about sending word to the D.A.'s office that I would tell them everything I knew about the Amatto crew members and the entire Amatto operation. I could, I thought, make a deal with the D.A. or the feds that would get me out of there, or at least get rid of the death sentence looming over my head. Then I remembered what Joe told me. I was on top of the hit list, and it would be carried out the moment I got out or was moved into the general population. The decision lay on my mind night and day for a week. I couldn't sleep, hardly ate, and suffered bouts of depression. What to do hounded me twenty-four-seven. Finally I came to the conclusion that I had to believe in Joe and what he told me. He wouldn't let me down.

Once I made the decision, I forced myself to come back to reality. I had to trust Joe and believe in him, and once I came to this conclusion, I actually felt that a burden had been lifted off of me.

It was ten minutes to twelve when the prison doctor had the guard unlock my cell door, and upon entering he said to me, "Please take off your shirt." He then put a stethoscope to my heart and lungs and also took my blood pressure. Sort of ironic, I thought, for a guy to have a physical just a few minutes before he was to be put to death. When he was finished doing this, he reached into his medical bag and drew out of a hypodermic already filled with a clear liquid.

Before I could ask, he said, "You have a very rapid pulse and a very significant high pressure reading. I'm giving you a sedative so as to prevent you from having a stroke or massive heart attack before you are executed. The State doesn't want to be cheated out of this. You are to die by electrocution in the chair, and not by any other means. To die otherwise is to be prevented. As ridiculous as it sounds, it's the law." He then gave me the shot, but I felt no change.

Then two guards came and got me and we started to walk step by step to the door leading to the death chamber, each guard holding me up by my arms. We were followed by the warden and the rabbi. As we made our way, I kept on thinking to myself, *Did Joe give me a load of bullshit? Why did he lie to me? Did the bosses get to him and order him to set me up? How could Joe do this to me? I trusted him. Maybe I could have won the appeal and got a new trial.*

All seemed lost…

# XLV

    I felt myself being shaken and my face softly slapped, and I instinctively opened my eyes. It was Joe peering at me, saying, "Marco, wake up. Wake up."

    I was still very groggy, but managed to look around and saw I was in a beautiful bedroom, laying in a big comfortable bed with real sheets with my head resting on two comfortable pillows, and was wearing silky pajamas. I wondered if this could be heaven, and if it was, I would be very happy to have made it here.

    When my eyes focused, Joe handed me a cup of something filled to the brim and said, "Drink this all up. It'll bring you back to reality."

    I drank what he gave me and fell back to sleep. I don't know how long I slept, but when I awoke, I felt great. When my eyes focused, I saw Joe sitting in a big easy chair opposite me. As I stirred, he said, "Welcome back to the living again, my brother. Try getting up on your feet, but do it slowly." I was able to get out of bed without much difficulty. "You ok?" he asked.

    "Just like new," I said.

    "You might just be."

    Little did I know how true it was, but at the time I let that pass.

    "You must be hungry," said Joe.

    I nodded yes.

    "Let's go down to the kitchen and eat."

    The kitchen was large and fully equipped. Joe took

some sandwiches from the fridge and we ate, washing them down with Coke.

After eating the best food I'd had in years, I told Joe, "You gotta tell me how the fuck I got here, my brother."

"Sit down at the table, and I'll make it easy, even for a dummy like you," he said, smiling, still with a boyish look on his face. "But first, I gotta go back a lot of years. After I tell you this, this conversation never happened."

He leaned back in his chair. "You know I was with the O.S.S. during the war," he said, "and when it was over, the O.S.S. was incorporated with the C.I.A. and I was recruited to join it. I was assigned to do covert operations all over the world. That's why I came back to the States and stayed until I received another assignment, and then left to see it through. Without bragging too much, my record of success was outstanding, so I was told, and big promotions were given to me. Because of my record, the company sort of owed me a favor.

"Like I kept telling you, you were on the hit list from all the five families. They took a vote and you lost. 'Why take chances?' the New Jersey boss said, and he won the other bosses over. On top of that, the young bastards that were pushing the drugs also decided you had to go because you whacked their main guy, caused their operation to shut down for a year, and they wanted revenge for not only taking Paulie out, but also for the loss of a lot of money.

"You had no choice here. Like I told you, if you'd got acquitted, you'd be a prime target, and believe me, they'd find you. If you were found guilty, and were put away in prison in general population, you wouldn't last very long. The families have guys on the inside that would be happy to take the contract to kill you for as little as a carton of cigarettes."

"How did I get out of being zapped by Old Sparky?" I asked. "I don't remember anything after I started to walk toward the door to the death chamber."

"The doctor who gave you the shot had replaced the regular prison doctor. He was one of ours. We brought him in just to take care of your situation. The shot he gave you was a special sedative to put you first in a daze for a minute or two and then knock you out by the time you got inside the death chamber. All the other cons in your cell block thought you were scared shitless on your way there."

"What happened next?"

"The C.I.A. is ingenius," said Joe with a grin. "They got a homeless, nameless stiff from the morgue and put him in your place in Old Sparky. He was about your height and weight. We had one of our funeral parlors color him up so that he even looked like you. They shaved him, put him in prison clothes, and sat him in the chair before you got there. Once you came, you were put in a double-layered coffin and the blinds were then raised to let the witnesses view what they thought was you, and the execution was carried out. Only it wasn't you. Just a homeless stiff. Once this was carried out, our doctor examined the guy, declared him dead, and signed the death certificate listing Marco Falcone as the deceased. His body was then put in the coffin with you. He had the penthouse, you had the cellar." Joe smirked. "The coffin was then taken by hearse to a prearranged, secluded place where our agents took you out of the coffin, changed your clothes, and switched you to one of our cars. And here we are.

"By the way, the stiff, according to your last will and testament that we created for you, was cremated, and the ashes dumped into the Hudson River. So it looks like all the loose ends have been tied up."

"Joe, I want you to know, I didn't plan to kill Paulie," I said. "I only tried to save Uncle Vito from Paulie, then had to save my own life."

"I know you're telling me the truth, and I know you shot Paulie in self-defense," said Joe.

"How can you be so sure?" I asked. "You have only my word."

"Uncle Vito told me."

"What? How could he tell you? He couldn't speak."

"But he could blink," said Joe. "It's an old Sicilian way

of communication that we also picked up and used in the war when silence was of utmost importance. It's one blink for yes, and two for no. It's a form of language that we used in the O.S.S. I recognized it when I went to see Uncle Vito before he died. I'll never forget when I bent over to kiss him, he kept on blinking his eyes ten times, and then stopped for a few moments, and then started to blink ten times again. He did this over and over until I realized he was trying to convey something to me. So I blinked back indicating that I understood. 'Will you be able to understand me if I speak to you?' I asked him. I got one blink back indicating he could. I then asked, 'Did Paulie try to smother you?' Uncle Vito blinked once. It was a yes. 'Did Marco shoot Paulie in self-defense?' One blink again. 'Did your doctor realize you could see and hear?' Two blinks that time. 'You didn't want the doctor to realize this?' One blink. 'I'm going to get in touch with Marco's lawyer and give him the good news that he has you as an eye witness who can prove that Marco killed Paulie in self-defense.' Two blinks. 'Is it because there are contracts out on him?' One blink. 'Can you stop them?' Two blinks. 'But you're still the Capo?' Two blinks. And with that, Uncle Vito turned his head to one side, signaling that the meeting was over. It was then I realized Uncle Vito was no longer Capo of the Amatto family, and Tony A was the new boss and as such had to carry out the decision of the commission to get rid of you. I keep on telling you you're a dead man, Marco, if you even think of calling anyone. Just sit tight and everything will work out good."

    I decided I had to take Joe's word and follow everything he was telling me. "What happens now?" I asked.

    "Go lie down and grab a nap," said Joe. "Tomorrow afternoon, you'll be picked up by two of our people around twelve o'clock. Not before. They'll knock on the door, and before you open it, ask for their names. If they answer any different than James and Tom, run over to the steel door leading to the basement, lock it, and phone the number listed on it. Tell whoever answers it that you have the wrong number, then hang up, and don't open the door until you hear knocking on it, and James and Tom replying by name to your asking who's there. What I'm telling you is just a precaution to make sure the guys with the contract don't get to you before our guys do. Once contact is made, you'll be driven to Floyd Bennett Airport and you'll board one of our nice comfortable planes."

"Where am I going?" I asked.

"You'll be told once the plane is in the air," Joe replied. "I gotta go now. I stayed a little longer than I should. So this is so long, my brother. I'll always think of you and remember all of the good times we shared." Joe grabbed me and hugged me, and I did the same, and he left.

The rest of the day, I napped and watched T.V. I hit the hay around ten at night and slept right through until a little after ten the next morning. I ate some food out of the fridge, and made coffee. I showered and moped around until a little before noon when I started to glance at my watch every few seconds. It was about five after twelve when there was a knock at the door.

"Who is it?" I shouted.

"It's James and Tom," said someone outside.

"Ok, I'll open the door." And in came two guys who could have been an ad for Arrow shirts and 3G's clothes; dark suits, white button-down shirts, red ties, and polished black Oxford shoes.

"Hi, Marco," said one of them. "I'm Tom, and this is my partner James." He pointed to the other guy. "Are you ready to take a little ride before you start your adventure?"

"Where are we going?" I asked.

"We'll tell you on the way, so let's get going. Don't take anything with you. It'll be supplied."

We walked from the house to a car waiting at the curb. Tom got behind the wheel, and James pointed for me to get into the back seat as he got into the passenger seat. As we drove off, I noticed that the car parked across the street from the safe house for the time I was staying there also took off, but in a different direction from ours.

    During the half-hour trip, there was little conversation going on. Tom slowed down as we approached a security gate where a large sign read "Floyd Bennett Field." Tom showed some papers to the military security guard, who then saluted him and opened the gate. Tom continued to drive to another gate in another part of the field, showed papers, and the gate opened, and he drove up to a small plane that was parked on a tarmac, set aside from all the other planes. The car then stopped before an open cockpit door and James motioned for me to leave the car and use the steps to get into the plane. As I started to climb up, James and Tom came over, shook my hand, wished me good luck, and James whispered to me, 'You have a very good friend who went to bat for you in a big way. He used up a lot of favors doing this for you, and from what I understand, you deserved it."

    Before I could say anything, he continued, "All the information you need to know will be given when you're in the air. You'll also find a suitcase in the overhead containing everything for the new you. Just take it easy, and don't push. Everything will be explained when it's determined it's the right time. Ok?"

    "Ok," I said,

    I finished climbing up the steps and entered the plane's cabin. The plane looked like it held about forty seats. I grabbed one around the center of the cabin and sat there. I tried sleeping but couldn't. Looking out the window and seeing empty runways became boring. I looked for magazines or newspapers. There weren't any. So I just sat, fidgeted, crossed my legs, and then uncrossed them. It seemed like an eternity before I heard one engine cough and start, and then the other one come to life.

    That moment, I saw two guys enter the plane and come into the cabin. One of them was carrying a small case. They looked like carbon copies of James and Tom. They just nodded to me and took seats two rows ahead of me.

    A few moments later, the cockpit door was closed, the plane taxied to a runway, and we took off.

We must have been in the air about an hour when one of the other passengers came over to me and said, "If you need to use the bathroom, there are two in the back. There are also some sodas in the galley. We'll eat later. Ok?"

"Ok."

We were up in the air about two hours when one of the other passengers came over to me and said, "I'm going to get something to eat. Want anything?"

"I would like that," I said. "And a soda too, if I can get one."

"No problem."

He brought back the food and drinks and said to me, "In about a half-hour we'll start the orientation session, and everything will be explained to you. Before we get started, everyone in your former life no longer exists. Agreed?"

"Agreed."

"And saying that, it is my sad duty to inform you your parents were killed in a hit and run accident two days ago."

The tears welled up in me as I started to shake uncontrollably. But I was able to regain my composure.

"The Company took care of all the funeral arrangements, and your parents were interned in a Jewish cemetery with a Rabbi officiating at the service. That's all I was authorized to tell you. You have our deepest sympathy. In order to give you time to mourn, we will delay the start of the orientation by an hour." And with that, he joined his partner.

I ate and drank slowly, thinking maybe the time would pass quicker, but it didn't. My mind kept racing back and my history kept unfolding. Could this whole mess have been some kind of spiritual payback for some of my former actions, bookmaking, shylocking, high-jacking, black marketing, extortion, abortion, murder, fraud, and accepting money from the mafia, kidding myself that it was just a loan? Am I getting just rewards for my actions? I only wanted to be a good doctor and save lives. And look, I said to myself, there I am disgraced, my loving parents dead, thrown out of the medical profession, and having to run away like a hunted animal. I was brought back from my depressing daydream by one of my fellow passengers who approached me and said, "Are you alright, Marco? Are you ready to get onboard with us?"

Reality sprang back, and I said, "I'm fine. What do you want me to do?"

"Nothing," he replied. "Just listen. My name is Ed, and my partner is Barry. I'm going to move the seats back so that we can face you." After this was done, both of them sat down.

Barry then started by saying, "Marco, we have here a complete dossier from the time you were born until now. We're not here to criticize or judge, but to lay out a program that will keep you alive and let you go on practicing medicine. But we need your complete cooperation."

Ed then joined in, "When my partner said 'cooperation,' he meant it. Violating our instructions will cost lives; not only yours, but others in our company. Before we continue, can we be assured that you will abide by our rules? If you can't, the plane will be turned around, and you'll be dropped off at Floyd Bennett, and you will be on your own. Even your friend Joe won't be able to help you once you get off the plane."

"I swear by whatever is holy that I understand and agree," I said.

"Understood," said Barry.

"Agreed," said Ed. "We're going to leave these papers with you. Memorize them so that they are second nature to you. We will be back to question you as many times as we need until we feel you are comfortable with your new identity. We know you are very smart. Otherwise, you couldn't get through med school. So go to work now and start studying, memorizing, whatever you have to do to block out Marco Falcone and replace him with your new you, Isaac Medina." And with that, they handed me the file and both walked to the front of the plane. They took the first row seats, and a few minutes later I heard them both snoring.

I went through the papers they gave me, and I had to admit that my identity was perfect. I was sure that I could, in a little time, fit into the mold that was created for me. I must have spent three or four hours going over and memorizing the details. I knew I had to master them in order to stay alive, and I wanted to live.

Barry got up first and walked past me on his way to the rear of the plane. I guess he was going to grab some food or use the toilet. As he passed me, he said, "Hey, Doc Falcone, how are you holding up?"

I didn't fall for the trap, and answered, 'I think you're mistaken. I am a doctor, but my name is Medina."

"That's funny," said Barry. "You look just like the doctor that treated my mother in Beth Israel."

"Sorry," I replied. "I never had privileges at that hospital. You must have me confused with another person. We all look alike in our scrub suits and white coats."

"Maybe you're right, doc. Sorry about the mistake." And Barry walked away.

Ed then came over and sat opposite me. "That was ok for a starter," he said. "You hesitated a bit in your answers. You have to be believable one hundred percent of the time. You'll probably run across pros that will spot you in a minute or two for not being who you claim you are. Be more natural and comfortable in your new skin. Keep rehearsing, and we'll keep testing you."

Somehow my mind took me back to my anatomy class in med school, where I had to memorize all of the bones in the human body. I did great in the class. I now tried to apply this concept to my new identity, and to my surprise it worked. So I kept going over and over all of the information I was given, and after a while I believed I had everything down pat.

At certain intervals, either Barry or Ed would come by, sit down facing me, and casually ask background questions, not in any particular order, trying to trip me up. The interval interrogations continued on and on, conducted by Barry and Ed, each taking turns. At the end of each session, I was given a critique of my responses and statements. At first, they were sort of understanding and kind, but as time went on, their criticisms became more and more intense and forceful, and even threatening. I felt as if I was being given the third degree. At the end of each session, I continued to be told, "Your life, as well as others, depends on being able to convince the pro interviewers that you are who you say you are. They are masters in tricking the ones they question. One small slip causes intensive further interrogations until the person questioned breaks down. You don't want this happening to you, so keep working on the things we find don't sound fitting to the new you."

    The question and answer sessions went on and on. We took a break every three hours to eat, go to the toilet, stretch our legs by walking up and down the cabin, and grab a cat nap. And then the question and answer sessions started again. It was after a really vigorous session that the three of us had coffee and I curled up in my seat thinking I would get my usual half-hour nap. The next thing I knew Ed was shaking me. "Get up, Doc," he said. "We land in about twenty minutes. So go to the washroom, clean up, and change your clothes. You look like shit."

    I did as I was told, and a few minutes later got back into my seat, looking and feeling refreshed. I looked out the window and saw it was getting light and there was land beneath us. From the cockpit came the announcement, "We are beginning our final descent. We should be on the ground in about ten minutes." And we were. The plane taxied up to a waiting car, and the three of us deplaned and entered it.

    "Where the hell are we?" I anxiously asked my two companions.

    "Welcome to Israel," said Ed. "We just landed at a military airport near Tel Aviv. Once we get through immigration and customs, others will be there to help you and we'll say goodbye. Make sure, Doc, that you have all your papers with you. One last thing, and don't ever forget it; if you come across someone you knew or you recognize, deny. Keep denying and tell them they are mistaken, and walk away. You are Doctor Isaac Medina."

We were let off at a far corner of the airport and were quickly passed through the authorities. Once we were officially in Israel and standing in the deserted airport, Barry said, 'This is where we both part company. You were a good student, and we know you'll fit the mold that was made for you." Ed nodded in agreement. They both shook my hand and started to leave, then Barry turned and said, "Just wait here. Your guide will be here in less than five minutes."

Here I was, in the middle of a deserted part of an airport in Israel, my suitcase at my side, waiting for what and for whom I had no idea. And Barry and Ed were right. I heard footsteps coming in my direction but couldn't see who it was until the person came into a lighted part of the terminal. I couldn't believe my eyes. I blinked, and blinked again to make sure, and then I heard the familiar voice asking, "Doctor Medina, is that you?"

I was about to reply, 'Stop playing games, Joe. Your brother is here.' But then I remembered I was now Doctor Medina, and as such, had never met this guy before.

"Yes," I replied, and he extended his hand to shake mine.

I was then told, "I'm Pete Ventura, and I'm going to show you around and get you settled." And with that, we both walked out of the terminal and into a waiting car, and that's the way it was.

## THE END

Made in the USA
Charleston, SC
10 June 2013